Brianne felt her heartbeat jumping crazily, felt those arms tighten around her and his warm breath fanning her cool cheek. She finally dared to look up into those golden eyes. The desire she saw in them made her shiver anew. Unable to bear it, she closed her eyes and leaned forward, feeling his arms tighten further until she was almost crushed.

Pierce Nolan looked into the exquisite face and his desire ran hotly through his veins. He could feel her body warming against his where her flesh touched his clothing. He had to kiss her—and yet, one kiss would lead to more, he knew. He was not the kind of man who would be satisfied with anything less than all of her.

Dear Reader,

We, the editors of Tapestry Romances, are committed to bringing you two outstanding original romantic historical novels each and every month.

From Kentucky in the 1850s to the court of Louis XIII, from the deck of a pirate ship within sight of Gibraltar to a mining camp high in the Sierra Nevadas, our heroines experience life and love, romance and adventure.

Our aim is to give you the kind of historical romances that you want to read. We would enjoy hearing your thoughts about this book and all future Tapestry Romances. Please write to us at the address below.

The Editors
Tapestry Romances
POCKET BOOKS
1230 Avenue of the Americas
Box TAP
New York, N.Y. 10020

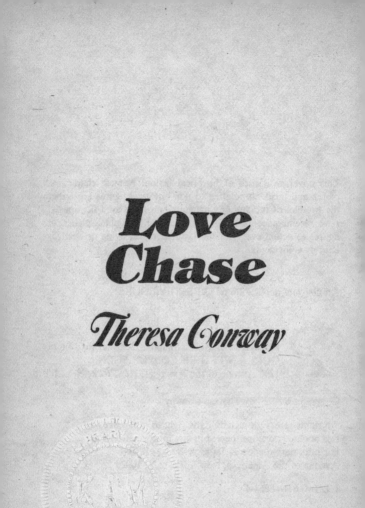

Love Chase

Theresa Conway

A TAPESTRY BOOK

PUBLISHED BY POCKET BOOKS NEW YORK

This novel is a work of historical fiction. Names, characters, places and incidents relating to non-historical figures are either the product of the author's imagination or are used fictitiously. Any resemblance of such non-historical incidents, places or figures to actual events or locales or persons, living or dead, is entirely coincidental.

An *Original* publication of TAPESTRY BOOKS

A Tapestry Book published by
POCKET BOOKS, a Simon & Schuster division of
GULF & WESTERN CORPORATION
1230 Avenue of the Americas, New York, N.Y. 10020

ISBN: 0-671-46054-4

First Tapestry Books printing March, 1983

10 9 8 7 6 5 4 3 2 1

POCKET and colophon are registered trademarks
of Simon & Schuster.

TAPESTRY is a trademark of Simon & Schuster.

Printed in the U.S.A.

For my mother Agnes,
with love

Love
Chase

Chapter One

A WARM, SOFT APRIL BREEZE FLOATED DOWN THE MISSIS-
sippi Valley, swirling delicately above the silvery-green
waters of the mighty river and over the moist, alluvial
lowlands of Louisiana. Fields of dark, rich, plowed earth
showed furrows cut deep into the soil which were just
now revealing the tender, green shoots of sugar cane
pushing up from the buried joints that had been dropped
in earlier in the year by the black field hands.

The breeze continued over the fields, where, by summer, it would be fluttering the tasseled tops of the cane
which would be six feet high or more by then. A little
apart from the fields and less than a mile from the levee
on the river, situated atop a small rise in the green earth
and surrounded by live oaks and bending cypress, rose
the white-plastered brick of Brian O'Neill's plantation
manor, Avonlea, its six delicately fluted columns soaring
thirty feet to the slate roof above. Iron grillwork enclosed
the second-story veranda from which steps curved outward on either side to the first-floor porch, a shaded, cool
place from which the master of the house, Brian O'Neill,
could sip his mint julep in relative ease.

The zephyr breeze played among the blossoms of pink
and white crepe myrtle for a moment before whisking
around the seated pair who sat in the garden at the side
of the house. Attentively reading from a book of poems,
a young man sat in cream-colored coat and trousers, his
apple-green waistcoat a startling contrast to the high
color in his cheeks.

1

Beside him, in a full-skirted dress of pink muslin, sat eighteen-year-old Brianne O'Neill ignoring the flowery phrases dropping from Carter Lowell's lips. Instead, she was thinking how dreadfully boring it was to be forced to sit quietly while everyone else was out among the trees and meadows, urging their horses in a spirited gallop.

Here she sat, tied to her wheelchair because of that stupid accident she had had last October during the hunt. She remembered the exhilarating feeling she'd had, urging her favorite mare to greater speed while keeping an eye on her companions. She'd been going along beautifully, sure she was going to bring the fox to bay, when her horse misjudged a hedge and leaped too late, its front hooves grazing the shrubbery, causing it to fall. Instead of rolling over the mare's neck and falling forward, Brianne had slipped off sideways and the horse had rolled onto her legs, pinning her agonizingly to the ground. She had had to wait some minutes before help came and by then, she'd already passed out from the shock and pain. The next morning she'd discovered, upon awakening in her bed that she couldn't walk or even stand without help.

With unconscious grace, she lifted a fashionably pale hand to tuck a straying curl into the gathered knot at the back of her head, smoothing the dark auburn strands at the side of her face with a fingertip. Her wide-set, turquoise-blue eyes gazed out at her companion with suitable fascination, although they barely registered the color of his hair. A sprinkling of light-brown freckles across the bridge of her nose, which tilted slightly at its tip, and the wide bow-shaped mouth were in repose, although now and then, she would catch at the bottom lip with small, white teeth, wondering when the others would be back.

"Do forgive me, Carter," she finally interrupted with a smile, "but I'm afraid I'm beginning to feel the heat out here. Do you think we might move onto the front porch?"

"Why, of course, Miss O'Neill," Carter concurred quickly. He drew the cane wheelchair closer to where she was seated.

Brianne hated the sudden vulnerability which always washed over her when someone helped her into her chair. The awkward, halting movements that were necessary for her to get from the stone garden bench to the wheelchair made her angry.

Carter, of course, was gentle, hardly daring to put his hands on her waist as he helped her to stand and then to turn and sit down in the wheelchair. When it was accomplished, Brianne sighed with relief and hoped the time would soon come when she would be able to walk again on her own. The physicians from Baton Rouge had promised her that, yes, she would walk again someday. The paralysis was only temporary and it was only that her legs were still weak from lack of use. She must do her exercises and, gradually, with God's help, she would be on her feet soon.

That had been six weeks ago, she thought with frustration, and still she was tied to this wheelchair, missing out on all the fun and gaiety, forced to listen to those silly sonnets from a young man who interested her not one ounce. Heavens above, why couldn't one of the more dashing young men have volunteered to stay behind and entertain her! She bit her lip peevishly as Carter wheeled her up the small ramp that had been installed from the garden to the porch.

"Ah, it is nicer on the porch," Carter said pleasantly, drawing up a chair to begin reading once again. "Would you like something to drink before I continue, Miss O'Neill?"

"No, Carter, and please do call me Brianne. I feel as though I must be on my best behavior with such formality." She allowed a soft twinkle in her eyes as she teased him just a little. It amused her to see the pink in his cheeks deepen even more.

He looked as though he might like to say something,

but instead opened his book and quickly began to recite once more. Brianne resigned herself and tried hard not to fidget noticeably. With returning elation, she heard the sounds of horses and young people coming down the oak-lined avenue from the direction of the levee.

Four riders and two loping hounds clattered up the graveled drive to the steps leading up to the porch where Brianne and Carter sat. One of the riders leapt off, his features very like his sister's, although his hair was much redder and the freckles more prominent on his skin.

"Well, I'm winded! What? No refreshments waiting for us, Brianne?" he asked hopefully, stripping off his hat and running fingers through his thick, wavy hair.

"You can very well call for your own refreshment, Winthrop O'Neill!" Brianne returned pettishly, still feeling sorry for herself to have missed the thrill of the ride. "What took you so long?" she added plaintively, choosing not to look at the expression on Carter's face.

"What's the matter, Brianne, honey?" one of the young men asked, eyeing Carter's flushed face with amusement. "Wasn't the company stimulating?"

Brianne glanced up at the tall figure of Josh Fontaine, his attractive face even more appealing today in contrast to Carter's pink cheeks. "You weren't in any hurry to volunteer to keep me company," she accused sharply. Then, with a coquettish smile that made her face dazzling, "But I forgive you, Josh, if you'll just bring up a chair and tell me about your outing." She included a third young man in her smile. "And you too, Gerald, unless you've got to leave?"

"Why, no, Miss Brianne. Nothing I'd rather do right now than sit next to you and converse," Gerald assured her, sitting on the step at her feet.

The fourth member of the party was Emily Turner, Winthrop's fiancée. Emily took a moment to greet Carter, he had been staying with her family for a month, visiting from Vicksburg, which was some ninety miles upriver. He was her cousin and she knew how timid he was. She pitied him for the yearning look on his face, as he watched the spell Brianne O'Neill was weaving around the other young men.

"Win," Emily said, "I think I'll go inside and wash up." She nodded to Brianne who threw her a smile and returned to her rapt audience.

"And so you did find the tracks of some wild animal?" Brianne asked Josh with mock concern.

He smiled. "Honey, it must have been a deer, nothing to fret about," he returned, winking at Gerald.

"Disappeared at the creek's edge," Gerald confirmed, staring lazily at the toes of the pink satin slippers that peeked out from beneath the piles of petticoats.

"Oh, I wish I could have been with you," Brianne sighed, leaning her chin in her hand as she looked directly at Josh. "I'd give anything to be able to ride—just down to the levee and back—but papa wouldn't hear of it! He'd probably lock me in my room if I threatened to go ahead anyway."

"You'll be riding soon enough," Josh soothed her. "Heh, those damn doctors don't know everything you know! Why don't you send down to New Orleans for one?"

Brianne laughed. "Don't be silly, Josh! You don't just send down for one like you would a bucket of shrimp!"

The others joined in her amusement.

"Honey, those gentlemen ain't tiring you out, is they?"

Brianne looked up to the veranda above where a round, black face peered down at her with some disapproval.

"No, Sara. I'm having a good time," she answered firmly to the woman who had been her nurse when she was younger. "Stop worrying about me. I've got two—," she glanced at Carter, "—three able-bodied young men down here to help me if I should need it. Win's inside with Miss Emily."

The black face disappeared, presumably to check on any "shenanigans" between the engaged couple.

"Brianne, you just say the word, honey, and I'll carry you inside," put in Josh, his eyes twinkling. "After all, we can stretch the rules of propriety in your case."

"Old Sara'd skin you alive if she caught you carrying me anywhere," Brianne giggled, enjoying the banter thoroughly and wondering what handsome Josh would look like without his skin. "I'll just have to call Win and poor Emily would skin *me* alive!"

"Brianne O'Neill, I think you're a hard-hearted girl who enjoys everyone waiting on you hand and foot," Gerald McLaughlin put in, coming closer to the truth than Brianne would have liked. "I think all this attention you're getting isn't going to get you back on your feet too soon."

Brianne stared at him, one eyebrow drawn up coolly. "Gerald, you're nasty to say such a thing and I—"

"Miss Brianne certainly isn't getting any more attention than what she deserves!" Carter put in heatedly, causing all three heads to turn toward him in surprise. "It's—it's just a shame that such a lovely girl has to suffer so. Why, I'd be more than proud to sit out the dances with you at the cotillion next month, Miss Brianne!"

"Why—I—thank you, Carter," Brianne managed, furious that Josh was barely managing to contain his laughter. "I'm sure I'll have plenty of people to keep me company, Carter." She saw his crestfallen look. "And I'll expect you to keep your promise, of course." She smiled at him.

"Why, thank you, Miss Brianne." Carter stood up. "I think I'll go in to see if Miss Emily's ready to return home now."

After he'd disappeared, Brianne turned to both Josh and Gerald in a pique. "And you two, I suppose, will be sitting out with me too?"

Josh choked on his amusement. "Aw, honey, it's not fair to the other young ladies to have the two best dancers out of circulation now, is it?" He leaned over to draw a gentle finger down the smooth, auburn wing of hair. "Besides, I'm betting you'll be so panicky at the thought of sitting with Carter Lowell all night that you'll force yourself to get out of that chair!"

Despite the pleasure his attention had inspired, Brianne was still angry. "Oh, you two act like I'm pretending I can't walk!" she burst out. "Lord, don't you think I want to ride and dance and walk again! I've tried, believe me, I've tried very hard!" (This was only a small lie, she reasoned.) "I'm just not ready yet!"

"Well, honey, when you are ready, you can bet we'll both have to stand in line for a dance," Gerald winked at her, atoning for his thoughtless words. "But it'll certainly be worth it!"

Feeling somewhat mollified, Brianne allowed him a smile. She lifted her eyes to look out over the smooth expanse of green lawn, divided by the oak-lined avenue of gravel, and thought about how dreary it would be to have to sit in this chair at the cotillion and watch everyone else having fun. Well, if she couldn't dance, she just wouldn't go! She forgot about her promise to Carter Lowell and made her decision. Why should she put herself through the torture of watching that simpering Annabelle Jackson waltzing with Josh or that empty-headed Mollie Corwin sitting for refreshments with Gerald.

"Brianne, it's close enough to supper, dear, why don't you invite the young men inside to eat? I'm not expecting your father home until after dark." The handsome woman standing in the doorway gazed fondly at her daughter with eyes almost the same shade of blue, although her hair was dark brown and she was shorter than the younger girl. The cool, poised exterior of the mother was mirrored in the daughter for a moment as Brianne looked up and smiled at the woman she most admired in the whole world. Then the Irish temper flared through, effectively snuffing out the New England side of her nature she'd received from her mother.

"I don't think either one of these boys deserves a

mouthful, mama," she teased. "If it were up to them, I'd
be sitting all alone at the cotillion next month."

"Darling, I'm sure you'll have plenty of company,"
Joanna Winthrop O'Neill assured her daughter, used to
the wayward flashes of temper and petulance. "I've
invited Emily and her cousin, Carter, to stay. We have
plenty of room."

"Oh!" Brianne bit back the groan she nearly let slip.
She eyed Josh who returned her glare with amusement.

"You'll not want us to desert you now, would you, fair
damsel. Your ears will probably fall off from the heat of
Carter's passionate declarations!"

"And besides, you do have the best cook in three
counties!" Gerald put in mischievously, standing up and
brushing off the seat of his pants.

Forgetting propriety, Brianne stuck her tongue out at
him, to which he responded with a chuckle. "You would
both starve if it were entirely up to me," she retorted,
wishing it were possible to make a dignified exit in a
wheelchair.

"Shall I have one of the servants wheel you in?"
Joanna asked, aware of her daughter's pique.

"No need, ma'am, I'll be honored to do so," Josh
quickly put in.

Gerald respectfully offered his arm to the mistress of
the house. "Where is Mr. O'Neill today, ma'am?" he
asked.

"My husband has business in Natchez," Joanna replied. "I'm expecting him home tonight."

"Wonderful city, Natchez," Gerald responded politely.
"I was there not too long ago myself."

"Yes, and nearly got himself killed by some drunken
seaman in Natchez-Under-the-Hill," whispered Josh,
bending down toward Brianne's ear. "He was coming
down to the levee to wait for the next steamboat and
decided to stroll along Silver Street—nearly a costly
mistake."

"Is it really as bad as I've heard?" she whispered back,

a thrill running down her spine, both from the mention of the notorious den of sin which flourished at the base of the bluff upon which Natchez had been built, and the proximity of Josh's lips near her earlobe.

"Worse," he responded dramatically.

"And how would you know?" she demanded, turning her head a little to see if he was teasing her.

He laughed. "I've been known to be a hell-raiser, myself, honey," he answered with an arrogant sniff, as though it were something to be extremely proud of.

They went into the dining room where Win, Emily, and Carter were already awaiting them, the servants standing like dark shadows behind them. As always, when she entered this room which was her mother's pride, Brianne felt a kind of awe. It was the only time she ever bothered herself thinking of the enormous sums of money that had been required to build Avonlea and to maintain it. One could not look at the gold and white French handblocked wallpaper, the identical white marble fireplaces, one at each end of the room, the Italian parquet floor, or the bronze chandeliers without being aware of the wealth they represented.

It had been over twenty years before that Brian and Joanna O'Neill had fled from Boston and her parents' censure to this stretch of fertile land which could be had for only sixty cents per acre. Since then, with Brian's loving skill and shrewd financial acumen, Avonlea had turned from a small weed infested farm into the sprawling plantation which produced enough sugar cane to fill a small flotilla of flatboats headed downriver to the port of New Orleans. Prices were continuing to rise despite the uneasy rumors of states' rights and Southern secession from the Union.

But now, on this lovely April afternoon, thoughts of war were far away from the people gathered at the long, polished oak table with its English china and Irish crystal. The food brought in by the kitchen servants was tasty and prepared with a flourish. Even Emily, who usually ate like a bird, appeared to enjoy the food enough to take second portions.

Brianne was proud of the fact that her father employed the best cook in three counties, that her house servants were the best trained (and perhaps, most fairly treated, due to her mother's New England upbringing) and that Avonlea itself was the pearl among most of the other plantation houses along this stretch of the river between Natchez and Baton Rouge. Someday soon, she knew, she would be expected to marry some fine, upstanding young man from one of the many proud and aristocratically wealthy families in the area. Winthrop had certainly been fortunate to have fallen in love with the only daughter of Marlow Turner, whose sugar fields were a close second to Avonlea's own. Not always did the sons and daughters of the plantation owners marry for love— more often it was a marriage of convenience when two plantations neighbored each other and the fathers wanted to see the lands joined.

Thinking of marriage, Brianne stole a look at Josh's boyish countenance. With his dark hair and lean height, he was certainly a catch worth contemplating. But when she imagined herself at Rosemont with Josh's four sisters her sudden enthusiasm was quickly quenched.

She turned her attention to Gerald and almost immediately discarded the notion of marriage with him. Gerald could be sharp at times, downright disagreeable to others. The Southern charm of Josh Fontaine was lost on Gerald when his Scottish blood took over. He would be a demanding husband, not one to allow his wife full rein with the purse strings. Josh would be more indulgent in that area, Brianne decided.

Of course, Josh had never hinted at marriage with her and she felt reasonably sure that she wasn't quite in love with him yet. There were other boys in the area who might be considered, and she did have at least another year before marriage became pressing. Her father would have most likely had her engaged before now if it weren't for the fact of her accident and the resulting "delicate condition." She realized abruptly that it was doubtful that any man would want her for a wife if she'd never be able to walk again.

"You're not very talkative this evening, my dear," Joanna reproved her daughter, noticing Brianne pushing the dessert of sponge cake spread with raspberry jam around on her plate. "Do you feel well?"

Brianne looked up, her cheeks coloring a little. "Yes, mama. I was just thinking."

Winthrop laughed a little. "My sister, thinking, when there's sponge cake in front of her nose—now that is an event!"

Brianne scowled at him. "Don't be silly, Win, food isn't everything. I was—I was thinking about the cotillion next month. I'm not at all sure I'll go." She ignored the look Carter gave her. "After all, I won't be able to dance and—"

"We'll discuss it later, Brianne," Joanna cut in, intercepting the young men's looks. "If you young men would like to stay longer you're quite welcome."

Josh stood up, shaking his head. "Thank you, ma'am, but I'd best be getting back to Rosemont before it's pitch dark. Father wants me home to discuss business." He bowed.

"I'll ride with you as far as Twin Oaks," Gerald said, standing also. "Thank you for supper, Mrs. O'Neill. Good-night, everyone." He gave Brianne a crooked smile and followed Josh out the door to call for their horses.

"Emily should be getting home, mother," Win said, giving his dark-haired fiancée an affectionate look. "I'll ride with her and Carter, if you don't mind."

"Of course I don't mind," Joanna said with a pleased smile at her son. She gave Emily a fond wave of her hand as she watched the three of them depart. "Ah, only a scant six months and Emily won't have to leave after supper. It will be nice to have her in the house, don't you think so, Brianne?''

Brianne nodded absently, thinking ahead to the marriage scheduled for early October. When, she wondered, would plans for her own wedding begin?

Chapter Two

"TIME TO STIR YOURSELF, MISS BRIANNE," SARA SAID IN her affectionate grumble as she entered Brianne's room the next morning, a slender coffee-colored servant girl in her wake. "Mandy, child, you open those windows over there and let a little fresh air in this room, hear?" The young maid hurried to do as she was asked, knowing that Sara's old eagle eye was on her, measuring her for the important duty of being the young mistress' maid.

Brianne did not feel much like stirring, although she knew it must be late in the morning already. She had kept herself up late last night, stewing about her chances of marriage. She knew very well that she herself would scoff at the idea of marrying a cripple—so what chance did she really have? It had definitely unnerved her to think that she might end up an old maid. Not she, not Brianne O'Neill, one of the prettiest Southern belles in upstate Louisiana and certainly one of the most eligible.

"Oh, go away, Sara!" she pouted into her pillow. "I'm tired!"

"Honey, I know you is tired," Sara commiserated, "but it's nearly nine o'clock, lamb, and breakfast can't wait all day. 'Sides your father is back and he has a guest with him." The negress' heavy brows drew together in a slight scowl.

"A guest?" Brianne pulled her face out of the pillow with interest. "Some gentleman from Natchez?"

"Gentleman! I don't know 'bout that, Miss Brianne,"

13

Sara warned, beginning to fold back the counterpane on the bed so that she could help Brianne dress.

"What do you mean, Sara?" Brianne demanded, sitting up in bed and swinging her legs out with Mandy's help. She pulled off her long nightgown and sponged her neck and arms with water, then waited for Mandy to pull the cambric chemise over her head and then the many voluminous petticoats that were required under the full skirt she would wear.

"Well, he's not like any gentleman I've seen 'round here before, Miss Brianne," Sara explained with a woeful shake of her head.

"Why would papa bring a man home who wasn't a gentleman?" Brianne asked, the sounds muffled as the sixth lace petticoat was pulled over her head and tied at her waist.

"Don't know," Sara admitted, though she had her suspicions from rumors which had already spread among the kitchen help. She'd heard that Mist' Brian had come in a few hours before dawn, drunk as a polecat, hanging on this stranger who claimed to have saved him from some riffraff in Natchez-Under-the-Hill. To Sara's mind, the man was not much above riffraff himself.

"Well, now you've created such a mystery, I suppose I'll just have to go downstairs and see what this is all about," Brianne continued as Mandy buttoned the back of the willow-green merino basque which exactly matched the full skirt beneath it.

As soon as Sara had brushed and combed Brianne's hair and fashioned it into a smooth chignon at the nape of her neck, a house servant was called for who would wheel her chair down the ramp next to the rear stairs. The graceful, wide spiral of pink-veined marble stairs at the front of the house was too beautiful an ornament to be cluttered by a wooden ramp, Brianne had insisted, and so the girl was obliged to go down to the ground floor by the rear of the house. In those days she, as well as everyone else, had thought that the ramps would be only temporary.

Arriving downstairs near the back door which led out to the brick building housing the kitchen and pantries, Brianne instructed the servant to wheel her into the dining room where, he informed her, everyone was still at breakfast.

"Brianne! Ah, there's my flower!" Brian O'Neill, a tall, florid Irishman with flaming hair and twinkling blue eyes quickly stood up from his place at the dining table to take charge of Brianne's wheelchair.

"Papa, you look terrible!" Brianne exclaimed, taking in the bloodshot eyes, tousled hair, and overall tiredness in her father's stance.

"What? Here I'm expressing my gladness at seeing my beautiful daughter and she berates me before breakfast!" He leaned over to kiss her cheek and the smell of whiskey smote her in the face. "God's teeth, puss, am I not to be greeted properly as a loving father should be?"

Brianne, knowing her father's weakness for Scotch whisky and Kentucky rye, wondered why in the world he hadn't stayed in bed until the hangover was gone. Usually, when he came home after a long night of drinking, no one saw him until well after luncheon. The reason for her father's appearance, though, was looking at her from across the room, where he was seated comfortably in front of a plateful of eggs and sausage.

In the flash of a moment, Brianne registered the fact that this stranger was handsome, a little aloof, and, somehow, dangerous. He was certainly tall, well over six feet, with wide, powerful shoulders that strained at his buff-colored coat. His hair was thick, wavy, and quite dark, though not black, which, with the bronzed tan of his skin, made him seem somehow foreign, perhaps Spanish or Italian. But the strangest thing about him was the color of his eyes, topped by dark-crescent eyebrows: they were a golden topaz, reminding Brianne of a panther's eyes.

She wanted to look away from them, but they seemed to hold her gaze, causing the smile that had shaped her lips at sight of her father to slowly die away. The stranger continued to stare back at her with an arrogance that made her soon begin to wish she could get up and slap him.

"Ah, I see you've noticed my friend over there," Brian O'Neill put in, breaking the taut silence. "Brianne, may I present Pierce Nolan, a most handy fellow with a pistol, my dear."

She wasn't surprised to hear it, although she was still in a quandary as to how her father had ever met up with someone like this, much less brought him home!

"Charmed, I assure you, Miss O'Neill," the handsome stranger said, standing up and bowing with an almost feline grace.

Brianne inclined her head toward him as regally as she dared and then, at the insolence in his slow smile, she felt foolish. To recover herself, she asked rather sharply, "I'm interested in knowing how you met my father, Mr. Nolan. Surely you are not one of his business acquaintances?"

Brian O'Neill looked extremely uncomfortable. "Now, honey, breakfast isn't the time to inquire about such things. Why don't we all finish eating and then there'll be plenty of time to answer your questions." He wheeled her over to the table.

Beneath the screen of long, dark lashes, Brianne watched for the stranger's reaction to her wheelchair. Unexpectedly, there was no look of shock or surprise, but a mere flash of something in those golden eyes that most resembled pity. She straightened her back, resolving not to show her discomfort.

Joanna, looking her usual cool self despite the promise of rising humidity, presided over breakfast with her own brand of Yankee poise and Southern charm. It was clear that Brian was still in the throes of a blistering headache and so it was up to her to make their guest feel at home.

Winthrop, as usual, was in a tearing hurry to get up from
the table and be about his business and Brianne, for
some reason, was watching the stranger warily as though
expecting him to stand up at any moment and begin
shooting his pistol in the air.

"Mr. Nolan, you must forgive us all," Joanna put in
politely, "for I must admit we are not at our best this
morning. I'm sure you'll find our company more entertaining at luncheon."

"Does Mr. Nolan plan to stay until lunch then?"
Brianne inquired with innocent curiosity, although the
flash in her turquoise eyes belied that innocence. She
hoped he was not going to stay much longer. His
presence irritated her extremely. She couldn't quite put
her finger on it, although she had to admit she was more
used to men making a fuss over her, admiring her,
however clandestinely, and showing their admiration in
their flowery remarks. But this man seemed to be
ignoring her, placing his attention equally on his food or
the others at table. Probably his pity at her disability
dampened any attraction she held for him. But, of
course, so much the better, for from the look of him he
might have been an escaped criminal or some renegade
gunslinger from out West.

The object of her inner turmoil turned to look at her,
meeting her eyes with a look of curiosity. "I don't quite
know how long I'll stay, ma'am," he answered her in his
slow drawl that didn't quite camouflage the sharp steel
beneath it. "That depends on your hospitality."

The words in themselves were quite correct, but the
way he looked at her when he said them made her well
aware that he knew of her disapproval.

"What do you mean, Nolan? You must stay at least—at
least a week!" Brian declared loudly. "God's teeth, man,
you saved my life last night. My home is yours, sir."

Nolan turned to him with a smile. "It was my pleasure,
sir. I'm grateful for your true Southern generosity."

Again, Brianne thought she detected a hidden meaning, some sarcasm that belied the politeness in his words. Was this stranger making fun of her father? "Your speech, Mr. Nolan, does not have quite the rhythm of everyone else in this part of the country. Are you not from around here?"

He laughed as though amused at her detective work. "I was born in St. Louis, Miss O'Neill. As you know, that city cannot quite make up its mind whether it is Southern or Northern in disposition. Because of that, my views and my speech are neither wholly with the one or the other. I consider myself neither an abolitionist nor a champion of slavery, ma'am, but an impartial outsider."

"Perhaps you are just unwilling to throw your weight behind one, sir, only to find that your judgment might prove wrong." Brianne was aware of her mother's stare of disapproval, but ignored it. She was determined to provoke this man out of his cool withdrawal even if she had to display the manners of a spoiled child!

His slow smile made her furious. "Without seeming too egotistical, Miss O'Neill, I must admit that my judgment in such matters has never proved me wrong thus far."

"Sir, in our part of the country such a refusal to take a stand behind one thing or the other would label you a coward or a fool!"

"Brianne! That is enough, daughter!" Brian O'Neill rose from his place at the table, his blue eyes mirroring his displeasure in her. "If you cannot find it in your heart to be civil to our guest, to a man who saved my life last night when I was foolish enough to find myself in a bad situation of my own doing, then you may excuse yourself from this table! I have personally extended an invitation to Mr. Nolan to stay at Avonlea for as long as he requires!"

Brianne felt her cheeks becoming hotter by the moment. Of all the times she wished she was not confined to her wheelchair, this had to be the most pressing. Without waiting for a servant to wheel her out, she grabbed the large wheels herself and rolled the chair from the table to the hallway. Outside, she waited a moment to collect her breath and still the trembling in her arms. How dare that man cause an argument between herself and her father! Why her father had never chastised her in front of a stranger before! She seethed with anger and was surprised to find slow tears slipping down her cheeks. Furiously, she wiped them away with the backs of her hands.

"What in God's earth came over you in there?" Winthrop whispered behind her, causing her to start in surprise. "Father's face got red as a beet and I thought mama was going to faint backward in her chair." He took the handles of her chair and pushed it outside onto the front porch.

"I don't know, Win. I—I guess I just don't like that man. Why did papa bring him to Avonlea?"

Winthrop settled himself in a chair next to her. "Well, I shouldn't be telling you this. Father'd have my hide, but I guess it's better that you know since it seems we'll be having Mr. Nolan for company for a while. Father had concluded his business in Natchez and was on his way home. Of course, he had to go down Silver Street to get to the levee to catch the next steamwheeler."

"Oh, Win, you're not going to tell me he went to Natchez-Under-the-Hill!" Brianne asked, remembering Gerald's experience there.

"Exactly," Win confirmed. "Seems father took the time to play a round of cards and have a few drinks at one of the taverns there. And he knew full well what kind of shenanigans go on in those taverns. There's been many a planter's body found floating in the river when he complained about cheating at cards. Well, father was sure they were cheating—"

"And they tried to kill him!" Brianne asked in alarm,

her anger at her father for causing her embarrassment forgotten. Heaven knew she loved him dearly despite his faults.

"Two toughs pulled him outside and proceeded to punch his brains out," Win went on, his mouth tightening at the thought. "They hadn't gotten too far when Mr. Nolan came up and took on one of the bullies with his fists. At least the odds were fairer then. Father said his memory's rather foggy on what happened next, and Mr. Nolan won't confirm or deny it, but there were a couple of pistol shots and then Mr. Nolan grabbed father's arm and told him to start running like all hell had busted loose. They waited at the docks for the next steamwheeler and stopped at Ferriday for a few drinks to steady pa's nerves before coming home."

"Oh, Win!" Brianne felt ashamed of herself for treating her father's rescuer so abominably. "I wish father had told me all this before I behaved so stupidly!"

"Honey, I knew something had put a bee in your bonnet and there was no stopping you. You just don't like that man, do you?"

Brianne shook her head. "Something about him just doesn't settle with me, Win, but I'm sure I can be civil to him after hearing what he did for papa. I—I don't know how to go about telling him I'm sorry." She bit her lip.

"Heh, now, where's that Southern charm I see oozing out of your every pore when Josh or Gerald or any one of the other young bucks in the county come around? If my sister can't find a way to make amends without making the man feel that it was all his fault, then I don't know what God made woman for!" Win teased her affectionately.

"Hmmm, we'll see about that," Brianne muttered, not quite as convinced as her brother about the ease with which she would save face. She started to ask Win if he knew what business Mr. Nolan had had in Natchez, then stopped as she heard her father and their guest coming down the hallway to the front veranda.

"Listen, we'd be pleased to have you, Pierce, for as long as you'd be caring to stay," Brian was assuring the other man. "Let me see if I can find my son, Winthrop, and I'll have him show you around. I'll have one of the house slaves take your things to our *garconnière.*"

"That's your bachelor quarters, I take it?"

Brian O'Neill nodded, surprised the man had understood the meaning of the Creole term. "It's just a few yards away from the side gardens so you'll have plenty of privacy."

"Thank you, Brian. I appreciate your hospitality, but I really don't feel I should impose on you and your family."

"I suppose you're referring to my daughter's display of ungracious behavior, sir, and I can't but offer my apologies on her behalf. She—has been delicate because of her fall from a horse last October."

"A shame," Pierce Nolan said, half to himself, as the two men crossed the threshold out onto the veranda.

"Win, there you are, son," Brian said heartily, glad that he could now leave his guest in good hands so as to go upstairs and sleep off his damnable headache. "Would you mind showing our guest around the house and grounds. And have Thaddeus take his things to the *garconnière.*" And when Pierce started to protest, "Don't worry yourself, sir. Southern hospitality is legendary and I won't have you refusing us. You're welcome to stay for as long as you wish." He shook his hand and retired inside.

"Let me go find Thaddeus, Mr. Nolan," Win said quickly, winking at his sister who gave him a horrified look at the thought that he was about to leave her alone with their guest. "I won't be long," he assured them.

For a moment after he left, there was silence on the porch as Brianne tried to find a suitable way to open up the conversation. She sniffed the pungent smoke in the air and realized that Mr. Nolan had lit a cigar. It unnerved her that he was standing a little behind her so that she couldn't see the expression on his face, but only the edge of his dark-blue trousers.

"Don't feel that you have to stand, Mr. Nolan," she said, clearing her throat a little. "Please bring up a chair. I don't mind the company."

"I had the distinct impression that you minded my company quite a bit, Miss O'Neill," he returned quietly.

She flushed, wishing he would at least stand where she could see him. "My remarks at breakfast were uncalled for, Mr. Nolan," she said with difficulty. "I didn't realize what you had done for my father until Win explained everything to me. I want to thank you for your intervention." When he said nothing, she continued, "And to apologize for my earlier behavior."

"Apology accepted," he said, remaining behind her.

That was all he was going to say! Didn't he realize what it had cost her to admit her own wrongdoing! Despite her good intentions, it seemed this man was bound to cause her to lose her temper.

"Mr. Nolan, if you insist on remaining out here with me, would you please have the goodness to stand or sit where I can see you!" she demanded, ruffled. "As you can see, I am rather confined as to where I am to be situated, but you are free to move about, I believe."

He chuckled and pulled a chair up next to her. "You make yourself sound like a prisoner, Miss O'Neill." He continued to smoke, surveying her over the top of his cigar.

She ignored his remark and pulled at her lip with her teeth. Where was Win? If she knew her brother, he was probably taking his time just to tease her! Well, she was not amused at being left with this ill-mannered bore. "I can't think what is taking my brother so long," she said, striving for neutral ground.

"Perhaps he wanted to give you time to extend your apologies," Pierce suggested with the hint of a smile.

"Oh!" Brianne turned to him, eyes wide in surprise.

"How extremely ungentlemanly of you to say so, sir!" she flashed. "I had thought we had pushed that episode out of the way!"

"And so we did, Miss O'Neill. I was only trying to give you a reason for your brother's prolonged absence."

"How insufferable you are, sir!" Brianne drew herself up in her chair. "If I could walk away from you, I would, but as I am constrained here, I would hope you would take it upon yourself to remove yourself from my company!"

"But I am a stranger here, Miss O'Neill," he reminded her. "Where would you have me take myself?"

The words itched on her lips as she thought about exactly where she'd like him to take himself, but years of stern discipline from her mammy and her parents would not permit her to utter them. Instead, she gave him what she hoped was a shattering look.

For a moment they were both silent. Brianne waited for him to speak, waited for her brother to appear, waited for someone to come who would rescue her from this aggravating situation. Finally, she felt she had to speak.

"Mr. Nolan, I am well aware that being from St. Louis you might not understand the manner and ways of Southern gentlefolk. But, I believe that even in the state of Missouri, when a lady asks a gentleman to depart her company, he does so!"

"I didn't think you considered me a gentleman," he reminded her, the hint of amusement once more in his voice. "I believe 'coward' and 'fool' were the exact words you used to describe me."

"I have a few others waiting to be added to the list," she fumed. But before she could break the years of breeding, her brother rounded the corner, whistling cheerily to himself.

"Sorry, I was so long, sir," he said quickly. "Your things have been taken to the bachelor quarters and my mother said to tell you that lunch will be served at two o'clock." Win hesitated when he saw the angry flash that came from his sister's eyes. "Has Brianne been behaving herself?" he chuckled with the slight touch of arrogance that was part of his father's legacy.

"Your sister has kept me highly entertained, Mr. O'Neill," Pierce assured him, not daring to turn and face the volatile female beside him. "Shall we go then?"

Chapter Three

"OH, BRIANNE, DO TELL ME HOW LONG THAT HANDSOME man plans to take advantage of your hospitality!" Mollie Corwin gushed as she sipped icy lemonade. "Did you say he actually admitted to being a hired gun! And a Texas Ranger! How thrilling! But goodness he does look terribly old, doesn't he? Perhaps not quite thirty—but, oh, whoever cares when one gets the feeling he could simply sweep you off your feet if you allowed it!"

"Or maybe if you didn't allow it," Annabelle Jackson put in boldly, passing a pointed tongue over her lips.

The three young ladies, all eighteen years of age, were sitting in the gazebo, looking down the hill at the small lake in which the young men were hunting for frogs. Two small negro children stood quietly, moving long handled fans back and forth to keep the flies off the young ladies. Now and then, Brianne would fill glasses of cool lemonade for them in deference to the heat. She had learned this kindness to slaves from her Yankee mother, who had never quite gotten used to the "peculiar institution" when her husband had brought her South.

"He's an ill-mannered brute," Brianne confirmed nonchalantly, although her eyes were drawn to him too as he stood in his shirtsleeves, up to his knees in the lake. "I can't imagine why Win seems so enthralled by him. Papa's about ready to deed Avonlea over to him, I swear, and even mama considers him a gentleman!" She sniffed and shook her head. "Of course, I know better."

Annabelle turned her dark head with interest. "And how do you know?" she inquired, her dark eyes filled with excitement.

Brianne shrugged. "He doesn't know how to carry on a civilized conversation with a lady. He has two nasty looking pistols which he carries around with him quite frequently, and I swear he's been trying to take Emily Turner away from my brother under his very nose! Of course, Emily is such a flighty thing she's all agog over the attention!" Brianne couldn't keep the sting out of her words. She refused to believe that she was jealous of the attention Pierce Nolan gave Emily when he had all but ignored her in the two weeks that he'd been at Avonlea. Two weeks! They had seemed like two years. When would the man take his leave!

"He hasn't tried to compromise her, has he?" Mollie demanded.

Brianne shrugged as if to say she had no idea, and couldn't care less.

"Perhaps there will be a duel between Mr. Nolan and your brother," Annabelle suggested dramatically. "How wonderfully romantic for Emily!"

"Annabelle, that's a silly thing to say!" Brianne put in hurriedly, shuddering at the thought of Win facing such a dangerous man. "I'm—I'm sure that Emily has more sense than to take a man like Pierce Nolan seriously," she added, reversing her earlier assessment. "Really, I suppose I shouldn't have said such a thing, when I don't really—"

"Hush, here they come," interrupted Mollie, spreading her blue-striped skirts to their best advantage. Beside her, Annabelle did likewise.

"Ah, ladies fair, have you been talking about us?" demanded Josh, satisfied at the pink stain on all three faces. He pointed to a large bucket which Win was holding. "There'll be frogs' legs for supper tonight," he promised with a wink.

The afternoon had already grown long, and twilight

was beginning to turn the blue sky to a dusky rose and dull gold.

"Ouch! Damned mosquitoes!" Annabelle's brother, Bruce, slapped at his arm. "Don't you ladies feel them?"

"Goodness, Bruce, a lady doesn't feel such things," Annabelle replied with dignity, risking a quick glance at Pierce Nolan who smiled at her, revealing his white, even teeth, so attractive, she thought, in the tanned face.

"What happened to Emily?" Win wondered, wiping a muddy hand over his brow. "Did she run to tell cook to start the grease frying?"

"I think she went to see about more lemonade," Brianne answered.

"I guess I'd better go up and help her then." Win shouldered the heavy bucket and hurried up to the house where twinkling lights were beginning to show through the curtained windows.

"How many frogs did you catch, Mr. Nolan?" Annabelle wanted to know, gazing up at the man with an innocent boldness which caused his smile to deepen.

"I lost count, ma'am," he returned, rolling down his shirtsleeves and buttoning his waistcoat. He nodded toward a place next to her on the bench. "May I?" All the men had taken off their high boots and replaced them with dry shoes, so Annabelle nodded eagerly, no longer worried at having mud splattered on her new frock.

"Brianne tells me that you have lived in Texas, sir," Annabelle continued, causing Brianne's cheeks to crimson in embarrassment.

Pierce did not even look at her, but kept his eyes on those of his attentive listener. "Did she? Why, I must have forgotten that I'd mentioned it to her," he answered easily. "Yes, I've lived in Texas, Miss Jackson. It's a marvelous, raw, new state, conducive to wanderers like myself."

"You consider yourself a wanderer, Mr. Nolan," Brianne put in sweetly, "and yet you have made yourself at home here for two weeks."

Annabelle looked at the other girl aghast. "Brianne, dear, perhaps Mr. Nolan finds the Louisiana climate to his taste."

"Or the Louisiana women," Pierce added smoothly, still looking at Annabelle though he wished he could pull that spoiled brat, Brianne over his knee and spank her.

"Mr. Nolan, you are a flatterer, sir!" Annabelle simpered, veiling her eyes with her lashes. "Bruce, we simply must have Daddy invite Mr. Nolan for supper this week. I declare he'd enjoy his company immensely!"

Bruce grinned. "Sounds fine. Pierce can show me some fancy shooting out on the target range."

"Josh, will you wheel me back to the house!" Brianne put in suddenly, not sure she could stand another minute of this. "These mosquitoes are eating me alive!" She turned her head to Pierce and retorted, "Yes, I know, Mr. Nolan, we all know that ladies aren't suppose to feel mosquito bites!"

Pierce smiled at her, a slow, lazy smile that told her he knew how she felt and why she wanted to get away. Her hand itched to slap him, but she forced herself to remain calm.

"I'll come back with you two!" Bruce piped in, continuing to slap at his arms. He glanced over to Mollie who'd been silently watching Pierce Nolan with adoring eyes. "You coming, Mollie?" There was no formal engagement yet, but both families considered there to be an "understanding" between Mollie Corwin and Bruce Jackson. Mollie sometimes chose to ignore that commitment, for she enjoyed flirting with men and, as she told Brianne, it truly wasn't legal until she had the engagement ring on her finger.

"Ummm? Oh, yes, Bruce, I suppose we should go up so that Win and Emily don't eat all the frogs' legs themselves," she giggled, rising to put her hand on Bruce's arm. "You coming, Annabelle?"

"If Mr. Nolan is ready—"

Brianne did not wait to hear if Mr. Nolan was ready or not, she wheeled her chair down the ramp to the ground.

"Heh, wait for me!" Josh put in. "Honey, I don't think you'd make it up that hill under your own steam!" He got behind her chair and pushed her up, puffing slightly by the time he'd reached the top of the incline. "Whew!" he whistled, wiping at his forehead with his handkerchief. "Honey, did you put extra weights on those wheels?"

For a moment, Brianne could only suck in air and then, in a sudden burst like a dam breaking open, she started to cry, the tears streaming down her cheeks onto her bodice. Josh, at a loss, hurried around to pull up her chin and wipe at her tears.

"Honey, I'm sorry," he whispered, hunkering down in front of her. "It was a stupid thing to say, I know! Sweetheart, stop crying now," he urged, realizing that his sodden handkerchief was not up to the job of staving a woman's tears.

How long she would have sat there crying, Brianne couldn't have guessed, but the next thing she knew a strong, long-fingered hand was pushing the tousled hair back from her brow and stroking her cheeks gently with his dry handkerchief.

"Feel any better?"

The words were uttered softly with no hidden amusement in them, and Brianne realized that he understood the reason for her tears, the release of tension that had been building gradually within her for so long, even before he had come into her life. She nodded, not daring to look up into those golden eyes for fear that some lurking insolence in them would spoil the moment.

"There now, keep the handkerchief," he urged her, still in that curiously soft voice. And then the hard edge returned, the underlying insolence she hated. "I have others, so don't feel obligated to return it."

She sniffed once more and dabbed at the end of her nose. "I'm perfectly all right now. Just the heat and it's been a tiring day. If you'll just—wheel me inside Josh, I'll go see what Win has done with our supper." She risked a glance at the challenging golden eyes. "And thank you for your handkerchief, Mr. Nolan. I'll see it gets laundered and returned to you in the morning."

"Oh, Sara, I don't understand why that man can upset me so!" Brianne wailed later that evening when the woman was helping her dress for bed. She twisted the handkerchief in her hands as though longing for it to be tied around his neck.

"Lamb, you just ain't used to a man like him!" Sara soothed her, dropping the fine lawn nightgown over her head and tying the pink satin ribbons at throat and wrists. "Just like I say when he first come here—he ain't a gentleman! Honey, you're used to being pampered by your men folk. That Mist' Nolan ain't no gentleman when it comes to knowing how to treat a delicate female—which you is!"

"Oh, I don't know, Sara. He seemed to treat Miss Annabelle with as much charm as Josh treats me! Why is he so hateful to me?"

"I don't know, honey, I just don't know!" Sara shook her head woefully. "Let's hope he's gone before too much longer, and then you won't have to worry your pretty head 'bout him." She prayed she was right about that.

"I certainly am not about to be worrying about him, Sara!" Brianne put in with more sharpness than she intended. "It's—it's just that he seems so different when he talks with mama or papa, and I really think he and Win get along as well as Win gets along with any of the other boys in the county. It's just when he's with me. Oh, I don't know! I don't know what he expects of me!"

"Honey, he don't have no right to expect nothing of you!" Sara flared, distressed at seeing her lamb so upset because of that drifter. "Just you get him out of your head, lamb!"

"I'd be much happier to get him out of sight, Sara."

"Don't worry," Sara repeated, signaling to Mandy to come brush her mistress' hair. "Now, this'll soothe you, Miss Brianne," the old negress assured her.

Brianne closed her eyes, giving herself up for a moment to the tingling relaxation of someone brushing her hair in long, smooth strokes. "Prettiest hair I've ever seen, ma'am," Mandy was saying timidly. Brianne barely registered the words. Wouldn't it be wonderful if life was as easy as sitting here having her hair brushed? But, of course, it really should be that easy—and it would be—except for the plain fact that she couldn't walk anymore.

Pulled out of her pleasant reverie at the thought, Brianne glanced down at her legs, pulling the nightdress up past her knees, surveying the slender, white limbs which had refused to do her bidding for the past six months. If only she could run away from that nasty Mr. Nolan, ride a horse again and leave him behind. There'd be no one for him to make fun of, to feel sorry for. She hated the thought that he might feel only pity for her. She remembered the gentle way he had brushed the tears from her cheeks. It had been only pity then. Humiliation welled up within her and, once more, her fingers pulled at the handkerchief he'd given her, proof of his pity.

"Sara, do you remember those exercises that Dr. Blackwell told me to do for my legs?"

Sara looked up from the depths of the armoire where she'd been putting away clothes. Her brow wrinkled. "Sure, honey, I seems to remember most of them."

"I want you to teach Mandy how to massage my legs and push my feet back and forth like Dr. Blackwell showed us," Brianne went on, her voice deliberate as she stared at her legs. "I want to do them twice—no three times—a day. Isn't that what he said to do?"

Sara nodded, a pleased smile breaking out on her broad face under the colorful turban. "Why, honey, I didn't think you put no account into those doctors' words!"

"Well, I've got to try something, don't I? I simply can't allow myself to sit in that chair the rest of my life!"

"Lamb, I'm so pleased to hear you say so!" Sara beamed.

Chapter Four

"PAPA, PLEASE LET ME TRY!"

"Brianne, I'll not have you falling and breaking your neck!" Brian O'Neill returned stubbornly. "Honey, you've got to be listening to reason. You can't try to ride a horse without the use of your legs! What if the horse reared or you lost hold of the reins? Sidesaddle is risky enough without—"

"Then I'll ride astride, papa," Brianne returned.

They were in the stables where Brian was getting ready to take his usual weekly ride around the perimeters of his plantation. It was a long journey which would keep him out from morning until late afternoon. He'd be foolish to let his delicate daughter accompany him.

"Honey, I don't like to be arguing with you! You've got less than a week before the county dance," he wheedled. "Now you wouldn't want to be laid up in bed for that, would you, puss?"

"Oh, papa, I'll get much more enjoyment out of riding with you than sitting at some silly dance, watching everyone else waltzing! I've been doing my exercises faithfully for the past week or more. My legs are getting stronger, I swear!"

Brian was ready to pull out his hair. He had to admit that his daughter was every bit as stubborn as he was, and she wasn't about to be put off without him becoming an ogre about it. He hated to give her a direct no; after all, she had so much to bear as it was, missing out on all the fun things that young people did in the springtime.

"Darlin', if you'd only wait until after the dance—"

"Papa, please!" she insisted, looking up at him with those great turquoise eyes shiny with tears. "I'll go crazy if I don't get out of this chair!"

"'Twas a horse that did you in, puss," he reminded her, although he was beginning to waver noticeably.

"Oh, excuse me."

Both O'Neills turned at the sound of Pierce Nolan's voice. Brianne couldn't help the frown that automatically shaped her mouth. Although they had become civil to one another. For the moment, her impatience at his interruption, just when she had almost persuaded her father to let her ride, overcame the admiration she might have felt at seeing him in his riding costume—a suit of buff buckskin that suited him perfectly with its tight trousers and fitted coat. She, herself, had worn her favorite riding habit of turquoise blue which almost exactly matched the shade of her eyes. She had put it on with Mandy's help this morning, sure that she could charm her father into letting her go with him.

"Pierce, good morning!" Brian greeted the younger man with a wide smile. "If you're going riding, sir, why not come with me? It's always nice to have company on the long ride around Avonlea."

"But papa!"

"Darlin', I said no. Now you'll be getting yourself back inside," Brian said sternly. "The ride is much too long for you even if you could sit a horse."

Brianne was about to give up when she heard an unexpected source of defense come from Pierce Nolan.

"Brian, I think if your daughter would like to try to ride, you should allow it," he was saying in that lazy manner of his. "If you'll pardon my impertinence, I think it might prove beneficial for her to be out of that wheelchair for a while."

"Thank you, sir, but I believe I can handle—"

"Oh, papa, just let me try for a little while!" Brianne

begged. "If the hours grow too long, I can come home by myself. Goodness knows I've ridden all over Avonlea since I was a child!"

"I'll accompany her," Pierce put in quietly, seeing the intense eagerness on the girl's face. He liked to see the petulance gone from her mouth, the spoiled sulky look replaced by a fresh glow that made her quite lovely. He admitted to himself that she might be quite an intriguing young woman if she ever stopped thinking of herself long enough.

"Mr. Nolan, I'm perfectly capable—"

"Pierce, that's a good idea," Brian interrupted before his daughter's anger could take root. "If she's going to be stubborn enough to insist on going, then I want to make sure she can get back all right." He gave his daughter a crooked smile. "Well, puss, it seems you're to be riding after all, thanks to Mr. Nolan."

Brianne flashed a glance at her champion and smiled rather sourly. "It'll be all I can do to express my gratitude," she replied with impudence.

Pierce laughed. "We'd best see if you're able to sit a horse, Miss O'Neill. I can collect my thanks later."

They chose the gentlest mare in the stables, a fact that infuriated her, since she hadn't ridden old Suzy since she was eight years old. Despite her protests, Brian was firm in his choice, not wanting to risk her on one of the higher-stepping fillies. They brought the horse out into the yard where one of the negro boys held the bridle.

Brianne, who had followed in her chair, wheeling it with some difficulty, but insisting on doing it herself, realized that she hadn't thought through exactly how she was going to get up on the horse. It was going to be awkward at best.

"Honey, if you can stand by yourself, I might be able to lift you—"

"I've a better idea, Brian," Pierce put in, estimating the distance from a nearby bale of hay to the horse's saddle.

"Have your boy bring the mare over here," he indicated the straw bale, "and you can swing her up to me and I can settle her on the saddle."

"I'm not a bolt of cloth to be swung about and tied to the horse, Mr. Nolan!" Brianne protested, not liking it one bit that she would be put into close proximity with him.

"Honey, he's got a point," Brian soothed her. "I know it will be a bit undignified, puss, but I think it's the best way. You're not strong enough to be given a leg up, are you?"

She shook her head, knowing he was right. She pushed her chair as close as possible to the straw bale, then drew on her riding gloves and made sure the ribbon of her riding hat was secure, before pulling herself up, haltingly, into her father's waiting arms.

"That's my girl," Brian grinned at her. He steadied her, then swung her up where Pierce was waiting on the straw.

"Steady the mare, boy," Pierce commanded, his arms strong beneath her knees and around her back. He looked over at his booty and smiled disarmingly. "Are you comfortable enough, Miss O'Neill?"

Brianne couldn't help the rosy blush that suffused her cheeks at the thought that this man was actually holding her against him, her hands clenched tightly at the back of his neck. She wished it were Win or Josh.

"I'll be more comfortable in the saddle, Mr. Nolan!" she retorted.

"I'm not surprised to hear you say it, Miss O'Neill." He leaned over the mare and dropped her lightly into the saddle, one leg on either side. Her arms were still about his neck until he could grab the reins to bring them up to her, and for a brief moment their faces were close together. Brianne was oddly aware that if she chose to she could turn her head just a little and her cheek would rub against his tanned, shaven one. She smelled his masculine scent of soap and leather, a rugged scent that she had always liked on her father or Win. Why did it disturb her now?

For his own part, Pierce had always liked the closeness of a woman, especially a beautiful one who had spirit. The trouble was, this one had a little too much spirit—the kind that had to be tamed. God, but how he would love to do the taming! Of course, this delicate piece of womanhood was out of his reach: she was too vulnerable, both because of her handicap and the fact that she was an innocent. Despite his resolution, he still enjoyed the soft verbena scent on her clothing and the tentative touch of her gloved hands on his neck. He felt her tremble and wondered what she was thinking.

"The reins, Mr. Nolan?" Brianne asked, slipping one hand from his neck to grasp them from him.

The contact was broken and Pierce straightened, looking down on the pert face with an introspective grin. Damn! He knew where to go when the ache for a woman came over him. Thank God, Win O'Neill was man enough to have tasted the fleshly pleasures of Mrs. Morrison's House of Pleasure up in Ferriday. When there was nothing but innocent, flighty belles surrounding a man, he had to get down to business sooner or later with a woman who knew what was what.

When they had all mounted their horses, Brian led the other two off at a leisurely pace, in deference to Brianne. Pierce couldn't help noticing, though, how ably she held the reins and guided her horse with them. The joy in her face totally transformed it and the beauty there was refreshing, with the morning sun lighting up the turquoise of her eyes and bringing out the reddish glints in her auburn hair.

They rode without speaking for nearly half-an-hour, the two men aware of the girl's happiness and not wishing to intrude on it.

"Papa, this is heaven!" Brianne burst out finally. "I can ride again!"

"Honey, it's the Irish in you," Brian assured her

merrily, his own joy great because of his daughter's. He
let himself wonder, briefly, if he had done the right thing
by sheltering her these past six months. Perhaps, he
should have encouraged her to do more things before
now. Ah, but who knew? She was his darling daughter,
his pride and joy, and he had had to make sure that she
was truly out of danger. "You'll be telling us now, if you
get too tired?"

"Yes, papa, I promise to tell you the minute I start
napping on poor old Suzy!" Brianne returned with a little
laugh.

They passed the acres upon acres of fields planted in
sugar cane, the mellow ground softer and damper here
than higher up by the house. The cane was rising thicker
and stronger now, unhampered by threatening weeds
which the overseer made sure were cut down by field
hands every day.

"When is the cane ready for harvesting?" Pierce asked
his host.

"The cutting is usually determined by the weather—
and my own judgment," Brian answered him. "I can't be
letting it go past mid-autumn or an unexpected frost
might cost me thousands of dollars in damage. If we get
too much rain, it could flood the fields and that would
ruin the crop just as badly as frost."

"Have you ever thought about raising cotton? I've
heard that's an easier crop to handle."

"I raised it when I first came here," Brian returned.
"But the land was better suited for the sugar cane. I'm a
richer man because of it, too, Pierce. Haven't you heard
it takes ten cotton planters to make in a year what a sugar
cane producer does? Come along now and I'll show you
where the sugar is processed."

They rode farther south, following the line of the river
until they were in sight of a large brick building with a tall
chimney. Brian pointed to it proudly. "That sugar house
cost me nearly seventy-five thousand dollars to put into
operation, sir. It's operated by those two large furnaces

you see encased in metal on the side. God's teeth, but you should see it when it's in full operation in the fall. We put half our field hands here while the other half's out cutting the stalks." Brian turned to the younger man and his smile was genuine. "Hell, Pierce, I'm hoping you'll consider staying 'til then."

Pierce returned the smile. "That's a few months away, Brian. I won't commit myself, nor do I want to strain your hospitality too much. I've enjoyed these few weeks."

"And you're welcome to stay for as many more as you like." Brian pressed his horse on to check with a group of field hands who were working in a section of land close to the river.

Pierce stopped his horse to let it graze, noting that Brianne had done the same. She was leaning forward in her saddle, staring out at the river which was visible between the moss-covered black cedars and the tall weeds that grew along the mudbanks.

"And what about you, Miss O'Neill?" he asked her boldly. "Is your welcome to stay included in your father's?"

She looked up at him, her eyes wary. "My father is master of Avonlea, Mr. Nolan," she said. "I usually concur with his wishes."

"I wonder," he laughed.

"I wonder, too, Mr. Nolan," she put in questioningly. "Of course, it is not at all unusual for guests to stay at Avonlea for a whole season. We do have the best cook in upstate Louisiana and no one can complain of a lack of comfort in the house. But still, you are, after all, a stranger to us." Her turquoise eyes gazed at him boldly. "Are you, perhaps, running away from something, Mr. Nolan?"

His amused laugh surprised her. "Is that what you would like to think?"

"I can assure you, I hardly bother myself about the reasons for your staying or going," she said quickly.

"I'm glad to hear it, Miss O'Neill, for I have no

intention of airing my reasons to—ah—strangers, as you put it.''

She folded her lips and turned away from him, and he wondered why he had deliberately drawn her anger. She would have been surprised, he thought, if he had told her the reasons for his staying overlong at Avonlea. Some of them would have surprised even himself. Was it an unconscious longing for those things that were old and settled and full of their own charm? Was it a momentary respite from the rawness, the wildness of Texas and the West, California and the mining towns? He had seen them all, traveled and slept under the stars more times than he had slept with a roof over his head. He had left his home in St. Louis when he was sixteen, almost thirteen years ago, rebelling as youth did at the rules and regulations of the old, established way of thinking.

Pierce thought back to the sweet, warm days of his youth in St. Louis, a city that was old and new, a melting pot of many nationalities—French, Spanish, English, and German. His parents had been strict, effectively disguising their love for him behind their stony ambition for their only son. They lavished money on his education, even sending him on the Grand Tour in Europe; they did everything they could to shape and form him into the object of their expectations. But, as he had grown older, the questions had begun to come with increasing frequency and intensity. When would he marry, whom would he marry, where would they settle, what position in his father's manufacturing business did he want? All the education and training, the output of money, had been there for his use only to fulfill *their* dreams and ambitions. They had had very definite ideas as to what he was to become: a sturdy pillar of the business community with his own rigid set of standards and conduct, exactly like his father.

Pierce had not been able, even at the tender age of sixteen, to accept implicitly such a way of life; to have his future mapped out for him so carefully that there was no

room for change, for excitement, for adventure! He had
run away, fearing that the longer he stayed, the harder it
would be to leave. He had gone off to find a different
kind of freedom in the raw newness of the West—the last
frontier.

He had lived with Indians, Mexicans, Spaniards, min-
ers; used his wits to avoid fights, and his gun when he
couldn't. He'd never made close contact with any of the
myriad horde of men and women he had met during his
travels, with the exception of the few comrades he'd
made in the Texas Rangers. Ah, those were human
beings a man was proud to call his friends!

An uneasy tug pulled at Pierce's memory as he
reflected on those good friends he'd made in Texas. It
was a damn shame when Texas had been made a state
and the Rangers had all but been put to rest. Now the
federal government was responsible for upholding law
and order in that vast new addition to its territory.
Somehow, Pierce doubted that they would do as fine a
job as the Rangers had done. In fact, one of the reasons
he had loitered in Louisiana was his reluctance to go
further from that state he had grown to love and the men
he had come to admire. On his trips into Ferriday, he
made it his business to check with the telegraph office for
any news of the Rangers. It was rumored that they were
to be called out again since the Union Army could not
keep the Mexican bandidos or the Comanche warriors
from raiding. It would be a simple matter to re-enlist in
the Rangers as a troubleshooter, which had always been
his specialty.

His thoughts returned to his home, his parents and
sisters, Rose and Mary. The two girls were probably
married by now, he guessed, and, no doubt, he was an
uncle already. The letters that had been so few, mainly
because of so many changes of address on his part, had
always ended with the hope that he would return someday when he'd decided on settling down. He shook his
head thoughtfully. He wasn't sure he would ever be

completely ready for that. He was old enough now to have grown used to his own independence. And yet, these last weeks at Avonlea, among members of a family who so obviously loved each other, had made him rethink his position.

Still, there was the problem of finding a suitable wife, someone who could share his own excitement for adventure and travel. None of these hothouse flowers in this part of the South would dare dirty the hems of their flounced skirts unless it were absolutely necessary. The things they cared about, the dances and picnics and barbecues, were so far removed from the things that mattered to him.

Pierce found his eyes studying the girl in front of him, tracing the elegant tilt of her head, the slender arch of her back, the way she sat her horse. He imagined that she must be beginning to tire, and yet, he would bet money that she would never say so. In this Southern hothouse blossom, he thought, was mixed too much of the wild, Irish rose. She was spoiled, yes, and terribly ignorant when it came to how to treat a real man. She knew how to flirt and toy and giggle and bat her lashes, but he wondered if she was capable of true passion.

Brianne, trying to concentrate on keeping her back straight and her demeanor suitably poised, felt Pierce Nolan's eyes on her. It took every ounce of decorum she possessed to continue staring straight ahead, praying her father would settle his business with the field hands and return to them. She hated knowing that that man was behind her, assessing her, waiting for her to fall from the horse in a faint or begin to complain that she needed to return home to rest.

Devil take it! She *was* beginning to feel tired. She had truly thought that she would be able to keep up with her father at the slow pace they had kept, but after an hour, her thighs were starting to ache and her back to protest. She knew full well that it would probably take them well into late afternoon before they would arrive back at

Avonlea. Well, she would stand it as long as she could, she told herself. She saw her father cantering back with relief.

"We're clearing out a section of wood there by the river," Brian explained for Pierce's benefit. "My overseer, Tom Benson, is in the fields today, so I've only got his assistant, Big Blue, to watch the slaves here."

"An unusual name," Pierce commented.

"That's the name he came with. He's a slave, you see. Bought him from a planter near Baton Rouge four years ago. He's a good worker and a natural boss."

"Might that not be dangerous then, giving him so much authority?" Pierce questioned, truly curious.

Brian shrugged. "He's always been loyal and there's been plenty of chances for him to try to escape. He has his own cabin, you see, with his wife and their three children. I don't think he'd be trying to leave them, and he's smart enough to know that the little ones would never make it."

"He's trapped then," Pierce murmured more to himself than to his host. Would he feel that way too if he decided to settle down with a wife and raise a family? Would he eventually come to feel trapped, not able to go, and yet, not happy at staying? He turned his attention back to O'Neill.

"Come on and I'll show you the lower fields, Pierce," he was saying, starting up his horse. "You okay, honey?" he asked his daughter.

"Yes, papa," she assured him, taking up the reins and pushing Suzy into a brisk walk.

They continued on for another hour, stopping briefly to let their horses drink from the creek that bisected the O'Neill land. Brianne felt the perspiration dotting her brow and sliding uncomfortably between her shoulder blades. She knew she was being foolish in not telling her father that she was tired and needed to start back for home. She risked a cautious glance to where Pierce Nolan was in conversation with her father, wondering

what sarcastic remark he would have if she admitted that
she was worn out. Stubbornly, she decided she'd drop
from her horse first before she'd admit it.

The May sun rose higher in the pale-blue sky, bearing
down on the fields of sugar cane and the riders who
surveyed them. Brianne felt the beginnings of a headache radiating from the knot of tension at the back of her
neck. She had had a drink from her father's canteen at
the last stop, but she felt thirsty again. Overriding her
thirst, though, was the need to stretch her legs out and lay
down somewhere. The muscles, long unused to this
position, were protesting painfully now. Lord knew, her
father would never let her ride again if she fell off her
horse or fainted. She'd never hear the end of it.

"Papa?"

"Yes, darlin'?" he questioned, stopping his horse and
turning in the saddle to watch her.

"I—think I've had enough for one day," she admitted,
swallowing her pride, although she refused to glance in
Pierce's direction.

"You've done well, daughter," Brian said with obvious
approval. "Maybe I was wrong in keeping you off a horse
for so long, eh?" He trotted up beside her and Brianne
was careful to keep the strain out of her face as she
smiled up at him. "You're a good lass, Brianne." He
turned to Pierce who had seen the struggle in her face to
hide its weariness when Brian had trotted up. "Pierce,
I'm entrusting her to you, sir."

"It will be my pleasure to see her back home," Pierce
said with a grin. He pulled up to Brianne's mare and
waited until Brian had gone on before whispering, "Do
you think you can make it?"

Her head shot up and she glared at him. "Of course, I
can make it, Mr. Nolan!"

He shrugged and set a slow pace, enjoying the leisurely
ride along the twisting path through fields and beneath
trees, feeling the sun on him and the intoxicating scents
of spring. Despite his preoccupation with the scenery

though, he was well aware of the tension emanating from the girl beside him. He only had to turn his head a little to see her teeth biting at her lower lip, the drops of perspiration on her face and the way she clutched at the reins. He was almost sure that she was going to pass out. He only hoped he would be able to catch her before she broke her fool neck.

They were following the river now, as it was cooler than cutting straight over the meadows. Out on the Mississippi, they could hear the splashing of a paddle-wheeler, and Brianne stopped her horse at the levee, outwardly to watch the progress of the steamboat, but truly to have time to collect herself for the last mile to the house.

She was aware of Pierce Nolan beside her, even as her eyes automatically slipped over the elegant lines of the packet boat with its white filigree trimming. Its two tall smoke stacks were blowing out clouds of white smoke while the huge paddle wheel in the back churned through the river water within its housing which stood nearly four stories high. They could see, even from this distance, the multicolored figures of men and women strolling along the wide decks and leaning over the rails to watch the churning water below.

"Have you ever been on a steamboat, Miss O'Neill?" Pierce wondered, lighting a small cheroot.

She nodded. "Yes. I had to go down to Baton Rouge on one when I had my accident last year. Unfortunately, the fun of the journey was lost on me."

"You should go again someday when you're fully recovered."

She turned her head to stare at him. "You believe I'll walk again, Mr. Nolan?"

He smiled. "I believe you're stubborn enough and gutsy enough, Miss O'Neill, to do just about anything you set out to do."

She tossed her head a little, although the effort cost her. "I didn't think you thought anything of the kind, Mr.

Nolan. I had the feeling you believed me unworthy of your notice or attention since you have so pointedly ignored me when others are present."

He flicked the half-finished cheroot out into the muddy water and laughed. "I wasn't aware you had suffered from my lack of attention. You seem to have plenty of young bucks around to offer themselves to your service." His golden eyes raked her. "However, if I have ignored you, Miss O'Neill, let me say it is only because I am not the kind of man who enjoys the mindless flirtations of silly, young women who can't seem to make up their minds whether it is a man they want, or an adoring puppy."

He heard her indrawn breath of outrage. "Mr. Nolan, I am neither silly nor mindless! And, when the time comes, I can assure you I will know the difference between a real gentleman and an insolent rascal, like yourself, who insists on insulting young women of good breeding!"

He clapped his hands and bowed from the waist. "Bravo! Well said, Miss O'Neill. You have, I take it, effectively put me in my place, so to speak."

"I am heartily glad that you are well bred enough to be aware of it, sir! When we arrive at home, I certainly hope you will take your attention elsewhere."

His golden eyes were insolent and his voice mocked her. "And yet, were you not just complaining of my lack of attention, ma'am?"

"Oh! You—you are the most—" She was sputtering ineffectually, seeking some loathsome name to call him while still retaining her own decorum. At a loss, she simply glared at him. "Shall we continue on, Mr. Nolan?" she finally suggested tightly.

He nodded, barely keeping the smile of amusement off his face.

They turned their horses up the lane of gravel, walking slowly beneath the arch of live oaks. For the few minutes that they had crossed swords, Brianne had forgotten about her aches and pains, but now, in the silence that

surrounded her, she felt them even more fully than
before. The weak muscles in her legs, coupled with the
forgotten strain on her back from riding, made her clench
her teeth to keep from crying out. She felt a slight nausea
rising in her chest and swallowed to keep it down.

They had come up to the circle drive now in front of
the brick steps that led up to the front door. The veranda
seemed to be swimming before her eyes now and she
took a deep breath to steady herself.

"M—my chair," she muttered, hoping to get off the
horse here and get inside.

"It's probably still at the stableyard," he replied, his
eyes watching her carefully.

The thought that she had to continue on around to the
back of the house made her want to scream in frustration.
Her head hurt, her legs ached dreadfully, and she felt as
though she were going to swoon any minute. Slowly, she
put her hand to her forehead, slumping down, feeling as
though the ground were rising up to meet her. With fear
in her face, she looked over to Pierce, watching as he
seemed to slide off his mount in slow motion.

"Pierce!" she cried out, her voice edged in disbelief.

Pierce was off his horse on the ground. In two steps, he
was with her, catching her in his arms as she fell sideways
off the mare. Cradling her against his chest, he stood still
for a moment, looking into her face where her lashes
fluttered against her cheeks. She must have fainted, he
surmised, aware of the tightening of her lips in pain as her
muscles cried out against the change of position. It was
the ache that brought her out of the faint.

"God's teeth, that hurts!" she swore softly, using her
father's favorite oath.

Pierce couldn't help but smile. "You're just not used to
it, yet," he assured her. "After a few more rides—much
shorter, I would think—the muscles will toughen up
again."

"Lord, I don't ever want to see the back of a horse
again!" she cried. And then she became aware that

Pierce was holding her easily against him, that her riding hat was hanging around her neck by its chin ribbons and that they were in full view of any house servant that happened to look out a front window. "Good heavens, you've got to put me down!" she said frantically.

"Don't be silly, Brianne, you'd fall flat on your face, and how would you explain a broken nose to your father?"

She was aware that he had called her by her first name, and remembered now crying out to him in kind. It made her somehow uncomfortable to be on this casual basis with him, but she realized there would be no going back to the old formality.

"Well I can't expect you to carry me all the way around to the stableyard," she put in.

"Then, it seems the only thing to do is for me to carry you in the house and you may call for a servant to fetch your chair." He proceeded up the steps to the front door, his knock answered by the majordomo, Thaddeus, who was careful not to show his surprise at the sight of Miss Brianne being held by their houseguest.

"Miss O'Neill was too tired to wait for her chair to be brought up from around back," Pierce informed him smoothly. "If you'll just have someone run get it, she can be taken up to her room and tended to."

Thaddeus nodded and left them to go into the salon.

"Thank goodness, mother wasn't about!" Brianne sighed with relief. She was aware that Pierce still held her. "You can settle me in one of the salon chairs."

His mocking grin disarmed her. "You're a light enough bundle for me to carry, Brianne. And look how you've managed to gain my devoted attention!"

"Oh! Put me down!" she burst out angrily. "I can wait here for my chair without your support!"

"What an ungrateful little imp, you are," he laughed, but obliged her by setting her down on one of the stuffed sofas. "Not even a word of gratitude for keeping you from breaking your headstrong little neck?"

She flushed and lowered her eyes. "I do thank you for catching me before I fell," she murmured. She looked up at him with wide eyes. "You—you won't tell papa what happened, I mean about me not being able to make it back all the way?"

He leaned closer and she thought he was going to swallow her up with those golden eyes. "My lips are sealed," he said. "You have got to be one of the bravest young women I've ever met, Brianne O'Neill, and one of the stubbornest!"

She was gratified to hear the admiration in his voice. She looked away from those mesmerizing eyes, then felt his finger beneath her chin, drawing it back to him. For a terrible, breathtaking moment, she thought he was going to kiss her and it was all she could do to keep her heart from jumping out of her bodice.

Pierce wavered for a moment over those luscious lips that were parted in an invitation she could hardly be aware of. With an effort, he merely brushed at her mouth with his free hand, a lingering caress which he was aware would leave her as unsatisfied as he. Then, straightening, he cocked a dark eyebrow at her.

"So, now that you have had my attention, Brianne, are you so sure that you want it?"

Feeling a sense of frustration, Brianne wished she were close enough to strike out at him. For a moment, they both stared at each other, each judging, wondering, before Pierce turned on his heel and started out of the room.

"Where are you going?" she cried, hating herself for wanting to know.

"To a place where a woman knows exactly what to do when she has a man's attention!" he replied savagely.

Chapter Five

THE MAY TWILIGHT WAS BLESSEDLY COOL AFTER THE HEAT and humidity of the day, Brianne thought as she sat in her wheelchair, watching Mandy press the last creases out of her ballgown of purest white satin. The gown had cost her father a pretty penny, having been sent up from New Orleans, but it had all been part of a calculated plan to make sure she would attend the cotillion. He had also bought her a new pair of shoes, white kid lined in blue satin with tiny blue heels. Dancing slippers! She might as well have gone barefoot for all the dancing her feet were going to see. Still, they were tempting, especially with the striped, silk stockings that went with them. Of course, she had given in against such brandishing of gifts, mostly because she had finally realized that sitting at home alone would be much worse than sitting among friends at a party.

"You'll look like an angel, I swear!" Mandy breathed in awe as she carefully laid the gown on the bed.

"Exactly as papa would wish," Brianne laughed, although a sad note had crept into her voice. "Is Sara coming up?"

"She helping your mama, Miss Brianne," Mandy replied. "She'll be here when she done with her."

By the time Sara puffed into the room, Brianne had already bathed herself with a sponge and pitcher of rose-scented water. Mandy had succeeded in tying the strings of the seven petticoats that would go beneath the dress, but they had waited for Sara to help with the gown.

Cautiously, Mandy helped Brianne to stand and to hold onto one of the bedposts for support. After the long weeks of exercising and practicing, Brianne's muscles seemed to be growing stronger.

"Honey, this is sure 'nough the handsomest dress I've ever laid eyes on," Sara hummed, pulling the dress over her mistress' uncorseted frame reverently. Ever since she'd found that the corset hurt her back too much when she leaned against her wheelchair, Brianne had received her mammy's tacit approval not to wear one, although neither one would dare reveal this to her mother.

The gown slipped over Brianne's lithe form, billowing its yards and yards of material over the petticoats and hiding the prized dancing slippers. The bodice was cut off the shoulder and the decolletage cut deep across the breasts, edged with expensive Brussels lace. That was the only ornament the dress boasted except for the wide silk sash which spanned Brianne's small waist and hung in twin streamers down the back of the skirt.

Sara worked her magic on the thick, silky tresses of auburn hair, pulling them gently back from Brianne's forehead and gathering them into a tangled knot of graceful curls that hung over her shoulders, accented by two fragrant gardenias on either side. With her embroidered gloves, ivory fan, and pearl earrings, Brianne looked truly breathtaking.

"Oh, Sara!" Brianne sighed deeply.

"Honey, I'm just bustin' with pride over you," Sara wept, brushing at the tears. "If ever God did the wrong thing, it was when he let you fall off that horse!"

Brianne reached up and touched her finger to the woman's lips. "Hush now, Sara, let's not talk of it now when the mood should be gay and charming." She laughed a little bitterly. "It is a lovely gown. Sad to think that it will be horribly creased by the end of the night because of this stupid chair." She straightened her shoulders and lifted her chin. "I'm ready, if you will call Thaddeus."

Downstairs, a smartly outfitted carriage awaited the women, the men preferring to ride their own steeds to all the public affairs. Winthrop carried his sister to the carriage, then helped place the wheelchair into a small cart which would be driven to Rosemont by a negro driver.

"Where's Pierce?" Win asked, glancing at his pocket watch. "I told him to be ready by seven."

He probably didn't have the required evening attire, Brianne thought sourly. Except when necessary, she had not spoken to their houseguest since last week after her ride. She had hoped her freezing silence had unnerved him enough that he would have the decency to stay at home tonight.

Finally, Pierce appeared, already mounted. "We thought you'd decided not to come, sir," Win said.

"Please accept my apology for being late," Pierce said smoothly, looking impeccable in a black suit of finest kerseymere. His shirt was snowy white with a pleated front and stiff, standing collar, beneath which he sported a handsome black tie. His waistcoat was indigo blue, embroidered silk, and Brianne thought she saw the wink of real diamond studs on the buttons. He had even borrowed a pair of gloves from Winthrop and one of his best black silk hats.

"The reason for my tardiness is this," Pierce went on, holding two corsages of flowers and gesturing toward Brianne and her mother. "My gift for the two loveliest ladies in Louisiana." He dismounted under the watchful eyes of Brian O'Neill, who was thinking that he should have thought of doing the very same thing himself. The fellow did have charm, after all.

Pierce bowed low at the door of the open carriage and leaned forward to hand one corsage to Joanna, who smiled graciously and fastened them to her lavender silk bodice. Pierce then turned his attention to the daughter of the house, his golden eyes appreciating the beauty revealed and enhanced by the stunning gown she was wearing.

"The flowers come in a poor second, ma'am," Pierce murmured. The corsage he had chosen for her was already fastened to a strip of pale-blue velvet which he tied deftly about her slender wrist.

"Thank you," Brianne got out, more surprised than anyone else about the gift. Her turquoise eyes questioned him, but the gaze she received told her nothing except how much he was appreciating her beauty.

Brian O'Neill, who had closely watched the exchange of glances between his daughter and the man who had become a close friend, felt the beginnings of a devilish Irish glee. God's elbow! They were made for each other! They were certainly a match in looks. He'd have beautiful grandchildren. Their temperaments were not always on an even keel, but that would only add spice to their relationship! Why hadn't he seen it before? He almost rubbed his hands together, but common sense returned as he realized how delicate such a plan was. After all, they knew nothing about Nolan's family, his background, except that he was from St. Louis. And there was the matter of Brianne's handicap. Her dowry would have to be enlarged.

"Brian? Are you daydreaming, my dear?" Joanna was asking. "We'd best be off or we'll be unforgivably late."

Brian O'Neill came back to the present with a thud. He looked at his daughter who was no longer gazing at Pierce Nolan, but seemed to be ignoring him. Pierce, himself, had pulled his horse up to where Win was waiting, impatient to be off to the dance and his Emily. Had he dreamed it?

He gave the driver the signal to be off, then laid the switch to his own mount to catch up with Pierce and his son.

The county cotillion was held each year at a different plantation house. Rosemont was the perfect choice this

year of 1850 since it was celebrating its twenty-fifth year
of existence. Because it had been built in a slightly
different era than Avonlea, Rosemont's lines were closer
to the ancient Greek temples that had been so popular
among plantation builders of the 1820s. Thick columns
rose in front and back of the house with pediments in the
manner of a Greek temple. It had a hipped roof, crowned
with a balustraded captain's walk so that Ben Fontaine
could look out over his vast domain from the highest
point on it. Of course, Rosemont's most beautiful claim to
posterity was its formal gardens from which it had gotten
its name.

Lettice Fontaine had a passion for gardens and flowers
and had made sure that every available inch of space
around her house was filled with both. All around the
house there were bushes of azaleas, camellias, roses, and
wisterias. Cape jasmine, lilies, and magnolias filled the air
with a heavy fragrance, and lemon and orange trees had
been planted in colorful tubs. The gardens were terraced
where the hill sloped down toward the riverbanks and a
latticed pavilion provided a cool refuge on warm summer
days.

As the carriage drew nearer the house, the flower
scents wafted out to Brianne, and she could hear the
sounds of carriage wheels and horses and people talking
and laughing. In the background, an orchestra was
beginning to play light music, and the sweet notes
mingled effectively with the chirping of the crickets in the
lawn.

For a moment, Brianne allowed herself to think of the
cotillion last year when she had been one of the belles of
the ball, had had every dance taken and been charmed
by every young gallant attending. She swept the thought
aside quickly, angrily. She would not be the belle of the
ball tonight, but she would not be a simpering ninny
either. If she had to, she'd keep Carter Lowell beside her
all night!

She was glad to see that her chair was awaiting her on the porch where it could easily be wheeled to the back of the house and outside to the gardens. She was relieved when Win came to carry her up the stairs, somehow fearing that Pierce Nolan might ask to carry out the task, especially after his unexpected gift of the corsage.

"Brian, Joanna, so glad you could come," Lettice Fontaine gushed warmly from the top step. "And Brianne, my dear, Josh will be overjoyed to see you!"

Ben Fontaine extended his hand to Brian and Win, who quickly introduced Pierce to him. "Ah, yes, I declare my daughters have been gaggling about you, sir, for the past month! I daresay it's not because you've a handy shooting arm, is it?" He winked broadly at Brian who grinned.

"I admit to having been thoroughly charmed by your daughters at one of the soirees Mrs. O'Neill had at Avonlea," Pierce replied smoothly, exhibiting a style that no one could have found fault with.

Brianne raised her brows, wondering at this demeanor from a man who seemed more at home exhibiting a mocking arrogance that would hardly have set well with Ben Fontaine.

"Honey, you look as though you've just descended from heaven!" Josh said, startling her a little as she turned her attention from Pierce Nolan. "Of course, I do know better," he whispered with a wink. "Will you allow me to escort you to the party?" Without needing an answer, Josh pushed her chair inside the massive hallway of his home, where all was lights and giggling girls hurrying from the powder rooms to the party, and servants rushing to and fro in a controlled frenzy.

"Wait until you hear the orchestra, Brianne. Father brought them up all the way from New Orleans by packet boat."

"I'm sure they'll be wonderful," Brianne returned soberly.

Josh seemed to recollect himself. "Sorry, sweetheart, I didn't mean to—"

"Josh! You sweet thing, I've saved the first waltz on my card for you!" Annabelle Jackson tittered, hurrying up as Josh wheeled Brianne out onto the back porch. She spared a glance for Brianne. "Hello, Brianne. My, you are looking lovely tonight, dear!"

Brianne smiled, though she thought the effort would break her face. How dare that simpering little flirt act condescending to her! If it weren't for this stupid chair, Annabelle wouldn't have had the courage to confront her. Josh wouldn't have so tamely entered his name on her dance card either. Brianne longed to fly out of the chair and claw at the tight curls of Miss Jackson.

"Oh, Josh, you must come meet my cousin Barbra, up from New Orleans! She'll only be here the weekend and she's dying to meet the most charming young man in the county!" Annabelle had hooked her arm through Josh's.

The "charming young man" looked from one young lady to the other in a quandary. His eyes looked about desperately and found Bruce, Annabelle's brother, coming toward them.

"Bruce, I've got a lovely lady for you to escort to the gardens!" he called. And after the exchange of escorts, "I'll be back later."

Brianne watched him go, Annabelle clinging to his arm, and ground her teeth together in a rage. She would never speak to Josh Fontaine as long as she lived! How dare he sweep her into someone else's hands!

Forcing herself to stay calm, she traded pleasantries with Bruce Jackson, wishing all the while that she had never come. By the end of the night, she knew her pride would be in tatters. It wasn't fair, she thought rebelliously! Sara was right. God must have made a mistake when He allowed her to fall off her horse! The night had started sourly and it could only get worse. Her melancholy finally wore down poor Bruce who gladly gave her up to

Gerald, who produced a glass of punch from the refreshment table.

"A lovely night for a party, isn't it?" Gerald offered pleasantly, his eyes watching the dancers as they took their places for the first dance. He cleared his throat uncomfortably, hating to desert Brianne, but remembering that he had promised Ellie Windom the first dance. He could see her now, her eyes scouring the crowd for him, her cheeks slightly pink at the thought that he might leave her standing there. "Ah, Brianne, I am sorry, but I've promised this waltz to Ellie—"

"Go on!" Brianne blurted, nearly spilling punch on her dress as she set her glass on a nearby table.

"Maybe I could find someone to—"

"*Will* you go!"

Brianne watched as the music began, striving to keep the tears out of her eyes, tears of frustration and anger that she blinked back quickly. She saw Win and Emily swooping past, their eyes lovingly on each other. The flurry of long, full skirts in all colors swept past, accompanied by the black trousers of their partners. Brianne refused to look at all the familiar faces, desperately afraid that she would see only pity in their eyes as they spied her sitting on the side with all the matrons and wallflowers.

"Surely, the most beautiful woman present tonight is not alone?" It was Pierce, his mocking voice causing her to panic at the thought he might see the diamond flash of tears on her lashes.

She kept her eyes lowered, waiting for the tears to evaporate. "Don't make fun of me tonight, Pierce, please," she said in a whisper.

He came closer, standing beside her so that the black kerseymere of his trouser leg pressed against the arm of her chair. "Feeling sorry for yourself again?" he wondered, taking a drink from the glass of brandy he had brought with him.

She looked up at him, but he seemed preoccupied with watching the dancers. "What—what do you mean?" she asked.

He looked down at her then, his golden eyes narrowed while his dark brows rose upward in sardonic crescents. "I mean that I have never seen a young woman more filled with self pity. You have charm, beauty, more than most, and yet you're letting that damned chair rule your life."

"Don't talk to me like that!" she breathed, turning her gaze stonily away. "How am I supposed to feel? Happy?"

"If you could manage gracious it would be an improvement," he replied, knowing that he was making her angry and liking it much better than the sullen, morose look he had seen upon coming up to her. "If you truly believe that you are more charming and pretty than the other girls here, then you wouldn't let that chair hold you back. The true test of a woman's charm is if she can carry it through despite a headcold, stomachache, or, yes, even a wheelchair."

She hated to admit that he was right. "Well, I certainly won't be wasting my charm on you, Pierce Nolan!" she nearly spat out. "You don't have to bother keeping me company any longer. The dance is about to end and I'm positive there will be plenty of young men to mollify me."

He laughed. "God, you are a vain thing! Heaven help the young men when you regain the use of your legs!" He threw her a sardonic glance. "You'll be able to make all of them pay for leaving you to wilt tonight."

"Oh, go away!" she shot back waspishly.

"I am," he responded in cavalier fashion. "I've been thinking of leaving for the last few days."

"Leaving? Leaving Avonlea, you mean?" She looked up at him in surprise.

"Yes, won't you be happy to see me go?"

She blinked at the way he had so casually announced his departure. Yes, of course, she would be happy to see him go—wouldn't she? "Where are you planning to go?" she wondered, curiosity getting the best of her, although she really didn't want to sound interested.

He smiled down at the auburn head, inhaling the fragrance of the gardenias in her hair. "I didn't think you would be interested," he began lazily, "but I must confess that it pleases me more than a little to hear that you are. Can it be that you will miss me, Brianne?" he wondered, with a teasing note in his voice. "Perhaps our stimulating conversations are having the opposite effect on you than I had thought." He saw the tiny frown of exasperation that shaped her mouth.

"If you must know," he continued before she could say anything, "I'm going down to New Orleans. It will put me in a better position to leave for Texas the minute I hear any news of the Rangers being called up again by the Governor. He has hopes that they can rid the frontier of the Indian threat; the government troops seem to be bungling badly and hundreds of settlers are paying the price with their homes and their lives." His voice had become passionate with purpose and Brianne looked up at him, startled.

"You told me that you had worked for the Rangers before," she remembered. "You were a—trouble-shooter?"

He smiled grimly. "Yes. A person who located and *eliminated* sources of trouble." He leaned down to meet her gaze. "The Rangers were my only family for a very long time. I trusted them like brothers and I feel I owe them a debt for helping me understand myself and what I wanted out of life. The captain I served under knows very well that I'll come back, if needed."

"And—you feel you are needed?"

"Not yet, perhaps, but it's inevitable, I think, that the Rangers will be called out again. I have to be free to go to them." He stopped, and Brianne could see the questioning look in his eyes, a question she was at a loss to comprehend. What did he really want her to say?

"I've heard my father talk of a 'man's duty' many times," she said softly.

He nodded, oddly pleased that she seemed to want to understand. "Even a man's duty to himself and his conscience."

How odd, Brianne thought, that this is the first serious conversation I've been able to have with him without one of us growing angry. She felt, for a moment, the insecurity of being on unfamiliar ground. It frightened her a little and she tried to steer the conversation back to safer lines.

"Well, I'm sure that everyone shall miss you—even I," she put in with a twinkle to her voice, the twinkle of a practiced flirt. "I have to admit it was quite refreshing at times to have such a rogue to cross swords with!"

"Refreshing?" The familiar insolence veiled his expression as he sensed her need to shy away from the seriousness of a moment before. "Brianne, are you flirting with me?" he asked her with a hint of laughter in his voice. "My dear, you'd best be careful, I'm not some fresh-faced boy for you to toy with."

Her smile was replaced by an impudent look. "Goodness, and you called me vain! I suppose you think that I, among others, am just waiting for you to hold out your arms so that I can fall right into them!" This was familiar territory now and she blinked her eyes with innocent guile while swooshing her fan back and forth with lazy purpose. It pleased her to think that she had the power to flirt with this rascal as nonchalantly as with Carter Lowell.

His loud laughter caused several people to crane their necks to stare at them. "Why, I do recall you falling into my arms not too long ago, ma'am, when you fell off the back of your horse!"

"How clever of you to twist my meaning, sir!" Brianne remarked tightly. "However, I do see Josh making his way over here, so I would suggest you make your departure."

"You're sure you don't want me to stick around in case you're deserted again when the next dance starts?" he questioned in mock seriousness.

She flashed an angry look at him. She would have said something, but Josh came up, his eyes showing his appreciation of the picture she made in her dress. Ignoring Pierce, she turned her attention to Josh. "So there you are," she purred, forgetting her earlier oath never to speak to him. "Have you been enjoying yourself without me?"

"Hell, no, honey! Nobody can dance like you, darlin'." He seated himself next to her. "Would you like something to drink?"

She shook her head. "I just want you to sit here and talk with me, Josh," she pouted prettily, using the fan to her advantage. "You looked so handsome out there on the dance floor, you near took my breath away!"

He grinned, pleased at her interest. A few minutes later, Gerald joined the group, having already come to the conclusion that Ellie Windom didn't hold a candle to Brianne O'Neill. Carter Lowell, who'd been busy making arrangements to head upriver the day after the cotillion, made his entrance and quickly came over to where Brianne was the center of the attention of four or five young men. It was a handsome group assembled around the fair white blossom, Pierce thought, joining in a conversation between Brian and Ben, who were talking politics with a group of older men.

Joanna O'Neill, glancing over to her daughter, allowed a pleased smile to come over her. She seemed to be enjoying herself. Joanna was grateful for that. She had been worried that Brianne might sulk all night, feeling sorry for herself, and spoil the entire evening. But looking at her now, talking animatedly with some of the handsomest young men in the county, Joanna felt positive that everything would be all right. Nothing could go wrong on such a perfectly lovely evening.

* * *

"Hmmm. What did you say, Carter?" Brianne asked, not really listening to the young man who hadn't left her side all evening, although the others had gone back and forth to honor their dancing commitments.

"I said, I was going to be leaving tomorrow, Miss Brianne," Carter repeated, staring at the shell-like quality of the tiny earlobe she was presenting to him. "I'll certainly miss—everyone here."

"Oh, thank you, Carter," she replied absently. She was watching the bright pattern of dancers, her eyes fixed for the moment on Josh and Marianne Deveau. Shifting her gaze, she was surprised to see Pierce Nolan dancing with Emily Turner. She had to admit, although grudgingly, that he was an admirable dancer. Wherever had he learned to dance so elegantly, she wondered. She could see the controlled strength in his movements as he swirled Emily around effortlessly, causing a blush to come to her cheeks. When the dance was over, they continued their conversation.

"Carter, have you seen my brother?"

"Winthrop? I—ah—yes, he was inside a moment ago, I think." The truth was Carter hadn't noticed anyone but Brianne O'Neill all evening.

Brianne barely heard him. She was watching in surprise as Pierce and Emily walked casually from the dance area into the darker edge of the woods beyond the torches where the formality of Lettice Fontaine's gardens stopped and the tangle of cypress and oak took over. In another moment, they had walked into the trees!

Suspicious, Brianne desperately wanted to find out what they were doing, but was prevented from doing so by Carter's presence. She certainly couldn't have him go with her. What if something scandalous were going on? Poor Win would be obliged to fight for Emily's honor, and Brianne had no doubts that Pierce was a much better shot with a pistol than her brother. And yet, why would Pierce and Emily have gone into the woods by themselves? She itched to know, and the longer she sat there, the more desperate she became.

"Carter, will you please go inside and bring me a plate of ham, and perhaps some biscuits?" she asked nervously.

"Why, certainly, Miss Brianne. Shall I—?"

"Please do go now, I'm famished," she implored, her eye still on the edge of the trees. She waited until he was up the steps before she wheeled her chair over to the far side of the dancing area. She glanced back, seeing that another tune had begun and all the other young men who might have wondered where she was going were otherwise occupied. She only prayed that no one had seen Pierce and Emily disappear a moment before.

Once out of the light of the torches, Brianne pushed at the wheels of her chair, following the gravel path that led through the dark woods. Here and there, Ben Fontaine had hung colored lanterns for the benefit of anyone wishing to stroll through the woods, over the shallow stream to the pavilion beyond. Brianne stopped once and listened, thought she heard voices and pushed slowly forward, coming to the stream. Of course, she could go no further, for the bridge had been built with steps on either side which prevented her from rolling her chair up. She wondered if Pierce and Emily had crossed it and ended up in the pavilion below. Her view of the bridge was obstructed by a heavy tangle of undergrowth and shrubbery and she pushed her chair closer to the stream in order to see around the greenery.

"I am sorry I will not be here to attend the wedding, Miss Turner," Brianne could hear Pierce's voice coming from the other side of the bridge.

"Both Win and I will be sorry when you leave, Mr. Nolan," Emily replied clearly. "You have no idea how much Win really likes you. I suppose, never having had a brother, he has appreciated your visit even more."

"With a sister like Brianne, I think he should be glad he didn't have a brother," Pierce laughed.

"Mr. Nolan, Brianne is shortly to become my sister-in-law," Emily reproached him gently. "She may be a little headstrong, but surely you can't begrudge her that, seeing how fate has dealt with her."

Brianne cringed at the idea that they were talking about her. She pushed her chair a little farther out, trying to make out where they were. In a moment, she saw them on the far side of the bridge, making their way back over.

"I felt I should thank you personally for all you've been to Win," Emily was saying. "He would never think of doing it himself, but I suppose that's the way with men. Does he know that you are leaving?"

"No, I haven't told him yet, Miss Turner," Pierce answered. He looked out over the stream casually, something having caught the corner of his eye. Through a thick tangle of undergrowth and bushes, he noted a flash of white which baffled him for only a moment until a thought came over him that made him smile. "Ah, Miss Turner, perhaps you had better go back to the dance area yourself, if you'll forgive me. I'm sure that there are plenty of sharp eyes and prattling tongues that would be all too ready to make something of this walk we've shared."

"What? Oh! Of course, Mr. Nolan, if you think it would be more appropriate. I—I really didn't think—"

"I'll wait here on the bridge for a decent interval." He bowed over her hand. "And the best of luck to you and Win in your married life," he said sincerely.

Brianne watched as Emily made her way back through the trees along the path. She saw Pierce Nolan, standing idly on the bridge, lighting a cheroot which he smoked in leisurely fashion, staring out over the stream at nothing in particular, but effectively preventing her from making her escape.

Brianne waited for long, excruciating minutes, afraid to move lest her chair make some sound which might draw his attention. She saw him throw the last of the cheroot into the water, then turn to walk down the bridge. Instead of taking the path back to the house, he began strolling casually toward her hiding place.

Terrified of being seen and desperate that he not catch her in her foolishness, Brianne panicked. Heedless of caution and the limits of her chair, she pushed it backward, jamming into a large rock which jutted out of the mudbank. She tried to swivel it around in the opposite direction by throwing her weight to the side and felt the chair teeter off balance.

For a horrified moment, the chair leaned backward, the wheels off the ground in the air. Then the slick wetness of the mudbank caused the chair to slide backward on its side, dumping Brianne into the stream.

At the sound of the loud splash, Pierce increased his pace and came to the edge of the stream, only to face a comical sight. Brianne, her beautiful dress mud splotched and sopping wet, her hair wetly plastered to her head, was in a sitting position in the shallow stream, leaning back on her hands, her legs straight out in the water.

Pierce, fearing he might break into laughter, wisely kept silent, aware of the anger written so clearly on Brianne's face.

"Well?" she demanded after taking a deep breath.

"Brianne? What are you doing in the water?" he inquired, barely containing his laughter.

"Get me out of here!" she cried out shrilly, fuming and sputtering, pushing wet strands out of her face. "Don't just stand there gaping at me!"

"You'll have to forgive my temporary paralysis," he explained, unable to succeed in keeping the grin from his face. "It's not often I see young ladies of your breeding, sitting in a stream in a ballgown."

"Ooooh!" She was speechless with rage.

Pierce, feeling he'd better say no more for the moment, waded in carefully, pulling the chair back out onto level ground. Meticulously, he pulled out his large white handkerchief and dried the seat as best he could.

Brianne, watching him with growing impatience, could stand no more.

"Will you stop fooling with that chair and pull me out now?" she demanded. "My dress is ruined, I'm all wet—and—and worst of all, you of all people have to see me like this!"

"I promise to tell no one," he assured her, wading back in to help her out. Then, suddenly, he stopped and looked curiously at her.

"Come on, hurry, before someone else comes!" she cried impatiently.

He continued to stand there in the water watching her, then slowly retraced his steps to the riverbank. Simmering with fury, Brianne glared at him, wondering what he was up to. Did he enjoy seeing her defenseless in the water? Did he plan on leaving her there and returning for more help? She waited, boiling, until finally her temper exploded.

"Get me out of here!" she screamed at him. "You get me out or I'll—I'll—"

"You'll have to get yourself out, Brianne," Pierce returned calmly, shaking his head and fixing her with a long look. He felt no desire to laugh now. He was dead serious. "A young lady with a temper as fiery as yours should be able to make herself stand up and walk right out of there."

"Why, you—you really do enjoy seeing me like this, don't you?" she cried indignantly. "You think it's all very funny!"

"What I think, Brianne, is that you'd better start walking soon if you don't want to stay in that chair the rest of your life. Now is as good a time as any since I've no intention of carrying you out and I'm not about to fetch someone to do it. I'm afraid you can sit there until someone wonders where you've gone, or get up and walk out on your own two legs." He walked to the base of a cottonwood and leaned against it, continuing to watch her sputtering antics.

"But I'm getting cold!" she replied, trying to bring back some calm to her voice, knowing that the more she screamed at him the more obstinate he would probably become. "I can't walk out! How can you be so cruel?"

"I'm not being cruel," he replied matter-of-factly. "You won't catch your death of pneumonia, you're a healthy girl. There's no reason why you can't begin walking now. I realize that you're in a highly charged state right now, but if you'll calm yourself down, I'm sure you can do it!"

"You'd have me crawl out of here!"

"I told you to walk."

"Damn you, Pierce Nolan, I could kill you for this! When my papa finds out—"

"Shut up and start trying to stand up, Brianne. You're only wasting my time and yours. If you don't stop screaming at me, I'm liable to just leave you here."

She was effectively silenced at this threat. She blinked back tears of rage, hating him a thousand times for this humiliation! Oh, if only she'd not followed him and Emily. What had gotten into her?

Well, she wasn't about to give him any more satisfaction at her expense. She'd show him! Clenching her teeth, keeping her Irish temper up, she drew herself up, then leaned forward onto her hands. With difficulty because of the heavy dress, she pushed herself to her knees. Refusing to look at Pierce, she took a deep breath and tried to move one foot beneath her. Her foot slipped and she nearly dove face first into the sandy bottom of the stream. Catching herself, she looked up at Pierce, who was watching her intently now.

"I suppose you're waiting for me to fall flat on my face!" she breathed, wishing she could manage to drown him somehow.

He shrugged. "That's up to you, Brianne. Do you think the others are beginning to wonder where you are? Frankly, I wouldn't put it past that meek Mr. Lowell to have the entire party begin searching for you. I'm sure the thought of all the guests assembled along the creek bank watching you during your ablutions in the water is an idea that doesn't appeal to you." He smiled with pure devilment. "I wonder what Miss Annabelle Jackson might think if she saw your predicament?"

At the thought, Brianne went cold. How dare he mock her? And yet, what he said was true enough if she knew Carter Lowell. The fool was probably even now searching for her. Grinding her teeth, she pushed the thought out of her mind. It would only serve to madden her further.

"You are a devil!" she threw out.

"And you, miss, are no angel, I'm afraid," he returned with a mocking grin.

"I hate you, Pierce Nolan. I swear you'll be sorry for this!"

"Spare me the undying threats, Brianne." He shrugged his shoulders. "I suppose, on second thought, that I could go and lead Mr. Lowell and his helpers to you—"

"Don't you dare leave me!" she wailed. "Damn you!" She took a deep breath and pushed as hard as she could on the floor of the stream. Suddenly, almost miraculously, she was standing up on her own two feet, a little wobbly, but standing! Hands outstretched before her, she lifted her head to see Pierce standing at the edge of the stream, ready to catch her if she should fall.

She'd done it! She was actually standing up without help! For a moment, pure joy made her smile and want to laugh out loud! She was standing!

"Bravo! Brianne, I'm proud of you!" Pierce said without mockery.

"You keep away from me. I'll walk out by myself! I will!" Brianne glared at him, refusing his outstretched arms. With halting, small steps, she moved slowly toward the embankment, the experience of walking engulfing her in its power. The movement of her legs was magnified a thousand times by the slow-moving water of the stream. She was unaware that her bare shoulders were flushed from the cool water, that her dress was ruined beyond repair, that a long streak of mud was coloring one cheek. She only knew that she was walking! God, how sweet it was!

Once at the embankment, she eyed the slippery mud with trepidation. It would be undeniably foolish to try to step onto it with her wet slippers and trailing skirts, but she'd be damned before she'd ask that scoundrel to help her Tentatively, she lifted one foot and set it on a rocky area, gathering herself to pull herself out of the water.

Suddenly, without warning, in the space of a heartbeat, she felt her footing going out from under her. Clutching the air, feeling her earlier joy die within her, she closed her eyes in defeat. And then, two strong hands were catching her shoulders, bringing her forward so that she fell against a hard chest, and two masculine arms were encompassing her, lifting her up and out.

Brianne felt her own heartbeat jumping crazily, felt those arms tighten around her, felt warm breath fanning her cool cheek. Hesitating, wondering at the sudden lightning-swift emotions that seemed to be running through her, she finally dared to look up into those golden eyes that seemed so very near her own. The desire she saw in them made her shiver anew, but not from the cold. Unable to bear it, she closed her eyes and leaned forward, feeling his arms tighten further until she felt crushed.

Pierce Nolan looked into the exquisite little face and felt desire run hotly through his veins. Damn, but she was lovely! But more than that, she was a brave young woman and a determined one with guts. He could feel her body warming against his where her flesh touched his clothing. He had to kiss her, he had to! And yet, one kiss would lead to more, he knew. He was not the kind of man who would be satisfied with anything less than all of her. Angry at himself for his own indecision, and at her for her flagrant invitation, he moved his head away from hers.

Feeling his movement, she opened her eyes. A rosy flush of embarrassment flooded her cheeks as she realized that he knew exactly how she'd felt a moment before. The golden eyes which had before been filled with desire, were now cool and arrogant as they flicked over her puckered mouth and heaving breasts.

"You'll have to do more than take a few steps to merit a kiss from me," he mocked her.

Stunned, she stiffened in his arms, her own turquoise eyes hardening with remembered anger. "As though I'd want a kiss from you!" she retorted, tears of anger and hurt filling her eyes. "You are the last person on this earth, Pierce Nolan, who would appeal to me in that way! Why, you aren't even a gentleman! Put me down in my chair this instant!"

"No, I'm not a gentleman," Pierce returned, careful to keep his voice under control. "And if that's what you want, Brianne, then you're right, I'm not the man for you. Better Carter Lowell or that peacock, Josh Fontaine, who would have waded right in and carried you out of the water!"

Biting her lip, Brianne refused to be baited any further, maintaining a stony silence as he placed her in her chair and began pushing her back to the house. It seemed hours had gone by since she'd left the dancing. Once again ensconced in the familiarity of her chair, she felt anger and bitterness creeping over her. She would never forgive Pierce Nolan for what he had done! Never!

They exited the line of trees and moved toward the lanterns that surrounded the dancing area. Almost immediately, Brianne saw Carter Lowell rushing forward, her parents and Ben Fontaine close behind. Suddenly, everyone seemed to be staring at her, their eyes flickering from her sodden dress and tangled hair to the man behind her whose arrogant expression mocked them all.

"Brianne, honey! What happened to you!" her father was demanding.

"Miss Brianne, I was so worried—"

"Brianne, your dress—"

The babble of excited and concerned voices seemed to be surrounding her. Brianne turned deep red, aware of the picture she must make. Her reputation was ruined, she had been made to look foolish. She wanted to put it all on someone—someone who could be blamed for doing this to her!

"Oh, papa, papa!" she wailed, pushing her fists into her eyes. "Oh, papa, I—I don't know how to tell you—"

"Darlin', tell me what?" Brian O'Neill looked from his daughter's downcast face to that of his friend and guest. "What happened, Pierce?"

Brianne's head shot up angrily. "Oh, don't ask him, papa! It's—it's all his fault! He—he—"

"He *what?*" Brian roared, his Irish temper, buoyed by several drinks of whiskey throughout the night, beginning to come to the surface. "What did you do?" he demanded of Pierce Nolan, who continued to exhibit such calm arrogance.

"He—he compromised me, papa!" Brianne blurted out angrily, deriving some satisfaction at the shocked looks she glimpsed among the party goers. "I fell into the stream—and—and he wouldn't help me out! He just stood there, watching me in the water—catching my death of cold, no doubt!" She looked at her father beseechingly. "Papa, you've got to do something! He—he wouldn't let me out unless I let him hold me and kiss me!"

"What!" Brian O'Neill turned beet red and Ben Fontaine, seeing the Irishman's hands curling into fists, caught him by the arm to restrain him.

"Papa, he compromised me!" Brianne repeated, nearly screaming out the words in a culmination of her anger, hurt, and frustration. "You can't let him get away with ruining me like this!"

Someone took her chair and wheeled her away from the scene, but not before Brianne had the chance to turn her head and glance at Pierce Nolan's face. She was

satisfied that the insolence had been effectively wiped
away. But before she allowed herself a smile of congratu-
lation, she saw him look at her, his golden eyes hard with
anger. She quickly turned away and was relieved to see
her mother's face before her.

"Brianne, are you all right?" she asked her gently,
stroking at still-wet strands of hair.

"Y-yes, mama. I just want to go home!" Brianne told
her, feeling suddenly, overwhelmingly tired and drained.
"Please—can we go home?"

"Of course, my dear. Win can stay here with your
father until this matter is settled—"

"Settled? What do you mean? I just don't ever want to
see Pierce Nolan's hateful face again! He's not a gentleman, mama. Papa was wrong about him!"

"Darling, everything will be settled in the proper
manner. If Mr. Nolan has compromised your honor, he
will be dealt with accordingly. I'm sure your father and
Mr. Fontaine will get to the bottom of all this."

"Mama, I don't want—"

"Hush now. I'll just see to the carriage and we'll be on
our way home." Joanna parked her daughter's chair
inside the house with the help of one of the young men
who had accompanied them. "You just rest here a
moment, honey, and I'll be right back."

Brianne closed her eyes and leaned her head back in
her chair. A headache was beginning to pound at her
temples and she kept seeing those golden eyes staring at
her, accusing her of the lie and promising a revenge that
made her shudder. But, oh, she mustn't worry, she told
herself. Certainly, her father and the others would know
how to deal with a scoundrel like Pierce Nolan.

Chapter Six

THE NEXT MORNING, BRIANNE WAS SITTING UP IN BED, drinking hot tea, her mind re-living the wonder and the humiliation of the night before. She had studied her legs thoughtfully, wondering if it was her imagination that they looked more developed, less scrawny than they'd been only a month ago. Were they actually stronger? They must be, for she'd actually walked last night, hardly more than a shuffle, to be sure, but still, she had walked! Whether it had been pure determination or Pierce's mocking badgering that had done it, it didn't matter. She had hugged herself in delight. If she did it once, she would surely do it again.

Incongruous as it sounded last night, she supposed in the morning light that she really should be thanking Pierce Nolan for forcing her to take those first few steps. But, no, she couldn't undo now what she had done last night. And yet, a tiny part of her mind remembered those golden eyes filled with anger and desire, staring at *her* as though to somehow hold her in their gaze. She felt a delicious shiver run down her spine, then stopped herself, trying to imagine what had transpired between her father and Pierce.

There was no doubt that her father had come to look upon Pierce Nolan with a genuine warmth. It had gone past the stage where it was just gratitude for saving his life in Natchez. Brian genuinely liked Pierce Nolan, trusted him. What must he have thought when he saw this man he trusted with his bedraggled daughter, who was screaming that he had compromised her? It was a serious charge in this age of Southern chivalry. No Southern gentleman would tolerate his wife's or his daughter's virtue being tampered with. And her father had looked so awful, the anger in his face mixed with the pain in his eyes. Brianne shut her own eyes, trying to blot out that picture.

"Good morning, dear." Her mother's voice caused her to open her eyes, focusing on the concern she read in Joanna's face.

"Mama?"

"Your father and I would like to speak with you, darling," Joanna continued with forced briskness. "He's waiting in the library downstairs. Ring for Mandy so she can help you dress."

"What is wrong, mama? What—did they do to Mr. Nolan last night?" Brianne inquired, feeling as though guilt were written all over her face.

"Your father will speak to you on that, Brianne," Joanna answered, ringing the small silver bell for Mandy.

A tiny flutter of fear started in Brianne's heart. Pierce must have explained the whole incident and now her father knew that she had lied, that Pierce had most certainly not compromised her honor. Oh, the scene she had made because of her anger and pride! How could she ever hold her head up now? Did everyone know?

Careful to hide her inner turmoil, Brianne allowed Mandy to help her dress. When she was ready, her mother pushed her chair downstairs to the library where her father awaited her behind his huge oaken desk, which had always intimidated her a little. Something terrible must be about to happen, she surmised, noting the stern look her father was leveling on her.

"Good morning, puss," Brian said gruffly.

Brianne drew hope from the familiar endearment. "Good morning, papa."

"Daughter, there is no easy way to say what I am

about to say," Brian began uncomfortably. He glanced from his wife to his daughter. "Last night, I'm sorry to say, you were part of an incident which is better left forgotten. Unfortunately, there were too many people who witnessed your behavior for any of us to do that." He took a deep breath and leaned back in his chair. "You put Pierce and yourself into a compromising situation, my dear."

"I? But, papa, I was only—"

"Quiet, Brianne," Brian said, his voice becoming stronger despite the fact that his head was still pounding from the long night. "If you had conducted yourself in a more genteel fashion, you wouldn't have gotten yourself into such a predicament."

"After what Pierce Nolan had done, papa? How could I have acted other than I did?" Brianne questioned, not about to admit her own guilt easily.

"Ben Fontaine and I both questioned Pierce at length, Brianne, and according to his story, there was no compromise involved. You had simply followed him into the woods and dumped yourself in the stream after slamming your chair against a rock. That would explain the state of your dress when you arrived back in the company of the other guests." He leaned forward in his chair, his eyes intent on his daughter's. "Tell me, Brianne, and I want no lies of embarrassment or pride, is this what really happened? Or was there something else?"

Brianne held her father's gaze for an instant, then lowered her eyes, her bottom lip caught pensively between her teeth. Yes, she could hold to what she had said last night, enmesh herself deeper into the lie, or she could tell the truth and lose the guilt feelings that had plagued her last night. Did Pierce really deserve the consequences of her lie?

"Papa, I—I lied to you last night," she said, still keeping her head down. "Pierce is telling the truth. He—did nothing which you would have found fault with." She remembered with a sudden vivid flash of memory the moment he had held her and how close his mouth had seemed to hers.

Brian breathed a sigh of relief. "I'm glad to be hearing you say that, puss," he said. "I can thank your woman's hysteria and anger at putting yourself up as a laughing-stock last night to account for your deception, but if you had continued with the lie this morning, I would have been deeply ashamed of you." He seemed to brighten a little. "And now that that has been taken care of, the rest of the matter can be settled with little difficulty, I'm hoping."

Brianne looked up. "The rest of the matter?"

"Yes, puss, I'm afraid that because of your damning words last night, you cast both your and Pierce's reputation into disregard. As I've said, there were too many people who heard what you said for it not to matter."

Brianne was shocked at the thought that her revenge on Pierce for mocking her had actually backfired. Not only had she ruined him in the eyes of everyone that mattered, but she had also ruined herself. By her own words, she was a woman compromised.

"But, papa, surely you can let it be known—"

Brian shook his head. "I'll not have secrets whispered about you or any of my family behind our backs. I'll not have young men turning down your hand for marriage because there are rumors of you and Pierce Nolan. I've worked hard to find my place here, Brianne. We Irish have not had an easy time of it in this land of America and I'll not have everything I've worked for thrown away because of a young girl's spiteful tongue!" He stood up from his chair, his words gaining momentum. "I've decided that the best way to still waggling tongues is to marry you off, puss, and soon! You're eighteen now; time you were married."

"Marry! But, papa, there's no one—" She stopped, wondering if during the course of the long night, one of the young men had offered for her hand, the gentlemanly thing to do under the circumstances. Could it have been

Carter? She doubted it. Despite his infatuation with her, he was too mealy mouthed to want to marry a compromised woman. Was it Josh then, her girlhood friend turned rescuer? She swallowed hard and posed the question to her father.

"Josh Fontaine!" Brian snorted in irritation. "He's a good enough lad, but, no, he didn't stand up for you, daughter. Despite the fact that Ben and I go back many years, Josh is his only son and he wants to see the boy married to a young lady of impeccable background with no slurs on her character brought about by her own careless words of compromise!"

"No, puss, I'm afraid there's only one man for you, and that man is Pierce Nolan. He—"

"Pierce!" Brianne cried out in pure shock. "Papa, you can't mean that you would have me *marry* him!"

"That's exactly what I'm meaning, puss," Brian admitted. "We've already talked of it last night. He agrees that it's the only way to salvage your honor. He's willing to marry you, Brianne—"

"I wouldn't doubt it," she snorted, anger bringing fire to her words. "After all, look around you, papa, at Avonlea. It's one of the richest plantations in the entire state! Don't you think a man like Pierce Nolan would enjoy getting his hands on some of the wealth it represents!"

"No, I don't think he would care about that," Brian responded seriously.

"Papa, he's nothing but a rogue, a scoundrel whom you met only because of an act of violence. How can you think of giving me to him?"

"Because there is no one else to give you to!" Brian exploded, losing his temper as well. "Who else in the county would be willing to marry a young woman who no longer has the use of her legs?" he asked her bluntly. "And, as if that were not enough, now there will be doubts as to your honor and your integrity! No, daughter, I'm afraid even the wealth of Avonlea is no match for the loss of a woman's honor, whether real or imagined, in the mind of a Southern gentleman!"

Brianne was close to tears at her father's cruel words, words she could hardly believe he had said to her. "Papa, I won't marry Pierce Nolan! You—you don't care about me, you only care about him! Ever since he saved your life and you brought him here you've fawned over him like he was some long lost son! You feel grateful to him, papa! And so you've given me as payment!"

Brian's face turned white, then red deepening to nearly purple. "Don't you ever be implying that I don't love you! Why, I'd sooner take my last breath than see any harm come to you!" He moved closer to her and she shrank back in her chair, feeling like a small child. "Maybe I've loved you too much, daughter. You've had everything you could have wanted. I've spoiled and petted you, especially after your fall from the horse, but now I'll not give in to your Irish tantrums or your tears! You'll be doing as I say and be damned glad you're getting a man like Pierce Nolan who'll at least be a match for you!"

Brian O'Neill drew himself up, the color beginning to lessen in his face. He raised a hand to his aching head, avoiding his wife's gaze. "God, I could use some sleep, but not before I've straightened you out on one thing, puss! You are going to marry Pierce Nolan whether you like it or not! He may be something of a rascal, but I've never known him to be other than honest, and by God, I'm betting he'll tame that swift temper of yours quicker than any of these so-called gentlemen around here who've been letting you run over them for years!"

"I'll not be civil to him, papa!" Brianne yelled angrily. "I'll be hateful!"

"Suit yourself, puss, but I'm warning you that it won't be long before the man is your legal husband!" Her father stormed out of the room, leaving his wife and daughter staring after him.

"Mama, how could he talk to me like that!" Brianne wailed, reaction setting in after a few moments. "Oh, how can he say that he loves me!"

"He does love you, darling," Joanna soothed, coming to pat her daughter's head. "He believes he's done the best possible thing for you, considering the circumstances."

"I'll run away!" Brianne declared, but they both knew the futility of her words. How could she run away when she couldn't even walk! "Oh, I hate both of them, planning all this behind my back! If papa only knew that scoundrel as I know him!" Brianne continued to fume while her mother tried to comfort her. Her father had said there would be no one to marry her, but he was wrong! Surely, her charms were not so tarnished that there was not one young man who would take her hand in marriage. But, she had to ask herself, was there any of them she wanted? And still the question that nagged at the back of her mind was, why had Pierce agreed to marry her?

At the sound of a knock on her door, Brianne looked up from where she'd been lying on top of her bed, alternately crying and pounding her fists angrily into the counterpane.

"Go away!" she called out. "I don't want to speak to anyone!"

"Brianne, I'd like to talk to you." It was Pierce Nolan's voice!

"Leave me alone!" She pulled herself up, wishing she'd had Mandy stay in her room with her. "Haven't you done enough without throwing your victory in my face!"

"Don't be tiresome," Pierce replied, allowing the mockery to edge his words. "You're acting like a spoiled child, Brianne, locking yourself in your room for two days! What do you hope to accomplish? I'll still be here when you unlock the door."

"You mean if I wish hard enough you won't disappear?" she returned with heavy sarcasm. "I don't want to talk to you, Mr. Nolan, nor do I want to see you, ever!"

"You leave me little choice other than to break your door in," Pierce continued arrogantly.

"You wouldn't dare! My father—"

"Your parents and your brother are gone, my dear, to an engagement party given in our honor. Ironic that the guests of honor are not going to show up!"

"I don't care about that. You just go away! What does my reputation matter now?"

"It might matter a great deal someday, when you allow yourself to think like an adult," Pierce suggested.

"I said—!"

Brianne was halted in midsentence as she heard the force of a booted foot crack against her door hinges. Another loud kick, followed by several more and suddenly the door jamb gave way, leaving her door to swing open forlornly on its hinges. She glanced in panic for her chair, but Pierce was far quicker than she and kicked it out of the way. Feeling vulnerable in her morning robe on the bed coverlet, she could barely force herself to meet his cool gaze.

"So, you've forced yourself into my room, sir, the act of a true gentleman, I'll be bound!" she taunted him, knowing instinctively that none of the house servants were about to come to her aid.

"No matter what you do, my dear, the fact remains that in little more than a month you and I will become man and wife, and I will have every right to break your bedroom door in, although you can be sure there'll be no locks on it then!" His eyes moved up and down her figure insolently, aware of the flush creeping up from her neck to her cheeks. "I'm afraid you've only gotten what you deserved, a husband who is not about to coddle you or treat you like some spoiled child. The female I'm taking to wife had better learn how to act like a woman," he warned her, "for I'll not have a ninny in my bed!"

"Your crudeness disgusts me!" she shouted back at him. "Leave me alone before I—before I—"

"Spare me your threats!" he answered her with a hint of impatience. "I'm afraid you are at a disadvantage, Brianne, as long as you sit there clinging to your covers as though they offer some protection!" His eyes flamed with a mixture of desire and arrogance. "I must admit, though, you make an enchantingly feminine picture, one I wouldn't be loath to join on the bed if I could be sure you wouldn't slash my face with those nails of yours." He laughed shortly. "And then I would really *compromise* you, my dear."

"You are loathesome!" she sneered although she flinched at his reminder of her lie. "Does it fan your male vanity to put on airs in front of me? Do you think I am dying to be alone with you?"

"I think it matters very little what you want," he put in, "since very soon we will both be thrown together in the greatest of intimacies."

She drew in a deep breath at the degree of his boldness. "How dare you speak to me of such matters!"

"You will know of them soon enough," he reminded her with even more insolence. "Perhaps that is exactly what you need, Brianne—perhaps even what you secretly want—a man who doesn't go sniffing meekly at your skirts all day, but tumbles you on your backside and—"

"Enough of your gutter talk!" Brianne bristled, telling herself she would be damned before she'd swoon at his words. "You think you're the man for me, but you're infinitely mistaken, Pierce Nolan! Why, I'd sooner marry poor white trash than you, no matter what fancy lies you let my father swallow about your family in St. Louis and your wonderful education!"

Pierce cocked an insolent brow at her and nodded. "Perhaps, after all, poor white trash would be most suitable for you, ma'am."

"Oh!" Brianne reacted as though he'd physically slapped her in the face. Gathering her feet under her, she stood up, holding onto the bedpost, her turquoise eyes stormy with anger. Haltingly, but deliberately, clinging to pieces of furniture, she made her way to stand before him, too angry to note the admiration that crept into his eyes.

"I'd slap your face, but I'm too much the lady to bring myself to your level!" she said haughtily. "Now, you get out of here—"

Before she could turn her face away, Pierce gathered her into his arms, forcing her to loose her hold and lean against him. He lowered his face and saw those same full, pouting lips he'd seen before, but this time he was not about to hold himself back from realizing their softness and testing their experience.

Brianne closed her eyes, rearing her head back, but he followed her with his mouth until it closed over her lips. The kiss was passionate, reckless, forcing her mouth open, shocking her with its intimacy. Brianne felt his arm supporting her head as his mouth continued to force her back, moving her lips to his will so that she could barely breathe, let alone think clearly.

Despite her conviction that his nearness only irritated her, she couldn't deny the way her blood was singing with new life through her veins. After the first rush of passion was spent, he still did not quit her mouth, but only moved with more finesse, seeking her tongue with his and introducing her to this different way of kissing that she'd never experienced. It shocked her as it fired her blood even more, and she locked her hands behind his neck to keep him there.

Clinging so tightly to him, she felt the pleasurable sensation of his hand caressing her breast outside the layer of clothing and felt a sudden swift urge to feel it on her naked flesh.

Finally, he moved his mouth from hers to trail tiny kisses where the pale freckles lay on her cheeks and where her jaw sloped down to her throat. Arching her away from him, he exposed the smooth column of her neck and began planting kisses along it, stopping at the vee of her robe which prevented him from going further. His hesitation brought her back to her senses.

"Stop! You must stop," she said breathlessly, trying to bring back the anger of a few moments before.

He pulled away from her, although his hands still supported her by the arms. Those golden eyes were smoldering with desire now, cloudy and remote from the force of his passion. He stopped himself from doing more with an effort that caused an ache in his groin. "Perhaps you're right, by bride-to-be. Better to save the best for the wedding night, although I could easily devour you right now!"

The words made her tremble, but she refused to concede to him, stubbornly trying to shake off his hands, telling herself she'd stand alone if she had to rather than have him touch her.

"You've walked to me once now on your own power, Brianne," he mocked her, "and you'll do it again when you come to me in your bridal gown on our wedding day. I'll not have my wife rolling down the aisle in a wheelchair or I'll be hard put not to turn you over my knee and spank you 'til you're black and blue. It would be a trifle incommodious for the rest of the night's events." He released her, leaving her to sway unsteadily for a moment before she drew herself up and stood alone, watching him leave with an insolent smile on his face and a jaunty lift to his walk that made her grit her teeth in fury.

Chapter Seven

"I'M GOING TO DO IT, SARA, I SWEAR I AM!" BRIANNE CRIED, her hands holding onto a chair in front of her for balance. "Since I cannot play the invalid to him, I must become strong enough to win this contest of wills. How can I do that unless I regain the full use of my legs?"

"Lamb, you sound like you're talking more 'bout a battle than a wedding," Sara muttered, shaking her head. "Honey, your papa ain't going to change his mind 'bout having that man for a son-in-law, so why don't you just accept it and make the best of it. You could do worse!"

"Oh, Sara, I thought you hated him too!" Brianne accused.

"Lamb, I ain't saying he's the prize, but I'm not telling you to kick dirt over him just yet!" Sara moved to take up a position some feet away from her mistress. "I saw a white butterfly this morning, honey, and that's a sign of good news."

"The only good news I'd want to be hearing is that papa's changed his mind, or that Pierce Nolan's gone to New Orleans and caught cholera!" Brianne snapped. "Oh, but I don't want to talk about him anymore. Let's get on with it."

She drew herself up and away from the support of the chair and began walking slowly toward her mammy, something she'd been doing now for the past week. The going was careful, deliberate, but she made it by herself, causing a smile to break over her face. She would show that rascal, Pierce Nolan!

Ever since the day he had broken into her bedroom, she had been determined to regain her ability to walk again. She'd taken Sara and Mandy with her to Natchez, on the pretext of visiting a friend, and secretly visited a doctor there, who had assured her that there was no reason for her not to be able to use her legs if she continued with the exercises and massage routine she had begun.

Each day, Brianne did her exercises and tried to walk a little farther, a little more surely, telling no one except Sara and Mandy. To everyone else, she remained bound to her wheelchair, outwardly refusing to bend to her future husband's wishes by trying to walk, taking every opportunity she could to throw in his face the fact that he would not be getting a whole wife. Pierce seemed to let it all wash right over him, ignoring her barbs or returning them with his habitual sardonic amusement.

Joanna O'Neill looked on the arrangement with reservations, behaving in a properly kind manner to her prospective son-in-law, but not going along with the idea of marriage as wholeheartedly as her husband and son. Brian remained firm in his decision, the banns had already been posted and the church selected, and the guest list drawn up for invitations. Nearly the entire county, at least those who mattered, would be invited to the wedding and the following reception on the grounds of Avonlea. For his part, Win was delighted at having Pierce as his brother-in-law, and hoped that he and Brianne would make their home in Louisiana.

Of course, Brianne had no intention of leaving the place where she had been born and raised. She had already informed Pierce that her father had promised her acreage at Avonlea. Pierce had been noncommittal, not about to make up his mind under pressure. It was enough, he'd said, that things were going as smoothly as they were considering the circumstances. He had written a letter to his family in St. Louis and they would be coming down the week before the wedding to stay at Avonlea. It was a meeting that Pierce admitted he was anxious to be done with.

"Honey, that was fine, just fine!" Sara beamed as she caught Brianne by her hands. "Just turn 'round now and go back where you was."

Obediently, Brianne turned and walked slowly back to the chair from whence she'd started. When she'd completed the task, she looked up and smiled broadly at her mammy. "Oh, I can just picture the stunned look on Pierce's face when I walk down that aisle in two weeks!" she chortled.

"Lamb, you don't want to start off on the wrong foot with your new husband," Sara warned, although she, too, had misgivings about this marriage. "Remember what your ol' mammy says, lamb, and try to make a good, happy life for yourself."

Brianne shrugged. "You sound like papa, Sara." She glanced toward Mandy, who had been setting out her day clothes. "Help me dress," she said, "and call one of the house boys to take me downstairs in the chair."

When she was dressed in the jonquille-yellow corded silk, her hair drawn back in a tidy bun at the nape of her neck, Brianne walked proudly to her chair without help and sat down, her own face reflecting the pleased smile of the two servants.

A short time later she was downstairs, trying to decide whether or not to go outside. The roses in the garden were beginning to bloom now and she'd always loved sitting among their splendor, sniffing their beautiful fragrance. She had started to wheel herself out when she heard male voices coming from the salon.

"All right, then, Mr. O'Neill, we'll be sure to have one of the negroes bring the ice over a few hours before, packed in straw. Father said you're to have as much as you need." Josh Fontaine shook hands with Brianne's father, then turned to leave, stopping short at sight of Brianne in the hallway.

"Why, Brianne, hello!" he said, after the briefest moment of nervous silence passed between them.

"Josh, how nice to see you," Brianne returned, throwing him a dazzling smile. "Come, you're just in time to take me out to the garden."

He smiled with hesitation. "I'm—not sure that would be appropriate, Brianne, now that you are to be a married woman shortly."

"Josh, what in the world is wrong with you?" she said lightly, determined now that he should abide by her wishes. "God's teeth, we are old friends after all! Are you afraid that my fiancé might make something of our being together?"

Josh sighed, then gave in, pushing her chair outside to the garden. Brianne settled back in her chair, enjoying the game she was playing with Josh Fontaine. It served him right for not speaking up and offering to marry her when he'd found out she was to be engaged to Pierce Nolan.

"It's lovely out here, isn't it, Josh?" she murmured, leaning forward to sniff at a flower. "What have you been doing with yourself these past few weeks? I haven't seen you since—well, since the cotillion at your house."

Josh cleared his throat. "Been busy as usual," he answered briskly. "My father's been bringing me into the business more and more. He figures that pretty soon I'll be ready to take over and he can retire." He chuckled fondly. "Not that he ever will, not really."

"So—you'll be settling down, Josh?" she asked innocently.

He reddened a little and pulled at his collar. "Well, you can't say as I'm the first, since you're beating me to the altar," he laughed.

"Oh, Josh, you know this is all just to keep rumors

from springing up about what happened at Rosemont," Brianne put in frankly. "If it hadn't been for what happened that night, I certainly wouldn't be marrying Pierce Nolan! But, as my father says, honor is everything in this blasted country, although I suspect he means his more than mine." She glanced up at him questioningly. "Still, I suppose I should be grateful to Pierce for saving me from a fate worse than death!" she interposed mockingly. "No one else was willing to do so."

She was not surprised to see him look away from her. "See here, Brianne, you know you're talking nonsense. Why, we grew up together, but that didn't mean—"

"—That you'd have the nerve to ask me to marry you?" she finished sweetly. "Why, Josh? Was it because I'm a cripple? Didn't you think you could stand being married to a wife who couldn't join in the dancing, who couldn't ride with the hunt? Or was it that your father had other plans for you, perhaps?" She snorted derisively. "As though anyone else in the county could bring you one-half the dowry you would have gotten at Avonlea!

"To tell you the truth, Josh, even if you had asked for my hand, I'm not so sure I would have accepted!" She pushed her chair away from him. "I'd prefer that you leave now."

She kept her face averted, listening to the sound of his footsteps on the gravel path. When she knew that he was gone, a strange sadness filtered over her, a sadness born from the fact that she knew things would never be the same as they had been before with Josh, or any one of the people she had known all her life. Had it all started on the evening of the county cotillion, or had it begun before that?

Suddenly, she felt a man's hand on her shoulder from behind her. She started, wondering if it could possibly be Josh, then realized he would never have taken such a liberty with her now. Forcing herself to remain still, she felt the hand move lightly down her arm, to the arm of the chair, to bring her around to him. As she'd expected,

Pierce was inspecting her with his golden eyes, the dark brows drawn in the familiar sardonic crescents.

"You were rather hard on Fontaine, don't you think?" he murmured, his eyes gleaming.

She shrugged, breaking away from his insistent gaze. "I don't care about Josh."

"Hmmm. That's an interesting turnabout, since I could have sworn you cared more than a little about him before the fact of our engagement."

"He's just a child, really," she said airily. "I doubt that I could ever have loved him."

"I'm glad to hear you say it, my dearest, for it makes me think that what you really want is a man, that you're tired of overgrown boys who know how to say all the right things, but don't know the first thing about satisfying a woman, especially one of your passionate temperament."

"And, of course, I need have no qualms that you will see to my baser needs," she put in boldly, beginning to enjoy the light banter.

He smiled ruthlessly. "Your baser needs are what delight me most, Brianne. If I didn't think you had them, nothing on earth could have forced me into marrying you. Oh, I know you pride yourself on your charm and your physical attributes, but, believe me, if there was no passion lurking behind those exquisite eyes of yours, I would have left you to the gossips."

She preened a little, disregarding most of what he said to concentrate on his comment about her eyes. "But with all the passion in the world, without beauty to go with it, I doubt if you would have stayed, Pierce Nolan."

He laughed. "I admit I prefer my women to have some looks."

"Your *women?*" she inquired huffily.

"The gambols of youth and reckless living, my dear," he smiled, taking her hand suddenly in his. "Can you find it in your heart to forgive me?"

She was silent, put out by the thought that he had had

other women before her, while she herself was inexperienced. She felt his mouth on her hand kissing the fingers one by one, then turning to the palm, going higher to the wrist, until goose pimples were breaking out all over her. His lips slid even higher, up to the crook of her elbow where her sleeve began.

"Why—are you doing that?" she asked breathlessly.

"Because I want to," he answered simply. "Isn't the prospective bridegroom allowed some improprieties with his future bride?"

"If I said no, would that make you stop?"

He laughed. "Do you want me to stop, Brianne?"

She shivered at the desire in his eyes. He leaned forward, his face coming nearer, until she knew that he was going to kiss her on the mouth. She turned her face up a little, meeting his lips with her own, feeling them move against hers in practiced artistry. His hands were tight on her shoulders, steadying him as he demanded the intimacy of her open mouth. Vanquished, Brianne gave in so completely that she felt lost when he straightened to release her.

"Ah, those baser needs," he whispered, a hand caressing the side of her face.

She came to herself and eyed him warily. "You think you have me, don't you?" she asked as though it were a challenge. "What kind of a wife are you expecting, I wonder?"

"I have no expectations at this point," he answered lightly. "I have never been married so I have nothing by which to judge. Nevertheless, I don't doubt you will be unique, Brianne. Why else would I have chosen you?"

"Why did you agree to marry me, Pierce?" she wanted to know suddenly. "Don't tell me it was because you were afraid of being tarred and feathered by papa and the others. And don't tell me you love me, because I know you don't!"

His golden eyes changed, became deeper. "You're

right, my dear. It wasn't your father's threats, or your snow-white reputation that concerned me. And, no, I don't love you. You're too incomplete—you're still a child in so many ways, my dear. Believe me, I'm not boasting when I say I've seen so much more than you. I feel twenty years older than you sometimes rather than ten." He laughed lightly and turned away from her eager expression, putting his hands in the pockets of his trousers in an oddly boyish gesture. "I don't know why I agreed to marry you," he said finally. "Perhaps it was destiny, something higher than our wills." The mockery was back in his voice now.

"You say I'm a child, that you don't love me, and I know that I don't love you," she said, almost to herself. "It seems a bad start to a marriage."

He watched her pensively, his hands balled into fists in his trouser pockets. "Would you believe me if I said I admired you?" he asked. "Despite your faults, and they are too numerous to mention, you do have courage, my dear, and I've always admired that."

"You are an adventurous soul," she commented lightly. "I can't imagine why you want to settle down."

"Who's to say?" he shrugged. "After we're married, I still may go back to Texas and take you with me." He eyed the wheelchair. "Of course, you must start walking again for I can't be carting you around in that thing."

"Do you think I can just get up and walk because you wish it?" she demanded, careful to keep her eyes averted so he couldn't guess at her secret. "You agreed to marry me, knowing full well that I might never walk again!"

"You'll walk again," he said slowly. "Because you're the kind of woman who won't allow herself to grow old in a wheelchair. You enjoy parties and dancing and riding too much to condemn yourself to a life in that chair." He eyed her speculatively. "Besides, the journey west would kill you."

She picked up on his last comment, her eyes widening

as she realized what he was saying. "You don't mean that we would leave here, do you? Why, I couldn't possibly live anywhere else but Avonlea. It's my home!"

"When you become my wife, Brianne, you'll live where I want you to live," he answered her swiftly. "Did you really think that I was going to start cultivating a few acres of sugar cane? I told you before; I owe a debt to the Rangers that I have every intention of paying."

She frowned slightly, her brows drawing together in irritation. "A debt of honor," she amended. "It seems that word continues to pop up in my life."

"Call it what you like, Brianne, you can't say I didn't warn you of my plans."

"But, with our marriage, I was sure your plans would change," she put in hastily. "Why, I've never been farther than New Orleans, Pierce! I know nothing of the frontier you've spoken of. What kind of life would that be for me?"

"A wife is supposed to follow her husband," he put in. "Would you honestly wish for me to go without you?" His golden eyes probed hers.

"I—I won't leave Avonlea," she said stubbornly, refusing to meet his gaze.

He was silent for a long moment. "Then, I may have to leave without you," he warned.

She looked up, a sudden panic overwhelming her at the thought of his leaving her behind, the abandoned wife. "You wouldn't dare!"

"Believe me, Brianne, you had better start getting out of that chair—and soon," he said shortly. He turned on his heel abruptly, then stopped and turned back to her. Digging in his breast pocket, he pulled out a small box, tied up with a blue ribbon. Carelessly he tossed it at her. "Here, I forgot to give you this earlier. Sorry it's not more, but I had to go to Natchez for it instead of New Orleans, like I'd wanted." Without waiting for her to open it, he walked back toward the house.

Hesitantly, Brianne untied the ribbon and opened the

box. Inside, nestled on a bed of black velvet, was a diamond ring, twinkling out at her. Gasping, she took it out and slipped it on her ring finger, seeing the way it flashed and sparkled in the sunlight. On either side of the diamond was a topaz, not as big as the diamond, but of good size. She stared at them, winking back at her with the blaze of the sun on them. She knew she would always see his golden eyes when she looked at them.

Chapter Eight

THE CROWD OF PEOPLE CRANED THEIR NECKS IN EXPECTA-
tion as the music changed, signaling the bride's procession. The church was overflowing with people, some of
whom were forced to stand toward the back because
there were not enough seats. At last they would see the
bride, always the high point of the wedding procession as
men eyed her beauty appreciatively and women gasped
at the lavish trimmings of the wedding dress. But now,
suddenly, there was a murmur of pity washing over the
audience, a drawing back so as not to seem too curious.

In her wheelchair, her father pushing it behind her,
Brianne sat, as white as her gown of cream silk. There
were two high spots of color on her cheeks, and if one
looked behind the veiling of lace over her face, one might
have seen the red-rimmed eyes that bespoke angry tears.

Tragedy had struck not two hours before the start of
the ceremony. Thinking of it as she was pushed down the
aisle to her waiting bridegroom, Brianne couldn't help
wincing, and the tears nearly came again.

She had been so happy and so proud of herself! She
was confident that she would walk down the aisle,
surprise everyone and prove to Pierce that she was no
ninny to hide in her chair from the world. Things had
been going so smoothly, despite the uneasy truce between her and Pierce after he'd revealed that he would
not remain at Avonlea. Brianne had met his family, his
parents and his two sisters, Mary and Rose, both of
whom were exceedingly pretty and very polite, a rigid

politeness that had slowly turned to warmth as they had gotten to know their new sister-in-law. Brianne had been gratified that they'd been suitably awed by the spendor of Avonlea. Yes, it all couldn't have been nicer.

Brianne had grown more and more confident, walking about her room, practicing in her wedding gown to make sure she could carry the extra weight of the wider skirts and heavy, long veil. And then, just two hours before the wedding, two *hours* before her triumph, she'd fallen. She remembered with startling clarity how she had seen the box of books, a wedding gift from someone, she couldn't recall who, in front of her, right as her toe stubbed against the side of it. She fell to the floor, the wind knocked out of her, one of her legs striking the top of the box with sickening force as she tried to brace herself for the fall. When she'd tried to get up, a flash of pain had burst from her knee to her ankle and a swelling bruise was already appearing on her shinbone. She had burst into uncontrollable sobbing and had continued to cry while Sara, clucking sympathetically, helped her to dress.

Brianne could see, through the veil over her face, the figure of her husband-to-be, standing at the end of the long aisle, his face watchful, his expression closed from her. She gritted her teeth, wanting to wail at the injustice of fate for dealing her this blow now. How different it would have been to walk majestically down the aisle, to meet Pierce's surprise and pride.

She let a muffled sob escape and felt her father lean forward. "You all right, puss?" he whispered.

She nodded, but doubted that she'd ever be all right again. She searched the crowd discreetly and saw the looks of mingled pity and contempt on some of those well-bred faces. Josh was not even looking at her, his eyes staring straight ahead. Annabelle Jackson's expression was a mixture of contempt and malicious pleasure to see this final embarrassment to her girlhood rival. Brianne closed her eyes, sick of the sympathetic looks on the faces of the older men and women. There was not one happy glance, one look of encouragement, unless one counted her mother and brother and Emily Turner. Even Mr. and Mrs. Nolan were carefully trying to conceal their look of dubious pity. How must they feel, she wondered, thinking their only son was going to be tied down to this handicapped woman? Damn them! Damn them all!

Now she was at the foot of the altar where the priest was awaiting them, no expression on his solemn face. Thank God there was no pity there. But Pierce, what was in his eyes? Dared she look? She remembered how he'd told her he'd wanted her to walk down the marriage aisle or he'd beat her black and blue. She really hadn't believed his threat, but then she'd actually thought she *would* be walking down that aisle.

The priest began to speak, intoning words that made no sense to her in her highly emotional state. She still had not found the courage to look at Pierce, although she could see his hands folded on the railing above the knee rest. She thought about those hands, so slim and long fingered, yet strong and tanned—a man's hands. Suddenly, she thought of those hands on her legs, massaging them like Mandy had done. A furious blush covered her cheeks.

After the required repeating of the formal vows, it was time for the ring ceremony. Brianne felt her palms sweaty, felt the tug on her wrist as Pierce pulled her hand up in order to place the wedding ring on it. She heard the words as some indistinct noise that made no sense at all. Please God, let it all be over soon! All she wanted was to crawl back to her room and hide away from all these people! But of course, that would be impossible! She could never call her bedroom her own again. From now on, it would be shared with this man beside her, this man she hardly knew, a stranger really, she thought with panic threatening to overwhelm her.

"You may kiss the bride," the priest directed solemnly.

Brianne knew that it was Pierce who had turned to her,

who was lifting the veil from her face. Breathlessly, she looked up, hoping to find something in his eyes which might help her get through the rest of the evening. She saw only disappointment and a terrible kind of quiet anger. His golden eyes bore into hers as his mouth came down to possess her lips. She tensed herself for the hardness of his mouth, but he barely touched her, his lips brushing hers with all the intimacy of a close friend. She shrank inside herself.

"Go in peace," the priest was saying, "and God be with you."

"Amen," Brianne heard herself saying fervently.

"Pierce! Where are you, son-in-law?" Brian was in a jovial mood, having drunk several toasts to the health of the bride and groom.

Pierce heard him as he stood alone on the back porch of Avonlea, smoking the last of a cheroot which it seemed he'd only just lit up. He threw the glowing stub down on the gravel path and folded his arms as he leaned backward to look up at the stars. They were beautiful tonight, winking softly in the black velvet of the sky. He thought about how those stars would look in the wide-open spaces of Texas. Wouldn't they look bigger, brighter out there? God, just now how he longed to feel a strong horse beneath him, a wind ruffling the hair on the back of his neck, the smell of wild, untamed places that beckoned to him.

Damn, but here he was saddled with a wife who suddenly seemed more trouble than she was worth. He'd been so sure somehow that she would meet his expectations, that she would walk down that aisle today with her head held proudly. But no, she'd been pushed in that damn chair, her head down, her whole bearing cowed and forlorn. He'd hated her for an instant, hated her because he sensed so much pity being directed toward him for being tied forever to a crippled wife. He felt strapped, hemmed in by a civilization he'd never been comfortable with. Already he wanted to reject it and be free. But no, he was harnessed by that miserable, spoiled child-woman who probably didn't know the first thing about satisfying a man, and wouldn't be too interested in learning.

His jaw clenched, as rigid as his mind as he thought of getting away from this hole he had dug for himself. He had to admit that there was definitely something he'd liked in Brianne O'Neill that had drawn him to her. He was not the kind of man, however, who would go running after a woman, seeking only to please her and forgetting his own needs.

"Pierce, there you are." It was his father, coming up to formally congratulate him, the handshake cold and reserved. The same emotions were mirrored in his eyes. "You're out here, alone?" he commented after a moment.

Pierce shrugged and moved a little away from his father, looking out over the dark expanse of lawn where lanterns had been lit at intervals for wanderers from the party inside. "I would think every new bridegroom might be entitled to a moment of privacy," he returned, striving for lightness.

His father guffawed shortly. "Pierce," he began, clearing his throat in the manner of someone who was about to begin a long and tiresome speech, "your mother and I have been discussing this surprising marriage of yours. We think—"

"I don't want to know what you think," Pierce interrupted him quickly, and at his father's quick intake of breath, "I'm sorry, but I just don't feel the need to discuss the marriage with either of you."

"But this girl! In a wheelchair!" John Nolan seemed at a loss for words. "Don't you realize what you could have had if you'd come back to St. Louis, boy? With your money and our good name, why, you could have had your pick of any of the finest, loveliest girls in the city!"

"I'm not sure that I'll ever go back to St. Louis," Pierce

put in reflectively. "Not if it means turning myself into your idea of what a son should be. I have other commitments right now, I'm afraid."

His father seemed not to be listening. "Do you think you made a mistake, son?" he asked gravely.

Pierce looked up. "I'm old enough to know what I'm doing. I've been making my own decisions since I was sixteen."

"Yes," his father agreed soberly. "But this young woman—"

"Let's not discuss my wife," Pierce interrupted. "I don't expect her to be a cripple for life; it's only a temporary affliction."

"So I've been assured by her father," John Nolan returned gruffly. He was quiet for a moment, then continued in a different vein. "So, you won't be returning to St. Louis in the near future, Pierce? You mean to settle here?"

Pierce shrugged.

"You're going to receive some prime acreage from O'Neill and enough money with the girl's dowry to start your own plantation." He smiled grimly at the startled look his son gave him. "Oh, I made it my business to see that you were well-compensated for marrying a young woman tied down to a wheelchair. I believe O'Neill is being generous. He knows he's damn lucky to be getting an able-bodied son-in-law with your background, considering the circumstances."

Pierce faced his father, anger darkening his golden eyes. "You talked to Brian about the dowry?" he asked tightly. "What business of yours was it?" he demanded.

"The business of an interested father," John Nolan put in.

"Dammit! You had no right to come down here and try to negotiate my life for me! Brianne's dowry isn't what made me marry her! And as for remaining here for the rest of my life, I'm afraid you've been misinformed. I'm heading for Texas as soon as the Rangers are recalled

from retirement. Why, I could no sooner be a farmer and
sit every afternoon on my front porch with a cool mint
julep in my hand than I could turn myself into a
gray-suited, stuffy businessman like yourself!"

For a brief moment, Pierce saw his father's cool
reserve begin to crack. Then, with an effort, he resumed
his habitual calmness. "Pierce, you were always an
ungrateful son," he began slowly, deliberately. "Your
mother and I did everything within our means to see that
you got a good education in preparation for a high
position in the business world. It gave neither of us any
joy to see you throw everything away and run off to some
vague idea of freedom and adventure.

"You were a disappointment to us then, and it seems
you are determined to continue in that vein. You roam
the frontier for nearly thirteen years and then decide to
marry a young woman who is not only a cripple, but, if
rumor is right, is the product of a father who is a habitual
drunkard! How do you expect you will take such a
woman into the wilds of Texas? You are no longer a free
man, Pierce! You've made ties for yourself now, the very
thing you seem to hate!"

"Enough!" Pierce growled.

John Nolan drew back from his son as though shying
away from a physical blow. With another effort, he drew
himself together. "As you say," he began, "it is your
wedding night and I suppose a new bridegroom is
entitled to some privacy. If you will excuse me?" He
bowed stiffly and left his son standing at the edge of the
darkness, watching him.

Pierce stood alone again, smoking and thinking. His
father's taunting words pricked at him like sharp thorns.
Was he tied forever to Avonlea now? He knew his new
bride was not eager to leave the life she was accustomed
to. Would it be impossible to leave without her? Was it so
important that he return to Texas and repay the debt to
the Rangers that he felt he owed? But if not that, then
what? He had rejected his father's world of business, his

wife's world of Southern farming—what else was there for him?

If he left his wife to go to Texas, he would be labeled a coward and a blackguard. But did he really care about such labels? And yet, he couldn't leave Brianne to face such humiliation. He threw his cheroot to the ground in disgust. There was nothing else but to bring her with him. Maybe they could compromise on New Orleans; she would enjoy the bright lights and the shopping. They could see doctors there that would be able to help her to walk. Surely, she would not be adverse to that!

He knew that she wasn't afraid of the frontier; he didn't believe she had a cowardly bone in her body. She was just spoiled, a Southern lady born to the indolent life of plantation living, used to being waited on hand and foot. Surely, he could make her see that there was more to life than Avonlea and its surrounding countryside? He sensed there was a free spirit within that pampered child-woman that was a match to his own, but she refused to see it for herself.

But she was his wife now, he thought, smiling suddenly. That should make things just a little easier.

It was late, Brianne thought nervously, quite late and she had to admit that she was tired, bone weary after trying to make small talk with the guests and keeping her head held up despite the wish that she could go up to her room and leave them all downstairs. She knew it was after midnight, but didn't dare to look at the small china clock on her dressing table, fearing it was later than she thought. She heard Sara fussing with her wedding dress, hanging it up neatly in the wardrobe while Mandy saw to the veil, touching it with adoring hands.

Her mother was helping her into the new nightgown made of real French silk, trimmed in blue-ribbon knots at the sleeves and hemline. Exclaiming over its prettiness was Pierce's mother, Alicia, who seemed to be trying very hard to be kindly reassuring. Brianne wished they would all go and leave her in peace. But the thought came that when they left, Pierce would enter—

"Mama," she whispered, taking her mother's hand in hers. "I'm a little nervous."

Joanna smiled and kissed her daughter's brow. "Darling, there is nothing to be worried about. You're lucky that Pierce is—experienced enough to treat you gently."

"But I—I'm not sure what to do," she admitted, trying to keep the fire from staining her cheeks.

"He'll know that, my dear, and help you," Joanna returned wisely. "Now don't go upsetting yourself; this is your wedding night and very special to you!" She kissed her again and called Mandy over to brush her hair—it would alleviate some of her nervous tension.

"I think, perhaps, we had better retire," Alicia suggested primly. "Pierce must be waiting—" She stopped and flushed.

"You go on. I'll be there in a moment." Joanna waited until Alicia had kissed her new daughter-in-law on the cheek and gone out into the hallway before leaning over and taking her daughter's chin in her hand. "Brianne, remember that you are Pierce's wife now. I know that things have not gone smoothly for you two in these past few days. It has been a strain on everyone getting ready for the wedding. But this is the beginning of a new life for you. You're still my daughter, but you are also Mrs. Pierce Nolan."

"I—I'll remember, mama," Brianne whispered in a hushed voice. She reached up to put her arms about her mother's neck, something she hadn't done spontaneously since she'd been a little girl.

When Joanna had gone out, Sara motioned toward Mandy to come out with her, giving her instructions should her mistress call for her during the night. "Good luck to you, lamb," Sara said, her eyes moist as she dabbed at them with her apron. "A big ol' yellow tom cat came 'round this morning, honey, and that means good luck for you." She rolled her eyes and smiled. "You be a good girl." She left, taking Mandy with her.

The silence was suddenly disquieting. If she'd been able to, Brianne would have liked to walk to her bedroom window and look out at the stars. She wished she didn't have to lie here in bed like a stupid chicken waiting to get its head cut off. She laughed nervously at the idea.

"Giggles from my new bride?" Pierce opened the door and walked into the room, clad in a dressing gown of fine cashmere. He saw her looking at him in surprise. "A gift from your brother," he explained pointing to the dressing gown. "He assured me it was my duty to enter the bride's chamber decently clothed for the occasion."

"How thoughtful," she got out, unaware that her eyes were as round as saucers and that there was a becoming flush on her cheeks.

He seemed in no hurry to climb in bed with her, but turned to lock the door. "I never did ask you what your father said after he saw the broken door," he commented idly.

"I—oh, does it matter what he said, Pierce!" she answered, her voice becoming strained.

He shrugged, then walked over to where candles had been placed and blew them all out, except for those by the side of the bed. He eyed the effect of the candlelight on her face appreciatively. The light made her deep auburn hair gleam richly as it fell in soft waves around her.

"Your hair is beautiful," he murmured, coming closer to the bed. He knelt to the side of her and put his hand on her head, then moved it down her back, enjoying the feel of the thick, silky hair against his flesh. When she started to move away, he caught a handful of the hair and brought her back to him, pulling gently to force her head to tilt upward. Without warning, his lips came down to claim hers in a deep kiss that sent shock waves through her entire body. It was bold and masterful as though he were laying claim to his property. His tongue darted commandingly at hers, and they parried delicately.

"You have learned well, my bride," he said, pulling away from her, "but there is so much more for you to know."

Brianne waited, her heart beating hard inside her breast. She smelled the whiskey on his breath, but it was not unpleasant and she knew that he wasn't drunk. He was leaning over her, his hands on her shoulders, pushing her back into the pillows. His mouth followed, continuing to kiss her lips and cheeks and eyes.

"Pierce, you—you must let me breathe!" she protested weakly.

He drew away and silently began to untie the belt of his robe. Brianne watched him, still drugged from his kisses, looking up as he towered over her on the bed. She gasped when he removed the robe for he was naked beneath it. Embarrassed, she turned her face away, but felt his hand commandingly under her chin, forcing her back to look at him.

"I'm your husband, Brianne," he murmured softly, as though reminding her of that fact would make his nakedness less of a shock to her.

Hesitantly, her turquoise eyes followed the line of his shoulders down his lightly-furred chest to the flat stomach muscles. Below that she refused to look, although she'd received a fleeting impression of something alien. She was not ignorant of how men were built, having seen young slaves in the fields. But this was so different.

"Pierce, why can't we—I mean, isn't it proper to slip under the covers?" she said cautiously, not knowing if the suggestion would offend him.

"And after I've slipped under the covers, I suppose it is also perfectly proper for you and I to do our mutual gropings?" he inquired mockingly. "No, Brianne, I'd rather you see what you were groping with. You see, I'm a rascal and a man without morals as you have told me on more than one occasion."

She bit her lip, not quite sure if she should be angry or embarrassed. "I forgot," she finally shot back, "that you aren't used to having ladies of breeding in bed with you. I daresay *they* wouldn't wear a nightgown either!"

He smiled. "No, come to think of it, they wouldn't," he replied, and without warning, he pulled the covers off her and caught at the hem of her nightdress. "Pretty thing," he commented. "But it's keeping me from you and so, I'm afraid, it has to go." He pulled at the stuff and, rather than see him rip the expensive gift, Brianne lifted her arms so that he could bring it over her head.

Almost as soon as the material had cleared the top of her head, Brianne reached down for the cover to draw it up over her again.

"Ah, no, my wife," Pierce chided her mockingly. "Now is not the time to hide your charms from me. I want to see what I'm getting in exchange for my freedom."

"In exchange for your—!" Brianne held the covers tightly under her chin. "Did you ever think that I was giving up my freedom too!" she demanded.

"No, I didn't," he admitted without regret. "Women, I've been taught, are too eager to give up any freedom in order to catch a man who will support them and keep them from being labeled an old maid." He lifted his eyebrows sarcastically. "And isn't that a fate worse than death?"

"Please don't imply that *I* caught *you!*" she put in haughtily.

He laughed. "Spunky even on her wedding night. What happened, my love, to the wide eyes and blushing cheeks I saw when I came in tonight?"

She shrugged. "I was afraid—until I realized it was only the same person that I've been sparring with ever since you came to Avonlea."

"Well, perhaps it would serve my interests better if I gave you back some of that initial fear," he returned. His hand caught at the blanket that covered her and succeed-

ed in pulling it away from her nerveless fingers. His eyes
raked her nudity, noting with satisfaction and pride how
perfect she was.

Brianne closed her eyes as he laid down beside her,
supporting himself on an elbow facing her. His free hand
reached out to caress the satiny skin of her breasts and
pinch the small, tight nipples between thumb and forefinger. Soon they grew swollen under his continued ministrations.

Finally, when Brianne thought she couldn't bear any
more, she cried out, "Enough!"

"No, never enough, my lovely wife," Pierce returned
tightly, letting his hand roam over the softness of her
stomach and abdomen. "You will learn to enjoy such
foreplay when you become more experienced, my
dear."

"Is that what you call this mauling of my bosom?" she
demanded, although she felt a pleasurable tingling in her
breasts.

"Mmmm, and other things besides," he warned her
before his hand sliced between her thighs and touched
the softness of her womanhood.

"Oh!" Brianne thought she might swoon from embarrassment. She had had no idea there would be such
lengthy caressing before the culmination of the wedding
vows. That the man who caressed her so boldly was
Pierce Nolan did little to alleviate her discomfort. She
wished only that he would get on with it.

And soon he did, forcing her legs open so that he could
kneel between them. Anchoring himself with his hands,
he leaned downward to kiss her breasts while his knee
was insistent between her outspread thighs. Brianne felt
pleasurable sensations from her neck to her knees now,
radiating outward and causing a wave of heat throughout
her entire body. She moaned softly and was surprised to
hear her own voice.

He covered her mouth with his and she felt the hot
probing of his manhood at the gate of her femininity. She

gasped against his mouth when he entered her, stifling the startled cries against his lips that were kissing her with greater passion than before. Something was throbbing inside of her, calling forth an answering throb that made her whole body quiver. He stopped kissing her to look deeply into her wide-open eyes.

"What do you feel, Brianne?" he asked her hoarsely.

"I've never felt this way," she whispered back, her arms going around his neck of their own volition. "Pierce!" she cried as he lowered himself deeply into her.

"God, Brianne," he murmured, nearly out of his mind with passion she was so wet and tight. "You are beautiful, my wife, my love!"

Briane heard the endearment and tightened her hold around his neck. She reached up to kiss him passionately, caught up in the mindless frenzy of their bodies as they slipped into the age-old rhythm of love. It seemed hours passed as they enjoyed each other fully, and then his swollen member burst forth its seed within her and she answered him fully, causing him even greater pleasure.

"Pierce, I love you!" she whispered passionately, her hand woven into the hair at the back of his neck. Having said the words, she stopped in confusion, not knowing how or why she had said them.

He heard the words and was aware of her sudden stillness. Hesitantly, he lifted his golden eyes to hers, seeking the truth in those turquoise orbs that jumped away from his gaze.

"What did you say, my dear?" he asked her tenderly.

"I said—nothing," she returned, biting her lip, thinking he was merely baiting her with the question. Did she love him, or had it been the passion of the moment putting itself into words? She shivered at the thought of how vulnerable she would be if she did love him.

He sighed and the golden eyes narrowed. Perhaps he hadn't heard her right. He pulled himself away from her, lying for a moment on his back, his arms folded behind his head as he stared up at the ceiling.

He was silent for so long that Brianne grew uncomfortable, wishing she could reach the water pitcher in order to cleanse herself. She turned her head to look at her new husband, wondering at the change from passion to quiet.

"Are we—you finished?" she asked tentatively.

In the candlelight she saw him smile with the old amused mockery. "For the moment," he conceded, "but we have more to do before the night is done, wife."

She looked at him in dismay—more of what she had just gone through? It was impossible to be lifted up to such heights twice in one night. A stealthy tiredness had begun to creep over her and she realized that she was very sleepy. She suppressed a yawn and looked over at him again.

"May I—I'd like to put my nightdress back on," she said quickly.

"Why?" he asked, turning toward her so that she looked away hurriedly.

"I'm tired," she whispered, trembling at the knowledge that he was staring at her body.

He reached over and laid his arm across her breasts. "I'm not," he said.

Chapter Nine

PIERCE NOLAN GAZED DOWN AT HIS STILL-SLEEPING WIFE and allowed a broad grin to shape his sensual mouth. She really was a little beauty, he thought. Still unused to the sexual antics of love, she nevertheless had pleased him enormously last night. He thought ahead to the sensual nights on the prairie with her under the open sky with nothing but the gentle breeze in their ears and the smell of the wild flowers in their nostrils. God, what a pioneer woman she was going to make.

He swiveled his gaze unwillingly from her face to the wheelchair, sitting like some dark specter in a corner of the room, and then beyond to the window where birds were chirping in the new day.

Beside him, he felt his bride stirring a little, and had to smile tenderly at the grimace that shaped her mouth when she moved her legs. Damn, he guessed he'd made her a little sore last night with all his attentions. Perhaps he'd overdone it. He hoped not, for he had every intention of pressing those same attentions on her again tonight—if not before.

"Good morning, Mrs. Nolan," he said softly.

Brianne's eyes fluttered open and stared at him for a moment before narrowing slightly. "Good morning."

He reached down to catch her chin in one hand and plant a light kiss on her mouth. "Hungry? I wonder what your fabulous cook is putting out for breakfast?"

She looked at him aghast. "You can't mean that you want to go downstairs—this morning?"

He tilted his head a little, trying to gauge the expression in those turquoise orbs. "What's the matter, Mrs. Nolan? Surely, you don't expect to remain in this room all day?"

"But, aren't we supposed to? I mean, aren't we supposed to be alone for a while?" she fluttered, blushing under his careful scrutiny. His fingers had begun tracing tiny patterns down her jawline to her neck.

"You don't know what such words mean to me," he said, gently mocking. "Only one night spent together and the woman never wants to leave my side."

She pushed his hand away in irritation. "Good heavens! Pierce, you're acting so—so different today. I hardly know what to say to you!" She sat up, hugging the sheet around her, feeling his fingers clasping the curling, auburn tendrils that hung shimmeringly down her smooth back.

"I suppose marriage must be good for the soul," he murmured, leaning to press his mouth against the flesh of her back.

Brianne felt a shiver up her backbone and hastily squirmed away. But his mouth pursued her, and soon she felt his tongue swirling over her ribs, climbing upward to the tip of her shoulder blade. She pressed the sheet more tightly against her bosom, although her breath had begun to come much faster. His wandering lips reached the ball of her shoulder, then swept inward, one strong hand pushing away the heavy length of hair to expose the tender nape of her neck.

Despite her uncertainty at this unfamiliar playfulness, Brianne couldn't help leaning her head back and closing her eyes as tiny tingles reached throughout her back and shoulders. The sheet slipped from her fingers and her new husband took full advantage of it to bring one hand around to cup a firm, high breast.

"So lovely," he murmured against her throat, bringing her back to rest against his arm. Softly, he lowered her back onto the mattress and continued his explorations, nibbling at the end of her collarbone and nipping gently at the flesh above her right breast.

Brianne began to squirm once more, but this time it was not because she wanted to get away. Pierce allowed himself a self-satisfied chuckle as his mouth descended to the tip of one breast and worked magic on it. Her hands were clasped around his neck and he could feel the slight pressure they were exerting to keep his head where it was.

"I could eat you up in little pieces, wife," he murmured, moving to the other breast.

"Mmmm," Brianne breathed, her eyes still closed, although her hands had begun to gently caress the nape of his neck where the dark hair curled slightly.

Pierce could feel the excitement mounting inside of him. God, he hoped that she wasn't too sore, for he sure as hell wanted her again, right now! His hands settled on either side of her, clasping the softness of her rounded hips.

A sudden, sharp knock barely fazed him, but Brianne's eyes flew open and her concentration was shattered as she tried to sit up in the bed, a guilty flush stealing over her cheeks.

"Damn!" Pierce muttered. "Who in the hell could that be at this time of the day?" He looked over at his bride, but she had averted her eyes in embarrassment. He shrugged and stood up, grabbing the cashmere robe to make himself decent before unlocking the door. Sara's broad, black face beamed back at him over a silver tray laden with steaming coffee, mounds of pancakes and crisp sausages.

"I's been told that married folk need lots of food to keep up their energy," she said slyly, winking at Pierce and trying to crane her neck around the door to see where her lamb was.

"They need some privacy too," Pierce grumbled, taking the tray.

"Does Miss Brianne need me for anything?" Sara

asked gently, unwilling to leave until she was sure her young mistress was all right.

Before Brianne could answer, Pierce shook his head and prepared to shut the door. "No, I'll be seeing to her needs for a while," he answered, before closing the door and locking it once more. He brought the tray to the bed, noting that Brianne had been able to grab her nightgown and slip it on. She looked up at him with a slightly defiant air that made him smile, despite the ache in his groin. "Breakfast is served, Mrs. Nolan," he announced.

"I'm not hungry," she answered.

"Come on now, wife, you've got to keep your strength up," he teased her, sitting on the bed and handing her a plate and a napkin. "I can assure you, I plan to keep mine up!" He laughed with only a trace of mockery. "After all, Sara did make a special trip up here with all this; the least you could do is do it some justice."

With a small sigh, Brianne accepted a crisp sausage and two steaming cakes. She ate slowly, stealing little glimpses of her husband as he sat, perfectly at ease, naked on the bed, eating his breakfast, having cast off the robe after locking the door. When they had finished and were both nursing a cup of hot, rich coffee, she felt Pierce's eyes on her and looked up to meet his enigmatic gaze.

"What are you thinking about?" she asked curiously.

He smiled. "I was just thinking what a magnificent woman you're going to be once we get you out of that wheelchair and into the frontier! I can just see the soft honey tone your skin will turn under the sun, making those beautiful eyes jump right out at a man!"

"Frontier!" she questioned, swallowing a big gulp of coffee. "But, I thought all that had been resolved!"

He frowned slightly. "What do you mean?"

She looked down at her coffee cup, then back to his golden gaze, her own holding a slight challenge. "I mean, I thought it was all arranged between your father and mine. Part of my dowry to go toward building a new manor house—our house—on two hundred of the best sugar cane fields my father owns. My father told me we were welcome to stay at Avonlea as long as we wished, until our own house was finished."

Pierce's mouth tightened involuntarily. "This was arranged, you say, between our fathers?"

She nodded. "They had our best interests at heart, Pierce," she returned, almost primly.

He longed to wipe that self-righteous look from her mouth. "Well, I'm afraid that everyone forgot one thing," he began tightly. "The permission of the husband!"

She blinked back at him. "But, I'm sure your father can speak for you—"

"Dammit, no!" Pierce jumped up from the bed and paced the room for a moment. He looked back at his wife, unable to erase the scowl that now formed on his face. "Dammit, Brianne, I told you more than once that I had no intention of settling here in Louisiana! Texas—"

"I don't want to hear about Texas," she interrupted, fear making her voice angry. "I don't want to hear about your gratitude to the Rangers and your—your commitments to them because they helped you to grow up! Pierce, surely, you didn't think I was actually going to follow you into a Godforsaken frontier where you, yourself, admitted there are all the dangers of Indian raids! What kind of man would force his bride to go into such a place?"

"A man's bride is supposed to *want* to be with her husband!" he reminded her wrathfully.

"But, I thought, after last night—"

"What does last night have to do with our future together?" he asked her, striving for calm.

She blushed furiously. "Well, you—you did seem to show that you cared for me and I thought that meant that you might care about my feelings and what I want from the future!"

"Brianne, of course I care for you," he admitted, "but I don't think you realize what kind of man you've married."

"Obviously not!"

"What I mean is, I'm not the kind of man who can calmly sit back and let life go slowly by, who marks time by the change in the seasons and the maturing of his cane fields! Brianne, I know you must share some of that spirit of adventure. You wouldn't be happy living on a plantation like Avonlea for the rest of your life. What about the world outside Avonlea?"

"I would be perfectly happy never to set foot out of this county!" she said stubbornly, not about to admit that the prospect was not a heartening one.

"Then, it seems, we were both wrong about each other," Pierce said quietly, his topaz eyes holding her gaze.

There was silence for a minute.

Finally, Pierce spoke, "I don't suppose it would do any good for me to try to change your mind, Brianne. The longer I stay here at Avonlea, the more firmly entrenched I would become here. I'm sorry, but this is not where I want to spend the rest of my life. I want to leave for New Orleans next week."

"Pierce, I don't want to go to New Orleans," Brianne said, spots of color in her cheeks.

"Dammit, you are my wife!"

"Your wife, yes, not your slave!" she threw back at him.

"I don't want a slave!" he responded angrily. "I want a wife who cares about me enough to want to be with me!"

She swallowed and the words stuck in her throat before she finally got them out. "Then you've chosen the wrong wife, Pierce!"

For a moment, he stood watching her, his eyes questioning hers. Then he turned away abruptly, striding to where he'd dropped his robe. "I'm going to Natchez today," he began, the anger and hurt mixed in his voice, "and I'm going to buy two tickets on the next steamer to New Orleans. You'll have Sara pack your things, Brianne, because you're coming with me."

"If you make me go with you, I'll never stop hating you for it, Pierce Nolan!" she said shrilly.

"And if you force me to stay, I'm afraid I could never stop hating you for it," Pierce said heavily. "It seems we are at an impasse, Brianne, doesn't it?"

"You can go if you wish," Brianne tossed at him, not really believing he would do such a thing, "but I'm staying right here. Sara won't be packing *my* bags!"

For a moment, she saw him ball his hands into fists and stride purposefully toward her. She wanted desperately to cringe against the pillows, but faced him, inwardly trembling, wondering if he would, indeed, strike her. He came closer to her, the terrible anger mixed with something else she couldn't quite define in those golden eyes. So suddenly that she almost hadn't time to catch her breath, he reached out and pulled her brutally toward him, holding her tightly as he bent to kiss her. His mouth mashed itself against hers, trying to suck the very breath from her body, it seemed. His hands were hard on her arms, his teeth clashed against hers. It seemed long minutes before he finally released her and stared down at her. She was trembling, both from his overpowering strength and the sudden force of her own emotions.

"Can Avonlea make you feel like that?" he asked her sarcastically. "Can you take this house to bed with you every night and caress those cold, stone pillars outside?"

"Stop it!" she yelled at him, shocked.

"Look at me, Brianne!" he commanded. "I'm flesh-and-blood, a man who is also your husband! Don't be a little fool!"

His taunts made her throw her head up and tilt her chin defiantly. "You'd best buy only one ticket to New Orleans on that steamer, Pierce, for I'm not going with you! But, I swear, if you do leave, I'll hate you forever!"

For answer, he swept her a mocking bow and strode to

the door to unlock it, letting himself out and slamming it behind him.

Twelve hours later, Brianne was sitting in her wheel-chair, gazing out one of her bedroom windows. Panic and anger took turns causing lumps in her throat, and she continued to brush away unwelcome tears that insisted on forming in her eyes. Surely, Pierce would have been back from Natchez by now, she told herself. Certainly, he wouldn't leave without telling her good-bye, leaving her like this with a houseful of wedding guests. Damn him! He was just nasty enough to scare her by staying over at Natchez and coming in tomorrow morning, hoping to have scared her into accepting his demands. Well, she thought stubbornly, she wasn't about to give up the fight so easily. She felt confident that given a few more days, she could persuade him to stay at Avonlea a little longer—and a little longer would gradually grow even longer. The new house could be started and papa could begin to teach him about the sugar cane. Perhaps, Win would ask him to be best man in his wedding in the fall. How could Pierce refuse? She allowed herself a small, jittery smile. It was quite obvious from last night that there were certain things a woman could do to insure a happy husband. She blushed at the thought, but decided that, quite frankly, with Pierce teaching her she could very easily come to look forward to going to bed at night!

Oh, if only she wasn't confined to this chair, she'd go down and have a groom saddle a horse for her. She could trot down to the levee and wait for Pierce to come back—and if he didn't tonight, she'd go down in the morning. It was odd how she missed him suddenly. So many weeks ago, she thought she would loathe him forever—and here he was her husband! She smiled once more to herself. Being married to Pierce was not quite the fearful dilemma she'd once thought it would be. In fact, it could be quite fun, she was sure, once they both straightened out this little difficulty of where they would be living. After all, he was quite attractive, capable certainly of being a gentleman, and also of being a teasing rascal.

She stared out into the darkening twilight. She laughed nervously, wondering what would happen tonight when he returned. A small thrill ran up her spine at the thought of her husband's dark countenance leaning over her after she'd fallen asleep in the chair. He'd kiss her awake and carry her from her chair to the bed and then—

Chapter Ten

BRIGHT SUNLIGHT TOUCHED BRIANNE'S FACE AS SOMEONE parted the curtains at her windows, and she rolled over, not remembering how or when she'd gotten into bed, but not willing to awaken just yet. If she opened her eyes, all the fear and anger would descend on her once again and she felt too tired to deal with it now. Of course, she must deal with her new husband sooner or later. Pierce was not the kind of man one could ignore.

Tentatively, she opened her eyes and pulled herself up, stretching languorously and stifling a yawn, while she wondered suddenly if it was Pierce who was opening the curtains. She glanced toward the windows and saw Mandy instead.

"Good morning, Mandy," she called out, smiling at the coffee-colored girl who returned the smile with her customary shyness.

"Morning, Miss Brianne. How 'bout a nice hot cup of coffee? I brought you up a tray with fresh brewed." She hurried to a low stool where she'd set the silver service and brought it to the bed.

"Umm, is there a cup for Mr. Nolan?" Brianne asked, trying to appear nonchalant.

Mandy shook her head, brushing back a springy tendril of black hair that had escaped from her turban. "Haven't seen Mr. Pierce since yest'day mornin', Miss Brianne," she said. "He rode down to the levee and I haven't seen hide nor hair of him since."

Brianne glanced at the girl, who seemed unaware of

the gravity of her words. "He—hasn't been at Avonlea all night?" she asked, her voice becoming strained.

"No'm."

"Mandy," Brianne began, pushing the tray away and very nearly spilling the coffee, "please go find Sara and send her up to me. I want to talk with her."

Mandy bobbed a small curtsey, her dark brown eyes watching her mistress' sudden agitation with open curiosity for a moment. Then she recovered the tray before any damage could be done to the counterpane and hurried out the door with it.

When she'd gone, Brianne glanced quickly about the room, as though to assure herself that Pierce wasn't actually sitting in one of the corners, deriving a vast enjoyment out of her sudden discomfiture. She refused to think—could not accept the fact that he might have, after all, actually made good his threat to leave for New Orleans. Surely, he wouldn't be so callous, so caddish as to do such a thing to his new bride.

He's just staying away to torment me, she thought nervously, so I'll think he's really gone. Oh, wait until I see him again, I'll let him know exactly what I think of a man who could stoop so low! She frowned, imagining him in Natchez-Under-the-Hill, gambling until the early morning hours, sharing drinks with all sorts of ruffians, caring not one whit that his new bride would be forced to greet her wedding guests without him. Oh, how like him to be so insensitive to society's dictates, she thought, with mounting irritation. After this callous display, she certainly would not accept his proposal to go to New Orleans with him—much less all the way to Texas! Why, he would be mad to think she'd bow to his whims when everything she really loved was right here at Avonlea!

She pushed the bedcovers aside, too distraught even to worry about the brown stains on the sheet that proclaimed her lost virginity. She wanted to talk to Sara right away!

"Oh, my lamb!" Sara came rumbling into the room,

her broad face streaked with tears. "My poor, poor baby!" Her arms closed around Brianne as she sat on the bed, bringing her head against her ample bosom.

Brianne struggled out of the clenching hold and looked up at the older woman. "What is the matter, Sara? Why are you crying?"

"Honey, there ain't no easy way to tell you this," the black woman began with loving concern etched on her face. "Mr. Pierce—he's gone away, child!"

Brianne reared back as though she'd been kicked in the stomach by a horse. "Gone away?" she repeated dumbfoundedly.

Brianne stared at Sara, receiving a look of pity in return. *"He left me!"* She was silent for a long moment as she wiped away the tentative feelings of hope she had begun to experience in connection with her marriage to Pierce Nolan. That scoundrel had actually left her exactly as he'd threatened! What did he expect her to do? Sit quietly, like a good wife and wait for him to return?

"Sara, does anyone else know of this yet?" she demanded.

Sara shook her head, her heart swelling for this girl whom she'd taken care of and loved since she'd been a newborn. Knowing how headstrong and determined Brianne was, Sara shuddered to think what she might do.

"I must speak to my father," Brianne announced. "Sara, please ask my mother to come here as soon as possible." Brianne was thinking furiously as she hurried into a morning gown. If they hurried, they might be able to find out on which packet that rascal had gone and go after him!

It was nearly an hour later when she'd talked with her mother and accompanied her to see her father. Brianne pleaded with her father to go after Pierce and drag him back here on his ear. She would not be humiliated by him like this!

"Can't you understand, papa?" she pleaded. "You can't let him go like this! We'll all be made laughingstocks because of this!" She didn't dare admit even to herself, that she'd practically given him her blessing to go. She'd never thought he would really leave her.

"Daughter, I'm sorry to say that nothing can be done," Brian said wearily, feeling this blow heavily. How could he have been so wrong about Pierce? He had truly thought he was the match for his headstrong daughter— that love would eventually grow from their spats and entanglements.

"Dear, we have no positive way of knowing where he's gone," Joanna put in softly, her hand on her daughter's shoulder.

"Where would a vagabond such as he go to?" Brianne asked herself. "He told me he wanted to go to New Orleans—"

"He may be in Natchez across the river for all we know, or Ferriday, just a few miles away," Brian put in gruffly. "The point is, my dear, he could be anywhere!"

"But, papa, you must try to find him! There must be some way of finding out just which way he was headed. Ask the stable boys, the slaves down by the levee, send a letter to your banker in New Orleans—"

"All right, all right," Brian snapped, getting up from his chair and pacing the floor. "I'll have inquiries made," he finished shortly. He looked up to his wife, his blue eyes reflecting the discouragement and bitterness at this turn of events. "I suppose, my dear, we had better prepare ourselves to explain this turn of affairs to our guests. There may be some embarrassing moments when Mr. and Mrs. Nolan come down to breakfast."

Three days later, Brianne sat in her wheelchair in her father's study, fervently thankful that the nightmare of the last few days was over with, and that just this morning, they had seen the last of their out-of-town guests depart. The Nolans (she kept having to remind herself that they were now her in-laws) had been horrified and coldly embarrassed that their son could have done such a despicable deed. John Nolan had offered to assist in locating his son in any way possible. Brian had assured him that he had enough contacts to find out Pierce's whereabouts.

By now the entire county knew that Brianne, although she had not been left standing at the altar, had been abandoned by her husband shortly thereafter, a fact which gave rise to some ribald remarks among some of the younger gentlemen.

Now, after sending out discreet inquiries, Brian O'Neill had received the news that, indeed, a man answering Pierce's description had taken passage on a riverboat heading for New Orleans.

"So, now that we know where he is, what do you suggest we do about it, papa?" Brianne inquired eagerly.

"Be reasonable, Brianne! What can we do?" Brian asked her, pushing his hand through his hair and shaking his head slowly. "The man is gone. We have to content ourselves with saying good riddance!"

"But I am still married to him!" Brianne objected.

"And what would you have me do—announce divorce proceedings? There can be no annulment since you've told your mother that the marriage was, indeed, consummated." Brian reddened slightly and looked away from his daughter. "Divorce, my girl, is something not to be taken lightly. A divorced woman carries a secret shame with her."

"The shame can't be worse than that of an abandoned woman, papa!" Brianne countered, pounding a fist against the arm of her chair. "You can't let him get away with this! Does he think he can simply leave me to face everyone—and then, sometime in the future, at his own convenience, return to find me waiting happily for him! No, I tell you! I'll not be made such a fool of! I'm prepared to seek a divorce, papa, if it can be done!"

Brian shook his head once more, imagining the long drawn-out proceedings, the messy courtroom scenes in which his daughter would be required to speak. And what of the opinions of others? What would his son's future father-in-law, old Marlow Turner, have to say? Would the marriage between Win and Emily be placed in jeopardy by all the attendant publicity of a scandal? He, Brian O'Neill, had cut through all the hate and fear of the Irish, the suspicion surrounding his Catholic religion, the tribulations brought on by his own youthful, Irish temper. He would not see all that he'd worked for destroyed and opened up for all the world to see! He'd be damned if he'd allow his life's work, his dreams for the future to be shattered!

He turned to his daughter, his eyes troubled, yet his mind already made up. "Brianne, I cannot allow you to proceed with a divorce. You are still legally wed to Pierce Nolan, and so you shall remain."

Brianne could not believe her father's words. "No!" she pleaded. "I have been abandoned by my own husband, papa! Why should I be held up for ridicule because of *his* actions? Why must I continue to live with the shame while God knows where he might be?"

"It doesn't matter where he is," Brian said stubbornly. "You're still his wife, in the eyes of God and government!"

Brianne clutched at the ends of her armchair, pressing so hard that her knuckles whitened. She looked up at her father and her turquoise eyes blazed furiously. "Papa, I could almost hate you for what you have done!" she spat out vehemently. "You forced me to marry him and now you keep me from casting him out after what he has done to me and to our family!" She felt her wrath against her father was just, since he was keeping her from her rightful revenge.

"Brianne! That will be enough!" Brian commanded, although he felt his guilt strongly. "You are a married woman now and I expect you to be conducting yourself like one!"

Brianne abruptly wheeled her chair around and pushed it out the door, her eyes refusing to shed tears as her temper continued to surge. Conduct yourself as a married woman, he had said! With the mockery of a marriage that was hers! She pushed herself furiously to the back of the house and called for a servant to wheel her upstairs. Once in her room, she was glad to see Sara awaiting her, her familiar, broad face more comforting than her own mother's arms right now.

"Oh, Sara!" Brianne burst out, leaning forward in her chair with her arms outstretched to her old mammy.

"Honey, now, now!" Sara soothed, pushing the girl's tears into her apron. "Oh, it can't be that bad, lamb!"

"Oh, it is bad, Sara—it's terrible! Papa—he won't let me get a divorce from Pierce—and he—he won't go after him!"

"Maybe that's for the best, child. I knew there was somethin' 'bout that man that fretted me when he first came here," Sara replied.

"But I thought, I actually thought that on our wedding night, he and I—we seemed to be growing closer. I thought maybe I would be able to keep him here. You see, he'd talked about l-leaving the morning after the wedding, but I r-really didn't believe him." She sniffed and took her face out of Sara's apron. "I thought I could make him stay, Sara, and all the time he knew he was going to leave!"

"Honey, don't fret—the man ain't worth it!"

"Oh, I hate him with all my heart, Sara! If only papa hadn't insisted on the marriage, this would never have happened! Now, look at me! Everyone will laugh! Here I sit like some ugly toad in this stupid chair, waiting for a husband who couldn't wait to leave me!" She looked at Sara, her eyes widening. "Sara, I must keep on trying to walk! I can't let him beat me! If—if I can walk, I'll go after him myself!"

Sara couldn't keep the shocked lines out of her face. "Lamb, you shush 'bout such nonsense. You ain't goin' nowhere, traipsing after some no 'count man like him!"

Brianne didn't answer her, but she swore she'd walk

by the end of the month! She would walk—and she'd go after that blackguard of a husband herself! She'd obtain a divorce decree in New Orleans and fling it into his mocking face! Maybe then he'd know some of the pain and humiliation that he'd caused her to feel! But first, and she looked down at her wheelchair in disgust, she would have to start again, get on her feet and begin walking. The sooner she could walk, the sooner she would see her plan carried out! And her father was not going to stop her!

Chapter Eleven

IT WAS THE END OF JULY AND THE WEATHER HAD BECOME almost unbearably hot and sticky. The stalks of the sugar cane tasseled at six feet or more and grew at will now, taking on a purplish tinge. The river water was muddy brown, because of all the rains they had recently received, which also served to bring out the hordes of mosquitoes to attack their helpless human prey.

Inside the mosquito netting that Joanna had hung around her bed, Brianne was not asleep, although she knew the clock showed nearly two in the morning. Beneath the light sheet she had pulled over her when her mother had come in to say good-night, she was already wearing a lightweight traveling suit of pansy-colored muslin, a dark color so that she would not be seen slipping down the darkened hallway of Avonlea.

It was not long before she heard the light footstep of Mandy coming into her room. She hoped Mandy had remembered everything she was to pack. Brianne herself had taken the money she had hidden in a skirt pocket from her mother's household accounts, telling herself it would be enough to last her at least a month. She threw her legs over the side of the bed and stood up, taking barely an extra moment to steady herself.

She was more than proud of the fact that she had kept her promise to herself to walk before the end of July. She recalled with infinite satisfaction the looks on her parents' faces when she'd announced a surprise for them and proceeded to get up out of her chair and cross the room to them. It had been a day of elation, and Brian had immediately told her she could have whatever she wanted because of her great achievement.

She had been tempted, like Salome, to ask for a man's head on a platter, but had no wish to alert her father to her upcoming plans and so, sweetly asked for money with which to buy a new riding suit and crop. Brian had given her quite enough to buy this new traveling suit and other suitable clothing besides. She had been pleased by her own cleverness.

Still, there had been moments when she had been afraid that Sara might suspect something was in the air. Brianne had worried that Mandy might let their secret out, but, to her relief, the girl had been able to keep her mouth closed. Sara with her sharp eyes had to be lulled into thinking that her mistress was not contemplating anything so rash as taking passage on a steamboat down to New Orleans! With only her servant for company!

Now, listening to Mandy's short spurts of breathing, Brianne walked over to her and put a cautionary finger to her lips. "Ssh! Quiet, Mandy! We don't want to awaken anyone!"

"Yes'm," Mandy nodded, showing her mistress the small bundle of clothing she had assembled per Brianne's instructions.

"Good, I've got my clothing in that small suitcase over there," Brianne returned. "Just let me get it and we'll be off." She couldn't keep the eagerness from her voice at the thought of the upcoming adventure. In her wildest dreams, she never thought she would actually be doing anything so daring as traveling with only her servant—and to the wicked city of New Orleans!

Stealthily, the two slender figures made their way to the outside hallway and down the lovely spiraling staircase to the main hall below. Brianne had decided to slip out the French doors of the library into the side gardens.

It would be less risky than taking the front doors or the back way which would put them too close to the kitchen building where some yawning slave might still be half awake.

Once outside in the warm still night lit by the brightness of a white moon, Brianne and Mandy made their way to the path which led directly to the levee and the river. At the levee, Brianne lit the torch, as she had seen her father do countless times when he had cargo or passengers he wished picked up by one of the passing boats. That done, they had nothing else to do but wait. Despite the odd hour, Brianne was sure that a boat would be passing by before dawn. There was so much commerce on the river that there was hardly a moment when some type of vehicle was not within a few miles of Avonlea.

Sure enough, she heard the swishing of a boat against the waves of the river and stood up to peer through the moonlight, trying to make out what type of boat it was. It was a small, steam-powered flatboat going upriver. Disappointed, she was about to take the torch and sweep it into two wide arcs, the signal to move on, when she stopped herself. Upriver was Natchez and a better opportunity to catch one of the packets for New Orleans. One might be moored there at this moment, preparing to leave first thing in the morning. It was certain they couldn't wait here at the levee 'til first light, for Sara would eventually discover they were gone and alert her father.

Quickly, she grabbed the torch and bobbed it up and down, relieved to see the answering torch imitate her action on the flatboat. In a few minutes, the boat had come alongside and she and Mandy were helped on board. Immediately, she was aware of the many pairs of curious eyes fastened on her. She adjusted her bonnet and looked to the captain of the vessel.

"We should like to be put off at Natchez, sir," she said, bringing out two coins from her reticule, aware of the heavier weight of the coins sewn into her skirt pocket. And as a further precaution, she said, "My slave is very sick and I fear she may be coming down with some swamp fever. She has been with me since we were both very small and I must take her to the physician in Natchez."

"She don't look sick to me," the captain spat, signaling for the boat to be put back out into the river.

"It's—a strange kind of fever, sir," Brianne stumbled, aware of the faces grinning at her, as though they knew the outlandishness of her lie.

"Listen, missy, it don't make no difference to me why you're leaving in the middle of the night. As long as you've got money to pay, we'll drop you off at Natchez, we're stopping there anyway so the men can *ease* themselves a little," he ended, winking at her with a definite leer.

"Aye, we'd be happy to escort you 'under-the-hill', ma'am," a faceless voice came out of the shadows.

"Hell, leave 'em be!" the captain ordered gruffly. "There's plenty more to your liking in Natchez, boys!"

The ten miles upriver seemed a small eternity to Brianne as she sat stiffly on a barrel, Mandy sitting next to her, trembling a little. She breathed a sigh of relief when she sighted the lights and heard the noise that was Natchez-Under-the-Hill, still lively even at this hour of the night.

When the boat had docked among the hundreds of vessels moored on the landing, Brianne soon found herself ashore, looking out over the water for a suitable packet to take them to New Orleans. She could see many flatboats like the one she'd just been in, laden with wheat, corn, turkeys, and pigs, and keelboats, big enough for crews of twenty-five or thirty men. There were barges and skiffs—and not too far away, she spied the tall smokestacks of a packet boat. Joyfully, she picked up her bag of clothing and hurried to where the boat was moored off the landing. A ramp leading up to the steamer was guarded by two eagle-eyed men who were not about to let two unescorted females aboard at this hour of the night.

Brianne looked at them in dismay. "But you must let us aboard. We have money to buy tickets!"

"Sorry, ma'am, but you'll have to wait 'til morning. You can talk to Captain Griggs then."

"And where do you propose we stay until morning, sir," she demanded imperiously.

One of the men grinned and his eyes looked beyond her to the garish lights of Natchez-Under-the-Hill. Brianne could hear the sound of tinny pianos, the clatter of games, and the laughter and whine of women mixed with the raucous roars of their customers. He couldn't possibly be suggesting they go there.

"Sir!" she said hotly. "I am not that sort of woman. As you can surely see, I am a gentlewoman looking for passage South."

"I suspect you are," the man returned, scratching his chin and glancing at his accomplice. "But orders are orders, ma'am, and I can't let you aboard."

Furious, Brianne sat down on a pile of crates and signaled for Mandy to do the same. "Then we'll wait here for the captain!" she announced, prepared to keep her eyes open for the next five hours if necessary until he arrived.

The men shrugged their shoulders and went back to their interrupted conversation. Brianne glared at them for a few more minutes, then realized it was useless and that they would just continue to ignore her. Everything was hot and sweaty here, congested and stinking, and she wiped at her face with a clean handkerchief, wondering if this had been the best of ideas after all. Perhaps a steamer might have come by if they'd waited a little longer at Avonlea. She shrugged her shoulders. It was done! At dawn, they would be esconced in comfortable quarters aboard the packet and the discomfort of this night would soon be forgotten. She did wish, however, that she could feel safe enough to close her eyes for a few hours. Still, she couldn't trust the two men standing guard, and God knew what manner of men might be roaming the levee at this time of night. She thought of her father and Pierce meeting on this same levee not so long ago and starting in motion the chain of events that had led to this desperate act on her part. She cursed the moment under her breath and resigned herself to keeping her eyes open. Already, she could hear Mandy snoring softly next to her and knew she couldn't rely on the girl to keep watch.

The long hours seemed to crawl by. She would begin to nod and then come awake at the sound of some piercing scream or frightened wail. Lifting her head above the piles of crates, she could see the squalor that existed on the steaming mud flats of Natchez-Under-the-Hill, the huddle of weather-worn huts leading to Silver Street, which climbed steeply uphill to Natchez where all was bright and cordial and proper. Oh, how she wished she were up there, sleeping in some comfortable bed instead of down here in this hellish hole where cheats and thieves and murderers thrived.

She shivered and widened her eyes, fighting the sleep that seemed to wash over her in waves. Was it her imagination, or was the sky actually beginning to lighten to the east? She watched it 'til her eyes began to ache and her legs to cramp. It was all she could do to keep awake. If it weren't for the fear that her money might be stolen, she might have risked dozing off.

"Good morning, Captain!"

"Good morning, Stokes, Jones! Uh, what have we here?"

Brianne felt a hand tapping her on the shoulder and started out of the light doze she had fallen into. When had she fallen off guard? She shook herself awake and

stood up groggily, glad for the man's arm under her
elbow to steady her as her legs protested wearily.

"You are Captain Griggs?" she asked hopefully, suppressing a yawn.

"Yes."

"Oh, I am so glad to make your acquaintance, Captain
Griggs. My servant and I need passage aboard your
vessel for New Orleans." She indicated her purse. "I
have the money to buy tickets."

The captain, an elderly man with whitened hair and
side-whiskers seemed to size up the two young women
before nodding his head slowly. "Yes, there's room for
two more aboard, Miss—ah?"

"Mrs. Nolan," Brianne answered firmly, glad that she
had her married name to afford her some protection. She
followed the captain up the ramp with Mandy behind her,
followed by one of the men who obligingly carried their
luggage.

When Captain Griggs showed them to their small
cabin, it was all Brianne could do not to throw herself on
the welcoming snowy-whiteness of the bedsheets. She
turned to the captain with a dazzling smile as she
removed her hat. "Thank you, Captain. The room is
more than adequate."

The captain, seeing the beauty of his young passenger,
wondered anew at her courage in waiting for him on the
Natchez levee. Was she escaping an evil husband? Or
fleeing to join her lover in New Orleans? He guessed it
was the latter, and quickly bowed himself out, extending
his invitation to see her at supper.

When he had gone, Brianne stared at Mandy for a
moment, then couldn't help hugging the other girl in her
glee at the completion of their escape. "We've done it,
Mandy!" she crowed, unbuttoning the jacket of her suit.
She sat down on the bed blissfully, kicking off her shoes
and working her feet in small circles. "Heavens, I could
sleep for the entire day!" she proclaimed.

"Me too, Miss Brianne," Mandy smiled, settling their

things while her mistress undressed down to her petticoats and chemisette.

Brianne unpinned her hair and lay back on her bed, half asleep before her head hit the pillow. She was fast asleep by the time the packet boat passed by the levee at Avonlea.

Chapter Twelve

BRIANNE LEANED ONE ELBOW ON THE WHITE FILIGREE OF
the railing on the promenade deck of the *Magnolia
Queen* and sighed deeply, hoping they would be sighting
the city of New Orleans sometime that afternoon. The
trip had taken longer than she'd supposed and she'd had
to use more funds than she'd intended. She had resolved
to be more thrifty with her money, but it was a habit not
ingrained in the daughter of a wealthy plantation owner.
Their cabin, even though it was small by packet standards, was still expensive with its plush curtains, thick
carpets, and oil paintings on the walls. Last night, she had
sworn to Mandy that she would not eat too much for
dinner, but the teal duck had been so superbly done and
the blanc mange with jellied peaches could not be given
up! She had had to make up for her gluttony by skipping
luncheon today—and now she was famished!

Out of the corner of her eye, she was aware of a
brown-suited elbow close by her own on the railing and
straightened up to stare curiously at her unasked-for
companion. He was much older than she, with graying
temples and a somewhat dissipated look. She eyed him
with suspicion as he turned and regarded her with raised
brows.

"Good afternoon," he offered pleasantly, tipping his
hat and bowing from the waist.

She answered him in kind and proceeded to wait for
him to move on. But he stood there, watching her for a
time, then spoke again.

"I've been noticing you since you came aboard in Natchez," he continued smoothly. "You are traveling alone, aren't you? I mean, except for your slave, of course."

"That is hardly your business, sir," she responded coolly.

He smiled. "I would like to make it my business, ma'am. That is, if you would allow me—"

Why, the impertinence! Brianne fumed inwardly. What did he take her for, some trollop that he might pick up onboard and then discard when they reached the city?

"Sir, I ask you to move on and I will forget this affair. If you insist on bothering me further, though, I will be forced to inform the captain!" She whirled away from him, feeling his dark eyes still on her.

He laughed. "I don't think the captain will do anything about it, ma'am—since I am the owner of the *Magnolia Queen*—Blaine Fielding, at your service, Mrs. Nolan." He smiled apologetically. "I took the liberty of looking your name up on the register—and your cabin number."

She turned back to him and her turquoise eyes were flashing angrily. "Mr. Fielding, I am not used to strangers taking such liberties. If I had known that the owner of this boat stooped to such devices, I would surely have waited for the next packet before boarding!"

Casually, he took out a cheroot and lit it, blowing the smoke into her face. "I doubt that you would have waited through another night at Natchez, Mrs. Nolan," he went on confidently. "Oh, yes, I was watching you from the deck that evening and saw you arguing with my men about coming aboard. I thought to myself then that you were a very determined young lady, and a very desperate one, perhaps." He flicked the ashes of the cheroot over the side into the rolling water. "A young lady, traveling alone, with very little baggage, in my experience, ma'am, that amounts to running away from someone or something!"

"Oh!" Brianne gasped at his uncanny ability to have solved her puzzle so neatly. She didn't know what to say to him, but stood watching him helplessly, wondering what he planned to do. Did he already know who she was, that her father would be looking for her?

"Ah, I see that I have gained your proper attention," he said, pleased. "I am aware, Mrs. Nolan, that you were not at luncheon this afternoon. If I may be so bold, I would like to invite you to a private little supper in my stateroom, for I was not able to eat in the dining hall either. Will you join me?" He proffered his arm and Brianne could only stare at it as though it were some snake ready to bite her.

"Mrs. Nolan?" he prompted her.

Thinking she would find out just exactly what it was he wanted of her, Brianne took his arm gingerly, allowing him to lead her to his stateroom, the opulence of which nearly dazzled her. The long vistas of white walls with their paintings and mirrors were overwhelming. The carpet under her feet seemed twice as thick as her own and in the center of the room was an ornately carved and appointed chandelier of wood and brass with hundreds of tiny prisms.

"Might I hope that all this impresses you?" he asked smugly, stubbing out his cheroot in a tray and instructing the silent steward just inside the door to bring food from the kitchens.

Brianne caught herself and eyed him with a smugness equal to his own. "My father's study was twice this big at home, sir, and—"

"Your father's study, Mrs. Nolan? But I was under the impression that you were a married woman and, thus, living with your husband?" he interrupted smoothly.

"I am a married woman, sir, you can be confident of that!" Brianne put in quickly. "But my husband was called away on business not long after our marriage. I am on my way to meet him in New Orleans."

"Hmmm. Not a very likely story, my dear, from the manner of your departure in Natchez. I am wondering if you really are married—if you have assumed the name to deter would-be predators along your journey." His graying brows reached upward, nearly touching the fringe of hair that fell over his brow.

"Like yourself," she put in.

He laughed. "Touché, my dear." He walked to a cabinet, opening it to reveal several crystal decanters filled with liquor. Without asking her, he poured two glasses with an amber-colored liquid that she thought might be brandy. "Have a drink, Mrs. Nolan, or may I call you by your given name?"

"I'm sorry, Mr. Fielding, but I think, under the circumstances, it is best if we not find ourselves becoming too friendly. My husband is an excellent shot with a pistol—and a very jealous man."

"If that is so, then why is he allowing you to travel alone downriver when he must know of the dangers of card sharps and gamblers and all the other disreputable types onboard the packet boats?" Fielding inquired smoothly.

"He—I'm surprising him," she got out, taking a sip of the liquor, then setting the glass down.

"I see." His dark eyes seemed to be laughing at her as he moved closer.

Brianne watched him step closer to her, felt his hand, warm on her arm. What an audacious old libertine he was, she thought, and pulled away abruptly, grateful for the knock on the door signaling the steward with the meal.

The meal was delicious, with a variety of cold meats, salads, and gelatins. A stab of guilt assailed her that she was eating so well while poor Mandy was probably nibbling on one of the fruits Brianne had slipped into her pocket from the breakfast table this morning.

As though he could read her mind, Fielding suddenly

ordered, "Take what is left of the meal and have it wrapped and sent to Mrs. Nolan's cabin, Darwin. And please tell the cook it was delicious."

When the steward had left, taking the tray with the remainder of the meal with him, Fielding once more poured drinks and sat down on a comfortable sofa beckoning to Brianne to sit next to him.

She shook her head. "I'm afraid I should be going, Mr. Fielding. My servant will begin to worry about me."

"Do the worries of servants bother you that much, Mrs. Nolan?" he inquired. "I would have thought not. No, I don't want you to go yet, my dear. Stay and keep me company this evening and I will take you to a late supper later on. We might visit the salon or I could smuggle you into the card room, if you wish."

"No, I don't—"

"Hush, I said you shall stay," he repeated, standing up and moving toward her. She had stood up also and he caught her arm, roughly this time. "I have allowed you to dine well—without payment, ma'am. And yet, I cannot but expect your gratitude in return."

"You have my gratitude, Mr. Fielding," Brianne said imperiously. The situation was becoming more complicated than she was used to handling with the young men at Avonlea. They had never been quite so insistent, nor had she ever felt their experience to be so much more vast. A small knot of fear started in her stomach. This Mr. Fielding was not the kind of man who would deal with her like a gentleman, she suspected.

"Come and sit with me, my dear," Fielding was saying, leading her to the sofa and applying enough pressure to make her sit. He sat down beside her and smiled. "Don't worry, I promise I will not seduce you, my dear, unless you absolutely wish it."

"Such conversation, Mr. Fielding, is hardly proper between a married woman and a man other than her husband," Brianne breathed, aware that he had taken her hand and was kissing it leisurely, from fingertips to wrist.

"I don't think you are married, my dear," he reminded her, his lips crawling up her arm to the crook of her elbow. "I think you are running away from your father who has forbidden you to be with your lover and that you are meeting said lover in New Orleans, according to a prearranged plan. Believe me, I have seen such things many times aboard this boat."

"Perhaps so," she said, taking her arm away, "but you are wrong about me, Mr. Fielding."

He laughed rather harshly. "I'm a man of considerable experience," he told her, the lines deepening in his face when he smiled.

"Considerable experience," she repeated deliberately, looking pointedly at his slightly receding hairline. "You are also a cad! To have offered me a meal with the full intention of making me pay for it in this way! How could you, knowing I was a gentlewoman!"

He stroked his cheek thoughtfully, but his eyes narrowed as though really seeing her for the first time. "Perhaps I have been wrong, Mrs. Nolan," he finally conceded.

"Enough!" she said, knowing that she had gained the upper hand. "If you will kindly allow me to stand up so that I may return to my own cabin?"

He hesitated, as though loathe to let her slip through his fingers, then shrugged and managed a half-hearted grin. "If you are truly married, my dear, your husband had better watch himself among the flesh pots of New Orleans. If you ever caught him with another woman, I'm sure you would demand pistols at ten paces!"

She did not deign to offer comment on such a remark, but stood up and brushed at her skirts, refusing to meet his eyes. Despite the near-disaster that could have befallen her, she felt rather smug at her ability to have maneuvered herself so skillfully out of the situation.

At the door to his stateroom, he bowed before her. "If I have made a mistake, Mrs. Nolan, please forgive me. A beautiful woman alone has always had the power to make me forget myself. On the other hand, if I am right, and you are running away to New Orleans, please feel free to avail yourself of my help while I am in port." He kissed her hand and let her out the door.

Once outside, Brianne breathed a sigh of relief and hurried back to her cabin where a surprised Mandy was sitting in front of a tray of appetizing meats and salads just brought in by a steward.

"Miss Brianne, where've you been?" she asked, her dark eyes troubled.

"I've been—talking with the owner of this vessel, Mandy," Brianne answered quickly. "He very kindly had a tray sent down to our cabin to make up for the lunch we missed." She shook her head when Mandy offered her a plate. "No—thank you, I'm not very hungry right now."

For the first time today, Brianne had begun to realize the full meaning of traveling alone. The blame for this afternoon she laid fully on the shoulders of her errant husband—if Pierce had not left her, she would not now be on the packet going down to New Orleans to find him.

No, not just to find him, she corrected herself, but to punish him for his humiliation of her! She would divorce him—she would! Her father had not been able to stop her and neither would Pierce.

Chapter Thirteen

PIERCE NOLAN LEANED BACK IN HIS CHAIR AND LOOKED AT the faces of the other four men around the card table. Carefully, he lifted his glass of liquor and drained it, then turned to the pretty barmaid who hovered at his shoulder and ordered another.

"Take your time, Nolan," one of the men smiled. "I've got you beat this time."

Pierce didn't smile back. He threw out several gold coins which raised the ante considerably, then stared back at the man who had spoken. "Fifty dollars to you, Cribbs."

"Nolan, I think I've got you this time," the other man said eagerly. "I'll see your fifty and raise you another twenty-five!" He threw out his money like a challenge.

Pierce eyed him, then his cards, and calmly placed twenty-five dollars in the pot. "Call."

Cribbs threw down three queens and two tens and cupped his hands around the glittering pile of money, preparing to rake it in. Nolan placed a restraining hand on the man's and laid down his own cards with great deliberation. Full house, kings over jacks. The other men gasped. Cribbs stood up, his hand going to the front pocket of his elegant waistcoat.

Before he could bring his hand back out, Pierce Nolan was aiming the tip of his pistol straight at Cribbs' heart. "Son, I wouldn't try that, if I were you," he said quietly. "It was a fair hand."

"Goddammit! My daddy'll skin me alive when he finds

out how much I've lost to poker this week," Cribbs pleaded.

Nolan shook his head, not at all moved by the younger man's pleas. "You shouldn't play if you can't afford to lose, son," he replied implacably, then stood up and scooped his winnings into his hat.

The barmaid who had brought his drink smiled up at him with open invitation. "I go upstairs at midnight with the customers," she said, her painted lips a dark shade of red. "You'll be around?"

Pierce grinned, then shook his head. "Can't make any promises, honey. Maybe I'll see you."

The girl pouted. "You said that last night."

He grinned again, then escaped the room. Once outside on St. Charles Street, Pierce took a deep breath and started walking toward his hotel. He'd been in New Orleans much longer than he'd intended. Well, no sense in cooling his heels and spending his money here—time to leave for Texas and offer his services to the Rangers.

He trod up the stairs of his small, clean hotel and unlocked the door of his room. Sighing, he sat down on the bed to remove his boots. Damn! What the hell was wrong with him?

He laid back on the bed, his arms folded beneath his head. He wondered what Brianne was doing now: probably thinking of ways to roast him when he returned —that is, if she believed he would return. He tried to think of the coming journey, the excitement of exploring the wide open spaces, but the image of his wife's face kept superimposing itself on everything else. Dammit, she was a beautiful woman with that fiery hair and those turquoise eyes—damnedest color he'd ever seen! God, and her body had been sweet—so sweet that night he had had her. He told himself he had been foolish to have left so quickly—it might have been smarter to wait a few more days, enjoy himself with his new bride. That was the problem, he decided. He'd left too soon—after only allowing himself a taste of her. He should have gorged himself on that sweet, alluring body before leaving, then maybe he wouldn't feel this need, this hunger for her. Well, he knew what he could do for such hunger: there were plenty of other women around who knew how to scratch a man's itch. He'd been at the elegant Madame Tourand's before and was positive she had the loveliest and cleanest girls in New Orleans. He'd have one sent over, a petite little brunette with big, dark eyes and a pouting mouth that could drive a man to frenzy.

Earlier that same afternoon, Brianne had been pacing up and down in her hotel room, a few streets away from where Pierce was lodged. She had been in New Orleans four days already and had finally found out where Pierce was staying. She had had to pretend to be in search of her dear brother to inform him of their parents' death—the romantic Creoles had been eager to help her.

She had to find a way to meet with Pierce so that she could demand a divorce from him. She had been lucky, she knew, to have found him at all, that he hadn't left New Orleans before she'd arrived. Now, she had to see him before her money ran out, and that time was fast approaching. Tonight, she would confront him and demand the divorce, telling him that she never wanted to see him again, that they would be free of each other. She could always concoct some well-thought-out lie about him having died of yellow fever or cholera in New Orleans, she thought, and then she would be the respected widow, Mrs. Brianne Nolan, with no loss of honor to herself or her family. It was the best way out of an unpleasant situation.

But now, she must plan for tonight. How to get into the hotel might prove a problem since it was a hotel for men only. As a woman, she would not get past the desk clerk in the lobby unless she thought of some way to fool him. She had no wish to make a scene and have Pierce hear of it, to his everlasting amusement.

"That Mist' Nolan ain't no gentleman, Miss Brianne,"
Mandy muttered as she pressed one of her mistress'
gowns. "Why, I heard his hotel is smack in the middle of
a bunch of sin houses! I know 'bout 'ho's: Sara tol' me
'bout them!"

"Whores!" Brianne repeated, clenching her teeth.
Then suddenly, she smiled in pure devilment. "Bless you
Mandy, you've just given me an idea!"

She'd make herself up as one of those "ladies" who'd
sell their souls for twenty dollars and tell the clerk that Mr.
Nolan had sent for her. It seemed the easiest plan. All she
had to do was purchase a mask to cover her face so that
Pierce, if he happened down the stairs, would not know
who she was until the best moment, when she would tear
the mask off and reveal herself. It would certainly save
her any unexpected embarrassment should the clerk still
refuse to let her go upstairs.

Brianne looked over her small store of dresses, wondering what might pass as the dress of such a woman. All
her gowns seemed far too prim and proper, but with
needle and thread she might be able to make some quick
adjustments. She sent Mandy out with enough money to
buy what she needed, hating to part with the precious
coins, but reminding herself that this should be her last
night in New Orleans.

When Mandy had returned and Brianne had finished
retailoring one of her most colorful gowns—a burgundy-
red satin—into the semblance of what she wanted, it was
nearly eight o'clock. She hurried into the dress, noting
with satisfaction the lowered neckline which revealed a
good deal of her bosom. She had no cheap perfume, so
dabbed as much of her toilet water on as she could, then
asked Mandy to fix her hair as daringly as possible. When
she was finished, Brianne studied herself in the mirror,
not entirely pleased, but realizing she could do nothing
more.

Mandy expressed caution about the advisability of
such a plan, but Brianne would hear none of it. She

would do it her way and then they could go home with a divorce decree and the story that her poor, dear husband had expired in New Orleans.

Brianne hired a hansom cab to take her to Pierce's hotel, not wishing to be mistaken on the street for the reality of her disguise. She could splurge a little, although she parted with the exorbitant sum the driver charged with reluctance. Inside the cab, Brianne smiled to herself with gleeful malice as she prepared herself to play her role to the hilt. How wonderful it was going to be to see the look of shock on his face when she tore off the mask and revealed who she really was! What would he think to see her there—the wife he had thought would remain a cripple forever! Oh, she would look into those golden eyes that had mocked her for the last time and tell him exactly what she thought of him! She would call him all the foul names she wished! She felt carefree and wicked tonight, and nothing was going to stop her from carrying out her plan. Heavens, what a triumph it would be!

At the hotel, she brushed her skirts and loosened her shawl before entering the lobby, telling herself she must act the part or she would never get past the desk clerk.

"Good evening, honey," she drawled, opening the top of her shawl a little. "I'd like to see Mr. Nolan."

The desk clerk stared at the lovely vision before him, the mystery of the mask adding a sexy intrigue to the rest of her costume. She didn't look like no whore he'd ever been with, he thought, but those girls at Madame Tourand's were something special, he'd heard. And Mr. Nolan had told him that one of them would be coming by this evening to entertain him. Jesus, he'd bet this one would cost him a pretty penny!

"Upstairs, miss—room twelve," the clerk said. "Just knock on the door."

If she was surprised at the ease with which she had been allowed up, Brianne was careful not to reveal it. Hiking her skirts up to allow the entranced boy a view of slim ankles, she made her way up the stairs to the assigned room. The brass twelve on the solid door made her pause for a moment, a small thought nagging at the back of her mind, that she could be making a mistake in coming here. But she shook it off quickly, knocked sharply, taking a deep breath.

"Who is it?"

Brianne heard the familiar voice of her husband and felt goose pimples rise on her flesh. Would he recognize her voice? She must try to disguise it. "A lady to see you," she responded huskily.

A moment of silence and then, "Well, come on in, sweetheart—you're early, but that's all for the better."

Brianne pushed open the door and turned to close it carefully behind her. The room was half in darkness, lit only by a fire and a few candles on a nearby table. Her eyes picked out the figure of her husband, half-immersed in a tubful of water.

"Sorry about the fire, it's damned hot in here, baby," Pierce acknowledged, "but I decided a bath might not be a bad idea, since I was going to be entertaining a lady tonight." He laughed and picked up the cheroot he had lain on a small stool nearby. "I'll drown the fire in a moment." He eyed her conspiratorily. "Or maybe you'd like to join me?" he offered.

She shook her head.

He eyed her, the dark brows arching so familiarly that Brianne felt her heart lurch unexpectedly. "Come over here so I can get a better look at you."

She moved toward him woodenly, taking care to keep out of arm's reach. She saw the golden eyes, reflected by the light of the fire, narrow and her heart started beating crazily, seeming to jump in her breast as he reflected on her over the end of his glowing cheroot.

"Dammit, you're not what I asked for!" he finally exploded, standing up in the tub and grabbing a towel to dry off. Brianne looked down modestly, but he didn't notice as he angrily dried himself. "Hell, I told Madame in my note that I wanted a petite little brunette—not a redhead! I'm sorry, but you're too tall and slender for my tastes, baby."

Brianne found her voice with difficulty. "I was the only one available at this hour, sir."

He shrugged. "Well, I told her I didn't want anyone before eleven. I was hoping for a game of cards tonight since I'll be leaving the city soon. I could use the cash, savvy?" He stopped talking and eyed her speculatively. "You must be new, girl, or you'd be over here trying to change my mind for me. What's the matter, you just breaking into the business?"

She nodded silently, staring at the floor, her mind racing as she thought of when would be the best time to take off the mask and show herself to him. It seemed things were not going as well as she had expected. She had made the mistake in letting him get the upper hand and now he was controlling the situation instead of her. She must find a way to turn the tables on him.

She glanced up as he doused the fire with some of the bathwater and walked toward her, completely naked. Brianne was glad of the mask covering the upper half of her face, for the blush on her cheeks would surely have given her away.

"Tell me, sweetheart, are you going to stand there all night? As long as you're here, we might as well make the best of it. I can play cards any time." He grinned contritely and put out his cheroot. "Now, come here."

Brianne forced herself to smile and shake her curls saucily as she had seen Annabelle Jackson do so many times at home when she wanted to catch a young man's eye. She, herself, had resorted to it more than once.

"Sir, you are too crude for me," she whispered huskily, slipping the shawl from her shoulders and letting it fall to the floor. "You cannot rush me!"

His grin faded at the sight of the lushness of the bosom she had exposed. "Damn, woman, let me see more!"

Brianne could see the state of his arousal by the turgid flesh that pointed from between his muscular thighs. She shifted her gaze to his face and smiled boldly. "The gentleman is in a hurry," she said softly.

"You're damn right I'm in a hurry—to see more," he responded, resigning himself to leaning back against the bed while he waited to see what this lovely woman would do.

Brianne walked slowly toward him, feeling a subtle sense of power. She reached out to trace the outline of his jaw which tensed rigidly at her touch. Her fingertips, emboldened by the fact that he had not moved, came to trace his lips. Suddenly, he caught the hand that was teasing him and pulled her closer with it. His mouth came down on hers, mashing her lips against his own, waiting only a moment before he forced her lips apart to explore the delicate interior of her mouth. The kiss went deeper and seemed to last forever as his arms went about her, crushing the softness of her breasts against his hard chest. Brianne felt dimly the motion of his hand as it crept upward to tug at the neckline of her gown. She was trembling as though a strong wind had taken hold of her and she felt powerless to stop him as he ripped away the fabric of her bodice to expose her round, high breasts.

"Oh, please, you must stop!" she half-sobbed, her fists coming up to strain at his chest. "My gown!"

"I'll give you enough money to buy three more just like it," he murmured against her lips as he nibbled sensuously on the bottom one, his tongue flicking where his teeth bit tenderly.

Brianne felt dizzy with feelings that seemed to be washing over her at breakneck speed. She clung to his naked shoulders, feeling his arms about her, arching her backwards so that her breasts were offered to him. Hungrily, he reached down, quitting her mouth to suck at the globes of pale flesh that bounced with quivering trepidation in front of him. Slowly, he turned her around so that it was she leaning against the bed, her thighs caught up against the footboard.

"My God!" she whimpered, "I must tell you—!"

"Not now, dammit," he murmured warmly against her flesh, taking the swollen tip of one breast between his teeth.

Brianne yelped as he bit gently. She would faint if he didn't stop this right now. She must tell him who she was. But somehow, she realized that that was not going to stop him from his purpose. It would only delight him further, she knew, to realize that it was his own wife that he was torturing so exquisitely. Brianne closed her eyes and gave herself up to him, her only determination now being that he *not* find out who she really was. Let him think her a whore and she would find another way to get the divorce later when his amusement at her predicament would not ruin her triumph.

Pierce sensed the resistance leaving the girl and pressed her backward onto the bed, his hands holding her around the small waist while his mouth continued its enjoyment of her exquisite breasts. He bit into the succulent flesh, hearing the moan of pleasure escape her lips and it was all he could do to push down the skirts of her gown without ripping them to shreds.

When she was naked beneath him, he pressed his own flesh on top of hers, glorying in the feel of silken breasts and belly against him, the satiny texture of firm thighs that would soon wrap themselves around him.

"Beautiful," he murmured, his lips traveling back to her mouth. It tasted of mint and something else, wine, perhaps, that she had had with her meal. The lips were soft and pouty full, maddening him with the need to crush them with his own, to suck the honey from them and leave them bruised from his kisses.

Brianne felt her blood singing through her veins, felt a need greater than rational thought as she gave him back kiss for kiss, her arms tightening around his neck, imprisoning him against her as her fingers wove into the waves of chestnut hair at the back of his neck. Her body strained against him as though trying to stab at his chest with the turgid points of her breasts.

Pierce moved from her lips to the tilt of her nose, then stopped abruptly as he felt the thickness of the satin mask stop his ascent to her eyelids. "Take that off now," he said thickly, reaching to untie the string.

Brianne was quickly brought back to earth as she put her own hand over his. "No, you mustn't!", she gasped.

"What are you hiding?" he wanted to know. "Some scar you feel might disfigure you or perhaps pimples on your forehead which might put me off?" He laughed tightly. "Honey, I don't care if your eyes are crossed—"

"Please," she whispered, thinking quickly, "let me be your mystery woman tonight!"

He considered only a moment. "All right, whatever you want, my dear. I'm in no mood to argue!" He unpinned her hair and let the rich, shimmering waves fall into his hands. Feeling the silky-soft stuff between his fingers, he was suddenly reminded of his wife's hair: it had had the same silky texture. Then he shook his head. Why was he thinking of his shrew of a wife when he had this lovely, warm creature beneath him, hot and wet and ready for the experienced mouth and hands of a man who appreciated her. Not like his wife who resisted and fought and who probably hated him for what he had done to her. He firmly put all thoughts of Brianne from his mind and concentrated on satisfying the beautiful woman beneath him.

He kissed her again and rubbed the soft masses of her hair against his face, glorying in its softness. Then he lowered his mouth once more to her breasts, toying with the pink tips until Brianne begged him for mercy. He disregarded her pleas and she felt the treachery of her own body as her nipples rose and tightened, swelling against his lips.

Brianne moaned low in her throat and felt the same tingling warmth she had experienced on her wedding night. She sought to quell the feeling, not wishing to give of herself so fully, but there was no stopping it as Pierce's hands began to stroke her hips and thighs and his mouth continued to tease her breasts. The tingling became a slow, steady throb, centered in her belly and spreading outward like the spokes of a wheel.

She moaned again, helpless to stop herself, and her hands moved over his tight-muscled back with feathery light touches, her eyes closed in an attitude of surrender. She started as his fingers moved up her thighs to their juncture and began to work their magic so that her legs seemed to be turning to jelly. She felt warm, her skin moist with a light film of perspiration.

Now, she thought, he will put his knee there and soon I will feel that part of him which will bring me release. She remembered how startled she had been on her wedding night, the slight pain and discomfort that had left its mark in the soreness she'd felt the next morning. Despite her passionate feelings, she tensed slightly.

Pierce felt the girl tensing beneath him, as though preparing herself for what was next. He smiled to himself, remembering that she had admitted she was new to the business. Perhaps some brute had ravaged her and the final act of love had not been a pleasant experience. But, God, she was so luscious and passionate, it seemed a shame to reinforce that initial fear. Instead, he moved downward on her, spreading her legs wide, spreading a trail of kisses down her soft belly until he reached the juncture of curls between her thighs.

He heard her indrawn breath of shock as his warm breath, followed by his wet tongue, touched that secret part of her. "No!" she cried, but he ignored her, applying himself expertly to pleasuring her. Her hands came down to try to pull his head away, but he continued his ministrations until he felt her relaxing, then tensing again, but not with fear. A gasp escaped her lips and he could hear her rapid breathing as she lay suddenly quiet beneath him.

"My God," she whispered weakly. "What have you done to me?"

He moved upward once more and kissed her softly.

"You will learn to enjoy such foreplay when you become more experienced," he murmured.

Brianne stiffened. Hadn't Pierce used those very same words to her on their wedding night? And now he was using them to a woman he thought to be a whore! How could he! She wanted to weep, but he gave her no time for that.

She felt him placing a hand on either side of her hips as though holding her for the plunge of his body deep within her. She cried out, but not in pain, as she felt him filling her up, their bellies pressed tightly to each other. His thighs were strong and he moved within her, faster and faster, making her head roll from side to side in mute protest of his sudden, rough usage of her. Instinct drove her legs upward to clench tightly around his waist, aiding his movements as she arched her back and opened to him like the petals of a blooming flower.

Brianne stopped thinking about her revenge, the divorce, the fact that Pierce thought she was a whore. She did not want to think of anything but this man and his flesh inside of her flesh, and this soaring feeling of excitement that was carrying her faster and faster toward its climax.

Her fingers pressed into his strong back and his mouth sought hers as, finally, everything seemed to explode at once, causing a soft scream to be torn from her throat. They stopped and lay together, he breathing deeply and she glad of his arms around her, holding her tightly against him still.

Privately, Pierce was amazed at the depth of his reaction to this girl. What was it about her that had driven him to pleasure her so deeply, deriving such full satisfaction himself? Was it the texture of her hair which looked almost the same shade as Brianne's in the candlelight? Was it his muffled hopes to have seen his wife walking before he left her, to have been able to feel her legs, newly strengthened, around his waist at the height of their lovemaking? He shook his head and reared back from the girl, afraid of his own feelings suddenly. If he could feel this way about a nobody, a whore, for God's sake, it was time to move on.

Brianne felt his withdrawal and opened her eyes carefully. "What—what is it?" she wondered aloud.

He frowned at her and Brianne felt almost ashamed of her nakedness. She drew her legs into a more modest position and crossed her arms over her breasts. He laughed as though to himself and walked to where a bottle stood on the table. Quickly he poured two drinks and offered her one, which she took automatically, glad of the feel of the hot liquid in her throat and stomach.

"Honey," he said slowly, licking his lips as he regarded her, "you're a damn good piece of tail. You'll be taking Madame Tourand's place before long."

Brianne felt the sudden heat in her cheeks. She could think of nothing to say to him. Now was certainly not the time to take off her mask and show him who she was. No, the best thing would be to leave as quickly as possible. She edged off the bed and picked up her clothing from the floor.

"Finished?" he asked, his hard-edged mockery covering the sudden pained confusion he felt. "I suppose you'll go back to Madame's and request another assignation for the night. After all, the evening is still young, is it not?"

Brianne did not answer, afraid of enraging him. She bent over to step into the first of her petticoats and felt his hand slap her on one buttock. Shocked, she straightened and glared at him through the slits in her mask.

He threw her an amused smile. "Sorry, I couldn't help myself," he said. "It was too tempting a morsel to pass up." He reached for his trousers where they reposed over the arm of a chair and fished for his wallet.

Brianne, meanwhile had succeeded in tying on her several petticoats and was slipping the ruined dress over her head, staring dismally at the irreparable rip in her bodice. She would have to wrap the shawl tightly around her: thank goodness she had had the sense to have brought it.

"I'll pay for a new dress," Pierce put in, his golden eyes looking at the damage he had done in his passion. He took a sack of gold coins and gave it to her in payment. "There now, you can't say I haven't paid you for your night's work."

"Thank you," she said coolly, wanting to throw the money back into his face, but realizing she might need it to get home. She could not afford pride at a time like this. "And now, if I may leave you—?"

She lifted her skirts and prepared to pass by him when his arm shot out and prevented her from doing so. Brianne caught her breath as he arched her backward against his arm, his mouth following her and taking quick possession of her lips, drawing the very breath from her. It seemed an eternity before he released her, trembling so that she held onto the doorknob to steady himself.

Pierce caught a lock of rich hair and wondered if the girl had bewitched him! The way she moved, held her head, even the quick flash of her eyes behind the mask, he could have sworn it was Brianne! But that was insane! His wife was tied to her wheelchair and her father's plantation! He wished, with a sudden, unexpected ache, that it was Brianne, that she would have followed him somehow—

"Get out of here!" he growled low, his hand at the small of her back, pushing her through the door. "Get the hell out of here!"

Chapter Fourteen

IN HER HOTEL ROOM, BRIANNE AWAKENED FROM A PLEAS-ant dream, her body aching with a sudden involuntary need to feel Pierce's arms around her once more, safe and warm and protecting. A soft smile curved her mouth as her eyes opened and she stared out the window, her arm cradling the pillow against her hair. Had it all been a dream last night, she wondered? But her eyes picked out the dress she had worn, lying in a crumpled heap where she had thrown it last night. As if that weren't enough proof, she could still feel the bruised tenderness of her lips and the renewed tingling inside of her at the thought of what her husband had done to her last night.

She sat straight up in bed, trying not to think about the events of the night before, but unable to stop herself, reliving the explosive passion that she had experienced in her husband's arms. But not as his wife, she reminded herself brutally.

"He wasn't making love to me, his wife," she said out loud. "He was making love to a nameless whore!" Hot tears stung the back of her eyes, but she forced them down. How could she have been so incredibly stupid! Had she been hoping that she would go to his hotel this morning and find him ready to return to Avonlea with her?

Well, soon she wouldn't have to worry about him anymore, she told herself. She'd be rid of him once she secured the consent for a divorce from him. It would be better for both of them, she told herself, throwing off the sheet and getting up from the bed. She looked at her reflection in the mirror and was startled by the look of a woman who had spent a night of love. Her lips were swollen, her eyes heavy with fatigue and remembered passion. She felt her breasts gently, amazed at their tenderness. She blushed hard, remembering suddenly specific details of the night before. Forcing such thoughts from her mind, fearing she would burst into unexplainable tears, she called for Mandy to help dress her.

"How could I have been so gullible? Why did I let him use me like that?" she wondered, snapping at Mandy in her impatience. "I'll see this divorce through if it's the last thing I do!" Surely, it would be a simple thing to find an attorney in the city who could draw up the necessary papers to undo the civil ceremony. She would worry about the Church later.

When she was ready, her hat tied jauntily beneath her chin and her reticule stuffed with the coins she intended to fling back in his face (having counted out enough to afford her passage back to Avonlea by packet), Brianne went downstairs and walked the few blocks to her husband's hotel.

"I wish to see Mr. Pierce Nolan!" she demanded of the same desk clerk, now sleepy-eyed and a bit groggy.

The clerk gave her a curious look, as though trying to place where he might have seen this beautiful woman before. He recovered himself when she flashed her eyes dangerously at him and shook his head. "Sorry, ma'am, but he's not here."

"Then I shall wait for him in the lobby!"

"I'm afraid, ma'am, that he has checked out of the hotel altogether," the clerk informed her, watching her mouth open incredulously. "He said he'd be catching the next steamer to Galveston."

"Galveston!" Brianne couldn't believe her ears. "When?"

"Left real early this morning, he did, ma'am."

Brianne stood silent for a moment, her cheeks red with

frustration and anger, then whirled from the lobby and marched back to her own hotel, furious that he had slipped through her very fingers. How could she have allowed this to happen when last night she had been with him? Why didn't she take advantage of the situation to tell him who she was?

She stopped her tirade long enough to admit that she had been in no condition to force the issue of divorce last night. She had been stupid, so incredibly stupid, to have let him gain the upper hand—to think that she'd actually thought she enjoyed his lovemaking! She was mad enough to chew glass and began to pace the hotel room, thoughts whirling through her mind as she tried to figure out her course of action.

There were not too many alternatives, she admitted. She had enough money for passage back to Avonlea on the next packet. She could, she knew, go home and be forgiven for her headstrong departure: her parents would be so relieved to have her back in one piece that they would dismiss her foolishness as natural under the circumstances. She could stay here in New Orleans for a few more days, but there would be no good in that, for she'd only be spending more money which she could ill afford. She knew that Pierce, bound for Texas, would not turn around and change his mind to come back to New Orleans.

No, there was only one thing to do—follow him! Follow him and catch up with him and rid herself of him once and for all! She had come too far, had gone through too much, to go home in defeat! How could she return to Avonlea and settle down to being her parents' spoiled daughter once more? She was married now, there would be no escorts to the parties and summer barbecues that she had loved so. What good was there in going, when there would be no one who could, in all honor, ask her to dance? She would sit along the wall with the other matrons, watching girls like Annabelle Jackson and Marianne Deveau flirt and dance with the young eligible men of the county! God, it was not fair! She was young and full of life—newly reborn now that she could walk again! Look at all she would miss! And all because of that scoundrel who had married her, then abandoned her! Oh, it would have been a thousand times better to have been a dishonored unmarried woman than an abandoned, married one! She hated Pierce Nolan for he had been the cause of both alternatives.

Well, it was time he was made to suffer a little, she thought, throwing clothes into her traveling case haphazardly. She'd follow him to the Pacific Ocean if she had to! She'd find him and get her divorce, but not before she made sure she had given him back a little of what he had given her!

"Mandy, get yourself packed!" she told the surprised girl. "We'll be going down to the docks today."

"To go home, Miss Brianne!" Mandy exclaimed eagerly.

"No, we're going to Galveston, Mandy."

The girl looked at her as though she had lost her mind. "Galveston? B-but I thought we was goin' home today."

"My husband has gone to Galveston, so we are going there!" Brianne informed her shortly. "I'll have this thing done with, Mandy! I won't be pitied by the whole county when I get back home!"

Mandy stared at her mistress, who was, after all, only a few years older than she. What had this Mr. Nolan done to her to cause her to behave like this? She was acting crazy, wanting to take ship for a place Mandy had never even heard of. Oh, Mandy found herself wishing she'd taken more heed of Sara's advice and left Miss Brianne's problems to herself.

At the New Orleans wharf, Brianne waited in line impatiently, studying the notice posted outside the shipping office which told which ships would be going where. Mandy stood close beside her, her big eyes moving from side to side, still unsure of the wisdom of what her mistress was going to do.

"I can't make heads or tails out of that shipping schedule!" Brianne fumed impatiently.

"Pardon me, ma'am, but might I help you?"

Brianne turned to the direction of the man's voice and couldn't help a gasp of surprise at seeing Blaine Fielding standing before her. "Mr. Fielding, forgive me for being startled," she explained quickly, seeing the slow smile on his face, "but I thought that surely you would have made the journey upstream by now."

He shook his head, allowing his eyes to travel at leisure over the becoming picture she made in lilac muslin. "I have more ships in my line than the *Magnolia Queen*, Mrs. Nolan," he said, tipping his hat to her. "As a matter of fact, I'm seeing to the delivery of some cargo from another of my packets this morning. Fancy meeting you here on the wharf." His smile was not altogether trustworthy. "I have to admit, though, that I thought it was you even though I hadn't seen your face yet."

She didn't want to ask him what it was about her that had sparked his initial attention. Although she knew better than to trust him, she was in desperate need of help to continue her journey and so she asked him, "Can you help me figure out this shipping schedule, Mr. Fielding?"

"Of course. Is it back to Natchez?" He couldn't help the smile that came to his lips. "I take it your visit with your husband was of a shortened nature?"

She grew angry under his glance. "That is none of your business. But no, I do not wish to return to Natchez, sir, but I want to continue on to Galveston."

He was surprised. "Galveston!"

"Yes, yes," she said impatiently. "I dislike standing here all day, Mr. Fielding, so if you don't think you can help me—"

"Mrs. Nolan, you'll forgive me for my surprise, but I find it hard to imagine a delicate young woman like yourself making such a journey alone with no one to protect her!"

"I am perfectly capable of protecting myself, Mr. Fielding!" she returned sharply, wishing she had never divulged the information to him of her destination.

He studied her for a moment, then nodded, as though remembering the incident on his boat in his stateroom. "If you insist on going to Galveston," he said, "then I must insist that you allow me to offer you accommodations on one of my own vessels, the *Nancy Lee,* which is scheduled to leave this afternoon, as soon as all cargo has been secured."

"Thank you, Mr. Fielding. And where might I purchase tickets for myself and my slave?"

"No need to purchase tickets, Mrs. Nolan," he told her, picking up her baggage and starting off in the direction of one of the piers. "You'll come as my guest."

"Mr. Fielding! There is no need for that. I do not want to be obligated to you. Believe me, I am quite able to pay for my own accommodations!"

"I'm not sure if you realize how much they might cost," he informed her, stopping in his tracks to allow her to catch up with him. "The journey is well over three hundred miles, my dear, and once you arrive in Galveston, everything is quite expensive, including hotel rooms —unless you wish to bed down in one of the wagon yards?" His eyes gleamed at the thought.

"Then I'll travel as a deck passenger!" she said haughtily, referring to the practice of many of the packets of allowing room for passengers to sleep out of doors on the decks.

"I'm afraid, Mrs. Nolan, that that would not be a very wise idea," Fielding cautioned her seriously. "There are very few women who choose to ride as deck passengers, unless they have men to protect them. Your chances of being raped on deck, ma'am, are infinitely greater than in your own cabin by me."

Brianne flushed at his bald comments, but considered

the truth of his words. Her tearing need to reach Pierce and cut the tie that bound them together as man and wife overrode her caution at taking this man's offer. She nodded finally and motioned for Mandy to follow them to the packet ship.

Once aboard, Fielding showed her to her stateroom, a magnificent room done in colors of blue and green, with velvet carpeting and marble washstands in the room. There was a small, adjoining closet where Mandy could sleep on a cot.

"It's lovely," Brianne murmured, secretly relieved that she would not have to part with any of her precious coin, but still uncomfortable about what price Blaine Fielding might demand. He certainly acted the sophisticated, older gentleman but still she doubted if he was feeling fatherly toward her.

"I'll see you at supper then?" he asked, bowing and kissing one of her hands.

"Of—of course, Mr. Fielding," she hesitated, a sense of panic suddenly overwhelming her at the thought that no one would know where she was going. There would be no way for anyone to trace her whereabouts once she left New Orleans. Her father might surmise that she had gone to that city to look for Pierce, but there would be no way he could know she had gone on to Galveston. He would never expect such a thing from his daughter—and she had not told anyone in the hotel where she was going.

Still, she straightened up. She could take care of herself, she knew, as long as she had to, to find Pierce. She smiled slightly at Blaine Fielding, then locked the door firmly behind him, hoping he had heard the scrape of the lock and realized exactly what it implied.

It was a grueling three hundred miles for the *Nancy Lee* as the packet made its way from New Orleans, into the Gulf of Mexico, skirting along the bayous and marshes of south Louisiana, and hugging the coastline of east Texas. The trip was taking longer than usual because there had been severe weather almost the entire length of the trip, with the threat of a hurricane up from the Gulf causing the ship's captain to stick as close to the coast as possible.

Throughout the journey, Blaine Fielding had continued to act like a gentleman, although more than once, Brianne had felt his hand on her shoulder or arm in a light caress, but he drew back always when she glared at him.

"Your eyes are shining like stars tonight," Fielding commented as he sat across from her at the dinner table in the ship's dining room. "I'm wondering what could have caused it."

Brianne glanced at him over the rim of her champagne glass. "I'm trying to imagine the look on my husband's face when he sees me in Galveston." She had told Blaine part of her reasons for going to Galveston, although she hadn't told him that she was actually seeking a divorce from Pierce. She had simply explained that her husband had left her in Louisiana to follow some idiotic dream, and that she was determined to find him and talk him out of it. It seemed better than to mention a divorce. She didn't want her status as a gentlewoman lowered in Blaine Fielding's eyes. It was probably one of the only things that protected her from him.

"I can easily imagine the look on his face," Blaine said, taking a sip of champagne. "It would be the same one that I would have if I saw you coming toward me, and I were your husband." He smiled provocatively. "You are so lovely, my dear. I'm afraid you have no idea how rough this trip has been on me, physically and emotionally."

"Your physical and emotional well-being are entirely your own concern," she returned impudently, although her eyes still sparkled.

"How I wish that they were yours too!" he sighed melodramatically.

"I have enough trouble with one man," she replied, laughing a little.

"Perhaps it would be easier with greater numbers?" he suggested, delighted with her repartee.

"Good heavens, you are bold, Mr. Fielding."

"Please call me Blaine, for heaven's sake. I hope we have become good enough friends for that!"

She thought for a moment, then nodded. "Yes, I suppose we have, Blaine. And you may call me Brianne." She glanced at him wickedly. "And now we must certainly consider ourselves on friendly terms."

"Yes, I should hope so." He swirled the champagne in his glass contemplatively. "What if your husband is not in Galveston when we arrive, Brianne? After all, he had a good head start on you. Maybe he doesn't plan to stay in Galveston at all, but continue west or northwest."

She shook her head, horrified at the idea. "He would have to stay the night, surely."

Blaine shrugged. "That depends on when his packet arrives in port. Perhaps he has friends who live in the Galveston area?"

"I don't know—I don't think so." She was suddenly unsure of herself.

"Ah, don't worry about it. He probably would stay there for some time, even if he'd decided to move westward. He'd have to outfit himself, buy a horse and such."

"Yes, yes, of course, he would," Brianne replied, relieved.

After dinner, Blaine escorted her to her cabin, walking her along the promenade deck as was their usual custom. They stopped to watch the antics of some playful dolphins in the gulf waters below. Brianne leaned on the railing, slightly tipsy from the champagne. She hated to admit how homesick she was. She missed her family, Avonlea, Sara. Why had she started on this crazy journey, she wondered suddenly? Was it so important to punish Pierce, to obtain the divorce right away?

As she thought, Blaine had moved closer, his arms encircling her suddenly and pulling her toward him. With experienced sureness, he brought his mouth down to hers and kissed her. For a moment, Brianne allowed the kiss, seeking the warmth and sureness of a man's arms around her, but when he tightened his hold and his tongue moved insistently along her lips, she pulled her head away, not willing to give more.

"I'm sorry, Blaine. The champagne—"

"It's not the champagne and you know it!" he returned, not able to keep the disappointment and anger out of his voice. "You want a man, Brianne!"

"No!"

"Yes, dammit!" He took a deep breath and his eyes narrowed. "I'm not willing to wait much longer, my dear, for what I'm bound to have in the end!" And he released her suddenly, walking quickly away from her.

Chapter Fifteen

BRIANNE GAZED OVER THE RAILING OF THE STEAMER AT THE rapidly approaching island on which the port city of Galveston was built. She felt nothing but relief to have reached her destination, knowing she would soon be off this packet. Ever since her quarrel with Blaine Fielding, there had been a studied coolness in his behavior that mixed uneasily with the stealthy looks of desire he had given her. She had become more wary of his generosity and fully intended to pay him for her cabin on board the *Nancy Lee* as soon as they landed: she did not want to be indebted to him.

Mandy, who stood beside her, with the luggage piled beside her, tapped her lightly on the sleeve. "Is this the place, Miss Brianne?" she wanted to know.

"Yes," Brianne answered, her eyes continuing to scan the land as they came closer. "I'm hoping to conclude my—business—with Mr. Nolan and return home as soon as possible." She looked away from the city and brushed at her skirts, then tidied her hair beneath the hat she wore. "Heavens, I wish I could afford a new dress," she sighed wistfully, tired of wearing the same dresses she had packed so many weeks before at Avonlea. She had only been able to bring six gowns and, since her husband's impetuousness had ruined the burgundy satin, there were only five left to fashion a wardrobe from. It was embarrassing, knowing the other passengers had seen her in the same frock more than once on

the long journey. "Maybe I could find something ready
made in Galveston," she continued.

"I'm sure you can," Blaine Fielding said, coming up
beside her, startling her a little. "There's everything
money can buy there," he continued. "Of course, there's
a heavy markup on all goods, but you can certainly
purchase a new dress, providing you have the money."

Brianne noted the slight question in his words and was
silent. She had never realized how important money was
to the process of living. Sheltered by the wealth of her
father, she had never had a pressing need for money,
and the realization that she could not get along without it
in this unsheltered world had come as quite a shock to
her.

"Have you decided where you will start looking for
your husband?" Blaine inquired when he realized she
had no comment for his previous statement.

"I hadn't thought in specifics yet, but I'm sure that,
logically, I would try the hotels first."

He seemed to consider for a moment. "There are quite
a few hotels in Galveston, Brianne, enough to keep you
looking for at least three or four days."

"Three or four—"

He nodded. "And then, if you don't find him there,
you might have to consider that he might have friends in
the city who would have put him up. There are at least
five thousand permanent residents in the city alone, not
including the plantation owners on the island and across,
on the mainland."

Brianne realized the hopelessness of the situation. She
felt frustration building inside of her. To have come all this
way to gain her revenge, only to find that she might not
be able to locate him! Perhaps her father had been right,
she thought morosely: perhaps, she should have listened
to him and waited, safe and secure, at Avonlea.

As though sensing her thoughts, Blaine reached over
to pat her hand as though seeking to comfort her. "Don't
worry, my dear. I might be able to help you make

arrangements to have others help you look for him. It will be expensive though."

Brianne looked at him doubtfully. "I can't afford too much," she said hesitantly, not liking to talk about expenses with him. "I feel I must, in all conscience, pay you back for the use of the stateroom."

"Nonsense, my dear. What are friends for, if not to help one another in time of need?" His smile was not as sincere as it might have been, but Brianne was too preoccupied to notice. "Let me help you now and, when you find your husband, I can settle the debt with him."

She nodded slowly, although she wondered what would happen if she wasn't able to find Pierce. Still, that was something she didn't want to think about now.

"Perhaps you could recommend a good hotel?" she asked him.

"Of course, but I have a much better idea. I have friends who live in Galveston and have an enormous house with plenty of room. I'm sure they would be delighted for me to bring a friend to stay with them—"

Brianne shook her head quickly. "No, I don't think so. I would feel more comfortable in a hotel."

He shrugged. "As you wish, my dear. I'll be happy to see you to one once we've disembarked." He bowed before her and was soon lost to view.

"Miss Brianne?"

"Yes, Mandy."

"Sara wouldn't want you 'round that man, for sure! Somethin' 'bout him don't fit right, you know?"

Brianne nodded, then sighed. "I know, Mandy, but there's not much I can do but accept his help for he's the only acquaintance I have here in Galveston. Don't worry about him. I'm sure we'll have no trouble from him." She wished she could convince herself of that.

Galveston was a colorful city, large and growing, and full of immigrants seeking a land of opportunity. Their ranks swelled the population considerably as they came to the city off of the many steamboats, packets and ocean-going vessels that docked in Galveston harbor. Brianne felt a little more at home as she gazed at the deep-South architecture which made up most of the city proper. There were even a number of stately frame mansions which caused a feeling of homesick longing to envelop her briefly as she thought of Avonlea. It was mid-August now and she could imagine the tall stalks of sugar cane waving in the fields, the songs of the slaves as they went among the rows upon rows of plants to cut the weeds that would have begun to grow with the wet rains of the hurricane season. She closed her eyes and saw her brother Win cantering on his favorite horse, probably with Emily beside him, as they followed the sniffing hounds through the marshes in search of critters to catch. Her mother would be her usual cool, poised self, despite the heat and humidity, and her father would complain of the weather and the crop while he sat on the cool veranda with an iced julep in his hand.

What was she doing here? She should have been sitting on the porch with her father, laughing at his terrible Irish jokes and riding with him through the fields of sugar cane, helping her mother to arrange the beautiful roses from the garden into vases all over the house, listening to her brother confide his plans for the future when he and Emily were married. Why wasn't she there, at Avonlea, within the loving, familiar circle of family and friends? Why must she be here in this alien place, whose slight references to Southern charm only made the ache inside her grow deeper? She wished, with all her might, that she had never come looking for her errant husband. All of this—all—was his fault!

She sat woefully in front of the mirror in the room she had obtained at the imposing public hotel in Galveston, studying her face without really seeing it. She hoped that some of the agencies who dealt with missing persons might be able to turn up something on Pierce soon. It had already been two days and she was anxious to be done with all this. Blaine had assured her that he had employed the best men to find him, but because of all the new immigrants that were continually passing through the city, it was hard to locate one lone man immediately.

Brianne had already gone to visit one of the many barristers in the city, telling him, with properly flushed cheeks, that she wanted to obtain a divorce from her husband, who had abandoned her the morning after her wedding. He had been a kindly, elderly man who, despite his obvious disapproval of her actions, had been willing to help her, for a fee. He would, he promised, have the necessary papers drawn up to absolve her from the marriage, but would, of course, require both signatures as well as those of two witnesses. Brianne had told him that she hoped to have everything tied up by the end of the week.

Now, as she sat in front of the mirror, contemplating the ill luck that seemed determined to plague her through this whole thing, she thought of the party tonight that she had agreed to attend with Blaine. It was not the sort of thing she was interested in now, but he had insisted that she certainly owed him a favor for all that he had done in her behalf, and she had acquiesced finally. He had even had the temerity to buy her a new gown so that she could not use the excuse of having nothing to wear. It had been too much, the idea of attending the party in such a lovely gown, and she had accepted. She was tired of traveling on boats and skulking in hotel rooms. It would be a chance to pretend she was home again, enjoying one of the county balls that she had missed.

Mandy had had reservations, but Brianne had brushed them aside. She would go.

Blaine came to pick her up in a hired carriage at eight o'clock, exclaiming in satisfaction at the lovely picture she presented in the new gown. It was of soft-green muslin with embroidered colors stitched along the flounces at the

sleeves and along the edges of the four deep flounces
that were layered upward from the hem of the wide skirt.
The waist was shaped in a vee in the front, which
emphasized the tininess of her waist, as the skirt was
gathered and fell in graceful folds from that point. A large
pink-and-white cameo was fastened between her breasts,
drawing attention to the creamy half moons that peeked
out over the top of the daring neckline. Mandy had found
a fresh flower to pin to the velvet band around Brianne's
neck and had dressed her hair in a mass of curls which
was gathered loosely at the back of her head and allowed
to drape becomingly over her shoulders.

Blaine took her gloved hand and kissed it, his eyes
speaking his admiration. "You look lovely, my dear. I'll
be so proud to show you off to my acquaintances
tonight."

Brianne thanked him and then changed the subject.
"Have you heard anything more about my husband?"

He seemed irritated. "No, I'm afraid not. But must we
speak of him when all I want you to do is enjoy yourself
tonight?"

"But he is the only reason I'm here in Galveston," she
reminded him.

"I had hoped your reasons might have changed since
our meeting," he returned. "But come along—time
enough to think about your husband in the morning.
Tonight is for fun!"

The house where the party was being given was truly a
splendid one done in much the same style as her own
Avonlea, although not nearly as grand. Brianne found
herself relaxing once inside and she began to follow the
familiar pattern of being introduced and exchanging
pleasantries, the entire program of repartee that was as
much a part of her upbringing as remembering to brush
her teeth in the morning. It was almost like being home,
she thought wistfully, beginning to smile and flirt and
laugh freely with these people who were strangers, and

yet, in their speech and actions, as familiar as those people she had grown up with at home. She remembered Pierce telling her of the rawness and the wildness of Texas, but surely he must have been talking of another place! All was civilized charm and graciousness here in Galveston!

She had just finished laughing delicately at some sally of Blaine's as both of them stood in a circle of people, when something made her turn her head toward the hallway and the receiving line where a tall, broad-shouldered man was just being introduced. She stood perfectly still, her eyes growing rounder, her heart beginning to thump crazily within her breast. Beside her, Blaine was suddenly aware of her change of behavior and followed her staring eyes to their source of attention. Almost as an afterthought, he moved closer, his hand going almost casually around her waist, as though to steady her.

Pierce Nolan turned from greeting his host and hostess, the former of which he had known in those years of service in the Texas Rangers, to find a young woman staring at him from across the room, her turquoise eyes pulling him toward her as surely as any magnet. Her face and bearing were so familiar that he could barely believe his eyes. Brianne? But it couldn't be! How could she be here! Questions flashed through his mind. If it was Brianne—and it sure as hell looked like it was—he would find out exactly why and how she had gotten here. And the identity of the man who had his arm so familiarly about her.

It registered with startling clarity that she was standing, no longer confined to that other extension of herself, the wheelchair. Pierce felt his composure slipping as he adjusted to the fact that she had learned to walk again. Despite her stubborn, pigheaded threats to the contrary, she had made herself walk again! Pierce felt a flood of something like relief inside of him, coupled with a boyish eagerness to know the reason why she'd come here to see him. It must be to follow him, surely, for there was no other reason on God's earth that she would have come to Galveston, that she would have left her precious Avonlea for the lesser charms of Texas.

He started toward her, saw her eyes grow wider still and her lips part as though she found breathing suddenly difficult. He could see the provocative rise and fall of her breasts in the gown she was wearing and he had the sudden, burning desire to rip the gown off of her and see those glorious twin globes in all their splendor.

She turned suddenly to the older man at her side and said something. Pierce could see the reassuring squeeze at her waist and felt a tearing need to find out just who the man was. He didn't remember him from his stay at Avonlea. Who was he? And what right did he think he had, treating his wife with such familiarity?

He was a few feet away from them now and noted how Brianne stiffened visibly, her mouth closing and drawing in tightly as though girding herself for a battle with him. He allowed an insolent smile to shape his own mouth: a battle with Brianne could only end one way— with him as the victor, he thought smugly.

"Good evening, Brianne," he said, as though her appearance had not shocked him at all.

"Pierce, I hardly expected to find you here at such a gathering," Brianne responded, her tongue passing nervously over her lips although she strove to keep her voice from trembling. "But, I am glad to see you."

"How fortunate for me," he replied softly, his golden eyes devouring every detail of her appearance. His eyes passed to the man beside her. "But will you kindly introduce me to your escort? I don't recall him from Avonlea."

"Pierce, it doesn't matter—"

"Blaine Fielding, sir," Blaine put in, bowing smoothly from the waist, beginning to realize that the relationship between these two was not exactly that of loving husband and wife. "I accompanied your wife on her journey downriver to New Orleans, and then, by happy circumstance, was able to secure passage for her on one of my steamers from New Orleans to Galveston."

"On which you also accompanied her?" Pierce asked, his voice edged in steel and his golden eyes beginning to turn hard and cold.

Blaine nodded, wanting the other man to come to the worst possible conclusion, and yet, seeing the look in his eyes, carefully taking his hand from Brianne's waist.

"Mr. Fielding had been very helpful in helping me to find you," Brianne put in quickly, wishing to avoid any embarrassing scenes.

The golden eyes softened considerably as they swung back to the young woman and the grooves on either side of his mouth deepened as he smiled. "So, you followed me?" he asked, his voice eager suddenly.

The change in his demeanor threw Brianne into temporary confusion. Was he actually so glad to see her? She could almost have thought that he wanted her with him. But how could he when he had so callously deserted her in the first place? Her resolve hardened and she lifted her head to meet his gaze, her own narrowed and far from loving.

"Yes, I followed you, since my father would not do so. I followed you to gain justice for myself, Pierce Nolan. A filthy villain like yourself, who so cruelly left me to face all the wedding guests the day after we were married, must have some idea why I put myself in such peril to catch up with you!"

The light in his eyes was effectively doused and the old, mocking amusement replaced it. "No, I must confess I don't have any idea why you would risk your person to the protection of strangers," he nodded toward Blaine Fielding, "in order to follow a man that you obviously are still very angry with."

"Because I wish to be rid of you!" she hissed, careless as to the others who might be listening. "I will not be tied to a coward and a scoundrel like yourself any longer!"

Before she knew it, he had reached out and taken her hand in his, holding it tightly so that she could not release herself. His eyes raked her up and down and there was neither tenderness nor kindness in them.

"I suggest, my dear, that we take our discussion elsewhere. I do not care to be made a laughingstock among these people, nor, I think, do you."

"I don't care!" she returned, furious. "I would love to make you a laughingstock in front of them! It would be only a start in making you understand how I felt the day after our marriage!"

"You are my wife!" he replied, his tone dangerously soft. "I will not tolerate my wife making a public exhibition of herself!"

"I'll make more than a public exhibition of myself!" she retorted, twisting her hand as she tried to free it from his clasp. "I'll yell at the top of my lungs that I've taken Mr. Fielding as a lover and you'll be forced to give me a divorce to save your pride!"

"You do that and I'll break your neck for you!" His hand squeezed hers so tightly she thought he would break all her bones. "And if I find out later that it's the truth, I'll make you wish you had kept it a secret from me, after I've put a bullet through your protector's heart!"

At such a threat, Blaine stepped back a little, his face reddening. This was definitely not the time to interfere he decided, wisely.

"Pierce, let me go this instant!" Brianne fumed, her eyes glancing about for help, but finding none. She threw out a silent plea toward Blaine Fielding, but he seemed, suddenly, to have grown even older, as though at the thought of serious injury to himself, he had drawn upon his age as a barrier.

"Brianne, I want to talk with you," Pierce responded, striving for an even tone, as he began directing her toward open French doors which led out onto a patio. "Be reasonable, for God's sake! I come to this party and find my wife here, the same wife I thought was back in Avonlea, rolling her wheelchair through the summer garden! My God, you can't imagine what a shock it was, seeing you standing there on your own!"

"Oh, I can imagine!" she threw back at him, refusing to let the words of praise mollify her. "You leave me like the cold-hearted cad you are back at Avonlea—"

"—at your own suggestion," he reminded her seriously, finally having been able to maneuver her through the doors onto the patio where they at least had a better chance at privacy. "You told me to go, if you'll recall."

She stopped to catch her breath, her eyes not quite able to meet his gaze. "But I never thought—" she began, after the hesitation.

"You never thought I would leave you?" he wondered with a grim smile. "I think you made it plain enough what you thought about me and my plans for the future, Brianne."

She continued to look away from him stubbornly, not wishing to recall exactly what she'd said on that morning that seemed a long time ago. She felt his hand enveloping hers tightly.

"Brianne, at least let's talk about why you're here and what we're going to do about it," Pierce interjected patiently. "Where are you staying?"

She tightened her lips rebelliously, not wanting to give him any information.

He shrugged. "All right, then we'll go to my hotel room. It's not far from here and I'm sure I can hire a carriage to get us there in reasonably fast time." He started for the garden exit, but felt a tug on the hand that was holding his wife's. He turned back to Brianne questioningly.

"We—we can't just leave like this!" she whispered. "The host—"

"—is an old friend of mine," Pierce grinned, amazed

at her sudden worry about the social amenities in this situation. "In fact, that's why I was here tonight; to talk to him about re-enlisting with the Rangers."

Immediately, Brianne's lips turned down. "How lucky for me," she returned caustically, "to have prevented you from doing so."

He frowned. "Come on. We can talk about whatever you wish in my hotel room, but for God's sake, let's get going. Someone might think we're trysting out here in the gardens," he added mockingly.

Brianne flashed him a dangerous look from beneath her lashes, but followed him out without further comment.

Once in her husband's hotel room, Brianne felt some of her icy resolve begin to slip, only to be replaced by a hesitant uncertainty. She hoped she hadn't been foolish to allow him to bring her here: it definitely gave him the upper hand, a situation she still recalled from the last time she'd been in a hotel room with him. Once inside, she hurried to stand by one of the twin windows, facing Pierce who nonchalantly went to a sideboard to pour brandy for both of them.

"Here." He held one of the glasses out for her as he approached the window. "This might do you some good."

"I don't need a drink," Brianne returned, as though it made her stronger than him to refuse it.

He shrugged. "You look beautiful tonight Brianne," he said suddenly, nearly disarming her. "A man would have to be a little crazy to leave a wife that looked like you."

She snorted derisively. "I quite agree with you, but it's not compliments I want to hear from you," she said. "Do you have any idea what I've been through, how far I've traveled to get here? Oh, but you don't care about that, do you? You're too selfish to worry about me. All you're worried about is you and your grandiose ideas of the future!"

He put up his hand. "Enough! As to how far you've come and what you've been through, I'd say I have an excellent idea of that, and believe me, I do care. But it seems that that fatherly figure who was hovering over your shoulder when I found you at the party might have some ideas of his own as to the future, specifically your future, my dear. I do hope you've conducted yourself as a good and gentle wife should?" He was mocking her now, although the thread of jealousy gleamed behind his words.

"You disgust me!" she spat out. "You and your loathsome inferences! I won't be alone with you any longer than necessary. I followed you here to obtain a divorce and now I'm determined to get one! I don't want to be married to you any longer!"

With a panther's speed, he was suddenly in front of her, his hands holding her wrists while his eyes grew hard as topaz. "A divorce, you say! What an absurd idea," he mocked her. "I don't think you know what you want, Brianne."

"Yes, I do!" she shot back, trying to twist out of his grasp. "I want to be rid of a husband who is a callous, ill-bred—"

She was stopped in midsentence as his mouth came down on hers punishingly, bruising her tender lips, then sucking apologetically at them, before mashing her mouth into another passionate kiss.

Brianne felt herself falling under his masculine spell once more, felt the now-familiar lethargy radiate from her head to every part of her body. God, she mustn't let him tame her like this! With a sudden spurt of strength, she grabbed at his shoulders and tried to bring her knee up into his groin.

Pierce instinctively sidestepped to protect himself and her knee ended up grazing his thigh ineffectually. He reached down to grab at her knee, causing her to lose her footing. With a startled cry, Brianne felt herself twisted around on one foot and thrown quite neatly onto the bed, where she struggled to right herself before he could imprison her there.

"Pierce, you let me go!" she warned, glaring at him through strands of tumbled auburn hair. "I don't want this!"

"You want it as badly as I do," Pierce mocked her, calmly unbuttoning his shirt and tossing it aside. "Come on, wife, let's satisfy ourselves first, and then we can talk about whatever you want." He shucked his pants under her staring gaze and came toward her.

Coming to her senses, Brianne struggled to jump off the bed, but Pierce held her fast, lowering his head to kiss her once more, while he unfastened the hooks at the back of her gown. Her squirming succeeded only in making him tear one or two of the hooks. He continued to kiss her until she stopped struggling and he could slide her clothing from her and position himself on the bed next to her. He had meant that first kiss only as a means of keeping her quiet, but it had quickly grown into something more, a need for her that consumed all other thought. He wanted her now, despite her anger, her bitterness. He remembered their wedding night, his feeling since then of how incomplete it had all been. He wanted to show her how wonderful it could be.

Brianne felt nearly suffocated as he continued to kiss her slowly and masterfully, working her lips to his will, parting them and tasting her tongue with his own. The kiss went on and on, devouring her with his need of her, his wanting. She shivered and felt his hands sliding along her collarbone, caressing her throat and settling on the peaks of her breasts.

He kissed with a knowing passion that was held in check by a mastery of his own will that would wait until he had broken her will to his. His lips were smooth and warm and encompassed her whole mouth with a totality that overwhelmed her. The kiss was long, drawn out, and breathless, his lips continuing to move with deliberate purpose on hers.

A new sensation was suddenly mixed in with the other. His hands were moving on her breasts, stroking and petting the firm-fleshed peaks, rolling the tips between thumb and forefinger until they were hard and pointed, aching for his enveloping lips which soon quit her mouth to encompass first one and then the other, laving the small, pink circles with his tongue and causing a quiver of excitement to pass up her spine.

Her mouth was free now, free to call him all the foul names she could think of, but nothing could come out as she twisted a little in his embrace as though shying away from it. He pulled her firmly beneath him once more, his thighs hard against hers, his mouth unwilling to release her breasts.

Rational thought eluded Brianne as she felt the magic his mouth was working on her flesh as it moved downward, leaving a trail of moist imprints that raised goosebumps on her flesh. Her breath was coming faster now as she moved her body as though to escape his caresses only to seek them a moment later with feverish curiosity.

Their bodies rolled about the bed, seeking sweet release. Breathing quickly, Pierce drew up on his knees, gazing down at the lovely vision beneath him. God, she must be mad to think he'd grant her a divorce after this, he thought, lowering himself down to her once more, holding her tightly against him, feeling the tense points of her breasts nipping at his chest.

He kissed her once more, then moved down to her satin belly, and lower still to kiss that womanly core that was his ultimate goal. He felt her body arch in quickened passion, straining against him until he lifted his head and brought his body back to mold itself against hers. His fingers moved to that spot that now lay open to him and he doubled his artistry until he could hear the sweet sounds of her moans, begging him to go on. His hands moved to her hips, his fingers curving around her to bring her up to meet his downward thrust. He heard her gasp, a small, choked-off cry.

God, she was wonderful! He could feel the excitement washing over him in continuous waves, building to the inevitable climax. He kissed her again as he doubled his rhythm in order to effect his release and hers. As they reached the high peaks of their sexual union, he heard the tiny scream that issued from her throat and quickly covered her mouth with his own.

He lay against her, their hearts beating in identical rapid tattoo.

"Brianne, you delight me beyond all hope," he whispered softly, nuzzling one of the ears that were half-covered by the tangle of her hair.

He heard her sigh and wondered if the anger was still there, hidden inside of her, waiting to be given renewed strength.

"Pierce, you—we shouldn't have done this," she whispered back, feeling foolish now that passion had spent itself. How could she ask him for a divorce now? Lying naked together in bed, having just enjoyed each other with sensuous delight? It all seemed so wrong—and yet, it had been wonderful! She could barely lift her eyes to meet his golden gaze that seemed to look through to her very soul.

"You took advantage of me," she accused, although there was very little anger in the words.

"I would say we took advantage of each other," he pursued, nibbling at her perfect mouth once more. "You have no idea how glad I am that you came to Galveston, my sweet."

She put her hands up to his shoulders and pushed him a little. "Now, let me up, for we must talk seriously,

Pierce." And when he refused to budge, "We must talk, for heaven's sake! I've been chasing you for over six hundred miles—it can't all end like this!"

"But it's such a perfect ending," he smiled, catching one of her fists and kissing the knuckles. Then when she continued to look at him so seriously, "All right, then, my dear, we'll talk. I suppose I do owe you an explanation for my surprise exit from Avonlea."

Remembering fired her anger once more. "I doubt that any explaining you might do will help to erase the humiliation and hurt you caused me!"

"Nevertheless, I will try to tell you how I felt," he said quickly, putting a finger to her lips. "You must understand, Brianne, that our marriage took place under circumstances that were somewhat less than ideal. When I saw you being wheeled down to me by your father in your beautiful white wedding gown, I wanted to wring your neck for causing the pity and the embarrassment I could feel in the many pairs of eyes directed at us both. I had been so sure that you were the kind of woman who would not accept what fate had dealt her. I thought that you would walk down that aisle proudly without help to meet me as an equal partner in a marriage that would work. But no, there you were, looking small and pathetic, defeated. I hated you then, and despised myself for allowing the marriage to take place."

"But how do you think I felt?" she demanded.

"Hush and let me finish," he commanded softly. "I didn't give a damn as to how you felt, I must admit. All I could think about was the fact that I was tied to a woman, hardly more than a child—and I didn't want to be tied. I wanted to be free. There was a sudden longing for freedom and open spaces, Brianne."

"Like New Orleans?" she commented sarcastically.

He shrugged. "A city full of life," he replied, "where a man can certainly forget his obligations."

"Yes," she agreed soberly, remembering how he had

made love to her when he had thought she was only a whore. She bit her lip, swearing to herself that she would never tell him about that particular episode.

"But then the glitter faded and the itch came over me again. I know that you can't understand what I mean, Brianne. You look at Galveston and think that Texas is no different from Louisiana, but if you would come with me and see all that awaits us on the frontier: the long, pine forests, the prairies, the desert!"

"I don't want to go to those places," she said sulkily. "Avonlea is the only home I've ever known. I'm so homesick for it now, I can hardly stand it! I don't want to hear your talk of deserts and forests! Just come home with me, Pierce, and I'll forgive you, I promise! But don't ask me to understand your need for freedom and open spaces. Your restless spirit scares me. I want security and safety!"

"I'm selfish, I guess," he admitted. "I want you, Brianne, and yet, I also have goals I must accomplish."

She pulled away from him on the bed and sat up, looking down with narrowed eyes. "Well, you can't have both!"

His smile was mocking and self-assured. "You're my wife. You've come to Galveston and put yourself in my care again. How would you get back home again?"

She allowed herself a smug look. "Mr. Fielding would be only too happy to take me back home."

He snorted in contempt. "That old jack-a-napes! My dear, if you cannot see the avarice in his eyes, then you are, indeed, too innocent to step a hundred yards away from Avonlea and your father's all-powerful shelter. Your marriage to me is the only thing that keeps him from letting himself into your bed."

"What a nasty thing to say! And so typical of the way you think! Just because you are no gentleman, you think all men are like you!"

"If you have the foresight to recognize that I'm no

gentleman, then you should easily ascertain that your Mr. Fielding is much less! I've seen his kind too often, my dear, preying on naive, much-younger women like yourself."

She shook her head. "I won't come with you, Pierce." She looked away from him and cleared her throat. "I want—I want a divorce from you. After what you've done—and what you intend to do—I should think the request does not come as a surprise."

He sat up and took her by the shoulders, forcing her to look up at him. "I'm not about to give you a divorce, my dear."

"Why not?" she demanded, making herself meet his gaze.

"Because I love you," he returned.

Her eyes widened and her mouth opened in surprise. He had said he loved her! He had admitted it! Was he lying? She took a deep breath and looked into his eyes, golden calm pools that were impossible for her to read. "If you love me, then you'll do as I ask," she said, finding her voice.

He shook his head. "Love isn't a leash that you can pull when you want the other person to do your bidding," he said gently.

"I see," she said, anger returning. "You love me, but you love yourself more!"

He smiled mockingly. "Perhaps you are right."

"Oh, you cad! I don't believe you love me at all! You're just trying to confuse me! Oh, how can I think when I'm naked in bed with you!"

"Don't think," he advised, reaching for her possessively. He leaned down to kiss her again. "Just love me back, my dearest, and everything will work out."

She pulled away from him, her voice crisp. "Love you!" she retorted cuttingly. "Whatever can you be thinking of, Pierce Nolan! How could I love a conceited, lying villain like you! Why, I suppose you'd really like to hear me say it, wouldn't you? Hear me say that I'll go quietly home and wait meekly for you to return at your own convenience!"

The softness in his face was gone abruptly, replaced by arrogance and a fleeting bit of something that she thought might be regret, but couldn't be sure. "You are a hardheaded woman, aren't you, Brianne? You're so determined to go home a divorced woman, free of the encumbrance of me! But, tell me, what do you propose to do once you've obtained this precious divorce decree! Ask Josh Fontaine to marry you—or one of the other young bucks in the county? I'm afraid your little nose would find itself seriously out of joint, if that is what you expect, my dear. No, as I recall from your chivalrous Southern code of conduct, a divorced woman is only one step higher than any common prostitute on the street!"

With all her might she slapped him. "I'll not go home a divorced woman!" she seethed. "I'll tell everyone that I found you dead of swamp fever or cholera! I'll become a highly respected widow with the considerable wealth of Avonlea behind her."

He snickered wickedly. "And what if, at some later date, I decide to make an appearance?"

"Oh, you would, wouldn't you!" she fumed. "You're just low enough to do something like that!"

He smiled at her, and the smile looked uncomfortably pitying to Brianne. "No, my dear, I wouldn't be that low. No, I'd leave you to your widow's weeds and your considerable wealth, as you put it. I'm sure they would make suitable bedfellows."

She got out of bed and walked to where he had thrown her undergarments over the back of a chair. "I don't feel the need to discuss my choice of bedfellows in the future," she said rather smugly, feeling she might hurt him by her words. "You can be sure, sir, that I will pick them more carefully than I did you!"

To her chagrin, he laughed. "Ah, I'm sure you will, my

dear." He watched her graceful movements as she started to put on her underclothes, taking full note of the delicious view of her backside and the gently curving legs that he had once thought might never walk again.

"I'm proud of you, Brianne," he said suddenly, seriously. "You got out of that chair and made yourself walk."

"I don't suppose you ever thought I would," she returned, telling herself she didn't want his praise, although she couldn't help the sudden swift glow that started inside of her at his words.

"I think I told you once that I thought you were stubborn enough and gutsy enough to do whatever you wanted to do," he reminded her, cocking one eyebrow with amusement.

"And what I want to do now is rid myself of an unwanted husband," she returned quickly, squelching the softer feelings inside of her.

"So we are back to that again, are we?" He got out of bed with one swift, fluid movement and began pulling on his trousers.

"I won't leave until you sign the necessary papers," she said, although some of her earlier conviction drained away from her tone as he eyed her.

"You are free to stay here in Galveston as long as you wish," he informed her. "But I'm afraid that I plan to be leaving tomorrow for San Antonio."

"San Antonio?"

"Yes, that's where I've got to go in order to sign up with the Rangers. They've been called out and are already re-forming troops. I'm hoping to find some remnants of my old outfit." He looked at her as though trying to make her understand. "Brianne, what they're going to do is help settle the last frontier, to make it safe for settlers to come in and grow their corn and raise their cattle. You've seen what Texas can be, here in Galveston."

"But, I thought you said you loved the wildness, the

rawness of the frontier," she put in. "And yet, as a Ranger, surely you would help in destroying that ideal?"

He shook his head. "The vast open spaces will be there for a long time, Brianne. Yes, I love the wild prairies and the majestic mountains and all the untamed wildlife that goes with them, but I also treasure human life even more. I can't stand by and see human lives forfeited every day to Indians and Comancheros and all manner of black-hearted men when I have the ability to help stop it!"

"And if I would go with you?" she asked suddenly. "Where would I be while you're out fighting Indians and the like? What kind of life would I have?"

He smiled. "A most rewarding one, my dear. If you come with me, we could build our own cabin close to one of the federal forts and—"

"But I'm no pioneer woman!" Brianne argued.

"You have more courage and fortitude than you give yourself credit for," Pierce told her. "Look what you've already proven you can do! And, it won't always be frontier, Brianne. Someday San Antonio will be a bustling, thriving city and we can have our own Avonlea on its outskirts!" His eyes were warm on her, urging her to come with him, to follow him to the culmination of his ideals.

"Pierce—oh, I can't do it!" she said softly. "You ask too much of me!"

"No more than I ask of myself," he said, the light going out of his eyes, to be replaced by the familiar mockery. "If you are determined to go back to Avonlea, Brianne, to the traditions and stagnant civilization that were once, believe it or not, the frontiers of yesterday, then go. Perhaps we have misjudged each other."

"But—but you can't leave me here?" she said.

He eyed her insolently, his dark brows arched in twin crescents. "Why not? I received the distinct impression that you wanted nothing more to do with me. I should think you'd be glad to see me gone from your life."

"Why, yes, of course—but I still need the divorce—"

"I'm sorry, my dear, but the answer is still no. For one thing, I would question the validity of obtaining a divorce decree here in Texas, since we were married in Louisiana under the laws of that state, and the laws of your church, I might add." He grinned lazily. "I was always under the impression that you Catholics didn't recognize civil divorce."

"I don't care about that!"

"But you would when you decided you wanted to marry again," he said remorselessly.

She turned away from him, her hands balling into fists, tears gathering in her eyes. "I hate being married!" she cried. "I don't care if I never marry again! I just want to be Brianne O'Neill again, the same as I was before I ever met you!"

He felt the stirrings of pity for her. "Ah, so that's what it is, is it? I'm afraid, my dear, that you can never be Brianne O'Neill again. You've gone from girlhood to womanhood, Brianne, and there's no going back." He shook his head. "You're still such a child in so many ways, my dear," he said softly.

"Don't talk to me like that!"

He shrugged. "I'll go down and get a carriage and take you back to your hotel. If you wish, I can secure your passage on another steamer to New Orleans. I'm sure you can make your way back to Avonlea from there."

She was silent, as though thinking hard on what he had said. He buttoned his shirt and was out the door, returning in a few minutes.

"And so now, you'll see me back to my hotel and arrange to have me leave on the next boat to New Orleans?" she questioned. "Everything neatly tied up and done with! And I will have come all this way for nothing!" she said.

Pierce stepped toward her and took both her wrists in his hands, shaking her. "God, woman, you try me!" he returned. "How could I have been mad enough to say I loved you when you don't deserve a man's love!"

"Please stop!" Brianne cried. "I am sick of talking about love! You don't really love me!"

"I love you as I would a wayward child, my dear, a child who must be protected from herself!" He pushed his hands in his pockets and took a few turns about the room. "But I'm willing to wait for you to grow up, Brianne! Because I think that once you do grow up, you'll be one hell of a woman and a fitting wife for me to be proud of, and that's when I'll come back for you."

"Oh! I don't want you to be proud of me!" she sneered, confronting him with hands on hips. "Do you think, in your great male vanity, that I'll be content to let you roam the ends of the earth, whoring and drinking, while I'm sitting at home contentedly awaiting your return? Hah! I *will* follow you, Pierce Nolan, and I'll hound you until you can't wait to be rid of me!"

He threw back his head and laughed. "So, you'll follow me, eh? Make my life a living hell? Brianne, you are priceless! Do you honestly think I'm going to believe a sheltered, spoiled brat like you could even begin to follow me across Texas?"

"I've chased you this far, haven't I?" she challenged him.

He shrugged. "We're still in civilized country, my dear. Galveston is the same sort of Southern charm stronghold as Avonlea. You've not been in any real danger up to this point."

She faced him, her finely drawn brows drawing upward. "Are you trying to scare me, Pierce?"

"My dear child, the dangers of the trail are real enough, the Indians, the poisonous snakes, and mountain lions, not to mention unscrupulous men who wouldn't think twice about eating up little girls like you!" He shook his head and cocked an amused eyebrow at her. "No, Brianne, I don't think you'll be chasing me anymore, if you know what's good for you. I think you would do much better to return to your family and try to grow up. Who knows, perhaps one of those dangers I spoke of will be my own undoing and then the messiness of a divorce will have been unnecessary."

"People like you, Pierce, are never caught unawares by the whim of fortune," Brianne said soberly, the thought of Pierce's death causing her to pause in her angry tirade.

"I would hope not," he answered, smiling. "But look on the bright side. Perhaps, after I am gone long enough, you will begin to pine for me and realize what an amazing fellow you have for a husband. Who knows? You might even begin to fall in love with me."

"That's something I heartily doubt, Pierce Nolan!" she seethed.

He shrugged and leered insolently at her. "Little girl, you break my heart. Perhaps I should let you have your divorce and let you see how miserable you would become when it changes nothing in your life."

"It could not make me any more miserable than I already am!"

"Ah, but I could have sworn earlier that there was something more than misery in your rather heated return of my embraces, my dear," he mocked her. "A real woman would at least admit that she enjoyed it."

"I'd admit no such thing to a varmint like you!"

For a moment, his hands itched to take her by the shoulders and shake some sense into that stubborn head of hers. Why, he wondered, was she so determined to throw possible happiness away with both hands? Well, he'd see her on her way back to New Orleans in the morning and let her stew on it all the way back to Avonlea.

He sighed. In some ways, they were both so much alike. She, not willing to grow up and become the kind of wife he wanted and needed. He, not willing to mold himself into the stereotypical gentleman farmer that she had grown up with. They would both have to make compromises, he knew, but how could they even begin when she was hanging onto this divorce idea with the stubbornness of an English bulldog?

Chapter Sixteen

BRIANNE STOOD IMPATIENTLY ON THE DOCK AT GALVESTON harbor, her lively turquoise gaze watching her husband as he made his way through the crowd with her purchased ticket. Despite her anger, she couldn't help noticing how fine he looked in his traveling clothes of buff buckskin that fitted him nearly like a second skin. Damn him for looking so ruggedly handsome, she thought with irritation as she found herself drawn to him.

She shook her head, wishing such thoughts away. How could she even consider him attractive when he was forever treating her like such a child? Patting her on the head, putting her on the boat, telling her to go home like a good little girl and wait for him. And, on top of everything else, he was not going to give her the divorce she had come all this way for! She twisted her hand around the beaded strings of her reticule, threatening to break them.

He had talked of loving her, she remembered, the idea coming unbidden into her mind. Did he really love her? How could she believe in him? She remembered him saying how much older he felt than her; it was true, sometimes she felt even younger than her eighteen years when she was around her husband. Why did he insist on treating her like a child? Was it because, she wondered uneasily, that she behaved like one? Quickly, she discarded the unwelcome thought.

"Brianne, you look like you're about to erupt," Pierce

said with amusement, seeing the pensive look on his young wife's lovely face. "Come now, let's not have our last moments here be filled with anger."

She looked up at him, meeting the challenge in his topaz eyes, then quickly looked away. He came closer, tilting her chin up with his hand.

"You're sure you want to go back to Avonlea?" he questioned softly.

She continued to avoid his gaze, although the idea of Avonlea caused her heart to quicken in glad expectation. And yet, the thought nagged her, would life at Avonlea be the same as before her marriage? Had marrying Pierce Nolan changed even that for her, she wondered with a small insistent feeling of panic.

It was an awkward moment when he handed her the ticket, practically stuffing it into her nerveless fingers. For some reason, her heart began beating jerkily as she realized that he was about to leave her there and go off on that damnable quest that was really taking him from her. She started at the thought and her eyes flew upward to meet his.

"Pierce," she began haltingly, seeing the impatience already written on his face, "I know it seems we've made a bad beginning to our marriage, but I—want you to know that, if anything happens to you—"

"What?" he asked her mockingly. "An attack of conscience, Brianne?" He shook his head and his white teeth gleamed in a smile. "You can be assured, my dear, that my last moments, if death decides to take me, will be spent thinking of you at Avonlea, kicking your heels with joy when news of my death reaches you. At least I'll have the supreme satisfaction of knowing I've made your life as agreeable as it was before our wedding."

"Oh, Pierce, don't talk like that!" Brianne snapped, although his words had caused her some shame. "If anything happened to you, I would be unhappy, of course!"

He took one of her hands in his. "Would you, my dear?" he asked her softly, a note of eagerness in his voice that confused her. "For, perhaps, that would make it all worthwhile, you see."

Brianne looked into his eyes uneasily, aware of the warmth of his hand enveloping hers. His words had caused her already erratic heartbeat to jump even more and she found herself wishing suddenly that he had been this tender to her before, when it all would have mattered more.

Pierce, watching the emotions in her expressive eyes, suddenly took off his hat and gathered her into his arms. Leaning her back in the crook of one arm, he bent over her and pressed a passionate kiss to her mouth, uncaring as to who might be looking on.

For a long moment, Brianne let herself relax in the safety of his strong arms, wishing that things could have been different somehow. But then she brought her hands up to push against his shoulders, reminding herself that she mustn't give in to this rascal's charm.

"Pierce, you are a devil!" she breathed, her cheeks coloring at the thought of the public scene they'd made.

He laughed outright. "My dear, you're my wife, and a husband has a right to say good-bye in his own way."

"A husband!" she scoffed, straightening her clothing primly. "I can think of at least a dozen other things I could call you, Pierce Nolan, that would be eminently more suitable!"

He laughed again, appreciating her spirit. "Don't worry, darling. I shall treasure such heartfelt expressions of love on those lonely nights when we can't even make a campfire!" For good measure, he kissed her once again, amused at her efforts to maintain her composure when he released her. "Come on, Brianne," he whispered, "one last smile to hold in my mind while I'm away from you."

She stared up at him, her insides suddenly confused at

the myriad rush of feelings that were awash within her. She saw a tenderness in those golden eyes that warmed her, and yet she couldn't make herself give him the smile he asked of her. Stubbornly, she kept her mouth set, the passage of events too dizzying to allow her to think. At length, he shrugged and put his hat back on with an air of regret.

"Take care of yourself," he said lightly, then he turned abruptly and was soon lost among the throng on the wharf.

Involuntarily, Brianne took a step to follow him, then caught herself, feeling suddenly bereft. Stubbornly, she crushed the absurd feeling inside of her that made her want to cry like a child. She had missed her chance and there was nothing she could do about it now, she thought wrathfully; he was gone, without her warm wishes to hold inside of him. Perhaps it was best this way; he going to follow his dream, and she returning to the only place she had ever called home. But, her suddenly aching heart cried out willfully, he loves you, you can't let him go!

Gritting her teeth, Brianne pressed at her temple with one hand. Everything was so confusing now. She looked at the ticket in her hand. How could she go back to Avonlea, feeling the way she did? She looked over at Mandy, whose deep brown eyes were watching her with something like pity.

"Mandy," she said unsteadily, "we can't leave on that steamer for New Orleans."

"But, Miss Brianne, Mist' Pierce say we are," Mandy replied, smoothing the calico fabric of her head turban nervously. "We—we can't stay here!"

"No, we can't," Brianne agreed uncertainly. Her eyes opened wide and she stared at the other girl. "We'll just have to continue the chase, Mandy," she said suddenly, with a little laugh.

Mandy frowned. "For the divorce, Miss Brianne? But—"

"No, Mandy!" Brianne laughed again, taking the girl's hands and holding them tightly. "Not for a divorce! How could I have been so stupid! Mandy, you can't love a house made of stone and marble; it's cold and remote, it never can love you back, can it? But a man! A man like Pierce Nolan—he's warm and alive and real!" She looked at the servant, tears sparkling in her eyes, no longer caring if she was making a spectacle of herself. "Come on, Mandy, we've got to get going!"

"Brianne, I came as soon as I received your message!" Blaine Fielding said, hurrying into Brianne's hotel room after Mandy had opened the door to his knock. He looked around cautiously. "Your—er—husband isn't here, I take it?"

"No, I'm afraid I was too stupid to realize it before he'd already gone, but, Blaine, I—"

"He's gone?" Blaine interrupted, a pleased smile creasing his face and causing the lines at his mouth to seem even more prominent, Brianne thought dispassionately. "And you, my dear," he began coming toward her to clasp her hands in his, "why, you must be beside yourself! The cad, leaving you like this! Well, I'm glad you turned to me, my dear."

"Yes, he thinks I'm on my way back to Avonlea, but I've no intention of doing that," Brianne said, trying to free her hands from his grasp.

Blaine's smile became even wider. "My dear, please allow me to take care of you now. Why, it's obvious that you need a man to—"

Brianne nodded. "Yes, that's exactly the point, Blaine. I want to go after him, to San Antonio!"

The smile began to fade. "But, Brianne, you can't possibly mean that you are going to travel across Texas to go after a man who's obviously deserted you! Why, the trail is no place for a well-bred young woman like yourself."

"Spare me the details of the dangers," Brianne pleaded, sitting down in a chair, having finally untangled her hands from Fielding's. "My husband has already outlined them thoroughly!"

"Well, he's right," Blaine remarked, wondering if he could inquire why she was going after the man, and still remain a gentleman about it. "Look, why not take the next packet back to New Orleans, Brianne, with me? We could have a wonderful time!" He moved closer and leaned down to look directly into her eyes. "Come on, you know how much I admire you, and you've told me more than once that you don't think me too bad a fellow. I'll take your mind off that scoundrel of a husband, I promise you!" He put his finger under her chin and leaned closer as though to kiss her, but Brianne quickly moved her head out of his reach.

"Blaine, please," she said, rising from the chair and walking away from him. "I ask for your help in this as a friend, but if you give it only for a price, then I must say good-bye now."

Blaine flushed and his dark eyes kindled with impatient anger. Nevertheless, he forced back his anger with admirable control and asked, "How can I help you?"

She looked back at him eagerly. "I'll need someone to go with me to San Antonio, some sort of scout, I suppose. I would think there would be someone whom I could hire in this city that would be trustworthy enough. Perhaps you could make inquiries for me, Blaine. I would be so grateful."

Blaine passed a hand through his silvered hair, not quite understanding the need for all this expenditure of time and money. He was, he admitted, not young enough to wait forever for the object of his affections.

"I'll want to leave as soon as possible, perhaps tomorrow morning, if you can find someone," she continued, the excitement of this new adventure beginning to show through her voice.

"You would need equipment and horses," Blaine added sagely, not willing to believe that she was actually going to go through with it, but playing the game for now. "A wagon to carry extra food and water barrels."

Brianne realized that she really had no idea of all the preparation that went into the trip she was contemplating. She had never driven a team of horses in her life, but nothing could have made her admit it now. She was beginning to see, though, why Pierce had been so sure that she would not follow him. If she hadn't been so stubborn and thick-headed, she thought, she wouldn't have to be following him like this, she would be with him now. The thought sent a pleasant shiver over her.

Seeing the softening on her face, Blaine felt suddenly heartened and moved closer to her again. Surely a man of his vast experience could change the mind of a chit of a girl who hadn't even seen her nineteenth birthday yet!

"Have I told you how lovely you look today?" he began.

Brianne smiled absently, her thoughts so obviously elsewhere.

"Brianne, look at me," Blaine continued, turning her around and standing close to her. "You know I find you desirable, my dear. I'm a man who is quite used to taking skillful care of women."

"I'm not sure I understand," Brianne responded, not liking the way he seemed to be pressing in on her.

"I'm talking about an arrangment, my dear," Blaine smoothly continued. "An arrangement between you and me that would work to both our advantages. You would have plenty of money with which to buy your lovely gowns and live in a proper townhouse, and I—" and he leaned even closer, "—would have a most lovely and desirable young woman to grace my arm at social functions and warm my bed in more private moments."

"Warm your bed!" Brianne repeated, coloring to her hairline. She stared at the man, causing him a momentary consternation. "Pierce *was* right about you, Blaine! I'm only sorry I didn't believe him."

She tried to pass him, but Blaine's arms suddenly wrapped around her waist from behind and his mouth was pressed against the nape of her neck. Brianne struggled, her nostrils quivering under the scent of his cloying aftershave.

"Blaine, let me go!"

"I do want you, Brianne," he whispered wetly against her skin. "And you know how much you need a man!"

"I've already got a man—a real man!" Brianne shrieked, beating at his hands at her waist. "My husband is three times the man you are, Blaine Fielding!"

His surprise was so great, his hands dropped from around her, setting her free so that she could face him, turquoise eyes shot through with angry sparks. "Your husband! But I thought, that is, I understood that you were about to leave him!"

"I love him!" Brianne shot back and, once the words were out, she realized just how true they were. "My God, I do love him!" she repeated softly.

She was rudely pushed from her romantic reverie by Blaine Fielding's hand jerking her arm. "Don't be a fool, my dear! How can you love a man who keeps running from you? Is it love, or simply the chase?" Fielding asked, the idea not entirely new to him since he had many times found that once the object of his desire was his, she held no more appeal for him. "Let me take care of you in the manner you should be taken care of!" he urged, his hand once more snaking up her arm. "You can't put yourself in danger by trying to follow such a scoundrel across the state of Texas!"

"I will do it!" Brianne returned, snatching away her arm.

Blaine allowed himself a tight laugh. "Then you'll have a lot to learn on the trail, my dear." He stood away from her and tidied his cravat, which had started to become untied in their struggle. He smoothed the silvered hair at his temples and reached for his hat in order to set it on his head at a jaunty angle. Walking to the door, he turned back to look at her, a cold-blooded smile curving his mouth. "I wish you the luck of the hunt, my dear!"

Chapter Seventeen

TWO DAYS LATER, BRIANNE SAT NEXT TO MANDY ON THE hard wooden seat of a small covered wagon which they had stored with enough water and provisions to see them to San Antonio, according to their guide, Bill Keane. Brianne straightened the overhanging brim of her bonnet which the general store manager had assured her would keep her delicate skin from sunburning, and adjusted the soft leather gloves she would be needing in order not to burn her hands on the rough rawhide reins she would use to guide the team of horses.

Ahead of her, atop a rangy horse, was the guide she had paid nearly two hundred dollars to take her and her servant to San Antonio. Bill Keane looked to be in his forties. He was a quiet, soft-spoken man, at least a head taller than Brianne and as rangy and tough-looking as his horse. She had gone to the hostelry where scouts could be had to take her to wherever she required. The men had all looked at her peculiarly as though she were some prize heifer to be branded. Bill Keane had seemed more trustworthy than the others, and for a steep fee, he said he would be willing to take her there. She'd accepted.

Now as they waited to be ferried across the inland waterway to the mainland of Texas, Brianne would not allow herself any disparaging thoughts about her decision to follow her husband to San Antonio. She glanced at Mandy, whose brown eyes were large and frightened as she watched the ferry coming back across the water for them. In spite of herself, Brianne found herself wishing it was Sara who sat next to her and not this young girl who needed comforting more than Brianne herself. Kindly, she patted Mandy's hand.

The crossing on the ferry was not nearly the ordeal it looked, and in no time it seemed they were on the other side and Bill Keane was yelling at her to get the horses going. She flicked the reins and the horses moved docilely, pulling the weight of the wagon with relative ease through the tamped, dry earth of the road.

Here, all was green and verdant, Brianne noted with surprise. She had always pictured Texas as a land of deserts and mountains, a primitive, alien land. But this was nearly like home with its gently rolling hills and profusion of hardwood trees. There was beech and red maple and cypress, even magnolia trees that were bigger than the ones at home. Along the road, live oaks arched to provide a ceiling of green, through which Brianne caught glimpses of haughty, pillared mansions in the same style as Avonlea. Cotton was king here, not sugar, she saw from the snowy-white cups of the stuff that drifted lazily in the slight, balmy breeze off the ocean.

What had Pierce been talking about when he mentioned dangers of the trail? Why, there were no Indians here waiting to take her hair and plait it on their war belts! She saw no sharp-toothed mountain lions waiting to pounce on her! True, there were probably snakes for they were still close enough to the bayou regions to warrant the existence of water moccasins and alligators, but they would keep to the high ground along this road and not be bothered by them. She began to feel more confident and eager to get to San Antonio and prove to Pierce that she was not the spoiled, childish brat he had called her.

Despite her eagerness though, by the end of the day she admitted to herself that she was exhausted from the long drive and the constant attention she had had to pay to the horses to keep them from stopping to graze along the side of the road. Bill Keane had kept the pace fairly strong, usually riding several yards ahead, but now and

again settling back to inquire how they were doing. He
kept his eyes properly respectful, Brianne noted with
relief, and seemed genuinely concerned as to their
welfare.

When it was time to settle down for the night, they
stopped in a large expanse of meadow that seemed
designed for just this purpose from the evidence of wheel
tracks and horse droppings. Here and there small circles
of grayish burnt ground testified to campfires, reflecting
the hopes of those who sat around them, looking always
westward to freedom and prosperity.

"I'm tired," Brianne said frankly to Mandy as the two
of them sat close to the fire that Keane had built, drinking
one last cup of the strong coffee he had promised to
teach Brianne how to make. She had felt so foolish, not
being adept at cooking, and Keane had been obliged to
make supper for them. She told herself that maybe
tomorrow she wouldn't be so tired and would try her
hand at cooking. "Tomorrow will be your turn to drive
the horses," Brianne reminded the other girl. "Do you
think you can do it?"

Mandy nodded, although her eyes held uncertainty.
"We sleepin' in the wagon, Miss Brianne?" she asked,
her eyes sliding to where Keane had just returned from
gathering more firewood.

"Yes and Mr. Keane will sleep under the stars in his
own bedroll. Don't be so afraid of him, Mandy, he's not
going to hurt you," Brianne reassured the girl briskly.
She passed a hand over her forehead and the movement
made her shoulder ache. She shuddered to think how
she would feel in the morning and was glad she could let
Mandy take the reins.

A soft breeze continued to blow and, as there seemed
no threat of rain, Brianne tied back the flaps of the canvas
to allow more ventilation after they were both in their
nightgowns. She was already asleep before her head hit
the pillow of her bedroll.

The next morning, as she had known they would,

Brianne's arms and legs ached and her eyes felt heavy with fatigue despite the fact that she had slept soundly all night. Poor Mandy, her eyes wide and frightened, pulled desperately at the reins, trying to keep the horses in line, but they continued to pull either to the right or left, seeking the tender green stalks of grass that grew prolifically. By the noon hour, the girl was in tears, unable to continue to drive the team. Wearily, Brianne took the reins from her, noting the impatience in Keane's face and determined that he not regret accepting their offer. Fortunately, the horses seemed to sense the authority in the reins now and dutifully plodded in the center of the road, only now and then wandering when Brianne let her guard down.

By nightfall, Brianne didn't think she could eat supper she was so tired. Bill Keane advised her to go and lay down and he would give her maid rudimentary lessons in cooking so that he would not be obliged to act as cook for the entire trip. Although Brianne knew that Mandy was frightened of the tall, silent man, she could not keep her eyes open and did as he advised.

The next morning, she was surprised to see that Keane had tied his horse to the back of the wagon and was fully intent on driving the wagon himself.

"You two women aren't fit to be driving today," he told her matter-of-factly. "You couldn't get through the day and your slave ain't no good with the animals."

"Oh, I suppose you are right, Mr. Keane, but I realize I didn't hire you on as driver—"

"Nor cook neither," he reminded her, stuffing a wad of tobacco into his cheek. "But I'll collect payment later," he continued, then spat a stream of brown juice past Brianne's skirts to the ground below. "You riding up front with me, ma'am?"

Brianne looked back to where Mandy was sitting in the wagon. "Yes, I'll sit here for a while," she sighed, tying her bonnet beneath her chin and pushing up the sleeves of one of the calico dresses she had purchased before

leaving Galveston. She tried to figure how much money
she had left, not knowing how much Bill Keane was
going to demand for his services as cook and driver. She
might have enough to pay him without digging into the
small horde of coins that she had sewn into the pocket of
one of her petticoats.

"You from Mississippi, you say?"

The man's question startled her out of her reverie.
"No, from Louisiana, but close to Natchez," she replied,
hoping she would not be required to make polite conversation with him for the remainder of the day.

"I been to Natchez once," he went on, alternately
talking and chewing. "Hell of a place, ma'am, if you'll
excuse me."

She had no comment to make and hoped he was
finished, but after a few minutes of silence, he continued.
"Heard 'Old Rough and Ready' died last month—
damned shame."

For a moment, Brianne had no idea what he was
talking about, then she realized he was speaking of
President Zachary Taylor who had died in office at the
beginning of July. The new president was Millard Fill-
more who, as vice-president, automatically succeeded
him. She remembered her father being cautiously opti-
mistic about the man since he was a devoted follower of
Henry Clay.

"I served with Taylor during the war with Mexico,"
Keane put in as though reminiscing. "Fine man, sorry to
see him die."

"Yes," Brianne replied, not quite sure what he expected her to say.

They sat quietly for a few minutes, Brianne waiting for
him to say something else. When he didn't, she allowed
herself to follow the scenery, finding comfort in the
heavily timbered and well-watered landscape that reminded her of home. After a while, though, she realized
she was fast becoming bored and wished she had
thought to bring some piece of embroidery or perhaps a

book to keep her occupied. The man beside her seemed no longer interested in talking and she had no wish to get him started, so she crawled into the back of the wagon to doze beside Mandy.

She was awakened by the creak of the wagon wheels as they came to a stop. There was a thickly shaded water hole where the horses were allowed to drink and Bill Keane mumbled something about "relieving himself" which reminded Brianne of the necessities of her own toilet. The respite was a brief one, though, and very soon they were on their way again, following the road past gently rolling hills covered with oak. Instead of the great plantations they had seen the first two days, they now saw much humbler homes with rough-hewn farm fences enclosing fields of straggling corn.

"How many miles will we cover today?" Brianne asked, seating herself next to the man once more.

"Maybe as many as twenty," he said, brightening her hopes a little. "Should be seeing the Brazos River 'fore long. We'll try to make it 'fore night fall and camp there."

Brianne agreed, telling herself the farther they got, the closer they would be to San Antonio. "I'll take the reins tomorrow," she volunteered. "You shouldn't have to drive us again if Mandy and I take shifts during the day."

He nodded. "You think she's up to it?" He jerked his head backward.

"Yes."

He laughed shortly. "Hell, a little gal like that, I'd take the whip to her if I had to. She'd do what she's told then!"

Brianne looked at him in shock. "Mr. Keane, how can you even suggest such a thing!"

"She's a slave ain't she?" he asked belligerently. "If a slave ain't doing what you tell him, the only thing they know is the whip. If you ain't got the heart for it, ma'am, I'll be glad to discipline her for you."

"No, thank you, Mr. Keane," Brianne replied uneasily, sure that Mandy must have heard his comments and was

probably trembling with fear. "My father taught us never
to use force with our slaves. There are other ways to deal
with recalcitrance, Mr. Keane!"

He eyed her suddenly with a look that caused a small
prickle of uncertainty to run up her spine. "I reckon I
catch your meaning, ma'am," he said ambiguously.

Chapter Eighteen

THE DAYS QUICKLY STRETCHED INTO A WEEK. THE SMART
leather gloves that Brianne had bought in Galveston had
deteriorated into shreds and she had been forced to use
an extra pair of Bill Keane's. Mandy had learned to
handle the horses more successfully and the two young
women had found that taking shifts in driving the wagon
was the best way to handle it. Brianne drove from early
morning until the noon hour and Mandy drove until they
stopped for the night.

Brianne went to bed each night with aching shoulders,
caused from the pull of the horses. Her legs sometimes
felt as though they were going to fall off from bracing
them against the seat so much. Had it only been two
months before that she sat, a semi-invalid in a wheelchair, servants at her beck and call? Surely, she was not
the same girl anymore, she told herself. Now she was
dressed in drab calico, an unattractive bonnet framing
moist auburn curls that accented the slight tan her skin
had acquired from the days in the sun. Her hands were
rough and cracked, her shins bruised from the wagon
seat. Sara, she thought with a faint giggle, would be
thoroughly horrified!

They had crossed the Colorado River the night before
and the log cabins they saw now were sparsely dotted
among the thinning trees and tall grasses that Bill Keane
told them was the beginning of the prairies. Now and
then, they would pass farmers on the road, heading for

the coastlands to sell produce or to buy necessary farm
equipment or hardware. Conversation was limited to
road conditions ahead or the weather and there were
almost never any women for Brianne to chat with.

She had learned to make coffee in the last few days
and could now make a passable meal over the cookfire,
although her skill was still limited. She cooked and
Mandy washed the dishes and rinsed out the clothes so
that they could dry during the day on the top of the
wagon canvas. It was hotter here than along the ocean
coast where breezes had cooled things off. Now, the sun
seemed to beat down with even stronger purpose,
adding to the humid conditions caused by the numerous
lakes and streams in the area. Brianne longed for a bath,
and even more for a day of rest, but Keane seemed
determined to drive them on, making good time, but
effectively wearing out his clients.

They had settled down and made camp for the night in
a clearing that provided good shelter in case of rain,
which had been threatening all day with big dark clouds
gathering from the west.

"Thunderstorm likely," Keane said in his short, taci-
turn way.

Brianne looked doubtfully at the stream that coursed
its way beside the clearing. "Do you think there's danger
of flooding?" she asked with concern.

He shrugged. "We're here for the night," he answered
as though to say they'd have to make the best of it
whether the stream reached flood stage or not. "I'll be
bunking with you ladies tonight, in the wagon."

Brianne's mouth opened to protest, but she quickly
shut it as he gave her a challenging glare. Nervously, she
went about cooking their supper, wondering how on
earth she and Mandy were going to be able to make
room for the long lanky scout. The impending rain would
make the interior of the wagon even steamier than usual.
As it was one could hardly breathe at night. She prepared
dinner with a feeling of trepidation, wishing, suddenly,

that she had taken the time to check into Mr. Keane's credentials. She could blame her hardheadedness for not thinking that through, she told herself. Well, now it might have gotten her into serious trouble.

Dinner was quiet, everyone in a hurry to eat and get out of the open in case the clouds should burst forth with rain. While Mandy washed up, Brianne went into the wagon to push things around as well as she could, moving Mandy's and her pallets toward the front of the wagon with a few sacks of flour between them and the location of Mr. Keane's blankets. The space inside the wagon seemed so small to her, but she forced herself to chase her harried thoughts away and present a calm face to Bill Keane tonight.

Soon, she realized they could no longer put off the moment. It was late and without the stars and moon, the night had taken on an inky blackness. Keane allowed them a decent interval to get situated, then pulled himself into the back of the wagon and closed the flaps so as not to get soaked should a sudden downpour start.

"You ladies comfortable?" he inquired after he had settled down on his bedroll.

"Yes, thank you, Mr. Keane," Brianne returned, hoping he would turn on his side and start to snore.

That was not to be the case, for now he seemed in the mood to talk. Outside they heard the sudden pitter-pat of rain. "See? I'm glad I'm in here where it's warm and dry. Besides that ground gets mighty hard after a few nights. Maybe I should make this my permanent residence, eh?" he chuckled.

Brianne could hear him moving, as though trying to settle himself, then the soft, anxious cry of her maid. "Mandy, you all right?" she asked.

"Hell, yes, she's all right, for God's sake!" came the belligerent voice of Bill Keane. "Jes', I only touched her by accident and she skittered like a lively filly!" He chuckled once more. "Damn! I never had no black girl before!"

Now the talk was becoming dangerous and Brianne felt a coldness in her chest that made her breathing erratic. Beside her, Mandy was trembling.

"I would hope, Mr. Keane," she said, sitting up to look at his dark bulk, "that you would refrain from speaking so! My maid, I can assure you, has been brought up a decent, young girl and—"

"Hell, there's not a negress who hasn't spread her legs 'fore the age of twelve, lady! You tryin' to tell me yours is different? I'll bet she's squirming for a real man to stick it to her right, aren't you, gal?"

"Miss Brianne, I don't know—"

A sudden crack of thunder was followed by the zigzag of jagged lightning, the glow of which was visible even through the heavy canvas. Startled, all three sat bolt upright. They could hear the scared whinnies of the horses, and then the sounds of their hoofbeats on the muddy ground.

"God damn it!" Keane roared, throwing back the flaps of the canvas and scampering out into the rain. "Those horses are going to bolt, less I secure them tighter! Fetch me some more rope!"

Brianne lit the lantern inside the wagon and rummaged through crates and barrels until she found a good, long length of rope. Jamming her bonnet on, she stuck her head out the front flap of the wagon and held out the rope.

Cursing the weather, Keane grabbed the rope and went back to the horses, leaving the two young women to shiver inside the wagon, wondering what would happen when he returned. Fortunately, it took him nearly an hour in the rain and wind to secure the horses properly and, by the time he returned to the interior of the wagon, he was too worn out to continue his earlier threats.

Nevertheless, Brianne kept her eyes open, even after she heard the beginning of his loud snores and the gentler ones of her maid beside her. She was glad he'd been able to secure the horses. Without them, they'd be stranded here with only Bill Keane to protect them, and she was beginning to find out he was not the kind of man she cared to trust with her life. As soon as they came to the next good-sized town, she told herself, she'd pay him any money she still owed him and hire someone else to finish the rest of the trip.

Lying there in the stifling wagon, she thought about the possibility of returning to Galveston and finding someone else to get them to San Antonio. But so much time would be wasted, and she was positive that she would get no money from Bill Keane if she declined his services. No, she would have to continue on and hope that Keane had enough of a sense of honor to leave his two charges unmolested.

Was she actually risking her life and that of her servant just to go on this wild-goose chase after a husband who thought her safe at home? She shivered at the thought. She must find Pierce again, she thought with renewed determination. She recalled with a familiar sickening feeling how he had left her on the Galveston dock, after having begged a smile to send him on his way and receiving none. Had her stubborn refusal to give him a warm send-off soured his attitude toward her, she wondered forlornly? Surely, by now, he must be caught up in the camaraderie and adventure of the Texas Rangers, thoughts of his childish wife far removed from his mind. She gulped at the thought that he might not be anywhere near San Antonio by the time she arrived.

Her head ached with the questions. How could she have been so stubborn and hardheaded? Why hadn't she gone with him when he'd asked her? Angrily, she twisted beneath the bedding, feeling the sweat trickling down her back and legs. Oh, Pierce, if it weren't for my temper, I wouldn't be in this mess, would I? After all, he had warned her about the dangers of the trail.

The rain was pelting down in earnest now and the lightning continued to light up the sky and the surrounding landscape. She wished she were under a decent roof instead of this canvas wagon which didn't offer much protection. If only Pierce hadn't left her after the wedding, she thought with regret, realizing that she had been partly to blame for that. Why had she tried to convince herself that their marriage would never work, that he felt nothing for her but pity? Why had she acted so self-righteously outraged when he'd talked of declining her father's offer of land at Avonlea? She had never even tried to listen to him, to really think about how he felt. She was ashamed to admit it, but she had acted exactly as he had said, like a spoiled, pampered brat!

She shook aside the negative feelings and tried to concentrate on what she felt now for her husband, recalling how madly her heart had raced that time on the dock of Galveston when he'd kissed her, how proud she'd been that her husband was surely the handsomest man there, and that she had every right to him! And when he'd made love to her earlier—she blushed in the darkness at the memory—but couldn't help the smile that came to her lips. She finally fell asleep, still smiling as she nestled into the blankets.

At the first light of dawn, Bill Keane was up tending to the horses and checking to see if the stream was passable after the flooding rains.

"Don't worry, Mandy. I plan to dismiss Mr. Keane at the next town we come to," Brianne assured her. "We'll hire someone else to take us the rest of the way."

"Oh, Lord, Miss Brianne, I'm so happy you decided that!" Mandy proclaimed fervently. "I'm mighty scared of him, Miss Brianne."

When Keane returned, Brianne was already on the wagon seat, waiting for him to harness up the team. When he'd done so, he showed her the place in the stream that they would be crossing and mounted his own horse, reverting back to his usual quiet, introspective self as though what happened last night had never been. Brianne could almost have thought she'd dreamed it except for the shifty-eyed look he passed her after they'd crossed the stream, as though sizing her up in some way. Brianne straightened her back and forced down the prickles of fear in the pit of her stomach. She realized that they might not see another town before they were forced to camp for the night again.

As they pressed on, staying to the road, which was now little more than a cattle trail marked indelibly on the clay soil, Brianne kept her eyes out for signs of civilization, but was unrewarded, except for a log cabin here and there, too far away for her to get to without arousing Keane's suspicions.

After the rain of the night before, the earth seemed to steam, the green, knobby hills letting off clouds of vapor. By midday the sun had broken through the fog and beat down mercilessly once more, causing sweat to envelop Brianne's entire body. She was glad for the leather gloves that Keane had given her, without them the reins would have slipped through her damp fingers. She longed to take off the tight-sleeved basque and drive in her chemise top, but she knew that would be too much of an invitation for Bill Keane to ignore.

When they stopped for lunch, she plunged her face into the coolness of one of the numerous streams, wetting her entire head in relief. She took out a handkerchief and dipped it into the water, tying it around her neck to relieve the sunburn.

"How much further to San Antonio?" she questioned Keane as they bit off pieces of dried beef, not wanting to take the time to build a fire at midday.

"Maybe a hundred miles, maybe more," he shrugged.

"A hundred miles!" God, the distance seemed endless. "Can't we go any faster?"

"Ma'am, if you want to wear out them horses, you can push 'em, but if you want to get to San Anton', you'll take it easy."

She tried to suppress her disappointment. "Will it continue this hot much longer?" she ventured.

"Hotter," he returned, allowing himself a smug grin that told her, suddenly, how much he was enjoying her discomfort. "We'll be out of these last little hills by tomorrow and you'll start to see the prairie terrain again. Forest trees don't grow there—not enough rain."

"Will there be adequate water?"

He nodded. "You might want to take a bath at one of the watering ponds." His eyes lit up dangerously at the idea.

Brianne said nothing, but signaled to Mandy to take her place on the wagon seat to allow her a short nap in the back of the wagon. She was achingly tired.

By nightfall, they were once again encamped for the night. Cautiously, Brianne and Mandy went to their beds after supper, dreading the sound of Keane's footsteps around the wagon, but to their relief, he rolled himself up in his blanket close to the fire and was soon snoring regularly. Maybe he'd forgotten about his desires of the night before, maybe he'd decided to leave them alone. But she knew her hopes were futile: he was probably as tired as they were. After all, they had another hundred miles to go. Time enough certainly to pounce on them whenever he wanted to.

Two days had passed and they were now out of the woodlands of eastern Texas and into the western plains. It had seemed to happen overnight almost, the sudden jump from green trees and thick tangles of underbrush to the sandier soil and the long grasses with mesquite bushes dotting the flat land. Along the streams there were cottonwoods and willow trees which provided some shade when they stopped to water the horses. Brianne thought longingly of Keane's suggestion to take a bath, but she didn't trust him not to ambush her while she was in the water. His behavior seemed to her suspicious eyes to become more furtive as he rode out past the trail to scout ahead, leaving them to plod along at their slower pace and then joining them again a few miles ahead. He no longer tried to make conversation, but kept his comments to giving directions. His eyes would slide leisurely over her figure as she sat on the wagon seat and then he would turn his horse around to the back of the wagon and look in at Mandy who was nearly out of her mind, he made her so nervous.

Brianne found herself wishing she had some kind of weapon with which she could protect herself and Mandy, but there was no other gun in the wagon and she wasn't sure she could bring herself to use a knife should Keane try to attack one of them.

In the evening, she watched him prepare the cookfire as he always did, then light one of his cigars and lean up against one of the wagon wheels, watching her prepare the meal.

"I need extra water for the coffee from the spring," Brianne said, straightening up and grabbing one of the buckets she used for such purposes. "Mandy, you want to run get some?"

"You can get it," Keane said, suddenly, making her start.

For a moment, she wasn't sure what he was getting at, then saw him stand up and prepare to go with her. She swallowed hard. "There's no need to—"

"I'll come with you," he offered, smiling slightly.

"Why, it's silly for both of us to go," she returned, trying not to sound desperate. She saw him waver, then shrug and lean back against the wheel.

"All right, go get it then."

With relief, she grabbed the bucket and went beyond the clump of mesquite bushes to where a clear spring bubbled up between overhanging willows. Brianne sat down on the smooth bank of the creek and passed a jittery hand over her forehead. She felt her heart thumping crazily and her stomach was threatening to empty its contents from lunch. If that loathsome man touched her, she'd kill him, she decided. She stayed at the stream longer than necessary, trying to make order out of the

chaos of her mind. She must protect herself and Mandy
—Mandy! She'd forgotten about the girl!

Dropping the bucket, she ran back to the wagon, her
eyes widening with horror as she saw her maid spread-
eagled on the ground, her dress ripped up the middle
exposing her legs and breasts. There was blood between
her thighs and scratches on the satiny skin of her small
breasts.

"Mandy, oh my God! Why didn't you call for me, why
didn't you scream?" Brianne ran to her, but was caught
by a strong hand on her arm, nearly jerking it out of its
socket.

"'Cause I told her I'd slit her pretty throat if she did!"
Keane hissed in her ear. "She's a smart little negress that
one, even if you were right 'bout her not havin' no man
before! I told her I wouldn't touch her again, I'd leave her
be if she told me where you hid your money!"

Brianne thought quickly. "Money—what money?"

"Come on now, lady! Bill Keane's not as stupid as you
might have thought. A woman like you has to have
money. What'd you pay me with, shoe buttons?" He
shook her a little and thrust his face into hers. Sickened,
Brianne could see the long furrow along one cheek that
Mandy had managed before he must have knocked her
unconscious. "Listen to me, gal. You tell me where you
hid your money and I might let you both go!"

"What—what exactly do you mean?" Brianne asked,
trying to borrow some time, but realizing, with a feeling of
dread, that there was no one within several miles who
could possibly come to their rescue.

"God damn it! Don't try me, gal, or I'll poke you just
like I did your little maid over there!" He smiled, more a
leer really. "Heh, come to think of it, why not have you
too? Come 'ere, gal!"

He pulled her close to him and tried to kiss her. Frantic,
Brianne pushed at him with her fists and twisted her face
away. "Let me go! Let me go and I'll—I'll tell you where
I've hidden the money!" she screamed.

He caught her chin in one hand, his fingers pressing on either side of it as he held her face still. "All right, honey, you show me the money and I'll make it fun for you, but if you're tryin' to trick me, I'll rape you like I did the other one!"

She nodded, her cheeks hurting from his squeezing fingers. He released her and followed her to the wagon, carelessly stepping over the prone form of the young negress.

Inside the wagon, Brianne pretended to rummage around while she looked frantically for something to use to protect herself. Her eye caught the long knife she used to cut strips of beef and she sidled toward it.

"Come on, give me the money!" he warned, popping his head inside the flap.

Startled, Brianne jumped and drew her hand away from the knife, hoping he hadn't seen her going for it. Quickly, she went to the petticoat and threw it out into his face, causing him to stagger backward, trying to reorient himself. Her fingers found the handle of the knife and she jumped out of the wagon as he tore the petticoat from his face.

"What the hell!"

Brianne half crouched, the wagon at her back, the knife raised menacingly in front of her. "Now, you get out of here and leave us alone!" she directed. "The money you want is in the pocket of that petticoat. That's what you really want. Now you've got it!"

He eyed her, gauging the distance between them as though contemplating trying to wrestle the knife away from her. He picked up the petticoat, feeling the weight of the coins sewn into it. "But I thought you and me—"

"Get going, Mr. Keane. I swear to God if you try to lay one hand on me, I'll stick this knife into you!"

He hesitated, but something in those bright, turquoise eyes convinced him she was telling the truth. He'd seen eyes like that in a female mountain lion protecting her young. Well, the hell with her! He'd relieved himself on the other one and now he had the money! Better to let her stay here and starve! Or better yet, hope a marauding band of Comanches might come down this far and show her what rape really was! He almost smiled to himself. She'd not be so high and mighty after the redskins had their way with her.

"All right, then, I'm goin'," he said, moving toward his horse, his eyes still on her. With an evil chuckle, he mounted his horse. "I'm leaving you, ma'am, and I'll be thankin' you for the coin from the bottom of my heart!" He bowed ironically and spurred his horse to a gallop.

Brianne watched him until he was out of sight, then lowered her aching arm. She looked around and suddenly fell to her knees, crying bitterly.

Chapter Nineteen

BRIANNE LEANED OVER THE STREAM AND WRUNG OUT THE clothes she had scrubbed against the rocks, then stood up and flapped them out smartly, laying them over one arm to return to the camp. She passed a weary hand over her forehead and picked up the bucket in the other. She tried not to think of what awaited her at the camp: the same wagon, the docile horses which she would gladly ride anywhere to get away from her responsibility here, the sick young girl who, despite the fact that she seemed to be healing physically after the brutal rape she had undergone three days before, had not healed mentally and lay like a life-sized doll, never speaking a word.

Brianne had never felt so alone, so helpless against this vast prairie where nothing moved, or at least nothing human. Sometimes she could hear the song of the wood thrush or the calls of the wren and screeching hawk. At night there were animal tracks at the stream. She was afraid to think they might be bear or panther. There was life all around her, but there was death too, which seemed to be waiting patiently for her to give up and lay down beside Mandy, refusing to get up again.

But she wasn't about to give up, she told herself, although her arms ached and her legs ached and she was so lonely she would have almost welcomed an Indian, at least he would be human flesh, someone she might communicate with.

She reached the camp, not having moved from the spot where Bill Keane had abandoned them, since she had no idea in which direction help might lay. She had thought about riding one of the horses through the prairie grass, but was afraid she might forget how to get back to Mandy, or worse, that while she was gone, some wild animal might attack the girl in her defenseless condition. There was nothing she could do really, but keep hoping and praying that someone would come along the road and aid them. She could only be grateful that they had plenty of fresh water available, although food would begin to grow more scarce if they had to remain here much longer. Bill Keane had taken some of the salted meat and corn meal with him.

She hung the damp clothes on a piece of rope she had stretched between two shoulder-high mesquite bushes, knowing the sun would soon bake them dry. She glanced up at the pale-blue sky and the white-yellow ball of the sun, seeing no sign of clouds to cool the intense late-summer heat. She felt sweat on her neck and running down her back, remembering how cool and inviting the stream had looked as she'd washed out the clothes. A bath would be heaven!

Wearily, she went to the wagon, looking inside, knowing she would see the same thing she'd looked on for the last three days. Mandy lay in a clean light dress, her curly dark hair damp and unbound from the usual cotton turban she would have worn. Her luminous dark eyes were staring at the ceiling of the wagon and Brianne could not even be sure that she was aware of her looking in.

Biting her lip, Brianne bit back tears that threatened to burst out and reduce her to hysterics. Poor dear Mandy who had come all this way unquestioningly, following her mistress to the culmination of all her schemes! The girl was so young, younger even than Brianne—and to have had a man like Bill Keane use her so cruelly! Brianne ached for the girl and felt the responsibility for what had happened to her like a lead weight in her heart. Mandy hadn't deserved such a fate and she, Brianne, must do everything in her power to restore her to health.

At night, when the prairie was quiet except for the howls of coyotes or the chirping of the night birds, Brianne would feel the fear pushing up from her stomach and threatening to spew forth in terrible screams. She dreaded when the sun went down, hating the darkness and fighting the urge to sleep that overtook her. She hated to let down her guard for a moment, not knowing what might come creeping up to the wagon during the night or what might be waiting to greet her in the morning.

Now, as she looked in on Mandy, she wished with all her might that she had listened to her father and her husband. She should have learned not to trust men. She had found out what a cad Blaine Fielding was, but had not learned enough to distrust Bill Keane before it had been too late. Well, she thought savagely, I'll never be foolish enough to trust another stranger again!

She climbed into the wagon and leaned over Mandy, laying a hand on her forehead to check for fever. It was cool to the touch, thank God!

"Oh, Mandy, why won't you talk to me?" Brianne pleaded, staring at those blank eyes. "I'm afraid, too, you know. I don't want to be here anymore than you do. I promise that if we make it out of this alive, I'll have the best doctors treat you! I'm so sorry for what happened! So sorry!" The tears trickled down her cheeks as she stroked the other girl's forehead, wondering if she even heard her.

"Did you hear that thrush outside, Mandy?" Brianne asked as though having a conversation. "You must have! It must have been sitting on the horse rigging, it was at least that close! Oh, please do try to get better, Mandy!"

Brianne wiped her hand across her nose and dashed away the tears on her cheeks. She sighed heavily and went back out of the wagon to make some broth for supper. God, if only Sara or her mother or father were here! They'd know what to do, how to make Mandy come around. Or Pierce, if only he were here, she thought morosely. His strength of will was what had attracted her in the first place, and what had caused the inevitable clash between them, and now she would give anything to have his strength beside her, telling her what to do. But God knew where Pierce was now. He must have made San Antonio days ago.

Brianne began preparing the soup, hoping to get Mandy to take a little more than she had at lunch time. She didn't want to think about the possibility that Mandy could actually die. If the girl died, what would Brianne do? Panic seeped through her at the thought of being alone. She could ride one of the horses away from the camp and try to find someone, but who knew how long that would take, or if she might not get lost along the way. No, Mandy would live and Brianne must just keep hoping that help would come soon.

"God, why is it so hot?" Brianne asked of the silent landscape as she sponged off Mandy's perspiring body. "Was it this hot back in Louisiana?" she asked the unresponsive girl. "If it was, I just didn't notice it, I guess." She shook her head. It must be September already for this was her fifth day alone with Mandy and Keane had left them at the end of August.

When she finished sponging off the prone girl and brushing her hair back, Brianne climbed out of the wagon, stretching her arms and rubbing at the sore spot on her lower back. If they didn't starve or go mad, the heat would surely roast them alive. She thought about the stream once more, thinking longingly of the bath she dearly needed.

"Heavens, what's the difference!" she said aloud, making up her mind. "If I drown or get eaten by some wild animal, so much the better!"

She took a cake of plain soap and a piece of cloth to

wrap her wet hair in and also a petticoat and chemise so that she could rinse out her dirty dress after she'd finished her bath. At the prospect of washing thoroughly, her spirits rose and she began humming softly as she trod the well-worn path to the stream.

She looked around cautiously at the water's edge, studying the tracks made the night before. Well, she couldn't tell what was what anyway, she shrugged. At least she didn't think there were any animals around here now. With only a little hesitation she pulled off her dress, then stripped down to her bare skin, laying her garments close by should she need them in a hurry.

Stepping gingerly into the lazy stream, she remembered suddenly, vividly another time when she had stepped into a stream. Her mind went back in time to the county cotillion, when she had stood alone and walked, all because Pierce had taunted her so after she'd fallen into the stream from her wheelchair. How long ago had that been—it seemed ages!

She waded into the cool water, seeking some depth so that she could wet her hair. Halfway across the stream she found such a pool and stepped into it, finding that the water reached to her shoulders at this point. She leaned backward, dipping her head into the water and letting the current swirl her hair about her like delicate seaweed. Heavens, that felt good! Smiling, she began to lather her hair with the soap, digging into her scalp with her fingers, loosening the dirt and dust that seemed to have clung to her all the way from Galveston.

When she'd washed and rinsed her hair thoroughly, she applied the soap to her person vigorously. God, it was so good to be clean again! She vowed that as long as she remained encamped here, she'd come down and bathe every day. Why deny herself this simple pleasure? It would be something to look forward to. She paddled around a little in the deeper pool, then sat down in the shallower part, lifting her face to the sun as though to defy its heat.

Suddenly, she opened her half-closed eyes wide. Turning her head quickly, she scanned the line of rocks on the opposite side of the stream, then looked over the thick clumps of shoulder-high mesquite that grew along the path from the camp. Something—she'd heard something! Had it been a loosened pebble, a rock kicked carelessly aside by human feet, or had it been some animal? Keeping still, she listened hard, straining to hear something that might identify the sound further. There was nothing to give her any other clues, but still she remained uneasy.

Could it be some animal, coming early to the watering hole, led by thirst and, perhaps, hunger? Could it be some half-savage Indian wandering off from his band? Or could it be someone like Bill Keane? Brianne felt the hair on the back of her neck rise at the thought and she wished she had thought to bring the butcher knife with her. Carefully, she began to move in the water, listening for any sounds, but hearing nothing but the birds and the flowing stream.

When she'd reached the sandy ledge where she'd laid out her clean clothes, she hurriedly began to dry herself and step into the petticoat, still watching the other side of the stream and listening. Almost casually, she wrapped her hair in the towel, beginning to think it was some wild animal and not wanting to startle it by any sudden moves. She pulled on the top of her chemise and began hooking it up the front.

Suddenly, a scream carried through to her, a high shrill scream that made her automatically drop the shoe she had begun to slip on her foot. That was Mandy's voice! Brianne began running toward the camp, heedless of the rocks that scraped her bare feet or the thorny mesquite that scratched at her bare arms. Her heart jumped in her throat as she entered the campsite and saw five men on horses, dismounting and running toward the wagon.

Brianne's eyes saw the booted feet of a man sticking out from the wagon flaps and she screamed wildly. My

God, they were going to rape Mandy again! They'd kill her for sure! She started for the wagon, her hands doubled into fists, her mouth open to bite, when she was abruptly halted by an arm that snaked around her middle and lifted her off her feet and back against a man's hard chest. Like a savage, she fought, kicking and screaming, clawing at the arm about her. Finally, she felt a hand winding itself into her streaming damp hair and pulling her head back so she could look up at the face of the man who held her.

"Let me go!"

"Wait a minute, ma'am! I'm not about to get clawed to shreds by some wildcat! Now you just calm yourself down and I'll let you go then!" The blue eyes that looked out from the darkly tanned face did not look menacing, but rather curious and concerned for his own safety.

"Warren, what in hell have you got there?" one of the other men was asking, moving from the wagon to get a closer look at the wild thing his companion had captured.

"I think it's a cross between a panther and a she-wolf, Hartwig," the man returned good naturedly, releasing Brianne's hair, but keeping an arm about her waist. "I'm afraid to let her go!"

Brianne watched as the booted feet she'd seen backed out of the wagon, showing that they were attached to a young man of rugged appearance. "There's a sick woman inside this wagon, men." He glanced over at Brianne. "What have you found there, Warren? Was that who I heard screaming like a Comanche a moment ago?"

"'Fraid so, captain," the man called Warren returned. "I think she thought we were trying to harm the other one." He hesitated. "She was down in the stream, taking a bath, sir."

Hoots of pleasure issued from the other men, but were quickly silenced by a word from their captain. Brianne knew now that she hadn't been dreaming when she'd sensed someone watching her. This man who held her now must have seen her bathing. Furiously, she felt her cheeks flushing bright red.

"Let her go, Warren," the captain ordered and when his order was carried out, he walked over to where Brianne stood uncertainly and took off his hat. "Captain James Walker, ma'am, of the Texas Rangers. These are my men," he indicated the five men behind him and pointed to the man who still stood behind her. "I believe you've already made the acquaintance of Ty Warren, there."

"Captain, I—"

"We've been scouting in the area for renegade Indians, ma'am. They usually don't come this far east, but we've had reports of two farmhouse burnings this week. Is there anyone else here besides yourself and the girl in the wagon?"

Brianne shook her head.

"You're all alone here then?" the captain asked in surprise, looking around the camp. "How long have you been here?"

"Five, no, six days," she answered, hardly daring to hope that these men would actually be able to help her. She looked hopefully at the metal star on his chest.

"But—were there others with you?" he pressed.

She nodded. "A scout, a man named Bill Keane. He raped my maid and left us here after stealing my money."

"Your maid needs a doctor, ma'am. We can take you to our outpost. It's not far from here, if you think you're able to ride. We'll have to improvise a litter for your maid, and I'm afraid that we won't be able to take many of your things with us."

"Oh, captain, you have no idea how happy I am that you and your men found us." She swayed a little and found herself immediately bolstered by strong hands at her waist from behind. The same man who had watched her at the stream, she thought, but realized how silly it was to be embarrassed about it now.

"Captain Walker, with your permission, I'll carry the lady to the wagon," the man behind her said.

The captain, who was, despite his controlled discipline, very much aware of the lady's breasts popping out from the top of her chemise, nodded, thinking it was best to get her out of sight of his men who hadn't seen a woman for nearly two weeks, especially one as lovely as this one. He shook his head, wondering how she'd managed, virtually alone for nearly a week. By the look and sound of her, she was no pioneer woman.

"I'm sure I can ride, Captain Walker," Brianne said, settling herself on one of the horses she'd used to drive the wagon, what seemed years ago. She glanced over at the other horse which was hitched to a litter which dragged behind it carrying Mandy. "Is that safe for my maid?"

"Perfectly safe, Mrs. Nolan," the captain returned, having already learned her name after a brief conversation they'd had after she'd been dressed. "We'll take you both back to our outpost. It's a few hours away in Gonzales, but we'll take it easy." He glanced back to his men. They had tried to take as much of her goods with them as they could. Unfortunately, most of the food in the barrels would have to be left for foraging animals. Brianne had brought what dresses she could and her small reticule which held less than twenty dollars in gold in it. Once again, she cursed Bill Keane for his treachery.

When Captain Walker gave the signal to push on, Brianne felt almost giddy again as she realized she was leaving forever the encampment that she had begun to hate. She was leaving behind the solitude and the sadness and now new hope began to grow that Mandy would be treated and she would find a way to send her back home. Home! She thought of Avonlea and her family with longing, but almost in the same moment, she thought of Pierce, and a twinge of sharp despair ran through her at the thought that the chase had ended for her. She wouldn't be going on to San Antonio now. She had to see to Mandy, and she had no money to pay a new scout to take her to the city.

She looked up from her thoughts and was aware of Ty Warren riding beside her, studying her thoughtfully. She straightened in the saddle, staring back at him.

He smiled suddenly and touched his hat. "Do you mind me riding beside you, Mrs. Nolan?" he asked cheerfully.

She shrugged. "Does your captain object?"

He shook his head. "Only if you do, ma'am."

She thought a moment, then nodded. "It doesn't matter. As long as someone is watching after the litter."

He grinned again, showing very white teeth in his tanned face. It was evident that this man lived most of his life out-of-doors. He had a clean, healthy look about him that reminded her irresistibly of her husband.

"How old are you, Mr. Warren?" she asked suddenly curious.

"Twenty-three, ma'am. You have to be young to be in the Texas Rangers. It's not an easy way of life." He watched her for a moment, then asked, "And now can I ask you a question?"

She nodded after a moment's hesitation.

"What were you doing out in the prairie land with only a colored girl for company?"

"I came to Galveston from New Orleans in search of my husband," she said truthfully. "I hired Bill Keane in Galveston to take me to San Antonio where I hoped to meet up with my husband."

"I see." He seemed to think on this for a moment. "And then you say this Bill Keane abandoned you on the prairie after raping your servant and stealing your money."

She colored and nodded.

"So, how do you propose to get on with the search for your husband?" he wondered, his blue eyes watching her carefully.

She was caught unawares by the question, having just

convinced herself that she would be forced to give up finding Pierce again.

"I don't know," she finally said.

He was silent then, and after a while galloped his horse ahead of her. Brianne watched him conversing with his captain for a few minutes, before pushing his horse ahead, presumably to scout the area they were traversing.

She concentrated on the trail ahead of her, not wanting to think of having to make any decision about Pierce. It would be enough to reach this town of Gonzales they'd spoken of and rest and get her bearings once more. She had to make sure that Mandy would be taken care of and then, perhaps she could know better what to do about her husband.

Chapter Twenty

GONZALES WAS A SLEEPY LITTLE TOWN ON THE COASTAL plains of Texas where the San Marcos River joined the Guadalupe. A small fort which had been erected twenty years before housed the small band of Texas Rangers who had been called out by the Governor to help with the Indian problem. Many of the inhabitants of the town were of Mexican descent and, as Brianne rode down the dusty main street in the middle of the afternoon, she saw brown-skinned men and boys dozing in the shade of porches.

"It's called taking a siesta," Ty Warren explained to her as he rode up to her from the rear patrol. "It gets so hot in the afternoons, they figure there's no sense in trying to do anything but sleep."

Brianne was aware of the heat, but thought that sleeping in it was the last thing she'd be able to do. What she'd like was another cool bath to get the dust out of her hair and throat and then a huge supper with anything but dried beef or salt pork.

"Is there a hotel?" she asked, and then recalled that she had very little money with which to pay for a room.

Captain Walker, who had heard her question, cantered beside her and doffed his hat. "You're welcome to stay with us, Mrs. Nolan. We have room to spare inside the fort and my wife can help see to your needs."

"Your wife?" The words had slipped out and she flushed afterward. "Forgive me, captain, but I can hardly believe any young woman would want a life out here on the prairie."

He cocked a curious eyebrow at her. "But she's my wife," he answered. "Wherever I go, she comes along too." He said it as though it was something she should have been able to deduce for herself. Brianne realized that, out here in the new frontier, the men expected their wives to follow them without question whether it was to some remote town on the prairie or to the wild plains and a mud-daubed cabin. It was what Pierce had expected, too.

They rode inside the gates of the fort and Brianne saw a pretty blond-haired woman waving from a shaded porch, a smile lighting her face and restoring its youth. Beside her, a small boy held on tightly to the tail of her apron, sucking his thumb.

Captain Walker ordered two of his men to carry the litter to the building which was used as the infirmary. He helped Brianne down from her mount and introduced her to his wife, Ella, who had run down from the porch to greet her husband.

"James, I'm so glad you're back!" she exclaimed, receiving his rather formal embrace. "We didn't expect you for another four or five days." She watched as her husband reached down to pat his son's head.

"We had to return unexpectedly with this young woman, Mrs. Nolan. We came upon her and her maid during patrol. She'd been abandoned by the man she'd hired to take her to San Antonio. She needs a place to stay."

"Why, of course, you must stay with us," Ella Walker replied, her smile genuinely sincere as she looked at Brianne. "We have plenty of room and, I must confess, it will be a joy to have another woman for company."

Captain Walker, tipping his hat, went back to his men while Brianne followed Ella Walker into the clapboard building that was her home. Inside, all was neat and tidy except for a few homemade toys strewn about the floor.

"Zachary," she scolded the little boy gently, "Mama told you to pick up your toys." She glanced at Brianne with a smile. "He's only four, but James wants to make him a little Ranger already. He has to pick up all his toys or he goes to bed a half-hour early."

"That seems rather strict for such a young boy," Brianne replied, reaching down to tousle the boy's hair. He looked up at her and smiled shyly. "Are you going to be a Texas Ranger like your father?" she asked him in a friendly voice.

He nodded, then went to where he had left his toys and began gathering them in his arms. After he'd disappeared into his room, Ella showed Brianne where she would be staying. The bedroom was dark and warm, with only one small window to allow light in.

"I'm sorry about the heat in here," Ella apologized, opening a cabinet to get out fresh bedding, "but actually it's one of the coolest rooms in the house during the day since it faces north. At night, it gets humid, but I have some lightweight sleeping gowns if you need them."

"Thank you, Mrs. Walker. I appreciate your hospitality," Brianne said, slipping into a chair as she fanned herself with one hand.

"Please call me Ella. Here, let me finish making your bed and then I'll start supper. James is always famished when he returns from patrol, although he thinks he's too tough to admit it." Ella smiled and sighed. "He thinks being a Ranger is the next best thing to being God sometimes."

Brianne was surprised at her frank talk. She was definitely not the simpering, adoring type who thought her husband was all knowing. "Can I help you with supper?" Brianne offered, watching her make the bed and feeling useless.

"Heavens, no! Why don't you take off those clothes and I'll have one of the men bring in some water for a bath. You can soak as long as you like and then take a little nap if you feel the need. Supper'll be at least an hour."

"You're terribly considerate," Brianne said, catching her hand and pressing it. "I'm very grateful, Ella." She was horrified to feel tears close to the surface.

Ella returned the squeeze. "Now, I don't want you to fret about anything. I'll have James send word to the physician in the town to come look at your maid. And I'll ask Ty to help fill up the copper tub for your bath."

"Ty Warren?"

Ella nodded, her blue eyes serene. "Yes. You met him then? He is—a good friend, Brianne." She turned away and Brianne thought she saw a hint of a blush in her cheeks. What, she wondered, was that supposed to mean?

She didn't feel that she had the right to ask and so, after Ella had finished with the bed, she closed the door and began to undress. Had it been only this morning that she'd been bathing in the stream? Heavens, she wouldn't have thought so by the dust and sweat that had collected around her neck and between her breasts. She stripped down to her petticoat and called out to Ella to see if the tub was filled. When Ella confirmed that it was and that she had set up a screen around it, she walked to the kitchen to find Ella busily preparing dinner, expecting Brianne to take her bath in close proximity.

It seemed a bit awkward, taking a bath in the middle of the kitchen, but Brianne supposed it had been easier to lug the water that way. She undressed and slipped into the tub, seeing the cake of soap that Ella had thoughtfully put out for her.

Soon, the knotted tension at the back of her neck was easing away. Brianne stretched out as much as she could in the tub and leaned her head back, savoring the release of tension.

"Heh, what's for supper, Ella?"

Brianne started at the young man's voice, recognizing

it after an instant as that of Ty Warren. Instinctively, she clutched her arms in front of her breasts.

"Why, Ty, you eating with us tonight?" Ella asked in evident surprise. "You know you're welcome, but I would have thought you'd go into town and eat at Maria's café. I think she's been lonely for you." Her voice was teasing, but there was a note of disapproval in it too, Brianne thought.

"I'll see Maria tomorrow," Ty returned, and Brianne could hear him walk into the kitchen. "Give me a kiss, Ella, my love."

"Ty!" Ella said gaily. "James is already half jealous, you know," she continued in a teasing voice.

"He's got every right to be, you know. You're the prettiest girl in town and there's fifteen love-starved males here at the fort who've all been secretly in love with you!"

"Whatever will our guest think, Ty?"

Brianne scrunched down in the tub, afraid he might come walking around the screen to make sure she was actually still there. Instead, she heard him raise his voice. "Hello, in there! Don't get the wrong idea, Mrs. Nolan. It's just that Ella and I have been secret lovers for years and—"

Brianne heard the swat of a wet towel hitting flesh and Ty's voice raised in protest. "Ty Warren, you are incorrigible!" Ella laughed. "Now you get yourself out of here! Goodness knows you must have something better to do than tease two defenseless females."

"All right, all right, I'm going. But I'll be back when supper's on the table," he promised.

Brianne was glad to hear the door slam behind him. "He's gone then?" she called out.

"Yes," Ella confirmed. "You ready to get out of the tub? I've got a nice, warm towel waiting for you over here." She brought it over and hung it over the screen. "Wrap yourself in it and run back to your room before

James walks in. In this house, I'm afraid you'll find men coming and going all the time!"

Brianne hurriedly wrapped herself and went back to her room to brush out her hair and towel-dry it before slipping on her lilac muslin gown, which was the only one that didn't need pressing too badly. She tied a ribbon to keep her hair back from her face, regretting not having learned to do her own hair. The thought made her think of Mandy and she was immediately guilt ridden for not having seen to her welfare sooner.

Slipping on her shoes, she hurried back to the kitchen where she saw Captain Walker washing up for supper. "Oh, Captain, I must go to the infirmary to check on my maid. She might need me for something."

"No need, Mrs. Nolan. I have one of the Mexican women from the town looking after her. She's feeding her some nourishing broth now. I expect the doctor may not be able to look at her until morning. There's only one in the town and he's kept pretty busy between snake bites and gunshot wounds and broken limbs."

"Well, perhaps I should just look in on her—"

"Why don't you have supper first, Mrs. Nolan, and you can look in on her afterward," he suggested reasonably.

Ella, who was just finishing setting the table, agreed. "You need to eat, Brianne. Your maid is in good hands, I can assure you."

Brianne smelled the food and realized she was very hungry. She knew there was nothing she could do for Mandy at the moment, and decided that the Walkers were right. Eagerly, she sat down at her place, allowing Captain Walker to push in her chair. A moment later, Ty Warren walked in, his hair still wet from being washed, and a new suit of clothes on him. They were tanned buckskin, the shirt open at the throat down to the middle of his chest. Without his hat, Brianne could see the dark bronze of his hair which complimented the deep tan on his face, and the startling blue eyes which were just now looking back at her with masculine appreciation. She looked away, feeling suddenly like a small child, although she knew this man was hardly five years older than she. What was it about him that caused a sudden flutter in her heart? Was it that rugged honesty she read in his eyes? Or was it some special air about him that reminded her of Pierce?

"Good evening, Mrs. Nolan," he said, seating himself beside her.

"Well, Ty," James began pleasantly, "you mean you're forsaking your little señorita in town for Ella's cooking?"

Ty grinned. "You know damn good and well that your wife is the best cook in the state of Texas," he answered. "That's one of the reasons why I'm half in love with her."

"As long as it's only half, I won't be jealous," James returned good naturedly. He began carving the joint of beef that Ella laid before him on a huge platter.

"You'll need an escort to San Antonio, Mrs. Nolan," Ty was saying as he munched on a homemade biscuit. "It wouldn't be wise to travel alone with the Indian threat."

She looked up surprised. "Oh, I hadn't planned to travel alone, Mr. Warren!" She looked back down at her plate. "In fact, I'm not sure if I'll continue on to San Antonio. I—I may decide to return to my home in Louisiana with my maid."

"But you told me your husband was waiting for you in San Antonio?" he pressed with a puzzled air.

Brianne was silent for a moment, then stood up, throwing down her napkin. "Mr. Warren, that is none of your business!" she cried sharply. Then, horrified at her unexpected outburst, she stared at the three faces looking up at her and ran to her room, slamming the door behind her.

God's teeth! What was wrong with her? She'd been out of sorts and as skittish as a newborn colt. She sat down on the bed and put her head in her hands. She felt nausea rising in her throat and fought it down, feeling the

heat in the room with a sudden intenseness. Lord, what
was the matter with her? Perhaps she had eaten something that hadn't agreed with her?

Carefully, she laid down on the bed, wishing she could
open the door to let in fresh air from the hall, but afraid
she might hear what the others were saying about her.
She felt tears stinging her eyes again, and instead of
suppressing them, she let them come, finding a relief in
letting them out.

Brianne rolled restlessly on her bed, clad in the light
nightgown that Ella had given to her after dinner was
over. Brianne had felt embarrassed to face her, but the
other woman had been so kind that she had felt foolish.

"I'm sorry for what happened at supper," Brianne said
sincerely. "I don't know what happened really."

"That's all right, Brianne. You've been under an
enormous strain for the past several days. I was wondering what you were made of to be able to act so calmly
when you arrived. It was all perfectly natural, I can assure
you. I've seen the men blow up many times after long
weeks of patrol. You just try to get some rest tonight and
you should feel better in the morning." She closed the
door behind her and Brianne heard her footsteps going
down the hall.

Now, as she lay restlessly, listening to the night sounds,
Brianne sat up in bed and walked to the door to open it.
Ah, that was better. It was so stifling in her room, she
longed to go outside and feel whatever hint of a breeze
there was on her perspiring skin. She listened for a
moment and heard nothing so decided to step outside
just for a moment.

Outside on the porch, she looked up and could see
men patrolling the cross walks in the moonlight. She sat
down in an old wooden rocking chair and closed her
eyes, enjoying the serenity of the night and the knowledge that she was safe and protected after so many
anxious nights in the wagon with Mandy.

"Feeling better?"

The voice startled her and she opened her eyes to see Ty Warren leaning down toward her as though checking to see if she were still awake.

"Yes," she whispered, wondering what he was doing there.

As though he knew her question, he said, "I couldn't sleep either. Some nights, when I get back from a long patrol, it's hard to settle down. You get used to sleeping under the stars and being constantly on guard. The first night is hard under a log roof."

"I'm glad to be here instead of under the stars," she answered, aware of her bare feet and tucking them underneath her in the chair.

"Yes, I guess you would be. A lady like yourself isn't used to open spaces, I'm betting. Where are you from, Mrs. Nolan?"

"Heavens, you can't keep calling me Mrs. Nolan," she said with a little sigh. "I'm nearly as old as you are so please call me Brianne."

"Mighty friendly of you, Brianne," he said, sitting down at her feet and a little to the side. "Call me Ty then." He chuckled. "Even though you are almost as old as I am."

She knew he was teasing her. "How long have you been a Texas Ranger?" she asked, changing the subject.

"I asked you a question first," he reminded her.

"All right, then. I'm from Louisiana, upriver from Baton Rouge near Ferriday, across the river from Natchez. My father owns a sugar plantation there."

He clicked his tongue. "I would have guessed it was something like that. There's something—reserved about you, even when you were bathing in the stream this morning."

Brianne blushed furiously, glad of the night that hid her face. "I would hope you could forget that incident, sir."

He chuckled. "Not likely, Brianne, not likely." He was

silent as though savoring the memory in his mind. "And now, what was it you wanted to know about me?"

The question seemed improper somehow, but Brianne deliberately brushed aside any embarrassment she felt. "I wondered how long you'd been in the Rangers?"

"Oh, about four years now, I guess. I was born and raised in Beaufort, Texas so I guess I was destined to be a Ranger, like my father."

"Does your father live in Beaufort?"

"No, he died when I was nine at the battle of the Alamo."

"I'm sorry," Brianne said, feeling suddenly awkward.

He shrugged. "He died a hero in his own eyes and those of Texas. I'm not sorry for him, for it's exactly the way he would have wanted to die." He sighed. "It was all I could do to stay at home until I was nineteen to help care for my mother and my brothers and sisters. Then I hightailed it for the nearest Ranger post I could find. Of course, that was after Texas had been admitted to the Union and the federal government took over the problem of law and order in the state. The Rangers were beginning to be phased out by the government."

He laughed slightly. "Well, the government found out that the army didn't know which end was up when it came to fighting Indians. To put it mildly, they handled the frontier problem poorly. Of course, you can hardly blame the army, since the government's only assigned a few thousand soldiers to patrol the entire state. Why, most of those men have never seen Apache or Comanche warriors, let alone tried to fight them on their terms! We just set our state capital at Austin this year and people are still being killed or carried off in its outskirts!"

Brianne's eyes grew round with fright. "You mean, there really are savage Indians around here?"

"Of course there are. Over half of Texas is still wild frontier! Governor Bell finally got disgusted with the army's efforts at 'peace making' with the Comanche and called out the Rangers again."

"And, of course, you were happy about that?"

"Damn right—excuse me, ma'am. Why, everyone with brains knows that the danger of the Indians isn't going to go away too soon. The Ranger companies guarding the frontier have more or less permanent duty because the danger never ceases."

"So, you Rangers are organized then?"

"As well as we can be under the circumstances. Governor Bell called us up, but the army's not too pleased about it. We don't have uniforms like the army, not even government-supplied horses or firearms, but we do the best we can. Which is a hell of a lot better than those bluecoats!"

"But how can you go around killing Indians?" Brianne wanted to know, shivering at the thought of facing a band of savages.

"Honey, when you hear about some of the tortures those redskins use on their captured white prisoners, you'd be able to pull the trigger too. Like heaping live coals on a staked-out man's genitals—"

"Oh!" She stood up from the rocking chair, rubbing her arms nervously, trying not to put into thought what his words had conjured up.

Ty stood up too and, quite naturally, put an arm around her shoulders and drew her up against him. "Sorry, Brianne, I didn't mean to upset you like that."

She shivered, not feeling quite so secure anymore despite the strong walls of the fort. In spite of her ambiguous feelings toward Ty Warren, she was glad of his arm around her. "Are there Indians close by?" she whispered hoarsely, as though they might be listening.

"No. Or if there are, it's just a few renegades that have wandered away from their main bands, like the ones who've been burning the farmhouses." He pressed her even closer against him. "You don't have to worry, Brianne. You're safe here."

Brianne was aware of the hard chest against one shoulder, the rough hand on the other, pressing her closer. She turned toward him to tell him good-night, and was suddenly faced with the fact that she was being held against him and his face was leaning down toward hers. In a single moment, she felt a riot of emotions, stemming from leaping excitement at the nearness of this very male man to girlish embarrassment at the fact that the thinness of her nightgown left very little to his imagination as her breasts pressed into his chest. She thought she understood why Ella Walker had such a special feeling for this man among all the others.

"Brianne?"

The question meant several things she knew. And she realized she was not fully prepared to answer him.

"I—should go in now, Ty," she whispered, aware of his lips only inches from hers.

To her relief, or was it her disappointment, he let her go regretfully, his hands caressing her slightly as they released her. For a moment, they stood looking at one another almost curiously, as though both were trying to figure out the reason for such all-powerful attraction with so little time of acquaintance. He stepped away from her and turned to go back to the bunk house.

"Good-night, Ty," she called softly and heard him stop and turn to look back at her.

"Good-night, Brianne," he returned.

Chapter Twenty-one

THE NEXT AFTERNOON ELLA WALKER AND BRIANNE WERE sitting in comfortable homemade chairs in the room that served as a parlor, watching little Zachary play with his brightly painted, wooden-carved blocks. Brianne let her eyes wander idly around the room, noting the touches that Ella had added with the hand-sewn chintz curtains at the windows, the brown braided rug that lay over the gleaming waxed wooden floor, and the fresh flowers in bright vases that brought a fresh scent into the room. Could she ever feel really at home in a room like this, she wondered? Ella had even admitted that she had it better than most pioneer women, who usually had only dirt floors under their rugs and splintery wooden chairs to sit on. Only this morning, Brianne had nearly fainted at the sight of a small scorpion scuttling from beneath the overturned water bucket outside the kitchen. She couldn't help thinking of the well-scrubbed hallways and cheerfully wallpapered rooms at Avonlea with a touch of longing.

"Have you decided what you're going to do?" Ella asked kindly, looking up from her sewing.

Brianne shook her head ruefully. "I can't leave Mandy here, Ella. She and I have been through so much together, I feel more toward her than just an obligation, and yet, I must try to continue on to San Antonio to see my husband." She looked over at the other woman. "You see, he left me in Galveston on a—misunderstanding, and I must clear all that up!"

"This life is hard for a woman," Ella commented with a sigh. "Of course, we do it because we love our husbands and we want to be with them."

Brianne bit her lip, folding her hands into the material of the dress that Ella had loaned her while hers were drying on the clothesline outside. "Oh, Ella, I just feel so confused! Sometimes, especially when Bill Keane left us all alone out there, I hate the prairie and this heat and everything else that goes with it. Last night I couldn't help thinking of the shaded veranda of my home and the security of that civilized world that I've always known up until now."

"Well," Ella began, trying to buoy the girl's flagging spirit, "what else can be expected of you at this point? Why, you're only eighteen and have never been away from your parents before. I'm sure you're quite used to plantation life, and it certainly is a far cry from life out here!"

"It's not really the plantation that I miss," Brianne said softly, as though coming to realize it herself. "It's not the slaves doing your bidding every minute of the day or the fact that I've never before had to do any hard work. I think what I really miss is the love I've become so used to with my family, the caring I always seemed to take for granted. Out here, no one cares about anyone else. It's always them against the frontier!"

Ella reached over and patted the girl's hand. "My dear, you do make it sound so uncivilized! And I suppose you are right, up to a point. People are more interested in saving their own skins and wondering where their next meal will come from and what to do if their children get measles because the nearest doctor is fifty miles away. But that doesn't mean there's no room for caring! Sometimes it just gets shoved back to the end of the line, I suppose." She smiled encouragingly. "It only makes it all the more worthwhile, Brianne. This life will take some getting used to, but if you have someone you love to do it with, then it will all work out!"

"Ah, Ella, when will I get some of your wisdom," Brianne responded.

"When you've been out on the frontier as long as I have," Ella winked.

Brianne wondered if she would last even that long.

"I'm sure your husband must be missing you terribly," Ella went on conversationally. "What is he doing in San Antonio?"

"He went to rejoin the Texas Rangers," Brianne said soberly.

"Why, I wonder if James might know him then," Ella said. "Of course, there are so many regiments springing back up what with the Governor calling them all out again. Still, there could be a chance that he would be able to send a message to his outfit, if he knew which one it was."

Brianne felt her heart begin to flutter at the news. She dared not hope for too much, though, she reminded herself. But wouldn't it be wonderful if Pierce could come for her here! But, oh, he didn't even know she was here! Would he be angry to find that she'd followed him like this, after telling her to await him at Avonlea? Would he remember her previous threat to follow him because she wanted the divorce and was determined to get it? She shuddered to think what his reaction would be. She must see him face-to-face and explain everything to him; it couldn't be done through a message.

"Ella, perhaps it would be best not to send a message," she began carefully. "You see, my husband thinks I went back to Avonlea instead of following him over the prairie. As I told you before, we parted with a misunderstanding and I'm not even sure he would be happy to hear that I've come this far. I know it all sounds confusing—"

Ella studied the young face, her brow troubled. "I'm sure there are things that you have no wish to discuss with me, Brianne, and believe me, I'm not one to pry when it's none of my business. But you *are* so young,

and I wonder if you know exactly what you're doing.
You've come all this way to see your husband, and he
may no longer even be in San Antonio. What will you do
when you get there, my dear, if you find he's gone? The
Rangers rarely come to the cities. They were commis-
sioned to patrol the frontiers and the borders. I'm sorry to
say it, but it really is highly unlikely that your husband will
be there when you arrive in San Antonio."

"But I can't go back now!" Brianne blurted out,
standing up from her chair in so violent a motion that
Zachary looked up and started to cry. Quickly, Ella went
over to reassure him, looking over her shoulder at
Brianne with a concerned air. "I've got to find him and
make him understand how very foolish I've been!"
Brianne continued, on the verge of tears. "That he was
right about my being a spoiled child and expecting
everything to be done my way! He—he told me he loved
me—and oh God, that's not an easy thing for a man like
Pierce to say! I only hope he doesn't hate me now!"

Ella finished quieting her son, then went to the other
young woman to try to comfort her. "Hush, my dear, I'm
sure he still loves you! And he must know that you love
him!"

Brianne shook her head. "No, no, that's just the point.
He doesn't know that I love him! He—he thinks I don't
want to be married to him. You see, that's why I came to
Texas in the first place, because I was determined to
divorce him. I chased him all the way from New Orleans!"

"To get a divorce!" Ella seemed shocked, but quickly
recovered herself.

"Oh, it was all so stupid really," Brianne said. "He
married me because I had put myself in a compromising
position. I thought it was only a marriage of convenience.
I never knew that he could love me! And then I practically
forced him to leave the day after we were married, and I
blamed him for it! Oh, how could I have been so
incredibly stupid!"

Perplexed, Ella put her hands out to encircle Brianne's shoulders. "My dear, stop berating yourself. The only question you have to ask yourself now is whether or not you love him and want to be with him. If the answer is yes, then I would travel to San Antonio or Austin or wherever he is to tell him that!"

"I do love him!" Brianne replied. "At one time, I was positive that I hated him because of the circumstances surrounding our marriage. Lord knows I've known enough grief because of that rascal," she sniffed with a little smile, "but when we're together it's the most exciting time of my life! He challenges me and I come alive!"

"Then go after him."

"And yet, I tell myself sometimes, that perhaps I still haven't grown up enough to be the kind of wife that Pierce expects me to be. Even loving him, I can still be attracted to other men. Even Ty Warren—" She stopped, blushing, not at all certain of what Ella would think, or what her own feelings were toward the charming Texas Ranger.

Ella smiled gently. "I know what you mean, my dear. I've loved Ty ever since I came here with my husband two years ago. I don't know what it is about some men. You want to mother them at first, and then you realize that mothering is not what's on their minds. Oh, I don't mean to say that I've ever entertained thoughts of cheating on my husband with Ty. But I do love him. Not the same way that I love James, but there's just something about him that pulls women toward him." She eyed the other girl sagely. "Some men just have that air about them, I suppose."

"But, do you love your husband because you've been married as long as you have?" Brianne wondered. "Or did you love him even before you were married?"

"I love him now, Brianne, and that's all that truly matters. I want to have more children and grow old with him, and see our grandchildren together. I wouldn't trade James for Ty in a million years, for, you see, James loves me, and Ty doesn't."

"Pierce told me he loved me," Brianne recalled thoughtfully, "but I didn't want to believe him."

Ella shrugged. "He's a man, like any other, with faults and misconceptions. Maybe he felt trapped by the marriage."

"Yes, he said that," Brianne admitted. "And I told him that maybe I felt trapped too!"

"Oh, dear! I'm afraid that men don't fancy their women being quite that bold, Brianne. They are, believe me, more fragile than we in so many ways."

Brianne sighed. "I suppose I just kept thinking so much about what it would take to make me happy that I wasn't all that concerned about making him happy. But then, he didn't want to compromise either. Sometimes I think it would have been so much easier if he could have stayed at Avonlea a little longer so we could have grown used to each other more gradually, and yet, he wouldn't even do that for fear things would tie him down too much eventually."

Ella shrugged. "Men and their sense of adventure!"

"What do you think I should do then, Ella?" Brianne wondered.

"I think you should go on to San Antonio, and pray he's still there!"

Brianne chewed on her lip and leaned back in her chair thoughtfully. "All right," she sighed at last. "I'll go to San Antonio."

Ella smiled in relief. "I'm glad to hear it. You need have no fears about your maid. As you saw this morning, the physician is quite sure that with additional rest and nourishment, her mind will heal. I'll see her safely back to Louisiana myself when it's time."

Brianne gazed at her in amazement. "You would do that?"

"I have family in Mississippi that Zachary has never seen. James will be glad to see me get away from here for awhile. He worries so about me."

Brianne stood up and felt a lump in her throat at the kindness of this woman who was hardly more than a stranger. "Thank you, Ella," she said sincerely.

Ella stood up and hugged her. "I'll let you go, only on the condition that you accept my hospitality for at least two more days. I'll miss your company when you go, Brianne."

Brianne returned the hug, then stepped away and laughed ruefully. "You know, I've always thought that women could never be friends. I don't know, I just thought there was too much competition between them, too much spite and distrust. But now," and she let out a long breath, "perhaps I can find something to like even in Annabelle Jackson!" And at Ella's puzzled look, "Oh, heavens, I'll have two whole days to tell you about her!"

Chapter Twenty-two

THE NEXT TWO DAYS WENT BY TOO QUICKLY FOR BOTH young women as they talked and laughed together in a way that they had both missed. Ella helped Brianne with the sewing repairs on her dresses and even made her a gift of one of her gowns, a soft blue silk that was simply styled. When Brianne told her she couldn't possibly take it, Ella shrugged and pressed it into her arms.

"What would I be doing with it out here on the prairie?" she wanted to know. "It'll be nice to have a dress to keep for when you find your husband again. You'll want to look your best so you can charm the devil out of him!" She had laughed merrily and Brianne couldn't help but laugh too, although she still had reservations about charming her husband out of anything.

Captain Walker had told Brianne that he would be sure to have one of the Rangers accompany her to San Antonio as a scout. "And it will certainly be a man that you can trust," he assured her, reading the faint worry in her eyes as she remembered her ordeal with Bill Keane. "All of my men are gentlemen, ma'am, and I can assure you that none of them would stoop so low as to take advantage of a lone woman."

Brianne had gazed over the rough tumble of men and still retained some doubts, but realized there was hardly anything she could say about the matter. She certainly wasn't about to take the trip by herself and she had to admit that, as Captain Walker had told her proudly, any one of them could outride and outshoot a Bill Keane or a Comanche warrior. They were, after all, Indian fighters and would ensure her survival for the next eighty miles it would take to reach San Antonio.

The evening before her departure was quiet, the heat permeating the house as Ella had insisted on lighting the cooking fire so as to make a special supper. Unfortunately, Brianne didn't feel much like eating and couldn't do justice to the tasty dishes that Ella had prepared. She apologized for her light appetite and excused herself to go and visit Mandy for the last time. In the infirmary, Mandy had started making her recovery, thanks to the special care the Mexican woman, Donida, had given to her. Brianne was relieved since she would feel better about leaving Mandy tomorrow morning.

She stopped for a moment outside the infirmary and looked up at the star-filled night, feeling the air heavy about her causing perspiration to dot her forehead. Could she honestly live in a place like this if Pierce asked her to remain with him, she wondered. It seemed so wild and untamed, the very things that Pierce had said he liked about it. Civilization as Brianne knew it held no charms for him. Could this wild raw land hold something for *her*?

She shook her head in indecision and started walking back to the house, trying not to think about the long ride ahead of her tomorrow. She and the scout that Captain Walker would choose for her would not be riding in a wagon, as that would take too long and draw attention to them should they cross paths with an Indian party. This way, they would be free of the cumbersome wagon and be able to ride swiftly away from danger on fast horses that the Ranger would pick out for them.

As she walked, she heard men's voices on the porch and looked up to see Captain Walker and Ty Warren talking in friendly fashion as they both relaxed in chairs, smoking cheroots.

"Good evening, Mrs. Nolan," Walker said, standing quickly, followed by Ty. "I trust you found your maid recuperating?"

"Yes, thank you, captain. My mind is eased a great deal, knowing she's on her way to recovery. I felt guilty about dragging her with me to begin with, and to leave her here in a strange place was weighing heavily."

There was a moment of quiet and then Brianne turned to Ty Warren. "I guess I should be saying good-bye to you, Ty," she said, pushing back the discomfort as she recalled that evening they had been on the porch and he had held her for a moment in his arms. "I'm leaving tomorrow and I know that you will soon be going out on patrol again with the Rangers."

Ty smiled and touched the brim of his hat. "Yes, we'll be trying to clear out any Indians between here and your husband," he said smoothly, although Brianne thought that she detected an underlying sarcasm. "I'm sorry I'll not be scouting for you, ma'am."

Brianne nodded and turned to Captain Walker inquiringly. The captain informed her that he had chosen one of the older men to accompany her since he had the most experience. Jess Moses would be meeting her at dawn the next morning, so the captain suggested she'd best go to bed and get plenty of sleep for the next day. He said good-night himself and went inside, leaving Brianne to stand uncomfortably with Ty.

"Better do as he says, Brianne," Ty suggested lightly, throwing his cheroot to the ground.

"I think I'm too nervous to sleep," Brianne confided.

Ty chuckled. "Yeah, I know what you mean. To tell you the truth, I probably do my best sleeping on the trail. There's something about the stars for a canopy and your saddle for a pillow."

"My husband said something like that once," Brianne said thoughtfully.

Ty shook his head. "I hate to say it, but your husband sounds like a man after my own heart."

"I'm sure you would be great friends," Brianne said. "You remind me of him a little bit, although he's older than you."

"Glad to think I've got something over on him," Ty said with a smile. "He's a lucky man, Brianne."

She looked away from his too-intense blue eyes. "Sometimes, I don't think he would agree with you, Ty."

"Then he's a fool, Brianne, if you don't mind my saying so."

They were both silent for a while, although neither felt like going inside. It was strange, the pull that Ty Warren seemed to exert on her, Brianne thought. There was just something about him, like Ella had said, that made him attractive to women. Pierce had that quality about him, too, she realized.

"Well," Brianne said finally, knowing she couldn't stand out here on the porch all evening, "I suppose I'll go in now." She stood awkwardly.

"Then good-night, Brianne." Ty hesitated, then leaned toward her, brushing her lips lightly with his. "You take good care of yourself, little lady," he added softly.

He turned and walked away, whistling a little in the still, night air. Brianne watched his silhouette in the moonlight, then turned and went inside, knowing already she'd not be able to fall asleep very soon.

"Wake up, dear, it's nearly dawn," came a disembodied voice that seemed attached to a candle that glowed in the semi-darkness.

Groggily, Brianne opened her eyes which seemed pasted shut. "What?" she asked, disoriented and aware that her nightgown was clinging stickily to her.

"Jess should be here shortly with the horses," Ella continued patiently. "Come on, I've got a hot breakfast waiting for both of you." She shook the other girl by the shoulder, then left the candle on the nightstand.

Tired, because she'd slept badly last night after she'd

finally been able to doze off, Brianne forced herself out of the bed. She took a moment to regain her bearings, feeling a sudden nausea come over her at the smell of the cooking bacon from the kitchen. Quickly, she sat down and put a trembling hand to her forehead. When she felt capable of standing again without feeling dizzy, she began to dress in a lightweight cotton dress that Ella had given her. The sleeves were cut shorter than usual, leaving her forearm bare, and the neck, instead of being high, was scooped around her throat. It would be cool during the day and she would only be wearing one full petticoat with it, instead of the usual five or six. Since Ella had no riding habit, it was the next best thing she could find.

After she'd brushed her hair and fashioned it into a knot at the nape of her neck and washed her face and teeth, she felt capable of facing the others at breakfast. The nausea had gone away, but she had been left with a tiny seed of dread, wondering, suddenly, if she might be pregnant. She had seen enough slaves pregnant to know some of the symptoms, even if Joanna would have fainted had she known how interested her well-bred daughter had been in such things. God, of all things to have happened! It had to have happened in New Orleans, for it would be too soon to show such signs if it had happened in Galveston.

Brianne nearly laughed aloud, thinking how like Pierce it would be to have impregnated her after only making love to her three times. Here they had never even really lived together as man and wife and, somehow, he had succeeded in getting her with child. It was, she thought, his way to seal his possession of her. She shivered, thinking how limited her choices would be if she truly was pregnant.

"Good morning, Brianne," Ella said with a smile, pouring steaming coffee into a mug for her. "Hungry?"

Brianne wasn't, but she nodded anyway, knowing it

would be best to try to get down some food before they started off. She knew, instinctively, that this Jess Moses would be a man who wouldn't put up with any female shenanigans. He would expect her to be able to keep up with his pace, despite the fact that she was a woman.

Both Ella and Brianne were startled when James Walker burst into the kitchen, his face stern, his manner agitated.

"What is it, dear?" Ella asked, getting up from the table to go to him.

"Jess got himself in a fist fight down at the saloon last night!" her husband returned testily. "Damn near got his arm blown off by a touchy Mexican with a shotgun when Jess started accusing him of cheating at cards. He's in the infirmary now where Doc Sutter is sewing his arm up." He looked at Brianne and then away. "Damn!" he muttered beneath his breath. "I can't spare another Ranger with those renegades about!"

"Hell, you can spare one and you damn well know it!" Ty answered him, coming in unexpectedly through the door. "I just saw Jess. He's not in bad shape. He can stay here at the fort and Ella'll be glad for the company." He gave her a quick grin.

"But what about Mrs. Nolan?" Walker asked tightly.

Ty shrugged nonchalantly. "I'll take her, Captain."

Both Ella's and Brianne's heads shot up in surprise.

"But, Ty, you're too damn good a scout to—"

"Someone's got to take her, Jim, and next to Jess, you know I know the territory between here and San Antonio a lot better than the other recruits." He looked around at the group, as though challenging them to offer an alternative. "The lady wants to get to her husband. The ride shouldn't take over four or five days there and another three or four back. That's just about a week. You can set a rendezvous and I'll meet you there."

"And what if the trip takes longer for some reason?" Walker asked.

"If I'm not at the rendezvous point by sundown, I'll make for the fort and meet you when you get back." He grinned mischievously. "That'll give me time to convince your wife how truly charming I really am."

Captain Walker sat down in one of the chairs, considering the possibilities. It was clear to Brianne that he didn't want to lose his best scout to what he must consider a completely unnecessary trip escorting a lady to her husband. And yet, who else was there that knew the territory as well, or that he could trust as completely? After a few minutes, he sighed wearily.

"All right, Ty, you know damn well you've got me. You're the only one who can take her now, although I hate to lose you this week."

Brianne felt conspicuously to blame and started to protest that she could wait another week or so, but Walker, once he'd made up his mind, stuck to his decision.

Ella got up and busily began to prepare things for the journey, packing food for lunch and salt beef and pork for the rest of the journey. Brianne came over to help, leaving the two men to discuss the possible rendezvous.

"You're not happy about Ty taking me to San Antonio, are you?" Brianne guessed.

"No," Ella answered truthfully, "but there's not much I can do about it. I always feel better, knowing Ty is riding with James. He is a good scout and he's ridden with James for the last two years. Then, too, I worry about you two alone on the prairie—" She let her words trail off so that Brianne wasn't positive of their meaning. Did she mean she was worried about them because of the Indian threat or because of their mutual attraction for each other?

She could think of nothing to reassure her, except to

say, "Everything will be all right, Ella, please. Here," and she took a letter from the pocket of her dress, "I've written a letter to my family, explaining everything that's happened to me. I would appreciate you sending it by the first post coach that comes through here." She thought about the unforeseen complication of pregnancy, but decided not to divulge her suspicions to Ella: it would only cause her further worry. Instead, she reached over and hugged Ella who returned the hug, admonishing her to be careful.

"You ready?" Ty asked, getting up from the table and putting his hat on his head.

Brianne nodded, thanking the Walkers one last time for their hospitality. Then she turned away hurriedly and walked out into the lavender dawn with Ty behind her. Outside, two horses were waiting with saddles and another with supplies, to which Ty added the food that Ella had prepared. Silently, he helped Brianne to mount her horse, giving her a leg up.

"You got everything?" he asked, as he swung himself up in the saddle.

Brianne nodded. She'd tied her clothing into a bundle, the easier to carry on the packhorse, and Captain Walker had already seen to it. Ella had thoughtfully given her a hat to keep the sun off her head and neck and Brianne pushed the thong under her chin almost defiantly. "I'm ready," she said.

Ty turned his horse and Brianne did the same, the pack horse following docilely behind, led by a rope tied to Brianne's saddle horn. The two figures passed under the gate of the fort and into the town of Gonzales which was still asleep for the most part at this hour. Riding through the main street in the town, Brianne realized that she had never even come here since she'd been at the fort. How odd: it had been almost as though time had stopped while she'd been safe and protected inside the walls of the fort. Now, here she was, riding out of that security and facing the unknown again on the wild prairies of Texas. And what was waiting for her at the end of this trip, she wondered. Would Pierce still be in San Antonio, waiting for her, welcoming her with open arms and words of love? She shivered, not wishing to think of the alternative.

Chapter Twenty-three

EVERYWHERE, IN EVERY DIRECTION, AS FAR AS THE EYE could see, the Texas prairie stretched its brown and green terrain in endless miles that seemed to soak up the heat from the sun and reflect it back on the two lone riders. For the hundredth time, it seemed to Brianne, since they'd left the fort at Gonzales that morning, she asked Ty Warren how much longer before they would stop for the night.

Ty turned around on his horse in front of her and wiped his bandanna over his forehead. "Another hour at most, Brianne," he answered.

"That's what you said the last time!" Brianne objected, feeling her shoulders beginning to slump despite her resolution that she would not allow herself to weaken. "I feel as though we've been riding for hours!"

"We have," he affirmed. He stopped to allow her to catch up with him as he scoured the land surrounding them with alert eyes. When she stopped beside him, vainly trying to tuck stray wisps of hair underneath the straw hat, he leveled a look at her from dark-blue eyes. "I thought you would be in a hurry to catch up with your husband in San Antonio."

Brianne lowered her eyes uneasily, not wishing him to see the turmoil in them at the thought of Pierce. "I'm just tired," she hedged. "I guess I've not been used to riding a horse for a long time."

He smiled understandingly. "There should be a water hole up ahead a few more miles. There's some small hills around it where we can find shelter for the night in case it rains."

Brianne looked up in surprise at the white-blue of the sky. There wasn't but a few wispy clouds streaked across the western horizon. "Rain?" she questioned. "Why, it must be at least ninety degrees out here and hardly a cloud in sight!"

Ty shrugged, took off his hat and swatted it against his leg to loosen the dust from it. "There's rain in the air," he avowed. "I can smell it, so can the horses. I'll be surprised if we don't get a downpour by morning."

"Oh dear, will that set us back some?"

He looked at her. "Do you mind riding in the rain?"

She returned his look. "I can do it, if you can!"

He laughed out loud and replaced his hat on his head. "Honey, I could ride through a Texas twister if I had to. Didn't I tell you we Texas Rangers are impervious to the elements?"

She smiled. "I forgot."

They started their horses up again companionably, keeping to a steady pace. After a few minutes, Brianne looked curiously at Ty, a question worrying her. "You didn't want to take me to San Antonio, did you, Ty?"

He kept his eyes straight ahead. "No, I didn't."

"Why not?"

"Jess was a better man for the job. He knows the territory around here better than anyone else in the outfit. He's an Indian fighter from way back and besides, he's the best cook we had." He let a moment of silence slip by, then added, "And I wasn't sure how I'd feel being alone with you for four days on the trail, Brianne."

She colored, understanding him perfectly since she had felt the same way. "Captain Walker assured me that all of his men were perfect gentlemen," she asserted rather primly. "I assume that means you, too."

He looked at her and grinned wolfishly. "Now, just what the hell did he mean by that?" he asked her, and she wasn't sure if he was teasing or not. "Did he mean that I'd go behind a bush if I felt the need to relieve myself instead of doing it out in the open, or did he mean that when it came time to bed down for the night, I'd be sure not to bed *you* down instead of the horses?''

Brianne's color deepened. "I would think both of the above would fit," she returned tartly.

He smiled enigmatically at her and spurred his horse a little, leaving her behind. Frustrated, she was obliged to spur her own mount, although it was hampered somewhat by the slower pack horse behind it. He continued ahead of her, topping a small rise and stopping to look around, as though to make sure that everything was in order. He looked over his shoulder at her, waiting.

"Why did you decide to go off in front of me?" she asked as she reached the spot where he was waiting on his horse.

He pushed back his hat and eyed her almost comically. "I get tired of women's chatter," he declared with a grin. "When I'm out in the open spaces, I like to hear what's going on around me without interruptions."

She straightened up in a huff. "Do you mean I'm expected to keep my mouth shut the entire trip?"

"I suppose that's too much to expect," he admitted, leaning away from her fist as she reached over to swipe at him unexpectedly. "Heh, now, settle down, Brianne. Don't get riled after we've only gone twenty miles."

"Is that all?" she asked, disheartened, although her turquoise eyes still twinkled angrily.

"Come on, let's get going or we won't be making that water hole 'til after dark. That's when the animals come down to drink and I don't want any cougars sneaking up on us while we're drinking." He started his horse again and Brianne could do nothing but follow although her thighs and bottom were beginning to ache.

The sun had slipped behind one of the rises as they finally reached the water hole that Ty had spoken of. He scouted the area, leaving Brianne in a protected place, to make sure there were no dangerous animals lurking about. When he waved her forward, Brianne spurred her mount eagerly, seeing the clear water of the spring-fed pool receiving the last pink and gold rays of the sun.

She slipped off her horse and went to douse her face in the cool water, glad of it against her burning skin. She would have loved to strip down naked and immerse her entire body, but realized, with Ty hovering about, it wouldn't be wise. She contented herself with wetting her kerchief and wiping it around her neck and throat. Some yards away, she saw Ty setting up their campfire, settling the horses and getting out food for their evening meal.

She walked up to him, her hat dangling by its chin strap down her back. Ty looked up and saw the sunburn on her face which only served to make her turquoise eyes that much deeper. The short sleeves of her dress had allowed the sun to burn her arms too.

"You're going to be a little uncomfortable tonight," he pointed out matter-of-factly.

She looked down at her arms and shrugged ruefully. After a moment, she hunkered down next to him, watching him set the fire to going. "What can I do to help?" she asked.

"Do you know how to cook over a campfire?" he asked skeptically.

She nodded. "I learned the hard way, while Mandy and I were stranded out on the prairie. I'm not the best, but it'll be edible, and I'm sure I could do a better job than you!" Her eyes sparkled defiantly.

"I'm sure you could, Brianne," he agreed without argument. He rummaged in the supply bags for cornmeal and strips of salted beef. "Bless Ella, look," he said suddenly, "she packed fresh fruit for us, blueberries and peaches!"

Brianne felt her mouth watering and she hurriedly laid the strips of meat into a fry pan to get them sizzling over the fire. She mixed the cornmeal with water to make a pasty johnny cake, and even added a few of the blueberries as an extra special touch. Ty made the coffee, and it wasn't long before they were sitting back against their saddles, enjoying the food that seemed even tastier out in the open like this.

"Delicious," Ty pronounced when he'd scraped the last of his cornmeal from his tin plate. "You really are pretty useful to have around, Brianne. Here I was thinking I'd have to be waiting on you hand and foot! A spoiled plantation girl like yourself!" He grinned to take the sting out of his words.

"And here I thought I'd be stuck with some illiterate cowboy who wouldn't know how to compliment a lady on her cooking if he tried," she returned pertly, standing up to clear away the cooking things.

Ty watched her speculatively as she stretched languorously, then hopped up to get water from the pool so that she could do up the dishes. After that was finished, they sat around the glowing embers of the fire, Ty smoking a cheroot and Brianne hugging her knees, her thoughts far away in Louisianna, wondering how her parents and brother were doing.

"My brother's supposed to be getting married in October," she offered. "I was hoping to be back home in time for the wedding—"

Ty shrugged. "You might still make it."

She couldn't help the sigh that escaped her.

"Oh, come on now," Ty said, leaning toward her, "don't tell me I'm that bad a company!"

She shook her head, smiling a little. "No, it's not you, Ty. I'm just feeling a little homesick, I guess."

"Don't think about it," he advised her. "Just enjoy the prairie. Listen to the sounds and relax."

"You really do love this kind of life, don't you?" she asked softly after a moment.

He nodded.

"Do you still wish you hadn't had to come with me?" she wondered.

He chuckled. "You're beginning to chatter too much again!"

She was quiet for a few minutes, leaning back against the saddle, until she realized that her eyes were beginning to close. She yawned and sat up, eyeing him questioningly. "What are the sleeping arrangements?" She looked around. "I don't see a tent set up anywhere."

He laughed. "You sleep out in the open while you're on the trail with me, Brianne. Here's a blanket. You can use your saddle for a pillow, or one of your dresses."

"But—is it safe?" she wondered, glancing around anxiously, as he handed her the rough blanket.

"I'm here," he said quietly, laying a soothing hand on her shoulder.

She looked up at him, trying to smile, though she wasn't quite reassured. His hand on her shoulder was warm and comforting and, she told herself, he had surely done this a hundred times before. He was used to sleeping out in the open: probably kept one eye open all the time. "All right, then. Good-night."

He took his hand from her shoulder and pushed his saddle closer to hers. In a moment, he'd wrapped himself in a blanket, pushed his hat down over his forehead and was silent. Lying in close proximity to him, Brianne could hear the regular cadence of his breathing and wondered at how easy it was for him to fall asleep. She was positive it would be hours before she could do the same, even though her eyes felt like they had lead weights on top of them.

A hand brushed her cheek and then settled on her shoulder where it shook her gently. Brianne rolled over, too tired to get up. Her bones felt as though they'd been on a hard slab of rock all night and she was positive that every piece of flesh on her body was bruised. She shook the hand from her shoulder and tried to get as comfortable as possible, fully prepared to continue the pleasant dream she'd been having.

A sudden smack on her bottom roused her completely and she started up, turning over to eye Ty Warren half murderously. "What do you think you're doing?" she demanded, her voice croaking from sleep.

"Waking you up," he said confidently. "It worked, didn't it?"

She glared at him for a moment. Then, with resignation, she got to her feet and rubbed at her sore bottom. "It wasn't bad enough that I had to sleep on the hard ground all night," she accused him sorrowfully. "Now I won't be able to sit a horse!"

"You'll be fine, once you're back in the saddle," Ty returned positively. He looked up at the sky, which had become a leaden gray overnight and looked as though it would pour down rain any moment. He looked back at Brianne, as though to say I told you so, then went to saddle the horses while she chewed at a piece of last night's johnny cake.

By the time they started off again, the rain had begun in little sprinkles. Brianne was almost grateful for it against her skin. They trotted along steadily, Ty glancing up at the sky now and then while Brianne concentrated on anything but the soreness of her bottom against the leather of the saddle.

It didn't take long for the rain to come down in earnest and soon it was pouring soddenly over both of them, soaking their clothing.

"We'll have to find some shelter," Ty said, moving his horse next to Brianne's. "This rain isn't going to stop very soon. I'm afraid we'll have to lose a day."

She nodded, feeling a greater urge to get out of the downpour whether it meant losing time to San Antonio or not. She pointed ahead to a copse of tall trees, bent and twisted by the winds that occasionally blew over the prairies. "There's shelter among those trees!" she said.

He shook his head. "If lightning starts, that's the worst place to be. I think there's a shelf of rock a few miles ahead over one of those ridges. There's plenty of caves in there where we can wait out the rain."

He broke his horse into a canter and Brianne followed

willingly, eager to get out of the wet drizzle. Half an hour later, they were both dismounted as Ty scanned the rocks ahead of them, searching for a suitable place to shelter 'til the next morning. "Up there," he pointed to a hollowed out place in the rocks. "It's high enough that we won't have to worry about wild animals. We'll have to take the horses around the ridge and tie them under that over-hang of rock. They'll be safe there."

Brianne resigned herself to the long climb through the rain. Once they had secured the horses underneath the rock, Ty led her along the narrow ledge to the cave he had spotted before. He made a hurried fire, then went back to the horses for provisions.

"You'll have to take those clothes off," he pointed out, "unless you want to take a chill. I brought your other things, but they've gotten soaked through the bag. At least the blanket is relatively dry on the underside; you can wrap yourself in that."

"But—I can't take off all my clothes," Brianne began in alarm.

"Dammit, now's not the time to worry about whether I'm a gentleman or not," he said quickly. "I don't want a sick woman on my hands for another sixty miles. You'll either strip down, Brianne, or I'll take off every stitch myself!"

She knew he meant it and, after directing him to turn around, she took off the sopping clothes and laid them out on the rocks of the walls to dry as best they could, keeping the blanket tight around her. When she turned around, she saw that he was still dressed.

"What about you?" she asked. "You're just as wet as I was. I don't want a sick man on my hands for another sixty miles," she mimicked him.

He grinned boyishly. "Hell, I'm used to being wet. Didn't I tell you we Rangers are impervious to the elements?"

"Why, that's not fair that you—"

"There's no fairness to it," he agreed, "but nevertheless, you'll be dry and your clothes will be too in a few hours. I'll have to suffer through the dampness." He eyed her appreciatively in her blanket which she'd pulled around in front of her and was holding tightly, although her legs were bare nearly to her knees. "A mighty pretty sight for a man's eyes," he commented admiringly.

She backed away a little, watching him warily. "Now, Ty, don't you start getting any ideas," she warned, seeing him take a step closer to her.

"Married or not, you are mighty appetizing," he said softly, stepping up in front of her until he was almost touching her.

"Ty—"

Suddenly, she heard, close by, a peculiar clicking sound, like a rattle. She sensed the stiffness that suddenly ran the entire length of the man next to her. Taking a shallow breath, Ty whispered, "Don't move, Brianne. Whatever you do, stay perfectly still!"

"What—?"

"Quiet," he said.

Brianne heard the rattling noise come closer, felt Ty's hand go slowly from her shoulder to the pistol he wore on his gunbelt. He seemed as tense as a coiled spring and she held her breath, waiting to see what he would do. Moving her head just a little, she looked down to the floor of the cave and saw the thick-bodied snake, its coiled body waving gently at the head.

Without thinking, fear drove her to move and she jumped to the side, screaming at the same time. Ty stepped in front of her, pulled out his gun and fired, causing a blistering echo in the cave. The rattling stopped.

"You killed it?" Brianne whispered faintly, hardly caring that she'd dropped the blanket to the floor of the cave and now stood naked in front of him.

She saw Ty nod grimly. She half expected him to come and comfort her after the ordeal, but instead, without looking at her, he stumbled backward to the floor of the cave, leaning up against one of the rock formations.

"What—what happened?" she asked, dreading the answer.

"The damned thing got me," Ty breathed, already pulling off one of his boots. "Come here, Brianne, you've got to help me now."

She obeyed out of fear, kneeling down and helping him to roll up his trouser leg. She could see on the back of his calf, a bright red mark, beaded with blood, already darkening ominously. She looked up, awaiting instructions, noticing the sweat popping out of his brow.

"You'll have to cut it," he said, "and suck out as much of the poison as you can." He pulled off the neckerchief around his throat and handed it to her. "Here, tie this just below my knee, not too tight. You'll have to make two diagonal cuts across the wound and suck as much of the poison as you can. The knife is here, in my other boot." He moved his other leg and she saw the thick handle of the knife showing just above the top.

Cautiously, she pulled the knife out, her eyes widening at the long, curving blade of the Bowie knife. Desperately, she gazed up at Ty, whose eyes were closed as he breathed shallowly. "Ty, I can't—"

"Do it, Brianne," he whispered, "or you may have to—find your own way to—to San Antonio."

Fear made her hand tremble and she willed it to be steady as she leaned over his leg and laid the blade of the knife against the wound. Taking a deep breath, knowing she had to do it, or the poison might kill him, she cut into the flesh one way, than turned the knife and cut across the other way. She felt him wince, and it took all her strength to lean down and suck at the wound, tasting the warm blood on her lips and spitting it out onto the rocky floor of the cave. She continued for a few moments, until she felt his hand touching her hair, signaling that she had done enough.

"Cold c-compress," he whispered, clutching at her arm, his fingers sliding ineffectually to the ground. He was already beginning to shake and Brianne loosened the tourniquet a little before reaching for the petticoat she had only discarded minutes before. Quickly, she ripped off a long strip and went to the mouth of the cave to let the rain soak it. When she returned, Ty was shivering all over and she quickly tied the wet cloth to his leg with another strip of cotton. She took the neckerchief from his leg, hoping she was doing the right thing, wishing he would wake up and tell her what to do.

But he seemed to have passed out now and she realized she would have to make the rest of the decisions herself. She gazed at him grimly, knowing that the wet clothes would have to come off. "Well," she said softly to herself, "you might be impervious to the elements, Texas Ranger, but a rattlesnake is something else again!" She proceeded to undress him, taking as little time as she could, feeling his brow beginning to burn with fever.

When he was completely naked, she covered him with the blanket she'd used to wrap around herself, passing by the dead snake and shivering uncontrollably. She tucked the wrap around him, stoking the fire with the few bits of dry tinder he'd kept in his saddlebags for such an occasion. She didn't feel cold in the least, having dried off by now.

Ty, though, had begun to shiver in earnest, rolling about beneath the blanket, pushing it off in his delirium. Anxiously, Brianne recovered him and, when he'd pushed the blanket off another time, she laid down beside him, covering them both, trying to warm his shivering flesh with her own.

Slow tears rolled down her cheeks as she couldn't help thinking of the sorry situation they were in. Here they were in some rocky cave, with Ty sick with fever and no medicine to give him for it. She could only hope that the poison had not traveled too far up his bloodstream before she'd been able to suck it out. She had no idea where to go for help, no idea really how to tend to such a sickness. She put her arms around him, drawing his head down to her breast, letting her tears spill unheeded onto his hair.

"Oh, Pierce," she said wistfully, "how I wish you were with me!"

Chapter Twenty-four

THE NIGHT PASSED SLOWLY FOR BRIANNE AS SHE LAY HALF awake throughout the long hours, listening to the rain, getting up occasionally to stumble through the darkness to add more fuel to the faltering fire, and trying to keep Ty as warm as possible. There were times when he would push against her, hurting her with his fingers as they squeezed at her arms and making her jump from the heat emanating from his skin. She would unclasp his fingers and put her arms around his shoulders despite the heat that nearly burned her.

Occasionally, she would doze off and her dreams would be filled with memories of Pierce: gently mocking her in the rose garden at Avonlea, daring her to get up and walk when she'd fallen into the stream, and making exquisite love to her on their wedding night. She would always awaken after this last dream, her cheeks as hot as Ty's fevered body and her mind longing passionately for the only man she knew she would ever love. But then it would be time to stir the fire or settle the blanket more tightly around Ty, and the dreams would be dispelled most effectively, leaving only a pleasurable tinge at the back of her mind.

When morning finally came, bringing an abrupt end to the rain, Brianne got up and checked the pan she had put out on the ledge to catch water. It was brimming over and she brought it back, pouring some into Ty's canteen for drinking water. She poured a little into a tin cup and pressed it to his lips, relieved when she was able to get him to drink some. He lay back, his head rolling uncomfortably on the rocky surface of the cave.

Laying her hand gently on his forehead, she could feel that it was still burning. She soaked another strip of her petticoat into a small puddle that had formed in a crevice in the ledge, not wishing to use up all the clean water, and pressed it against his fevered brow, wetting it again and again when the heat from his body continued to dry it up.

She slipped on her dress which had dried a little in the night, although it still felt dampish against her skin. Steeling herself against choking nausea, she picked up the dead snake and threw it outside the cave, deriving a small satisfaction from watching it roll down the muddy side of the hill. Briskly, she set about tidying up the cave as well as she was able, stirring the fire and making herself some hot coffee with a little of the clean rainwater she'd collected. She laid out Ty's clothing along the rocks, disgusted when a huge, hairy spider scampered out of her way and wiggled into one of the cracks in the rocks. But, she thought, she wasn't about to let all this beat her! She'd done well enough so far, surprising herself at her own ability to stay calm. If this was part of being a pioneer woman, she thought with determination, then, by God, she'd make a good show of it!

The morning hours slipped by slowly as Brianne tended to her patient, striving for patience when he threw off the blanket and spilled water over the front of her skirt. At noon, she fixed a meal of salted beef and cornmeal mush, trying to get Ty to eat a little. She was gratified when she got two whole spoonfuls of mush down him, then aghast when he promptly threw it back up.

"Oh, Ty!" she sighed, stripping off more of her petticoat and dipping it in the cave water to clean up the mess he'd made. Tiredly, she sat down on a rock and nibbled at the beef, washing it down with more coffee. Was he going to get better, she wondered, wishing she had more skill with medicine. Perhaps there was something she should be doing that she wasn't. Hesitantly, she lifted the covers off him to check the snakebite wound. It was still quite red, but not as swollen, she thought with renewed hope. She changed the makeshift bandage and tucked the blanket around him once more.

During the afternoon, she thought he must be getting better, for she was able to get more of the cornmeal down him, this time keeping it down. He opened his eyes, trying to focus, then closed them again so that she had no chance to discern whether or not he had passed out again or was sleeping naturally. By evening, all her hope vanished as he began tossing restlessly again, his brow burning once more.

Determinedly, she continued changing the cloths on his forehead and leg until the water was nearly gone. She had enough left in the canteen to make coffee in the morning and give him a few more swallows, but if he didn't get better, she would be forced to leave the cave to look for water. The prospect dampened her confidence somewhat, but she told herself she would be able to deal with that when the time came.

When exhaustion finally overcame her, she lay down beside him as she'd done the night before, holding his body close to her own, having removed the damp dress, knowing she'd be warmer without it. Softly, she brushed at the moist shock of hair that fell over his forehead as gently as a mother with her child. She stopped suddenly, realizing the action would have been totally foreign to her only a few months ago. That old Brianne O'Neill, the one who had thrown a tantrum at the county cotillion, would never have been able to handle this situation, she thought with considerable pride at how well she managed it now. *That* Brianne would have sat on a rock and cried and wailed at fate for having done this to her. She would have cursed God and Pierce Nolan for bringing this all about and laid none of the blame on herself.

Brianne found herself smiling in the darkness, remembering that other girl with a kind of mature indulgence.

What else could have been expected of her? She had been brought up by parents who'd always seen to her every wish, servants that hurried to her commands and young men who'd fawned over her, admiring her for her beauty and her charm.

My God, she thought, if it hadn't been for Pierce, I might have actually married one of those men! The thought caused her to frown, imagining herself the mistress of some plantation manor, as silly and spoiled a wife as she had been a daughter.

Yes, Pierce had been right to call her vain and shallow then, but now, she thought proudly, she had proven to herself that she could be exactly the kind of wife Pierce wanted. Ty was going to get well and guide her to San Antonio, and if Pierce wasn't there, then she'd just continue the chase until she found him and gave him that smile he'd requested on the Galveston docks, and much more besides.

She hugged Ty next to her, willing him to get better. And after several hours of restless turning, he finally seemed to settle down. Brianne felt his forehead, finding it suddenly, blessedly cool, sweat popping out all over his entire body. Her eyes felt so heavy, she knew it would be impossible for her to keep them open and she allowed herself to drift into a restless sleep.

She awoke groggily in the morning. She'd been dreaming of Pierce and was aware with a sudden rush of emotion that she was on her back and that Ty was lying half on top of her, his arm held possessively across her breast, while one of his knees nudged against her hip. His body was cool and, when she turned to look at him, she saw that his blue eyes were open, watching her with slow-dawning realization of the situation. She felt his hand tense against her breast, then cup it softly, before sliding away.

"You're better," she whispered, reaching a hand to push back the fringe of hair that had fallen forward on his brow.

He nodded. "I'm thirsty."

She slipped out from the blanket, pulled on her dress, and brought him a cup of cool water to drink. He drained it and watched her for a moment, with an almost-puzzled look. "How did you manage to save me, my beautiful lady?"

"You told me what to do," she answered.

"I did? I must confess I don't remember much after shooting the snake and then seeing the blanket slip off you."

She turned around quickly to see him grinning at her in the old, cocky way. She smiled back, unable to help herself. "Well, I've seen quite a bit of you too," she answered saucily.

His grin widened. "And did you like what you saw?"

"Well, except for a few old scars, it was rather nice, I admit," she answered, her eyes sparkling, she was so glad to see that he was going to be all right.

"I suppose I could say I was lucky, being bit by that rattler," he grinned ruefully, looking beneath the blanket to where she had bound his wound with clean cloth. "It's probably the only way I'm ever going to get you to sleep with me, isn't it?" He looked up at her, a fleeting expression of regret passing over his face.

She looked away, biting her lip, her cheeks aflame. "A question like that doesn't deserve an answer," she whispered huskily.

He was silent a moment, then, "Well, I'm thanking you, Brianne, for all you did for me. I would never have thought you capable of it, I have to confess. Maybe you're made of sterner stuff than I thought." He gave her a sincere smile. "You are a brave lady."

"Thank you," she said, recalling suddenly another time that a different man had called her thus. It seemed a million years ago that Pierce had told her how brave he thought she was.

"You're miles away," Ty said softly, watching the glow

in her turquoise eyes and the way her mouth softened irresistibly.

She looked down at him and smiled. "I just realized, Ty, that I'm pretty pleased with myself right now."

"You've got every right to be damned proud!" he confirmed, pulling himself up to a sitting position, leaning against a formation of rocks behind him. "If your husband doesn't appreciate the kind of woman he's got for a wife, you can always come back to me, honey, and I'll show you what real appreciation is," he promised, his eyes twinkling.

She eyed him boldly, hands on hips. "I'm sure you would, Ty Warren," she laughed. And then, changing her mood, "Do you feel like eating something?"

He nodded. "You. But if I can't have first choice, then I'll take whatever you can round up out of those sacks."

Brianne set about making a meal, then strode to the edge of the cave to look down below. "Is there water close by?" she asked, looking back at Ty. "We'll need some fresh to make more coffee."

He nodded. "On the other side of the ridge there's a small stream. It dries up sometimes in summer, but after this rain, it should be flowing. You can walk to it around the top of this cave and down the other side. The horses will need watering too, but they'll have to wait until I can hobble around a little better."

"How long will that take?" she wondered.

He shrugged. "Swelling should be going down. I'd say we'd be able to leave by tomorrow morning."

She sighed, hating the delay, but knowing it wouldn't be wise to push him.

Later that evening, as she tended the fire, having brought fresh wood, the driest she could find, Brianne thought about Pierce again, finding it nearly impossible to keep him out of her thoughts. She was glad she hadn't been plagued by any nausea in the last few days and wondered if, perhaps, she could be wrong about being pregnant. She couldn't decide whether she'd be relieved or not. She could hear the soft sounds of Ty's breathing. He'd fallen asleep right after they'd eaten their evening meal, and she was glad he was getting plenty of rest. They'd have to start off again in the morning if they didn't want to run out of food before they reached San Antonio.

Restlessly, she fidgeted with the fire, then stood up to take a few turns to get her legs stretched out. Finally, she realized there was nothing else to do but get some sleep herself. She went over to where Ty was sleeping and lifted the edge of the blanket carefully to check the binding around the snakebite. Then, carefully, she eased in next to him, keeping her dress on this time, and tucking the blanket around them both. Instinctively, he turned in his sleep and put one arm around her, forcing her head into the hollow of his arm. After a moment of hesitation, Brianne relaxed, telling herself that very soon it would be Pierce holding her like this while they slept.

The following morning, they both awoke simultaneously. Brianne looked over and smiled at Ty, stretching vigorously to awaken her stiffened muscles. "How do you feel?" she wanted to know.

"Like thanking you properly for what you did for me," he answered, taking advantage of her position to pull her closer to him. He reached down and kissed her gently, then released her. "See, I told you I could be a perfect gentleman," he offered, watching her scramble to her feet.

She threw him a dubious look. "I really think it's time for you to get some clothes on, sir," she said, having just been made aware of his nakedness when he'd held her. She drew out the buckskin shirt and breeches which she'd washed in the stream the day before and dried outside in the sun. She'd folded them neatly last night, anticipating the need for them this morning. "Here are your clothes. Shall I turn around?"

He laughed. "No need, honey. I'm sure you've seen all there is to see in the last couple of days." He threw off the blanket and proceeded to pull on his trousers.

Brianne quickly turned to busy herself with breakfast. By the time she was finished, he was dressed again, although he'd left his boots off until they were ready to leave.

"The boots might cause the wound to swell again because of their tightness," he explained. "You'll have to help me with them and, hopefully, we can get another twenty miles in today. The horses have had such a long rest, we might get thirty out of them, but I'm not promising anything," he added quickly, seeing the expectant look in her eyes. "If we can get thirty miles today, we should see San Antonio by twilight tomorrow."

"Tomorrow!" she gasped, her face eager.

He held up his hand. "Now, remember, I'm not promising anything!"

She shook her head, but the eagerness remained on her face as they went about breaking camp and resaddling the horses. Brianne was obliged to help Ty with his boots and she could see him wince as the top went over the wound on his leg.

"I could cut it," she said thoughtfully. "Just slit the top a little so that it wouldn't feel so tight."

He nodded, grimacing against the discomfort. Brianne took the heavy Bowie knife once more, testing its weight in her palm, before slipping the blade under the top of his boot and ripping upward. A neat slash resulted and she could see the relief pass over his face.

"Feels better," he declared and stood up, testing the boot against the floor of the cave. "We're ready then?" He looked at her, his blue eyes dark and fierce for a moment, as though he almost regretted leaving this isolated spot, knowing that today would only bring her closer to the husband that stood between them.

"Yes," she answered, looking back at him steadily.

They went outside and began making their way back

down the rocky ridge to the prairie floor below. Once remounted on their horses, they swung into a mile-eating gallop, both wanting to make up for lost time. After an hour or two, they were forced to slow their gait because of the pack horse, although Ty continued to canter ahead every now and then to scout the countryside. He'd seen pony prints in the earth, still damp from the deluge they'd received earlier, and so he advised Brianne that they must proceed cautiously, since the only kind of ponies that made shoeless prints were usually Indian ponies.

"Do you think we'll actually run into some?" she demanded, feeling more nervous than she liked to admit.

He shrugged. "The prints are fairly fresh. My guess is that they rode through here on their way back to the plains in the West. It might not be the same ones who we thought were burning the farmhouses. Still, we have to keep a sharp eye out."

She nodded in total agreement. At the noon hour, they stopped to eat, taking up very little time as Ty was anxious to keep moving. He'd seen more pony prints and wanted to make another sheltered spot where they could camp for the night. He didn't like to think of meeting Indians out in the open with a female with him. There'd been over a hundred women carried off last year by the Comanches, and, although he wasn't sure that these prints belonged to Comanche ponies, a woman with Brianne's coloring would surely tempt the most complacent savage.

"There looks to be two or three of them," Ty explained to Brianne. "They're moving the same direction we are, maybe a day or two ahead of us. We'd better settle down our pace if we don't want to run up on their heels."

"What if we do meet them?" she asked, her turquoise eyes large and frightened.

He patted the pistols on either side, on his hips. "I've got my Colt pistols," he assured her, "and a rifle." He glanced at her. "You don't know how to shoot do you?"

She shook her head. "It wasn't one of the things expected of the daughter of a plantation owner," she answered.

He shrugged. "Then if we see anything, you lean low over your horse and head for the nearest bit of shelter you can find, even if it's just a clump of mesquite. Keep your head down and don't come out until you hear me calling you." His blue eyes bored into hers. "Do you understand me?"

She nodded. "Yes, I'll head for the nearest shelter."

They continued to ride, keeping to a slow trot, Brianne aware of the tense alertness in the man who rode beside her. She wondered if his leg was bothering him, but decided against asking. She knew it must pain him, but he wasn't about to let that get in the way of his scouting activities. She hardly noticed the heat, although the sun was shining with a vengeance after the previous rain.

After a few more miles, she could see a bluish clump of rocks on the horizon and realized that that must be what he had been making for. The sun indicated it was late afternoon already and she longed to ask him how far he thought they'd come.

"Ty?"

"Quiet!" he answered, his eyes scanning the ground in front of him. He raised his head and squinted at the far-off rocks. His head swiveled to the side and he could see another mass of rocks situated to the north, not as far away. He gave Brianne a serious look and pointed to the rocks. "Start angling your mount toward that rock formation," he instructed quickly. "I'll follow you."

"But, why—?"

"I have a pretty good idea that those Indians are up ahead in those rocks. If they've seen us, they must know that we're making straight for them. They won't give us a chance to make cover. When I tell you, you push your horse to a gallop."

Brianne nodded wordlessly, her heart in her throat. She cantered her horse to the right, catching the rope of

the pack horse in her hand. She stole a look backward at
Ty and saw the look on his face which conveyed an utter
absence of fear, as though he were sure of his ability to
save both her and himself from danger. His lack of fear
made her own that much less.

She risked a glance to her left and her eyes widened as
she saw a small cloud of dust behind a team of riders.
They were too far away to be able to tell what they were,
but, from the look on Ty's face, she realized they must be
the Indians. As though to punctuate her conclusion, two
high yells were sent into the hot, still air.

"Move!" Ty yelled and Brianne leaned low over her
horse and urged it into a gallop. She heard him right
behind her and felt the tug on her hand of the rope of the
packhorse. Suddenly, it slipped from her grasp and she
stopped for a moment to see what had happened.

As she turned, she saw Ty whirl his horse briefly in the
direction of the approaching Indians, sight through his
rifle and fire a shot. Then he turned back, his expression
exasperated when he realized she had stopped to watch
him.

"Get going!" he yelled. He leaned down and swatted
her horse on the rump.

Brianne felt the horse jump beneath her and then she
was once more lying low over its neck as it went at
breakneck speed, with her trying to direct it toward the
sheltering rocks. As she came nearer, she realized that
they were little more than rocky outcroppings with a few
boulders strewn among them. Nevertheless, she rode
straight for them and, once there, she instinctively
jumped down off the horse and pulled him around to a
clump of mesquite where she tied him down. Anxiously,
she turned to see Ty right behind her, the Indians quite
close now, as he jumped down and pulled her behind a
rock. From its cover, he pulled out both pistols and
sighted down one, waiting for the Indians to get closer.

The sound of the pistol going off made Brianne jump
and she craned her neck around the rock to see what had

happened. One of the Indians seemed to be dangling at a crazy angle from his horse while the other continued straight ahead.

"Get down!" She felt Ty's hand pushing on her shoulder so that she sprawled face first in the dust of the prairie. She felt a whoosh overhead and realized that the Indian pony must have jumped over their position and was now behind them. She heard Ty's other pistol go off and then heard a thud as two bodies collided.

Fearfully, she turned her head in the dust and saw Ty fighting hand to hand with the Indian, the latter hideously painted with streaks of red and black and yellow that splashed the entire upper portion of his body. She heard the men's grunting as they each tried to get a stranglehold on the other. Horrified, she saw the gleam of knives clutched tightly in sweaty fists, the blades catching the last rays of the sun.

Brianne stuck her fist in her mouth, watching with wide eyes as Ty twisted and turned beneath the Indian warrior, trying to gain the upper hand. So engrossed was she in the terrible death struggle being played out before her, that she had no idea the other Indian she had assumed was dead, was crawling stealthily toward her from behind.

"Aiyeee!"

The terrible cry caused her to turn around swiftly, feeling a strong hand on her arm, pulling her backward. Terrified, she looked into the dark eyes of the warrior, reading the pain hidden there caused from the bleeding wound in his side. But despite the pain, he was bent on pulling her away from the rocks, away from Ty!

Brianne screamed and kicked at him, trying to free her arm. Despite his wound, the Indian seemed much stronger than she and quite capable of pulling her out of the safety of the rocks. Relentlessly, Brianne struggled, twisting and turning in his grasp. It was her long hair that proved her undoing, for as she fought, it came loose from its pins and spread out on the ground, providing the

Indian an easier way of holding her. He grasped her hair and pulled her along the ground slowly, inching his way back into the open, closer to his pony.

Brianne saw the hatchet gleaming in one of his hands and closed her eyes, already feeling the coldness of the metal against her throat. Would he kill her right away or take her back to his encampment and put her through some horrible tortures? She continued to struggle despite the certainty that she was not going to be able to free herself.

She heard, suddenly, a whoosh-thump in the air above her head and, in the next moment, the Indian had released her hair and fallen forward next to her. Brianne lay for a moment, stunned, on the ground, afraid that if she tried to move, he might grab for her again.

"It's all right, Brianne," she heard Ty saying as he hovered over her anxiously. "Did he hurt you?"

She shook her head mutely. "Is—he dead?" she wondered, her throat dry.

Ty nodded. "I got him with my Bowie knife. The other one too." He smiled grimly. "They probably thought we were unwary travelers and would be an easy mark. You would have been a great prize to bring back to the camp, honey."

Brianne shivered and sat up, rubbing her scalp where the Indian had pulled on her hair. "Are you hurt?" she asked, seeing a trickle of blood beginning to soak his sleeve.

He shrugged. "Just a flesh wound. Come on, do you think you can help me drag the bodies behind these rocks?" He was already taking the legs of the Indian who had been trying to kidnap Brianne. "We shouldn't leave them lying out here in case they had friends who might be rendezvousing with them later."

Brianne stood up, feeling nausea building inside of her. Dizzily, she bent down to take one of the Indian's arms and caught sight of the gaping wound in his chest where the knife was still imbedded. Lurching sideways, she fell to her knees and began retching uncontrollably.

When it was over, she took off her neckerchief and wiped her mouth, glancing up to where Ty had dragged the body of the Indian to where he'd killed the other one. His glance questioned her and, when she nodded that she was all right, he set about covering up the bodies as best he could. He slapped the ponies smartly and they immediately took off to the south.

"Are you well enough to ride?" Ty asked with concern, coming back to where Brianne was standing uncertainly.

She nodded, although her stomach continued to roll. "I don't know what came over me," she gasped. "The blood and the heat—"

He patted her shoulder. "It's all right. Come on, let's make for those rocks to the West and we'll camp for the night. You need your rest."

Brianne bit her lip, wishing she could divulge her suspicions of her pregnancy, but deciding that it would just be one more burden for him. "What about you?" she questioned as he helped her back onto her mount and then went to retrieve the packhorse which was standing docilely in an open space, munching the sparse prairie grass. "Your leg?"

"We can see to that once we've found a place to rest." He mounted his own horse lithely, although she was positive she saw him wince as he hit the saddle. Then they were off again, heading toward the rocks where he told her there should be water and shelter.

"Do you think there might be other Indians?" she asked fearfully as they neared the rock formation.

He shook his head. "They would have attacked before now. Look," he pointed. "There's a natural spring here and we can rest comfortably under those trees. I think we'll be safe for the night."

She smiled, heartily hoping that that would be so. Once they'd made camp and seen to the horses, they sat

together companionably, eating an unhurried dinner.
After she'd finished, Brianne stood up and motioned to
Ty to take off his shirt. "I need to see that arm," she
advised him. "And your leg."

They moved closer to the small pool and while Ty took
off his shirt, Brianne wet a piece of cloth to wash the
wound as thoroughly as possible. It was, as he had told
her, merely a flesh wound, although long, and she
wished she had something beside water to treat it with.
His leg was swollen around the snake bite area and she
pressed a cool compress against it, gazing ruefully at the
remains of her petticoat.

"Let's hope we can get to San Antonio without further
need for bandages," she sighed.

"I never thought a woman's petticoat could be so
handy," Ty grinned, his eyes teasing. "I've always
thought they just got in the way of a man's pleasures."
He reached up to bring her head down to his, but she
pulled back, busying herself suddenly with rolling up the
rest of the petticoat. He frowned slightly. "I just wanted
to thank you, Brianne."

"For what?" she asked, laughing shakily. "You've
done all the work. I'm sure if you hadn't had me along,
you would have been in San Antonio long before now."

"Stop it, dammit! Why, I'd be dead from snake bite if
you hadn't been there! Brianne, don't sell yourself
short!" he urged, taking one of her hands in his and
holding it despite her resistance. "Of all the women I've
ever known, and believe me there've been a few, you're
the only one I'd ever have ride with me again. I know I
could count on you to keep your head and not act like
a—well, like a woman, for God's sake!"

She laughed a little. "Oh, Ty, if only my husband could
hear you saying that!"

Ty pressed the hand he still held. "Why, if he can't
appreciate you the way I've learned to, then you come
back to me. I promise you won't regret it!"

He sounded so earnest, sitting next to her in the

moonlight that she could almost believe him. Almost gaily, she reached over to tousle the bright, burnished hair which had grown longer since she'd first met him. "I'm afraid Ella was right," she sighed, "you are much too lovable, Ty Warren!"

He grinned, pleased at her about-face in temperament. "I try to be, ma'am."

They sat silently for a few more minutes, before Ty suggested they turn in for the night. "Tomorrow," he reminded her, "I want to try to make San Antonio before nightfall. The sooner I see you safe to the city, the easier I'll breathe at night."

Brianne nodded and followed him back to the small circle of fire, her mind leaping ahead to what tomorrow might bring.

Chapter Twenty-five

Twilight had just lent the darkening sky streaks of pale lavender and gold and pink when Brianne and Ty rode slowly into the bustling town of San Antonio. The city was an old one, built by the Spaniards more than a century before. It was a town of contrasts, of old brick and stone buildings that had stood for one hundred years or more standing beside newly constructed wooden structures that housed the settlers that were beginning to pour into this place and make it one of the most important cities in the new West. It was, as Pierce had told her before, the jumping-off place for Mexico or California, and the ranks of the army had swelled its population even more.

As they rode down the wide main street, Brianne could see horses tethered to hitching posts, a crowd of them in front of the saloons where tinny pianos and loud drunken laughter reached out into the street. An occasional buckboard passed them, and then a contingent of soldiers, looking hot and dusty, having just come in from the frontier, Ty explained to her.

They passed the monument to Texan pride and courage, the Alamo, which stood dark and lonely, weeds growing in patches here and there around its perimeter. Brianne saw Ty look at it almost longingly, as though wishing he had been fortunate enough to have died there with the rest of the one hundred or so martyrs to the higher cause of liberty.

"Is there a hotel nearby that's not too expensive?"

Brianne asked hopefully, as they passed a large two-and-a-half story building that boasted a brightly painted sign reading, *The Menger Hotel.* She could see inside as they passed the windows and sighed longingly at the sight of the solid Victorian splendor, where army officers sat conversing with travelers whose rich garments boasted wealth.

"That's too expensive I'm afraid for us," Ty said apologetically, seeing the direction of her gaze. "The only ones who can afford that are the rich *hacendados* up from Mexico to do business, or the ranchers from California on their way back East."

Brianne sighed, but told herself it really didn't matter where she stayed. She only wanted to find Pierce, and hoped that he hadn't already gone on to wherever it was he was to go.

Ty led her down a narrow street, away from the bright lights and laughter of the main street of the town. Here things were quieter, the buildings older. He dismounted in front of a two-story hotel, explaining that their accommodations were reasonable and clean, and that he had stayed here before on visits to the city. After tying their horses to the hitching post, they went inside to inquire after a room.

The accommodations proved to be more than adequate, Brianne thought, gazing wearily about her at the room the clerk had given her. A large comfortable-looking bed sat in one corner with a couch made of some bright material in the other. Brianne sank into a chair, then looked up questioningly as Ty followed her inside.

"I've ordered a bath for both of us," he grinned, divesting himself of the saddlebags he'd slipped around his neck. "Followed by a sumptuous feast when we're finished."

"But—you can't bathe in here!" Brianne objected. "Where is your room?"

"Honey, I'm afraid that even at these reasonable rates, we can only afford one room for the both of us. Now, I'm willing to sleep on the couch, but I'm not about to bunk down in the hall outside."

She knew it was useless to protest. She hadn't the heart to forbid him the use of the couch after all he had done for her. "All right," she agreed. "But you will be leaving tomorrow morning, won't you?"

He nodded. "I've already missed the rendezvous with Captain Walker, so I'll have to hightail it back to the fort and wait for him there."

Further conversation was interrupted by the appearance of two hefty men carrying copper tubs, followed by two women, each balancing two large buckets of steaming-hot water. When the tubs had been filled, it was all Brianne could do not to rip off the gown she wore, regardless of Ty's presence. Fortunately, there was a small leather screen that could be pushed between the two tubs and Brianne quickly slipped behind her side and undressed, knowing from the sounds of his movements, that he was doing the same.

"Jesus, that feels good!" Ty sighed.

Brianne agreed and sniffed the aroma of his cigar as he lit one up while soaking. She didn't care if her situation seemed incongruous. It was heaven to be soaking in the hot water after the hectic days she'd just passed.

After bathing, she waited for Ty to get clean trousers on while she slipped on her petticoat and camisole and drew a robe on over them. They sat down to a veritable feast of food which one of the maids brought in and set on the table. There were cold meats, salads, hot Mexican beans, and fruits. Chilled wine had been brought up to wash everything down and, by the end of the meal, Brianne felt as though she couldn't possibly stand up she was so stuffed.

"God's teeth," she smiled, remembering her father's favorite oath, "that was wonderful!"

Ty leaned back in his chair and nodded. "I almost forget the nuisance of this damned snakebite," he added.

Immediately, Brianne straightened, concern on her

face. "I'm sorry, Ty, I nearly forgot about your leg. Is it bothering you?"

He shrugged. "I think it just knows it's going to be losing one hell of a nurse in the morning," he stated with a crooked smile.

Brianne stood up. "Well, as long as you're still here, I might as well have a last look at it. Come over here and stretch out on the bed. Roll your trouser leg up so that I can have a look at it."

He did as she asked, enjoying the feel of the mattress after the nights spent on rocky cavern floors and hard dusty ground. Brianne knelt beside him, peering down at the wound, satisfying herself that it was healing properly.

"You know, I could have a doctor look at it while I'm in town," he suggested sniffing the clean smell in her hair as it trailed its shining splendor down her shoulders. The deep auburn seemed to glint with reddish lights and he reached out involuntarily, clasping a deep curl with his fingers.

"Oh, I don't think it will be necessary," she answered, then her voice trailed off uncertainly, as she looked in his eyes and saw them watching her purposefully.

Slowly, he pulled on her hair, causing her to lean down closer to him until she lay on his naked chest, her lips inches from his. His free hand came around and pressed against the back of her head, bringing her even closer until his mouth almost closed on hers.

"Ty, let me go," she said softly.

He groaned harshly. "Brianne, honey, you just don't know how damned beautiful you look! Why don't you let me, for God's sake?"

"Because I'm a married woman," she reminded him gently, wishing it wasn't inevitable that he was going to be angry with her. "I love my husband, Ty, and tomorrow I'm going out to try and find him. When I do find him, I don't want any feelings of guilt overshadowing our reunion. I've come too far for that."

"Dammit!" he cursed, pushing her away from him in

keen disappointment. "All I can say, Brianne, is that husband of your is the luckiest son-of-a-bitch in Texas with a wife like you waiting for him!" He swung around and picked up his shirt from the chair, pulling it over his head. Sitting on the couch, he pulled on his boots and jammed the dusty hat over his head, eyeing her impatiently from beneath its brim. "I think," he said flatly, "I'm going to go out and get drunk!"

It was two hours later that Ty, having drunk nearly half a bottle of Tennessee whiskey in a saloon frequented by Texas Rangers, felt a hard hand catch him by the shoulder and spin him around. Prepared for the worst, his hand went to the Colt at his belt despite his drunken state, but then he heard the friendly voice directed to him and eased up a little.

"Ty? Ty Warren?"

Ty looked blearily into the smoky-golden eyes of the man who was staring at him with all appearances of recognizing him, and tried to think where he'd seen those topaz eyes before.

"Jesus, man, don't you remember me? Pierce Nolan, I rode with you under Captain Hays for a year, three years ago!"

"Pierce Nolan!" Ty slapped a hand on the older man's shoulder. "I'll be damned! I thought you'd quit the Rangers," he continued, his brain beginning to clear a little from the mist that had begun to engulf it.

Pierce shook his head and grinned. "I was away for a while, Ty, but couldn't get Texas out of my blood. I came back to rejoin my old regiment, but I've been cooling my heels in this town waiting for old Rip Ford to get back from patrol out on the border. I've done a little scouting work for some of the wagon trains pulling out for Santa Fe, but not much else."

"You're waiting for Captain Ford?" Ty repeated blearily. "Damn, I thought he was up Amarillo way, Pierce."

"He's due back from the border any day now," Pierce

repeated, realizing his companion was on his way to getting quite drunk. "I've heard there's been plenty of trouble closer in and there's a great need for new troubleshooters."

"Yeah, you were always good at that kind of work, weren't you, my friend?" Ty grinned, ordering another round of drinks.

"'Course I hear the federal government's not too pleased about Governor Bell calling out the Rangers. It's just costing the state more money, and Bell's a good one to send all bills straight to Washington," Pierce continued, sipping at the smooth whiskey.

"What money?" Ty put in sarcastically. "Shit, this is starting to be volunteer work, my friend. If I were you, I'd head on out to California where the talk of gold is beginning to reach epidemic proportions. That's where I'll be headed once the Rangers finish their job here!"

"You tracking Indians?" Pierce wondered, feeling the hot liquor coursing through his veins rather agreeably. "I heard there's been some firings, a couple of farmers killed."

Ty nodded and ordered another bottle of whiskey. "What are you doing back here in San Anton'?"

Ty shook his head. "Escorting a lady to town," he said, swigging his drink with sudden anger. "Tried to bed the ungrateful wench, but she wouldn't have me."

"Damned ungrateful!" Pierce agreed.

"I didn't think escorting women through the prairie was something the Rangers were expected to do these days," Pierce went on trying to keep back his amusement. "With the Indians on the frontier, I would think you'd have better things to do."

"Hell, I guess Walker's gone soft or something. We found her abandoned out on the prairie and he felt it was his duty to see her to her destination."

"Speaking of women, I could use one myself," Pierce said rakishly, letting his eyes explore the crowded room as he leaned back against the bar railing. He didn't feel the need to tell Ty Warren that he was now a married man. He had to admit that he hardly felt like one himself.

"You should see the one I just left in the hotel," Ty went on morosely, staring into his glass. "Prettiest thing I've seen in a long time, the kind of woman that makes a man start thinking of settling down. Too bad she's already married." He whistled softly and downed his drink again.

Pierce slapped him on the back good naturedly. "Hell, if she's that good, maybe I could help persuade her to be a little more giving," he said affably. "Come on, finish your drink and bring the bottle. We'll have a little party, all by ourselves."

"She's a hard-hearted woman," Ty warned, grabbing the bottle and stumbling after his new-found companion.

"We'll just have to soften her up a little," Pierce returned. "Lead the way, *hombre*."

They made their way to the hotel and up to the room where Brianne was just about to go to bed, despite the nervousness that had kept her pacing for the last two hours. She heard the demanding knock on her door and started.

"Let me in, honey," Ty's voice came to her, slurring over the vowels. "Your husband won't do you as much good as I can."

She should have guessed he'd go out and get himself drunk, Brianne thought, angrily. How like a man to drown his sorrows in liquor! She strode to the door, intent on telling him to sleep it off elsewhere and that he couldn't expect her to let him sleep on the couch after the way he'd acted earlier.

Angrily, she threw open the door, her mouth open to say something, when her eyes went from the drunken smirk of Ty's boyish face, to the man next to him, whose topaz eyes were turning dark and hard with sudden shock. Brianne felt a stinging sensation in her chest that seemed to reach up to engulf her throat, making it impossible for her to speak. Her breath came in a fluttered gasp as she gazed at the man she had chased all the way from Louisiana. Suddenly, she had no idea what to say.

"Brianne!" She heard him say her name, but there was no tenderness in it, only hard suspicion and anger at seeing her here.

"Pierce," she managed, her turquoise eyes widening into enormous orbs that drank in the tall physique, the tanned face, and dark hair that seemed longer than it had been in Galveston. "Oh, Pierce, I'm so glad to see you. I—"

"Glad to see me?" His golden eyes narrowed. He turned on Ty Warren with sudden violence and, before the other man could even imagine what his next action would be, Pierce had landed a sharp blow to his jaw that flattened him to the floor. That, combined with the whiskey he'd already drunk, served to cause him to pass out cold in the hallway.

Brianne spared hardly a glance at the prone man, her eyes were all for her husband as she felt something inside of her bubbling up with joy, despite his obvious anger directed at her. Why he was angry, she had no idea. All she wanted from him was some sign that he was as glad to see her as she was to see him.

"I was afraid you might have already gone off before I could find you," she said, feeling him push her back into the room so that he could step in and close the door.

"Find me?" he repeated, his eyes narrowing even more. "So, I have a wife who's part bloodhound. I see you've stuck to the trail even better than I would have thought. Of course, you did get help from no less than the Texas Rangers!" He moved away from her as though afraid of his own violence.

Brianne stared at him in confusion. "What do you mean? Why are you so angry? I told you in Galveston that I could chase you across the whole of Texas—"

"Oh, yes, just so you would fling a divorce paper in my face, wasn't that it?" he questioned mockingly. "Well, my dear, I would never have guessed at the depth of your tenacity. I must admit to applauding it, even if it always was a bit misguided!''

"But, Pierce, about the divorce—" she began, licking her lips with her tongue as she tried to think how best to tell him of her burgeoning love.

"Christ, spare me the listing of all the grievances against me, all the reasons why we shouldn't be married," he interrupted angrily, coming over to where she stood and putting his hands on her shoulders.

The contact affected both of them. Brianne felt the warmth of his hands even through the robe she wore. It seemed to reach through and sear her flesh as though he were putting his brand on her. Pierce couldn't help but be aware of her turmoil despite his inebriated state, seeing the turquoise eyes meeting his with a questioning look, an uncharacteristic timidity that startled him coming from this woman.

"Pierce," she got out steadily, "I don't want a divorce from you any longer."

His golden eyes widened with surprise and doubt. "You don't want to divorce me?" he repeated, one dark brow going upward in a sardonic cresecnt. "Then, my dear wife, why did you chase me all the way across the prairie? Surely, you did not find things that boring at home that you must spice up your life with the threat of Indians, sunstroke, and snakebite?"

Brianne suddenly broke away from him, needing to break the contact that made it difficult for her to think straight. She turned away, then looked back, and he was aware all over again of how beautiful she really was with her thick waving auburn hair and those exquisite turquoise eyes that seemed to jump out at him from the attractive pale tan that she had acquired during her journey. Suddenly, he ached for her as he had never ached for any other woman in his life. She was his wife and she was here—they were together. He had every right to her, he told himself, moving involuntarily closer.

She wrung her hands together uncertainly. "I know, Pierce, that both of us didn't start off this marriage very well. You accused me of being spoiled and a child, and I thought you were too hard and unconcerned to make the marriage work. But now—"

"Yes?" he prompted, when she hesitated. "I'm waiting to hear just what you discovered on your way to San Antonio." He was almost touching her again.

"That I love you." She stopped as he took her suddenly in his arms and leaned down to kiss her. A soft, almost tentative kiss that surprised her and, at the same time, touched her deeply. It was as though he were exploring, trying to find out her feelings as well as his own. The kiss deepened, molding their lips together, breaking apart, and then coming together again.

"So you missed me?" he wondered, then kissed her again before she could answer. His teeth nibbled gently at her lower lip, pulling it out and then releasing it and kissing the spot tenderly. "I've missed you," he admitted against her lips.

"You—you have?" she breathed before he stopped her words with another kiss.

He nodded and pulled her tighter into the circle of his arms. God, how he wanted to make love to her now. He bent her backward against his arm and his mouth kissed hers once more before quitting it to concentrate on the pale-tanned arch of her throat. He kissed the length of it before stopping at the barrier of her robe. Impatiently, his free hand worked at the hooks in front until he had them undone and could slip the robe from her shoulders.

"I want you, Brianne," he murmured against the flesh above her chemise, where her breasts swelled enticingly. "I can't wait for you any longer."

He swept her, unresisting, into his arms and strode quickly to the bed, the covers of which were already pulled down in blatant invitation. Gently, he laid her down, then hurried out of his own clothes, his golden eyes blazing down on her so that she felt weak in the knees, anticipating his muscular, masculine body soon joining hers on the bed. She loved her husband, no matter what, and she wanted him as badly as he wanted her!

Invitingly, she held her arms up to him and he joined her quickly, planting kisses all over her face and neck, before dealing with the hooks of her chemise which, in his passion, he nearly ripped off of her. His eyes raked the length of her as she lay nude beneath him, her turquoise eyes meeting the lust in his gaze without flinching. She had spurned the arms of other men, she knew, for just this moment with the only man she could ever truly love.

"Pierce," she whispered softly, "love me now."

His heart leaped at the words she spoke. Slowly, he swept her body with his hands, as though trying to mesmerize each curve. No part of her body was safe from his tender exploration as she turned her head from side to side, caught up in the exquisite sensations he was rendering to her. He cupped her breasts gently and circled the tips with his thumbs, watching as they sprang to life, hard and pointed.

He leaned down to nibble once more at her neck, then went lower to her breasts which he still held in his hands, sucking at the firm, ripe flesh while his hands slid down her ribs to her hips, grasping them strongly as he pulled them toward himself. Brianne gasped as he enveloped the tips of her breasts, one by one, with his mouth, torturing them lovingly with teeth and tongue.

"Oh, my God!" she gasped, bringing her hands up to press his head, weaving her fingers through the thick waves at the back of his neck.

Pierce brought his head up once more to look into those marvelous turquoise eyes which had turned cloudy with desire. Smiling in satisfaction, he opened her legs, slipping his hand between her thighs to caress her, his smile deepening as he felt her jump under his experienced fingers.

Something subtle was happening, Brianne knew, as she felt her whole body softening, moistening, readying itself to receive him. The tight ball in her belly was unraveling, spreading its honeyed-warmth up to her breasts and down her legs.

Pierce knelt between her legs and pulled them up and around his waist, feeling her warm, wet inner core pressed against his throbbing maleness. Gently, he leaned forward over her, propping his weight on his hands as he prepared to thrust into her.

Their mouths found each other once more as Brianne put her arms around his neck, willing him to go on, to begin the final surge of mindless pleasure. Her body was crying out for domination by him and all her guards were down. She lay, open to him.

Gently, Pierce lowered himself, feeling that part of him slipping into her tight, slippery interior, bringing exquisite sensations that exploded inside his head. Brianne's breath caught in her throat as she felt the rigid head within her until his body was flat against hers and they were locked together in the most passionate embrace. She closed her eyes as he leaned down to kiss her deeply. The kiss, his tongue twisting against her own, his chest pressed to her heaving breasts, all made a tingling in her belly that seemed to be answered by his thrusting.

A soft moan escaped her throat as she met his thrusts boldly, exciting them both beyond belief. The pressure was building faster now, faster and faster until Brianne felt the spontaneous cry issue from her throat at the same time that he rammed himself deeply into her and released his seed into her boiling interior. She clasped him tightly, her legs entwined around his waist, clamping his body against hers. His face was hidden in the softness between her neck and shoulder and she felt his mouth open, breathing hard as he expended all his energies into her.

"Pierce, oh, Pierce," she breathed, returning his kisses passionately. "This is why I followed you all the way from Avonlea! Because we belong together!"

He lifted his head, his golden eyes meeting her turquoise ones tenderly. "You are wonderful, my sweet, my dearest love."

Brianne wanted to tell him now that she suspected quite strongly that she was pregnant. But she was afraid it might put a damper on their newly affirmed love. After all, she was not positive she was pregnant. With all that had happened in the last few months, it was quite possible that her monthly time could have been put off its normal routine. And yet, she was almost positive, deep inside of herself, that she was carrying his child, the product of that wild, passionate bout of love in New Orleans when he hadn't even known who she was.

"Pierce," she began carefully, her fingers moving caressingly through his hair. "Darling, we do need to talk about the future."

He looked at her, smiling as his golden eyes deepened. "It's looking very bright from my side," he declared, leaning down to nuzzle her throat and breasts. "Lord, Brianne, I must have you again tonight. I'm starving for you."

"But, Pierce, we need to talk about what will happen after tonight. I mean—what if—what if we went home to Avonlea first. Would it be so terrible to stay there until I get more used to the idea of following you around the entire country?" She smiled, hoping to lighten her words. She remembered suddenly, how Ella had told her about the fragility of men.

He looked at her and she hated to see the old mockery creeping into his eyes. "Good God, Brianne, look how far you've come from Avonlea, from all that you were there! I can see you're not the same girl I married. And I'm not just talking about the fact that you can walk again and ride a horse across Texas! Don't spoil it by harping about home again!" His lips curled faintly in disgust.

Despite the warning that flashed inside her head, she couldn't help disputing him. "What has going home got to do with the girl I used to be?" she demanded. "I'm not going to become her ever again! I love you, Pierce. I've proved it by chasing you almost a thousand miles!"

"Dammit, Brianne! Don't try to make bargains with me!"

"No! You're wrong, Pierce!" she put in, wishing she could make him understand.

"Then what is it, Brianne! Christ, why can't we go on from here instead of turning back?"

"Because—I'm pregnant!" she flung at him, not wanting to tell him like this, in anger, but seeing no other way to convince him that she couldn't go with him.

His eyes grew brighter for an instant, lit with an inner joy, and then they shuttered themselves once again, the light going out. "Pregnant?" he asked insolently. "You can't possibly be pregnant, Brianne!"

She flushed. "Quite possible, Pierce," she replied tightly.

He looked at her as though trying to see through the outer flesh to the inside of her. "You don't look as though you could be carrying a child from our wedding night," he claimed. "Certainly, you'd be much farther along and showing somewhat. Despite the fact that I'm a man, my dear, I do know the look of a woman with child. And Galveston, why you couldn't possibly be sure about that!"

She swallowed. "It was before Galveston, Pierce."

He looked genuinely puzzled for a moment, before dark anger surfaced and he grabbed her arms, digging deep into the soft flesh. "What do you mean?" he demanded, his voice dangerously soft. "The child couldn't be mine if it didn't happen at Galveston!"

She tried to twist away from him, but he held her too tightly. "The child will be yours!" she said. "You—you had me in New Orleans, Pierce. You didn't even know it was me, your wife, that you were making love to. You thought it was some whore you'd asked to come spend a few mindless hours with you in your hotel!" Her turquoise eyes gleamed with her own anger.

"What, in God's name, are you spouting!" he demanded, feeling murderous as his mind refused to listen to what she said, and instead dealt with the twisting pain of her imagined unfaithfulness.

"I'm trying to tell you—" Her words were cut off as she felt his hands encircle her throat.

"Perhaps you've grown up too well, my shy bride!" he ground out softly. "You remind me of the poor son-of-a-bitch lying out in the hall. I seem to recall you and he had come to this city together. I'm trying to think why a man like Ty Warren, a Texas Ranger with better things to do, might want to bring a lone, young woman like yourself across the prairie—"

She jerked away from his hands angrily. "What are you saying, Pierce? That you think I went to bed with Ty Warren? Well, why not Blaine Fielding too then? Or Bill Keane, the man I hired in Galveston to take me to you. The man who raped my servant and left us both abandoned on the prairie? I suppose the child could be any one of theirs, couldn't it?" she threw at him, her cheeks fiery with her rage.

Blindly, Pierce grabbed her and threw her on the bed, his hands pinning hers back as his knee inserted itself between her thighs. "So, you've gotten used to a man on top of you?" he questioned sardonically. "You were learning more things than how to walk and survive out on the prairie!"

"Pierce, you're crazy!" she shouted at him, before he smashed his mouth down onto hers. She pushed him away with her body. "Why—how did this happen? You've got to believe me! I only said those things because I wanted to hurt you, like you were hurting me! Don't you remember, in New Orleans, the woman with the black mask—"

She was abruptly cut off again as he kissed her hard,

his teeth grating against hers, his tongue fencing with hers in frantic rage as he closed his mind to reason. He was jealous, God knew he was! He didn't want to think about her and Blaine Fielding or her and Ty Warren, riding together out on the prairie in God knew what kind of intimate circumstances! The jealousy was a grinding need to hurt her like she had wounded him!

He knew he was achieving his aims, for despite her earlier anger, she was beginning to acquiesce, her perfectly formed body responding to his demands. He felt himself inside of her and closed his eyes at the excruciating tingling that encompassed him. God, she was so lovely.

He felt the climax building within him, and her answering response. He drew out the exquisite torture as long as he could, then felt himself exploding, emptying himself into her. With his passion spent, so, too, was his earlier anger. Tenderly, he reached down to kiss her and was surprised at the tears on her cheeks. The moment was too raw for either of them to speak and he pulled himself away from her, lying next to her on the bed, his arm possessively around her stomach. She was so quiet, he guessed she must be asleep, or at least pretending to be.

He thought back for a moment to New Orleans, the memory fuzzy at best. That had been a long time ago when one measured days on the frontier. A woman with a black mask— He felt his eyes closing wearily from the effects of the loving and the whiskey and the spent anger. He would have to think about all this in the morning, and they would talk then about their future.

Chapter Twenty-six

PIERCE AWAKENED QUICKLY, AS WAS HIS WONT, HIS HAND going immediately to the empty space beside him in the bed. He scanned the room and realized that Brianne was gone, her things nowhere to be seen.

"Damn!" he uttered softly beneath his breath. That woman had to be the most exasperating one he'd ever encountered. God knew where she'd gone now! Maybe back to Galveston to try to get a boat back to New Orleans. He started to remember what she'd said about being with him in New Orleans.

The woman in the black mask. He frowned, his topaz eyes going dark as he tried to remember what she'd been talking about. His brows peaked suddenly and he found himself recalling that night when the whore had come over to his hotel room. The more he thought about it, the more he remembered thinking at the time that she'd reminded him of his wife. Damn! Could it really have been Brianne? At the time, he hadn't known that she could walk so hadn't given his suspicions a second thought, but now—

He jumped out of bed, throwing off the covers and standing naked in the middle of the floor. Damn, it must have been her! He couldn't have known such enjoyment, such fulfillment with a woman who was only doing it for the money! Christ, why hadn't he been listening to her last night? Knowing her, his intimations about her suspected adultery with other men would have infuriated her enough to leave him. Damn, he'd bet she was on her way back to Galveston right now, determined to go back to Avonlea without him!

And now that he remembered the events in New Orleans, he realized that she probably wasn't lying about the fact that she was pregnant. Jesus, how could he have blundered so with her! Here they had finally begun to come together, to appreciate one another and he had driven her away—and this time, he knew, he would have to be the one to do the chasing.

He dressed quickly and was about to go out the door when a diffident knock sounded. Bounding over to the door, he threw it open, hoping that Brianne might have changed her mind and returned. Much to his disappointment, it was not Brianne, but Ty Warren, a long purple bruise on his jawline and his eyes bloodshot after all the whiskey he'd drunk last night.

"She's gone," Ty said, almost enjoying the desperation on the other man's face.

"I know it," Pierce returned, retreating behind his habitually cool exterior. "I'm on my way to try and catch up with her somewhere between here and Galveston. I'm surprised she didn't ask you to escort her back." His left brow peaked sardonically.

Ty grinned. "If you go that way, toward Galveston, I'm afraid you'll miss her altogether, my friend. She's taken the stagecoach for Austin where, I presume, she'll stay until she can wire home for money to get her to Galveston."

"How do you know all that?" Pierce asked suspiciously, stepping closer to the other man warningly.

Ty shrugged. "I happened to be awake, nursing my sore jaw, when I saw her stealing out of your room with her things. I figured she was running away and, being the gentleman I am, I asked her if I could help her in any way. She told me no, and where she was going. I gathered you and she hadn't had the coziest of reunions." He eyed the other man questioningly.

"That's private business between Brianne and me,"

Pierce returned gruffly, putting his flat-crowned, wide-brimmed hat on his head and adjusting his gun belt. "Now, if you'll excuse me, I've got to try to catch up with her and talk some sense into her stubborn little head."

Ty boldly put an arm out to stop the other man despite the impatient look Pierce gave him. "Listen, if you want to talk about talking sense into someone's head, why don't you let me talk to you for an hour before you leave?" he asked. "I want to tell you just what that little lady went through to get to you!"

"I'm not interested—"

"Dammit, Nolan, you've got to listen to me and then, maybe, you'll understand enough to treat her with a little more kindness. She's not the kind of woman who's going to respond to anger."

"And how would you know that?" Pierce demanded, his eyes holding a threat.

"Dammit, man, I went through a hell of a lot out there on the prairie with her! She saved my life, for God's sake!"

Pierced stopped, becoming interested now. He realized it might not be a bad idea to listen to what this man had to say about his wife. God knows, he'd started off on the wrong foot enough times, maybe he could start to learn from his mistakes. He was not so proud that he wouldn't admit he would accept help to get his wife back. She meant too damn much to him and he wasn't about to lose her!

"All right," he said finally, almost wearily, "I'll listen to what you have to say, Warren. But for God's sake, be quick about it, for I'll not have her slip through my fingers again!"

In the stagecoach which jolted her from side to side every time it hit a rut in the dirt road, Brianne gritted her teeth and forced herself not to become sick. This morning the nausea had seemed to hit her full force and it was all she could do to sit stiffly on one side of the seat, trying to maintain her balance. She was glad that the heavyset man in the opposite corner had, at least, put out his cigar, enabling her to breathe easier in the crowded confines of the coach.

Her decision to leave her husband and return to Avonlea had been well thought out all night. While he had slept beside her, she had turned to him, tears glistening in her eyes as she thought of how hard it would be to leave him now, after all she'd been through to reach him. But how could she stay with him under such terms as he had put out? There was to be no flexibility, no room for her opinions. She knew she couldn't live like that. She realized now, that she loved him too much not to have his respect as well as his love. She would go home and wait for him there and, perhaps, he would come home too after he had finished his work in Texas and they could sort things out together. Deep within herself she knew how much she was hoping that he would follow her to Austin, would even try to catch up with the stagecoach before it reached the capital. That was why she had told Ty Warren her destination.

But so far, Brianne had seen no rider that resembled her husband and her hopes were beginning to diminish. Come after me, Pierce, she thought to herself. Come after me and show how much you love me, please!

Ahead of her, the endless dusty miles stretched out to Austin and she thought about the fact that she would have to wire her father for funds once she arrived in the capital. Would her father be angry with her for her headlong flight after a husband who continued to be at odds with her? True enough, her first thought when running after him had been to sever her ties with him, to make herself into an independent woman who could be guided by her own choice as to a new husband. But, somewhere along the way, that tearing need to divorce him had changed to a need to be with him, an acceptance of the fact that, after all, she loved him. He was, as her father had said, a man worthy of her, a man who was every bit as stubborn and arrogant as she. But that stubbornness was what continued to keep them apart, each one unable to give in enough to keep them together.

Brianne sighed and looked out the dirty window of the stagecoach, wondering how much longer it would be to Austin. It seemed these last few months that time had always been measured by distance. She had been traveling so long, she was tired of it. The pull of home was strong within her and the thought of Avonlea, with its green lawns and the chanting of the Negro slaves in the fields called her like a beacon.

She leaned back in the thinly cushioned seat and closed her eyes, imagining her parents and brother on the veranda welcoming her home. The warm lights of Avonlea with its marble columns and multi-flowered gardens eased her mind as she endured the rough ride to Austin. The only thing that would mar her happiness, she knew, was the fact that she would not be returning home with her husband.

It was late in the afternoon by the time the stagecoach reached Austin and Brianne thought there must be a bruise on every part of her body. Her legs and feet ached from sitting in the same position for so long and her back hurt from trying to keep it stiff so as to avoid knocking into the person next to her on the seat.

She looked around curiously at the newness of this town and made her way to a respectable looking hotel, intending to get a cheap room for the night. She needed a bath and a nap and then she would send the wire to her father via his banker in New Orleans.

Once in her room, having parted with nearly all of her money by now, she sank to the bed, too tired even to ask for a bath to be brought up. She tried not to think of Pierce back in San Antonio, or his probable anger upon awakening and finding her gone. He had probably gone off West, telling himself he was well rid of the kind of woman who would go running off while he slept. He would be glad, she was sure, not to have her to worry about on the trail with him. She told herself this was the only way she could have done it, and yet, tears kept glistening just below the surface, threatening to spill over as she thought about having their baby back at Avonlea without him there. Feeling woefully depressed, she turned on her side and allowed herself a self-indulgent cry, hoping she would feel better afterward. Her tears gradually lessened and she finally felt herself beginning to doze off.

It was over an hour later that Brianne, awakened by some small noise, opened her eyes slowly to encounter two dusty, black boots in front of her. Fearfully, afraid to let her joy surface too quickly, she raised her eyes to buckskin breeches encasing long, muscular legs, then higher to a dark burgundy shirt open at the throat to reveal the patch of dark fur on a bronzed chest. Above that, she saw his face, tanned and angular, the golden-topaz eyes leaping out at her from beneath the brim of his black hat.

"Well, Mrs. Nolan," he asked softly, "do you like what you see?"

She continued laying there, savoring the moment a little longer, her turquoise eyes bright with happiness. "You came after me," she answered him softly.

He smiled, a smile devoid of mockery. "You're much too special a woman for me to let you get away. You're brave, honest, beautiful, intelligent—everything that makes you special to me. How could I not chase you to Austin when you chased me down Louisiana, across the Gulf of Mexico, and half-way across Texas?" He whistled softly. "That's a mighty tenacious woman."

She smiled too. "My husband might call it mule-headed," she broke in, sitting up on the bed and facing him.

"Then he's a damn fool!" he said wrathfully, and leaned down to bring her up against him, encircled by his strong arms. "He just began to realize it a few hours back. He told himself that despite the fact that he and his wife are destined to call each other stubborn and pigheaded, they must also be destined to tell one another how much they love each other." He bent his dark head, took off his hat and kissed her gently, first on the corner of her mouth, then more fully with building passion. Suddenly, he took his mouth away and eyed her, one brow cocked thoughtfully. "And," he went on, pressing her even tighter against him, "he's decided that he's going to bow to her wishes and return to Avonlea—at least until the baby arrives. After that, well, we'll have to see."

She nodded eagerly, hardly believing her ears. She had been on the verge of telling him that she'd follow him anywhere—hadn't she proved she could do it? She couldn't help the little thrill of laughter that bubbled up in her throat. "You know, Pierce Nolan," she said, tracing his lips with her forefinger, "I'm beginning to think you're quite a lovable fellow."

His golden eyes gleamed with a hint of mockery. "And I'm beginning to think you're a damn desirable woman!" He pushed her gently back onto the bed and sat beside her, pushing a stray curl from her ear and planting a soft kiss there that made her shiver. "What in hell was the matter with me that I was trying to run away from you all this time?" he wondered in amazement.

She clicked her tongue and pouted deliciously. "Why, you just wanted to see how far I'd chase you!" she answered, before he silenced her with another kiss that quite took her breath away.

"The chase," he said, looking deeply into her eyes, "is over."

THERESA CONWAY began writing because of her interest in foreign countries and history, and she is now the author of the best-selling *Paloma* and *Gabrielle,* as well as three other historical romances. She is a native of St. Louis, Missouri, where she now lives, and is married with two children.